My Grandpa's Second Wife

Lois Jean Thomas

Seventh Child Publishing, LLC

Saint Joseph, Michigan

This book is a work of fiction. Names, characters, and incidents are the product of the author's imagination or are used fictitiously. Any resemblance between events or persons, living or dead, is coincidental.

Cover design by A. R. Thomas

In honor of all the beautiful diversity on this wondrous planet. May we one day come to know that we are all united by one spirit.

CONTENTS

ACKNOWLEDGMENTS

My deepest gratitude goes to my husband, who has been extraordinarily patient with me during the writing of this book. He assisted with research and formatting, and worked with me on a cover design. He helped with editing by listening to multiple readings of each chapter. This has truly been a joint project.

My Grandpa's Second Wife

CHAPTER 1: MERCEDES MALDONADO

"Who's this, Mommy?" Javi asked, holding up a dog-eared photo he'd pulled from the clutter in one of his grandmother's kitchen drawers.

Mercedes looked up from the drawer she was cleaning. "That's you, sweetheart," she said, "when you were a baby. Your daddy and I took pictures of you on your first Christmas. I gave one to your grandma." Her voice took on a bitter edge. "I guess she just shoved it into a drawer, like she does with everything else."

She glanced into the living room, where her mother was lying in her broken-down recliner wearing her usual shabby tee shirt and pajama pants. Her eyes were half-closed, and the large mound of her belly rose and fell with her labored breathing. As always, a vodka bottle and an empty glass were sitting on the table next to her chair.

Mercedes slammed the clean drawer shut a little harder than she needed to. Then she yanked open the next drawer, where she found the usual array of random junk: chewing gum wrappers, twist ties from bread bags, a plastic fork, ketchup packets from a fast-food restaurant, the cap to an ink pen, and a sticky cherry lifesaver covered with grime.

"My God, Mom!" she called out. "You're such a slob! I might as well turn all these drawers upside-down and dump everything straight into the trash."

Her mother's eyes popped wide open. "Don't you dare, Sadie! There's good stuff in there. Stop being such a brat!"

Mercedes rolled her eyes and muttered under her breath, hating the job she was faced with, yet determined to get it done.

Years ago, her mother's house, located on the north side of Goshen, Indiana, had been owned by Mercedes' grandparents, Andrew and Norma Covington. Their marriage had been short-lived. But Norma had stayed on in the home, where she'd raised their only child, Mercedes' mother Denise. And then, Norma had raised Mercedes in the same home.

After Mercedes had left home to marry Javier nine years ago, she'd come back once a month to clean the house. Sentimental feelings kept her tied to the place that her late grandmother had kept in pristine condition, and it pained her to see it in a state of decline.

However, when the Coronavirus pandemic hit the country the previous year, accompanied by social distancing protocols, it had become impossible for Mercedes to keep up with the cleaning. She'd been terrified of unwittingly exposing her mother to the virus, who, because of her innumerable health problems, had been at high-risk for developing life-threatening symptoms.

Furthermore, Mercedes' energy had been depleted by the strain of her own household problems, which had resulted in a marital separation five months ago. She'd had to scramble to find her footing after Javier moved out.

So, while she had delivered food and other essential items to her mother over the past fourteen months, she had never lingered in the house.

Because of Denise's lack of motivation and limited ability to clean her own home, the place had rapidly deteriorated. Now that family members were protected by the Coronavirus vaccine, Mercedes had a lot of catching up to do to bring the house back into an acceptable condition. And there was a special urgency to the project: the family home was about to be put up for sale.

One by one, Mercedes picked up the useless objects in the drawer and threw them into the garbage can next to her. The only items she salvaged were a pair of scissors and a roll of Scotch Tape. She set them on the cracked countertop and proceeded to scrub out the grimy drawer with a rag and a bottle of spray cleaner.

It seemed to Mercedes that she'd been working on the project of deep-cleaning her mother's home forever, although it had been less than two weeks. When she'd met with the realtor about selling the house, the woman had expressed dismay over its condition. She'd agreed to list it only after the place had been thoroughly cleaned, which Mercedes had promised to do.

Even then, the realtor had warned Mercedes that her mother would never get what she wanted for the home because of its rundown state. She said she would have to list it as a fixer-upper, a house with "potential."

Moving out of her lifelong home was the last thing Mercedes' mother wanted to do. But her doctor had insisted that it was no longer safe for her to live alone. He'd given Denise a choice: either move in with a family member who could take care of her or go to a long-term care facility.

At first, the obvious choice had been for Denise to move into Mercedes' apartment in the neighboring city of Elkhart. Even though Mercedes had detested the idea of it, she'd been willing to take her mother in. As much as Denise abused her, took advantage of her, and drove her to the edge of her sanity, she could not bring herself to walk away from her.

But then, Mercedes' estranged husband had come to her rescue. He'd said in no uncertain terms that he would never allow their son to live in the same home as Mercedes' alcoholic mother. He'd warned Mercedes that if she moved ahead with her plan, he would go straight to court to get full custody of Javi. Mercedes had no doubt that he meant what he said. Javier was a man of his word.

So, after weeks of carrying on about what a despicable fellow her son-in-law was, Denise had accepted an alternate plan: she'd agreed to move in with her stepmother June.

June lived just minutes away on the west side of Goshen. Thus, the new plan would entail only a move across town, as opposed to moving to Elkhart ten miles away. Denise did not adjust well to change, and Mercedes knew that her mother would've been bitterly unhappy in the unfamiliar surroundings of Elkhart. Fortunately for everyone, June worked as a home health aide, so she possessed the skill, along with the willingness, to deal with Denise's declining health.

Mercedes was profoundly grateful to June for agreeing to take Denise in, although she had a hard time expressing such a sentiment to a woman she disliked so intensely. She knew June's commitment to moving her stepdaughter into her home wasn't made entirely out of kindheartedness. It gave June the satisfaction of having someone to control. She was already proclaiming that the first thing she was going to do when Denise moved in was to cut her drinking in half and get her to eat vegetables.

Mercedes had laughed the first time she'd heard June say that, knowing the ferocious battle that would inevitably ensue between the two hardheaded women.

Whenever anyone would ask Denise the reason for her upcoming move, she would recite a litany of health problems, some real, some embellished, some fabricated. Truthfully, she could no longer negotiate the stairs to her bedroom on the second floor of her home, or to the laundry room in the basement. "My balance isn't what it used to be," she'd say. "My doctor told me I have vertigo. Sometimes, I can't even walk across the room without falling over."

Mercedes knew the reason for her mother's incapacitation was quite simple. It all boiled down to a pattern of self-abuse. At the age of forty-nine, Denise was morbidly obese from decades of heavy drinking, a poor diet, and a sedentary lifestyle. Her so-called dizzy spells were nothing but a product of the alcohol that never left her system. And years of smoking had created her hacking cough and shortness of breath.

However, Mercedes knew the futility of confronting her mother with the truth. It would only lead to an angry exchange between them, and it wouldn't budge Denise an inch toward bettering herself. Denise would denounce Mercedes as an uncaring, ungrateful, and irresponsible daughter. That was the note on which their fights always ended. So, it seemed best to allow her mother to maintain her delusions.

As Mercedes opened yet another drawer and began tossing items into the trash can, Denise leaned forward in her chair. "I told you to stop throwing my stuff away," she bellowed.

"I have to," Mercedes yelled back. "The realtor said we have to get this junk cleaned out before she'll agree to list the house. Either shut up and let me clean or hire someone else to come in and take care of your mess. I know you don't have the money for that."

Then she grinned, deciding to goad her mother. "Do you want me to ask Javier to pay for a cleaning service?"

Denise bristled at the sound of her son-in-law's name. "Don't be a smart-ass, Sadie. That son-of-a-bitch isn't going to do anything for me. Anyway, I don't want strangers coming in and poking around in my stuff."

"Then stop yelling at me," Mercedes shouted, "and let me do my work."

Denise settled back into her recliner and closed her eyes, her voice dropping to a whine. "You're cold, Sadie. You're hard and cold. This is where I was raised. Where you were raised. Where you ought to be raising Javi. You should be moving back in here instead of making me move out."

Mercedes shook her head, trying to dismiss her mother's selfish comments. Truthfully, she had given a momentary thought to moving back in with her mother when she and Javier had agreed to separate. Being financially dependent on her husband, she'd had no idea how she would make it on her own.

But Javier had been one step ahead of her. In addition to paying child support, he'd offered to continue paying the rent on the apartment they'd shared, so that she and Javi could continue living there. He was determined to prevent, at any cost, the scenario of his wife and son moving into Denise's dysfunctional home. Then, he'd signed a six-month lease on an apartment for himself in South Bend, close to his job.

A tug on Mercedes' arm disrupted her rumination. "Who's this, Mommy?" Javi asked, holding up another photo.

Mercedes stopped her work and put her arm around her eight-year-old son's shoulders. "That's you on your second birthday. See all the presents we bought you? Your mommy and daddy spoiled you rotten."

She caressed his sleek black hair, then bent to kiss the top of his head. "Now, stay out of these drawers and let your mother get her work done."

But a minute later, Javi called out for the third time. "Who's this, Mommy?"

5

"It's probably you," Mercedes sighed. "Any baby pictures you find in your grandma's drawers are going to be of you. You're her only grandchild."

"No," Javi said, "it's not me. It's a girl. She's wearing a dress."

Mercedes put down her cleaning rag and took the photo from her son's hand. The picture was older than the previous two, taken with a Polaroid camera.

"I think it's me!" she exclaimed, peering closely at the picture. She walked into the living room and held out the photograph. "Is this me, Mom?"

Denise opened her eyes and looked at the picture. "Yup, that's you, Sadie."

Abandoning her cleaning task, Mercedes sank down onto the couch, continuing to stare at the photo. It was a picture of a dark-haired, dark-eyed toddler sitting on the lap of a middle-aged woman, whose sad blue eyes belied her sweet smile. Hanging on the wall above them was a painting so large, so vivid, and so beautiful that it overshadowed the human subjects in the photo. The painting was of a little girl gazing into a pond, tended to by a magnificent angel.

Vague memories teased the back of Mercedes' mind, something to do with a sweet moment cut tragically short. But try as she might, she couldn't bring up a clear recollection of what was haunting her.

She held out the photo to her mother. "Who's this woman holding me?"

Denise took the photo and glanced at it again before handing it back. "Oh, that's Dora," she said.

"Who's Dora?" Mercedes asked.

Denise looked as if she'd fallen asleep, and her labored breathing became a snore. "Mom, who is Dora?" Mercedes repeated loudly.

Denise startled, then rubbed her eyes and brushed wisps of stringy blonde hair out of her bloated face. "Dora was your Grandpa Andy's second wife," she said irritably. "Now leave me alone. I'm tired."

Javi scrambled up next to Mercedes, took one more look at the photo in his mother's hand, then turned around to stare out the large window behind the couch. Mercedes knew he'd be listening to everything she and his grandmother were about to say to each other. Javi took everything to heart, and he sometimes heard more than his young mind could handle. Yet, she pressed on.

"Tell me about Dora, Mom."

"I already told you. She was your Grandpa Andy's second wife. After my mom and before June."

"What?" Mercedes exclaimed, dumbfounded. "I thought Grandpa Andy had only two wives, Grandma Norma and June."

"Nope," Denise said. "He had another one in between those two." She grinned evilly. "I guess the man got around."

"Did I know Dora?" Mercedes asked.

"Obviously." Denise gestured toward the photo. "You're sitting there on her lap."

"I mean, did I have a relationship with her?"

Denise was silent for a while. "I guess you could say so," she finally said. "Your grandpa was married to Dora when you were born. She really took to you. She treated you like you were her own grandbaby."

An inexplicable sorrow stirred in Mercedes' heart, and her eyes welled with tears. "Was she nice?"

"I suppose so," Denise replied. "I never held anything against Dora. If you ask me, she was too good for your son-of-a-bitch grandpa."

"What do you mean by that?" Mercedes asked sharply.

A dark look crossed Denise's face. "Sadie, not everything is your business. Now, shut up and leave me alone."

But Mercedes persisted. "Whatever happened to Dora?"

"Goddammit, Sadie," Denise growled. "What do you think? She and your grandpa got a divorce. Probably not too long after that picture was taken. Then your grandpa and June got married. Now, enough said. Get back to work and let me sleep."

But Mercedes was too agitated to let things go. She jumped up and stood over the recliner, forcing Denise to look up at her. "I'm not done talking, Mom," she hissed. "Not until you tell me the whole story."

Denise reached over to the bottle on her table. With shaking hands, she poured herself a drink. "Okay. But I'm telling you the truth. There isn't much to say about Dora."

Sighing in exasperation, Mercedes sat back down on the couch. "Why didn't you tell me about her a long time ago? Why did everyone keep this from me?"

"Don't act like we were trying to do you wrong," Denise snapped. "Dora wasn't around all that long. I guess we all forgot about her."

She took a long drink of her vodka. "Except for your Grandpa Andy. I don't think he ever forgot about Dora."

Mercedes leaned forward, eager to hear more. "What do you mean?"

"A couple of months before he died, your grandpa came to me with a letter. He asked me to give it to Dora. He said it was important. He was all emotional about it."

"Did you do it?" Mercedes asked. "Did you give her the letter?"

Denise shook her head. "Nope."

"Why not?"

"It just didn't work out."

Anger boiled in Mercedes' veins. "Where's the letter now?"

Denise shrugged, pointing toward the kitchen. "Probably in one of those drawers you've been working on."

Mercedes stomped to the kitchen and yanked open the last three drawers she hadn't yet cleaned, rifling through the contents. There was no letter. "It's not here," she bellowed.

"Then look in there," Denise said, pointing to the broken-down desk in the corner of the living room.

With her frustration mounting by the second, Mercedes ransacked the desk drawers, tossing old junk mail and random papers onto the floor.

"Settle down, Sadie!" Denise yelled. "You don't need to wreck my goddam house over some stupid letter."

Just when she was about to give up hope, Mercedes spotted an envelope in the back of the bottom drawer. It was slightly yellowed, with a coffee stain on one corner. As she pulled it out, she saw two words written on the front in shaky handwriting: *To Dora.*

"Is this it?" she asked, waving the envelope in the air.

"Let me see," Denise said.

Mercedes handed her the envelope. Denise turned it over in her hands. "Yup. This is it."

"You didn't respect Grandpa," Mercedes hissed, jabbing her finger in the air. "You didn't respect his last wishes about this letter."

Denise looked up at Mercedes, her eyes hardening. "I didn't owe him any respect."

"He was a nice person," Mercedes insisted. "He never did anything to anybody."

Denise smirked. "That's what you think."

"What are you talking about?" Mercedes asked.

"He was a no-good drunk. My mom divorced him when I was just a little kid, because she couldn't take it anymore. He had a problem with his temper, too. I remember how he used to blow up."

Mercedes stifled a bitter laugh. Clearly, her mother had no right to point fingers at anyone else for their drinking or their bad temper. But Mercedes knew that if she wanted to get anywhere on the subject of her grandfather's letter, she couldn't get hung up on her mother's hypocrisy.

"I never saw Grandpa Andy get drunk," she said. "I never saw him drink at all."

"Yeah, but he used to," Denise retorted. "He did some drugs, too. Then when he quit, he got all high and mighty about it. He thought he was better than everyone else."

"Still," Mercedes pressed on, "you should've respected your father's last wishes. No matter what a person has done in life, you should respect their wishes at the end."

"Well, I tried." Denise sounded defensive.

"How did you try?"

Denise shifted her heavy body in her chair, wincing as if the slight effort hurt her. "When your grandpa told me to give the letter to Dora, I asked him where I could find her. He said the last that he knew, she was at some weird religious place in Kalamazoo, Michigan. An ashram, I think he called it. He was hoping we could send the letter to her there.

"So, I looked up the phone number and called the place, but the people I talked to said Dora didn't live there anymore. I asked them where she went. They acted like they didn't want to give out any information. I had to get pushy with them, and they finally said she'd moved to Saint Joseph or Benton Harbor, up there in Michigan."

"Why didn't you keep on looking for her?" Mercedes asked.

Denise smirked. "What? Did you expect me to run all over Michigan trying to track her down? Anyway, June found out about the letter, and she got upset. So, I stopped trying to do anything about it."

"Of course," Mercedes muttered. "You always take June's side." Even though Denise and her stepmother argued on a daily basis, they'd end up siding with each other against any other adversary. It didn't surprise Mercedes that Denise had put June's wishes over those of her dying father.

"As it turned out," Denise continued, "your grandpa took a turn for the worse right about then, and it didn't seem like the letter mattered anymore. It was a stupid idea anyway. It's all water under the bridge now." She tossed the letter, aiming for the small wastebasket next to her chair. The letter hit the edge and bounced off, landing on the pile of dirty dishes that cluttered the floor.

"You missed, Grandma," Javi called out. He hopped off the couch to retrieve the letter.

Denise held out her arm to block his way. "Leave it alone, Javi," she barked. Sulking, he went back to the couch to stare out the window again.

Silence settled over the room, while Mercedes' mind churned with questions. "Mom," she said softly, "what's Dora's last name?"

Denise yawned. "As far as I know, it's Covington. Same as your grandpa's. Same as mine, same as June's. Same as yours was before you married what's-his-face Maldonado. I don't think Dora married anyone else after she and my dad split up."

"June's here," Javi announced from his lookout post at the window.

Seconds later, the front door opened and June bustled in, wearing her work scrubs. She was a short woman with curly gray hair framing a face that would've been pretty if not for her perpetual scowl. Mercedes could remember the first time she'd met June. She'd been cute and petite, almost two decades younger than Mercedes' grandfather Andrew.

But over years of marriage, June had put on weight, and her tiny body had grown square. She reminded Mercedes of a sturdy little bus that never ran out of gas, always plowing forward, running over anyone who got in her way.

Mercedes had never thought of June as her grandmother. The only person she'd ever called Grandma had been her mother's mother, the sweet, indulgent woman who'd raised her while Denise was out running around and getting into trouble. The death of her Grandma Norma seven years ago had been the most difficult loss of Mercedes' life.

No, June wasn't Grandma, even if she had been married to Mercedes' grandfather for more than twenty years. She hadn't earned the title by any stretch of the imagination. Not even Javi called her Grandma. June was just June.

The minute June stepped into the living room, she surveyed her surroundings with angry eyes. "What the hell, Sadie?" she barked, pointing to the papers littering the floor around the desk. "This house looks worse every time I come over. You're making more messes than you're cleaning up. At this rate, it's going to be another ten years before we get this place sold."

"Well, if she'd keep her mind on her work, she might get somewhere," Denise said. "But she's been sitting here asking me questions about Dora."

June stiffened, and Denise grinned. Mercedes knew her mother was stirring up trouble just for the excitement of it. She hoped she wouldn't go so far as to mention the letter.

"I don't want to hear anything about that damn woman," June growled. "All Andy ever said was that he couldn't live with her. She must've been a real bitch."

Pleased with herself for having triggered June's outburst, Denise laughed so hard that she ended up in a coughing spell.

June stomped off to the kitchen to inspect the work Mercedes had done, fussing and cursing as she opened drawers and doors and slammed them shut again. All the while, she and Denise exchanged harsh words and ugly accusations. The two women, only six years apart in age, were purportedly best friends. But they could swear at each other like sailors.

Mercedes' estranged husband Javier lumped her female relatives into one category: loud-mouthed women with nasty attitudes. But there was a difference between Mercedes' mother and her late grandfather's wife. While Denise was a heavy drinker, June never touched a drop of alcohol, even though Mercedes had heard stories about her partying when she was younger. Now, June was as strong as an ox, while Denise barely had the energy to heave herself out of her chair.

When June came back into the living room, she stood with her hands on her broad hips, glaring at Mercedes as if waiting for her to get back to work. Feigning humble obedience to June's demands, Mercedes got off the couch and began picking up the mess around the desk.

Then, she walked over to her mother's chair and picked up the pile of dirty dishes on the floor. In the process, she picked up her grandfather's letter, sliding it under the stack of papers in her hand. Carrying the whole mess to the kitchen, she deposited the dishes in the sink and tossed the papers into the trash. Except for the letter.

As she stared at the envelope, she sensed there was something special in it. Something that should be passed on to its intended recipient instead of meeting the fate of the garbage can.

Knowing she had only moments before June's spying eyes would be watching her again, she stuffed the envelope into the pocket of her jeans. The letter seemed to burn her thigh. She thought her pocket might burst into flame from the incendiary material she'd shoved inside it.

"Sadie, when is that worthless husband of yours coming over to help?" June barked from the living room. "I thought he was going to haul this junkheap of a desk out of here."

"He's not going to come over here just to have you and Mom cuss him out," Mercedes retorted as she walked into the room. "He knows the two of you hate him."

Behind his back, Denise and June called Mercedes' Mexican husband the ugliest of terms applied to Hispanic immigrants. Such name-calling pierced Mercedes to the core. Despite the problems she had with Javier, she still loved him, and she couldn't bear to hear him disparaged like that. Besides, even though she was born in the United States, she herself was half Mexican. And her precious Javi, the light of her life, was three-quarters Mexican.

The truth was that Javier had as much disdain for Denise and June as they had for him, possibly more. While he managed to be respectful to their faces, in his worst moments he referred to them as white trash. His name-calling also hurt Mercedes, as it denigrated her racial heritage on her mother's side.

"You're better than they are," Javier would tell her. "I don't like you spending so much time with your mother and June. Those women bring you down."

And he hated having his son around people he thought were terrible influences. He constantly bemoaned the fact that Javi did not have the benefit of spending time with his refined Mexican grandparents.

"You need to find yourself a new fellow, Sadie," Denise said, her voice dripping with disdain for her son-in-law. "Jared next door is single now. He just threw his girlfriend out."

Mercedes contorted her face, shaking her head. "Jared is disgusting, Mom. He's a creep. My God, you should give me credit for having better taste than that."

Then June announced that she was going to the store, and she asked Denise if she needed anything. Denise rattled off a list of items.

"I've got to get going, too," Mercedes said. "I have some studying to do."

"What do you mean, studying?" June asked.

"I'm taking a summer class," Mercedes reminded her. "I've already told you that."

June and Denise looked at each other and smirked. Mercedes knew they were mocking her for trying to go to nursing school. Neither of them expected her to succeed. Time and again, they'd remind her that she never finished anything she started.

"My mom spoiled her," Denise would say. "So, Sadie thinks she should get anything she wants without having to work for it."

As Mercedes ushered Javi out of the house, she heard June say, "We'll see how long this idea of hers lasts." Tears sprang to her eyes when she heard the two of them share a boisterous laugh at her expense.

She was relieved to step out into the freshness of the late spring day, to escape the smoky, boozy air of her mother's house. As she and Javi headed toward her car parked along the curb, she heard a rough male voice call, "Hey, Sadie!"

Without even looking, Mercedes knew who it was: her mother's next-door neighbor Jared. His use of her mother's nickname for her irritated her. It seemed too familiar. But she knew that was exactly his intent.

Grudgingly, she turned to see Jared sitting on his porch steps, his scraggly brown hair pulled back into a ponytail, his unkempt bushy beard covering half of his face. His unbuttoned flannel shirt, with the sleeves torn out, revealed the contours of his bulging belly. He was playing with an orange tabby, dangling his car keys so the cat could bat at them.

Javi stopped in his tracks. "That's a nice cat!" he called out.

"Come over and see him," Jared called back in a voice of contrived sweetness.

Javi glanced up at Mercedes, a questioning look on his face. Mercedes nodded, then reluctantly followed her son the short distance to Jared's house. She knew she was being lured.

"That is a pretty cat," she said grudgingly. "I've never seen one with markings like that."

"This little schmuck is good-looking and he knows it," Jared chuckled. "He thinks he can get away with all kinds of crap. Half of the time, he's got my foot up his butt."

Javi looked sad at Jared's ugly description of his pet. "If you don't like your cat," he said, "we'll take him."

"No, Javi," Mercedes said quickly, "we can't do that. We aren't allowed to have pets in our apartment. I've told you that a hundred times."

"Well, Javi," Jared said, "you can come over here and see him any time you want." He glanced up at Mercedes with a leering grin. "I'd be glad to have you."

Mercedes' jaw clenched in irritation. Jared tried to hit on her every time she came over to help her mother. She knew he'd seen her car parked out front, and that he'd been sitting there on his porch steps waiting for her to come out.

"Jared," she snapped, "don't think you're going to get anywhere with me. You know I'm married."

Jared laughed. "That's not what your mom says."

"Well, she's wrong," Mercedes retorted.

"She says you and old Javier are finished," Jared insisted. "Sadie, when are you gonna wake up and realize that dude isn't gonna give you what you want?"

Not willing to stand there and argue in front of Javi, Mercedes nudged her son toward the car. "Come on, Javi, we've got to go."

But Jared tried a different tactic to keep her attention. "How's your mom doing?" he asked, his voice softening to feign concern.

Mercedes turned back. "Not too well. Her doctor doesn't want her living alone anymore. So, we have to get her moved out and get this place sold."

"Yeah," Jared said, "I heard something along those lines. That's too bad. I won't get to see you if you're not coming over here anymore."

Choosing not to respond, Mercedes took her son's hand and headed toward her car.

"Mom," Javi said as they buckled their seatbelts, "why did you tell Jared you're married? You and Dad aren't together anymore."

"Legally, we're still married," Mercedes explained. "We're just separated."

"What does that mean?" he asked. "Are you going to get a divorce?"

"I don't know, Javi," she sighed. "Your dad and I haven't figured out what we're going to do. We've been talking about getting back together. Don't you want us to?"

"Yes. But it doesn't seem like you guys are trying very hard. All you do is yell at each other." Javi turned to look at her, a somber expression on his face. "You should talk nicer to Dad."

Mercedes swallowed the lump that had formed in her throat. "I know I should, Javi. I'm sorry."

"If you ask me," Javi said, "you'd be better off with Dad than with Jared. Dad's a nicer person."

Mercedes threw back her head and laughed. "Don't you worry, Javi. I wouldn't be with Jared if he was the last guy on earth."

Javi grinned at her, and she reached over to ruffle his hair. Then he resumed his serious expression. "Mom, I don't like it when you act so ugly with Grandma."

"Well, how about the way she acts with me?" Mercedes retorted.

"Yeah, she acts bad, but..." Javi turned his eyes upward, as if searching for a thought. "But she's ruined. She can't help the way she is." He looked at Mercedes accusingly. "But you should know better. You're not ruined."

Mercedes stared at her son, flabbergasted. "You're just like your father, Javi," she said, more sharply than she intended to. "Too smart for your own good. Always pointing out to me how I should do better."

Javi turned away from her, staring out the window. Mercedes knew she'd wounded his sensitive feelings, and that he was trying to hide his tears from her.

Javier is right about one thing, she thought as she turned her key in the ignition. *I probably shouldn't have Javi around my mom. She really isn't a good influence. And it's too hard on him to see me fighting with her.*

She put the car in drive and pulled away from the curb. "That would make Javier happy," she muttered under her breath. Once again, she didn't know whether she wanted to try harder to please her husband, or whether she wanted to thumb her nose at all his suggestions for self-improvement.

That night after she tucked Javi into bed, Mercedes went to her own room, intending to spend an hour on her phone scrolling through her social media accounts. When she and Javier were living together, he'd complained about this habit of hers. He'd told her that looking at electronic devices at bedtime wasn't good for her, that it overstimulated her and made it difficult for her to fall asleep. Furthermore, he'd insisted that spending endless hours on her phone was a waste of time, and that it interfered with taking care of her responsibilities.

Hearing her husband say such judgmental things had always infuriated Mercedes. Now that they were separated, this was one piece of his advice she happily ignored.

Before changing into her pajamas, she pulled the letter from the pocket of her jeans. As she held the crumpled envelope in her hand, something inside of it seemed to call to her. She stared at it for a moment, then shrugged and laid it on her bedside stand. Phone in hand, she climbed into bed.

But the letter kept hold of her attention, refusing to let go. It seemed alive, something more than an inanimate object. When Mercedes glanced over at it, the envelope seemed to glow in the darkness. Time and again, she turned to her phone, but her eyes kept wandering back to the letter.

Sighing, she finally switched on her bedside lamp and reached for the letter. She stared at the two words written on the envelope in the spidery script of an elderly man: *To Dora.*

Mercedes had a hard time imagining her grandfather as someone who would write those words. She'd never paid much attention to the old fellow. No one had ever regarded him as an important figure in family life. Long ago, he'd resigned himself to sitting in the background of family gatherings, looking as if life had sucked everything out of him. He seemed to have nothing else to do but submit to the demands of his bossy wife and ungracious daughter.

Mercedes had known that her grandfather was a Viet Nam war veteran, and that he had a prosthetic leg related to a combat injury. But that was about it. She'd never even seen the artificial leg, which had always been covered by his baggy trousers. The only evidence of his having lost a limb was that when he got up and moved around, his gait was markedly impaired.

Now, Mercedes wondered what thoughts had been in that silent man's head. She doubted that anyone had ever known what his mind harbored. Suddenly, she felt remorse about having treated him with such indifference.

"Grandpa, what did you have to say to Dora?" she asked aloud.

Her intense curiosity agitated her more than her social media ever did. *I could open this, read it, and then reseal it in another envelope,* she thought. *No one would ever know.* She inserted her pinky finger into the gap on one end of the seal, ready to break it open.

But then, she looked at the old man's laborious handwriting, and she knew that his effort to write the words, *To Dora,* was an irreplaceable part of the whole message. Her own handwriting on a crisp new envelope would never substitute for it.

This letter is not for your eyes! The commanding thought rang clear in her mind, echoing in her heart. *It does not belong to you. It was meant for the eyes of one person only: Dora. Your grandfather had a reason for writing it. It's your duty to pass it on to her.*

The thought stunned Mercedes. She sat motionless with her hand on her heart. "Grandpa," she whispered, "I'll get this letter to Dora if it's the last thing I do."

CHAPTER 2: MERCEDES AND DORA

Mercedes stood at the front door of the Harbor Lights apartment building, feeling as if she was about to pass through a portal into another realm of existence. The unrelenting June sun beat down on her bare arms and shoulders, intensifying the perspiration generated by her anxiety. *My God,* she thought as she wiped the droplets of moisture off her neck and chest. *What kind of impression am I going to make on Dora if I'm drenched with sweat?*

It hadn't been that difficult to locate the residence of Dora Covington. Mercedes had done an internet search focusing on the twin cities of Saint Joseph and Benton Harbor in southwest Michigan, which had led her to this adults-only facility on the south side of Saint Joseph. The three-story building was located on a highway that ran close to the shores of Lake Michigan.

That morning, Mercedes had driven to South Bend to drop her son off for a week-long stay with his father. When she and Javi had arrived at Javier's apartment, he had offered to take the two of them out for lunch.

Even though many of the state's pandemic restrictions had been lifted, Javier had thought it best to play it safe by choosing a restaurant with outdoor dining. Mercedes hadn't been able to refrain from mocking his prudence, telling him he needed to get over his paranoia about the virus.

The freedom to enjoy such a family outing felt like an unbelievable luxury. Numerous times during quarantine restrictions, Mercedes had grown so frustrated with her confinement that she'd been ready to throw caution to the wind. But Javier had insisted that she follow the recommended safety practices, pointing out that her heedlessness would endanger him and Javi as well.

As the family walked toward the restaurant, Javier had reached for Mercedes' hand. His touch had sent a shiver of excitement through her.

They'd had a pleasant meal. Trying to avoid bickering, Mercedes and Javier hadn't talked much with each other.

Instead, they'd allowed their son to be the focus of their attention. But several times, Javier had caught her eye, flashing her an alluring smile. She could tell how pleased he was to have the three of them together.

After the meal, Javier had invited her to come back to his apartment to spend a little more family time with Javi and him. Javi had looked at Mercedes eagerly, hoping for a positive response. But she had declined, saying she had somewhere else she needed to go. The affectionate look on Javier's handsome face had changed to one of suspicion. Their relationship tended to run hot and cold like that.

Feeling guilty for disappointing her husband and son, Mercedes had headed up U. S. 31 to Michigan. And here she was, about to enter the lobby of the Harbor Lights apartment building.

She didn't like the fact that she was showing up at Dora's home unexpected. She would have preferred calling or emailing to request a meeting. But she had found no contact information on Dora Covington other than her address. She'd even searched a telephone directory of the area, hoping that Dora would have a landline phone. But there had been no trace of her in the phone book.

Standing there, Mercedes felt like an intruder, a busybody showing up at a place where she had no business being. Imagining judgmental eyes on her, she glanced furtively at her surroundings. At the dentist office to the left of the apartment building, a mother coaxed a reluctant child in for his appointment. At the strip mall to her right, an elderly woman emerged from a beauty salon, her short gray hair freshly washed and set. On the other side of the highway, a young couple sat at a picnic table in a small lookout park, gazing at the tranquil waters of Lake Michigan. All of the people were absorbed in their own lives. None were concerned about Mercedes' mission.

Fighting the urge to turn around and leave, she slipped her hand into the pocket of her shorts. The letter crackled under her touch. *It would be ridiculous to turn back when I've come this far,* she told herself.

She reached for the door handle, then pulled back. *They*

might still require masks in this building. I don't want to get thrown out of this place the minute I walk in.

Reaching into her other pocket, she pulled out her mask and put it on. Then, mustering every ounce of her courage, she opened the door and stepped into the lobby.

The place certainly wasn't what she would think of as upscale, although it was pleasant and clean and appeared to be fairly recently constructed. The pale blue walls were accented with dark trim and wainscoting. Large potted plants sat here and there, giving the lobby a homey look. To her right, three elderly women sat on upholstered chairs clustered around a small table, enjoying a leisurely conversation. Mercedes had the distinct impression that the building's "adults only" designation actually meant housing for senior citizens.

It's not a bad place to live, she thought. She was glad not to find her grandfather's former wife residing in dismal conditions.

As she glanced around, she saw that some people were wearing masks, while others weren't. She noticed the office straight ahead, where a middle-aged woman sat at a desk languidly scrolling through her cell phone. Mercedes took several steps toward her, thinking the woman might be a source of information. She noted a plaque on the desk inscribed with the name *Audrey,* followed by the title *Receptionist.*

She was about to open her mouth to ask Audrey whether Dora resided in the building when she spotted a bank of mailboxes to her left. So, she changed course and wandered in that direction. Finding the name of Dora Covington on one of the boxes would confirm that she'd come to the right place.

Suddenly, it occurred to her that Dora might not be at home. Saturday afternoon might well be a time for her to run an errand or visit a friend.

"Can I help you, Miss?" the receptionist called out in an indifferent tone.

Mercedes jumped at the sound of Audrey's voice, wondering whether she suspected her of being a trespasser. "What is your mask policy in this facility?" she asked.

"If you are fully vaccinated, you don't need to wear a mask, so long as you are visiting with a vaccinated resident," Audrey replied. She looked at Mercedes suspiciously. "Are you vaccinated? If not, you need to keep your mask on."

"I'm fully vaccinated," Mercedes said. Audrey glanced at her doubtfully, and Mercedes couldn't muster the nerve to remove her mask.

"Who are you coming to see?" Audrey asked.

"I'm looking for Dora Covington," Mercedes answered. "Does she live here?"

Audrey nodded impassively, her eyes returning to her phone. "Yes, she does. On the second floor."

"Do you know if she's home?"

For a brief moment, Mercedes hoped the answer to her question would be no. She would then ask Audrey to put the letter in Dora's mailbox. After that, her mission would be accomplished. She could turn around and leave, telling herself she'd made her best effort.

"As far as I know, Mrs. Covington is home," Audrey said. "I haven't seen her come down today." She raised her head and smiled at Mercedes. "She lives in apartment 204 on the second floor." Pointing to the signs for the elevators and the stairs on both sides of the lobby, she added, "The stairs to your right will take you closest to her apartment."

"Thanks," Mercedes said. She walked over to the recommended staircase and climbed it to the second floor. Passing apartment doors on both sides of the hallway, she stopped in front of the door marked 204. She could hear the faint strains of music coming from inside the apartment, so she knew someone was home.

Panic fluttered in her stomach, making her feel nauseous. *What do I say to her when she opens the door? Oh my God, what the hell am I doing here?*

Taking a deep breath, she tapped on the door. She heard the soft thump of a recliner returning to a sitting position, then feather-light footsteps crossing the floor. The door opened a crack, and large blue eyes peered out at her.

Mercedes instantly recognized the eyes from the photo Javi had found in her mother's drawer. But something deep inside her recognized them in another way, from a memory she couldn't articulate.

She suddenly thought of the many predators and scammers who target vulnerable senior citizens, and she imagined the woman might be fearful of the masked stranger standing there in the hallway. "It's okay," she assured her, "I'm not going to hurt you." Immediately, she felt foolish for saying such a thing.

The woman opened the door a little wider, but still appeared hesitant. "Don't worry," Mercedes blurted out, continuing to embarrass herself. "I don't have Covid. I've been vaccinated."

The woman smiled. "I've been vaccinated, too," she said in a tremulous voice. "So, I guess we're safe. Come on in."

Mercedes stepped into the apartment, removing her mask and stuffing it into her pocket. For a few seconds, she stood staring at the elderly woman, who gazed back at her with questioning eyes.

The woman was small and thin, her posture slightly stooped. Her long white hair was pulled back into a braid that hung to her waist, and wispy curls framed her soft face. Her silky gold blouse topped a full ankle-length skirt shimmering in shades of purple and gold. She wore gold bangles on one wrist, and her feet were bare. The essence of her seemed airy, translucent, more spirit than human flesh and bone.

Standing there in her sweat-drenched tank top and shorts, Mercedes felt awkward and oversized in the presence of someone so delicate. "Are you Dora Covington?" she asked.

The woman nodded. "Yes, I am. And you are…?"

"Mercedes Maldonado."

Dora tilted her head, looking at her quizzically. "Do I know you?"

"I-I think so," Mercedes stammered. "At least, you used to know me."

She glanced around Dora's apartment. It was clean and

tidy, set up for efficient living in a compact space. Adjacent to the small living room was a tiny kitchenette. A slightly open door leading off the living room revealed a small bedroom.

The unusual décor in the living room piqued Mercedes' interest. Like Dora's long silky skirt, her living quarters exuded the exotic. A few statues of angels were displayed here and there, but Mercedes could not recognize the subject matter of most of the decorative objects in the room. She thought they might be symbols of some foreign religion.

A sweet, musky scent permeated the apartment. *Is that a candle?* she wondered. *Or incense?* The droning strains of the music barely audible from the hallway were now louder, and hauntingly sweet. The overall effect of the surroundings struck Mercedes as other-worldly.

This sure isn't your typical old lady apartment, she thought.

Then her eyes traveled to a massive painting hanging above the sofa. It depicted a stately angel seated on a rock in a lush garden, lovingly attending to a tiny dark-haired girl gazing into a small pond. It was a stunning piece of art.

Forgetting her nervousness, Mercedes gasped and pointed. "That painting! I've seen it before!"

She caught herself when she saw the startled expression on Dora's face. "Well, I don't know if I've really seen it. But I know for sure I saw it in a photograph."

She suddenly wished that, along with the letter, she'd stolen the picture of her and Dora from her mother's house. It would've explained everything. But in her effort to rescue the letter, she'd left the photo on her mother's couch. It had probably fallen between the cushions by now.

Dora gestured toward the painting. "I painted this more than twenty-five years ago. I've given away most of my paintings, as I don't have space for them anymore. But I kept this one because it's my favorite. It has always hung in my living room wherever I've lived."

Her brow furrowed. "But I can't imagine how you could've seen it." She looked at Mercedes pointedly. "I don't mean to be rude. But how do we know each other?"

24

Mercedes thought carefully before phrasing her response. "I think you knew me when I was a little girl. As Mercedes Covington. But back then, everyone called me Sadie."

Suddenly, Dora's eyes lit up with recognition. "Oh! You're Andrew's granddaughter! Little Sadie!" Her slight body began to tremble, and Mercedes was afraid the elderly woman would collapse from shock.

But Dora steadied herself, hanging onto the apartment door for a moment before closing it. "Come, let's sit," she said in a breathless voice. She took a few steps to her recliner and sank into it, as if the shock had completely drained her store of energy. Hesitantly, Mercedes seated herself on the end of the sofa nearest Dora's chair.

Dora placed both hands on her heart. "Oh, Sadie, I never expected to see you again. Never, never, never! I thought you were gone from my life for good."

Then she leaned her head against the back of the chair and closed her eyes. Mercedes noticed that her breathing was labored, and she wondered whether her surprise visit was proving to be too much for her grandfather's former wife.

"I'm sorry," she murmured. "I didn't mean to upset you. Maybe I shouldn't have come."

Dora's eyes flew open. "My dear girl, please don't apologize. I'm delighted that you came. What a wonderful surprise this day has brought me! I can hardly take it in."

Her hands fluttered self-consciously over her hair and clothing. "If I'd known you were coming, I would've fixed myself up a bit."

She glanced toward an old-fashioned CD player sitting on a bookshelf on the other side of the small room. "I'm afraid the music is a bit too loud. Let me turn it off so we can talk." She eased herself out of her chair, then walked across the room to push a button on the player.

"I've never heard music like that," Mercedes said. "It's relaxing."

"It's the music I listened to when I lived at the ashram," Dora explained as she seated herself again. "We chanted a lot of Sanskrit mantras there. I still do. They quiet my spirit and soothe my soul."

Mercedes had never known anyone who'd lived in an ashram. She wanted to ask questions, but decided it wasn't the time.

Then, as if she'd reclaimed her strength, Dora reached toward Mercedes, grasping her hand. "My dear little Sadie! You have no idea how thrilled I am to see you!" She hesitated. "Perhaps I shouldn't call you Sadie. You go by Mercedes now?"

"Yes," Mercedes replied. "I prefer that."

"Of course," Dora said. "You're all grown up now. The last time I saw you, you had just turned four. You were such a pretty little girl, and so bright. As I might've expected, you've grown into a beautiful young woman. So tall and elegant."

Mercedes winced. No one had ever before referred to her as elegant, although Javier worked relentlessly to get her to behave in such a manner. Still, Dora's compliment warmed her heart.

"How old are you now?" Dora asked. "In your early twenties?"

"I'm twenty-nine," Mercedes answered.

"Unbelievable," Dora murmured. "The years fly by, don't they?" She looked at Mercedes curiously. "I just have to know. How did you find me?"

"Through the internet," Mercedes admitted sheepishly. She suddenly felt like a stalker.

Dora jolted slightly at Mercedes words. "Oh. I guess a person can find anyone or anything on the internet these days. I don't know the first thing about such matters."

"I tried to find you in the phone book," Mercedes explained. "I wanted to call you instead of just showing up. But your name wasn't there. So, I figured you didn't have a landline phone."

"No," Dora said. "All I have is the cell phone my daughter gave me." She gestured to the phone lying on the end table next to her chair. "Corina wanted me to have something I could take with me anywhere I go. Although I don't go many places these days."

Nervously, she smoothed her colorful skirt over her knees, then turned to smile at Mercedes. "Well, I'm glad you found me. But I'm surprised you even remembered me."

"Actually, I didn't remember you," Mercedes confessed.

When she saw the puzzled look in Dora's eyes, she spoke quickly to provide a context for her visit. "Last week, I was cleaning my mother's house in Goshen. My son found some old photographs in her kitchen drawers. One of the pictures was of you holding me when I was a little girl. I didn't know who you were. So, I asked my mom about it, and she told me you were my grandpa's second wife."

Dora nodded. "Yes, I was married to your grandfather Andrew for a few years." Her confused expression told Mercedes that Dora was still unsure of her motive for tracking her down.

"It wasn't that hard to find you," Mercedes explained. "My mom told me she thought you lived in Saint Joseph or Benton Harbor. So, you weren't that far from us, just across the state line."

Then, the conversation lagged. Mercedes had no idea what to say next to move her mission forward. But after a few moments, Dora spoke hesitantly. "How is your grandfather Andrew?"

Oh no! Mercedes thought. *How do I tell her this?* She sensed her answer would be difficult for Dora to hear. Taking a deep breath, she said, "Grandpa Andy passed away three years ago."

"Oh!" Dora slumped back in her chair, her chest heaving. "Andrew is dead?" She fumbled for a tissue from the box on the end table and coughed into it several times.

"Excuse me," she said as she attempted to struggle to her feet. "I need to get myself a glass of water."

Mercedes jumped up. "Let me get it for you."

"Would you please?" Dora's voice was barely above a whisper. "The glasses are in the cupboard above the sink."

Good Lord, what am I doing to this poor woman? Mercedes thought as she walked the few steps to the kitchen. She filled a glass with water from the tap and brought it back to Dora.

Dora took a sip of the water, then cleared her throat. "I suppose this news should come as no surprise. We're all getting older. Still, I can't believe Andrew is gone."

She dabbed at her eyes with a tissue, then looked down, slowly wringing her hands in her lap. After a few moments, she raised her head and turned toward Mercedes with a dutiful smile. But Mercedes could tell that the news of her grandfather's death had dampened the elderly woman's spirit.

"I'm sorry," Mercedes mumbled. Mentally, she berated herself. *Why didn't I think this through? I just walked into this woman's life and turned her world upside down. I should've known something like this would happen.*

She knew there was only one thing to do. The moment had arrived for her to complete her mission. She reached into her pocket and pulled out the envelope. Handing it to Dora, she said, "My mom told me that Grandpa Andy wrote a letter to you before he died. That's why I came here today. To bring it to you."

With an astonished look on her face, Dora held the letter in her delicate hands, as if she'd just been given a gift of incomparable value. She read aloud the two words written on the front of the envelope: "To Dora." Then, with trembling fingers, she broke the seal and pulled out a single handwritten page. Mercedes watched the tears pour from the elderly woman's eyes as she read the letter.

When she was finished, Dora refolded the letter and laid it on her end table. Then she bent over, hands to her face, her frail body heaving with quiet sobs.

Dora's reaction to the letter frightened Mercedes, and she wondered again whether her mission was only serving to cause pain and distress.

After a few minutes, Dora raised her head and wiped her tears. "Please forgive me for my outburst," she said.

"It's okay," Mercedes murmured. She reached over and awkwardly patted Dora's shoulder.

Dora picked up the letter again and slid it back into its envelope. "These are such precious words written by your grandfather."

Mercedes could hardly contain her curiosity. She wanted to ask if she could read the letter. But she knew that would be an invasion of Dora's privacy, and her grandfather's as well. "Grandpa must've loved you," she said.

"And I loved him," Dora responded. "Oh, I loved Andrew with my whole heart. We had our challenging times, and it became too difficult for him to stay with me. But it's such a comfort to know that even though we couldn't be together in our physical life, in the end we're together in spirit. The thought warms my heart."

She clutched the letter to her chest. "Thank you, thank you, Mercedes, for bringing your grandfather's words to me. Recently, I've been thinking about Andrew, grieving over how things ended between us. My dear girl, I believe you've been an instrument of divine will. The spirit knew what I needed for healing, and you brought it to me."

Mercedes stared at Dora, dumbfounded. She could hardly fathom how her poorly-conceived mission had turned out to have such an important purpose in someone else's life. She was used to being known as a mouthy diva among her friends. To being called a brat by her mother. To being reprimanded by Javier for her impetuous behavior. Even to being scolded by her son. She'd never imagined anyone referring to her as an instrument of divine will.

"And it was so gracious of your mother to forward the letter to me," Dora added.

Old familiar anger welled up inside Mercedes, dispelling the unfamiliar wonderment she'd been feeling. "Actually, it wasn't gracious at all," she said. "Shortly before he died, Grandpa asked my mom to give the letter to you. But she didn't follow through. She hung onto it for three years. I learned about the whole thing just last week, after my son found that photo of you holding me. Mom tried to throw the letter away. But I sneaked it out of her house."

"Why?" Dora asked. "What motivated you to rescue your grandfather's letter?"

Mercedes paused, thinking back to the surreal feelings she'd had when she first laid eyes on the letter. "Because I wanted to honor my grandpa's last wishes. And because I thought you should know what he wanted to say to you. The letter seemed important to me, too important to throw into the trash."

"Oh my, oh my!" Dora exclaimed. "I'm so glad you saved it. I can't possibly express what this means to me."

Once again, she retreated into silence, head bowed, holding the letter to her heart. She seemed to have withdrawn into a world of her own.

The moments passed, and Mercedes felt uneasy. *I should probably leave her alone,* she thought. She scooted toward the edge of her seat, ready to stand. "Maybe I should go now."

Dora shook her head as if to rouse herself from her reverie. "I'm sorry. I was lost in thought. Please don't feel you need to go. It's been so many years since I've seen you, and we have so much catching up to do."

"Okay." Mercedes settled back onto the sofa. "I guess I have time to stay a little longer."

"Wonderful!" Dora beamed at Mercedes. Then a shadow crossed her face. "Mercedes, I just have to ask this. How's your mother doing? I've thought about her over the years, wondering how her life turned out."

Her concern for Denise took Mercedes by surprise. "Did you have a close relationship with my mom?" she asked.

"I can't say that we were close," Dora replied. "But I did see a lot of Denise when I was married to your grandfather. The last time I saw her, I was so worried about her. Things weren't going well in her life. I hope she's doing better now."

Mercedes sighed deeply. "I don't think anything has improved for my mom. Things have probably gotten worse. She has a drinking problem, and her health is going downhill. Diabetes, high blood pressure, liver problems. You name it, she's got it."

"I'm so sorry to hear that," Dora murmured. "She's still a young woman."

Mercedes nodded. "Mom is only forty-nine. But she's never taken care of herself. And now, her doctor says she's not capable of living on her own anymore. So, she's going to be moving in with her stepmother June."

At the mention of June's name, Dora's face darkened. Mercedes wondered whether she had struck a nerve.

But after a few seconds of silence, Dora said, "I'm so sorry, Mercedes. It must be terribly hard on you to have your mother in such a condition."

Dora's kind words brought tears to Mercedes' eyes. No one had ever expressed sympathy for the pain she had to endure in dealing with her mother. "Yes," she said. "It's hard to watch someone destroy themselves. Mom refuses to do anything the doctor tells her to do. Every time I see her, I can tell she's a little worse off."

Anger welled inside her again. "It makes me so mad that she's let herself get to this point. It puts a burden on everyone else. Right now, I'm working on getting her house cleaned up so we can sell it. It's a terrible mess. I don't have the time to deal with it, but I have to."

"I'm sure that's a lot for you," Dora replied. She paused, furrowing her brow as if deep in thought. "Mercedes, our conversation has brought up a question I've wondered about for years. Did your mother and grandfather ever make amends with each other?"

The question bewildered Mercedes. "What do you mean?"

Dora brought her hand to her mouth as if to stop herself from divulging any more information. "I'm sorry. It's not in my place to talk about your family business."

"There's a lot about my family history that doesn't make sense to me," Mercedes said. "So please, tell me what you meant by your question."

Dora hesitated, as if uncertain about the wisdom of saying anything more. "Well, your mother and grandfather had a falling out a few months before he and I parted ways. Denise stopped speaking to her father. At the time Andrew left me, they still hadn't made up."

Mercedes chewed on her lip, thinking back to her early childhood. "They must've made up somehow. Because I remember at my sixth birthday party, my mom brought a strange man and woman up to me and said, 'Sadie, this is your Grandpa Andy and your Grandma June.' It was like they showed up out of nowhere. I didn't think much about it at the time because I was just a little kid. But it seems weird to me now. From that point on, Grandpa Andy and June were in my life." She grimaced. "June is still in my life."

Dora chuckled. "I take it you don't care for her?"

Mercedes shook her head vehemently. "No, I can't stand that woman! She's bossy and overbearing and always has her nose in everybody's business. She thinks it's her job to point out every mistake I've ever made in my entire life. I don't know what Grandpa saw in her."

Dora turned her face away for a moment, but not before Mercedes caught a glimpse of a satisfied smile. She took a few sips of water, glancing vacantly around the room as if trying to collect herself.

Then she turned her attention back to Mercedes. "Tell me more about your life," she said. "You mentioned that you have a son?"

"Yes." Mercedes was relieved that the conversation was taking a lighter tone. "He's eight years old, and his name is Javier. We call him Javi. He's named after his father. Actually, he's Javier Maldonado III, and he's really proud of that. I just dropped him off at his dad's place to stay for a week. Javier lives in South Bend. So, it was convenient for me to drive on up here."

Dora's eyes held a questioning look. But she made no comment, and Mercedes decided it wasn't the time to explain her marital status.

"Javi is the light of my life," she continued. "He's the best thing that's ever happened to me. Would you like to see pictures of him?"

"Oh yes!" Dora said.

Mercedes pulled her phone from her pocket. Holding it out for Dora to see, she scrolled through half a dozen photos of her son. Dora peered closely at the pictures of the dark-haired, brown-skinned boy. "He's so beautiful," she sighed. "He reminds me of you when you were a child. Of course, you were much younger, just a toddler when I last saw you."

She gave a joyful little laugh. "My great-grandson! May I call him that? May I call you my granddaughter?"

Mercedes responded without hesitation. "Yes, you may!" She took the elderly woman's outstretched hand. "And that means I can think of you as my grandmother."

Hearing those words come out of her mouth shocked Mercedes. She was amazed at how comfortable she felt with a woman she'd known for less than an hour.

"Did you know you were the only grandchild I ever had?" Dora asked. "Neither of my two children produced offspring. And I only had the privilege of being your grandmother for a few years."

"That's sad," Mercedes said. "For both of us." She was surprised by a sudden surge of grief in the pit of her stomach. "I really wish you'd been in my life for longer than that."

Dora smiled. "I wish the same. But life has brought you back to me. Life sometimes gives us second chances."

Dora's words served to banish the last of Mercedes' doubts about the wisdom of her visit. *This really was meant to be,* she thought. *Divine guidance—or something—brought Dora and me back together.*

"So, you have children, too?" she said. She knew Dora's offspring couldn't have belonged to Mercedes' grandfather. It made her wonder about Dora's life prior to her marriage to Andrew Covington.

"Yes," Dora replied. "I have a daughter and a son. Corina is my oldest. She's had a career in nursing. She lives in Florida, and she works as an administrator for a traveling nurse's program."

"That's interesting," Mercedes said. "I'm a nursing student myself, at Indiana University in South Bend."

"Good for you!" Dora exclaimed. "Nursing is a wonderful career, filled with many opportunities. Corina has done very well for herself in that field. You met Corina a few times when you were little. Of course, you wouldn't remember her."

Mercedes shook her head. "I'm sure I don't."

"And then there's Wesley," Dora continued. "He works for the International Red Cross. His entire career has been with humanitarian aid organizations. He's been all over the world. Most recently, he's been in the Middle East. Syria, I believe."

Mercedes had never paid much attention to international news. But she was aware of the unrelenting conflict in the Middle East. "Aren't you afraid for your son's safety?" she asked.

Dora's eyes clouded with sadness. "Of course, I am. I've been worried about Wesley's safety for the past thirty-five years. There's a part of me that wants to plead with him to come back to the United States and find a different line of work. But I know my son is living out his soul's purpose. He's doing what he came into this world to do. And I'd never want to stand in the way of that. So, I just pray. Every day, I pray for Wesley."

"Your children are so far away," Mercedes said. "Do you ever get to see them?"

Dora's face brightened. "Oh, I see a lot of Corina. She flies up to spend a few days with me about once a month. She's really good about looking after her old mother. She takes care of my financial affairs now."

She indicated the entirety of the apartment with a sweep of her hand. "I'd never be able to afford this place just on my meager income. Corina pays for a portion of my rent. And whenever she comes to visit, she fills my refrigerator with food."

"And how about your son?" Mercedes asked. "Does he ever come to visit?

"Wesley comes home every couple of years," Dora replied. "So, I don't get to see him often, not in person. And much of the time, he's not in a place where he can call me. But I do get to video-chat with him from time to time. And I video-chat with Corina almost every day."

She held up her cell phone. "She's spent hours teaching me how to do that on this little phone. I've been such a slow learner."

Mercedes thought about her relationship with her own mother. Although the two of them could never manage to be civil with each other for more than a minute at a time, a week never passed without Mercedes making a trip to Goshen to check up on Denise. "I'm sorry you don't have children close by," she said.

Dora pondered for a moment before responding. "I suppose I am, too. But I'm so glad they're both following the callings of their hearts, even if it has taken them far away from me. In my younger years, my world was very narrow. For my children, the whole planet is their home. That pleases me."

A soft tap on the apartment door interrupted their conversation. "Oh," Dora said, glancing at the clock on her kitchen wall. "That must be Elliott."

"Come on in," she called.

The door opened, and Mercedes looked over to see the figure of a tall, powerfully built African American man filling the doorway. He was impeccably dressed in a dark suit and colorful tie. White hair and a well-groomed beard framed his broad, handsome face. The dark eyes behind his black-rimmed glasses seemed to hold bottomless wells of kindness. He was carrying a canvas tote bag.

Mercedes had difficulty determining the man's age, although she presumed him to be Dora's peer. But when he walked into the room, she was unsure. His movement was light and graceful, belying his bulky size.

"How are you feeling today, Dora?" he inquired. Mercedes was enchanted by the quality of his voice: deep, resonant, and commanding, yet warm and gentle.

Dora smiled fondly at him. "I'm doing fine, Elliott. As good as can be expected."

"I see you have a guest," he said. "Am I intruding?"

"Oh no," Dora said. "Let me introduce you. Elliott, this is my granddaughter, Mercedes Maldonado."

Elliott shot Mercedes a puzzled glance. "Your granddaughter?"

"Andrew's granddaughter," Dora explained. She reached over to pat Mercedes' hand. "But I claim her as my own."

Elliott smiled broadly. "Of course." He shifted the bag to his left hand and extended his right hand to Mercedes. "It's a pleasure to meet you, Miss Maldonado. I hope you're enjoying your visit."

Dora continued the introduction. "Mercedes, this is Dr. Elliott Jordan." Mercedes reached out to shake his hand.

"Ladies, I'll get out of your way and let you continue your visit," Elliott said good-naturedly. "Dora, I brought you some strawberries from the farmer's market on the bluff. I know how much you love them. Should I put them in your refrigerator?"

"Yes please, Elliott," Dora said. "Thank you so much for bringing me such a nice treat."

Elliott lifted a small container of strawberries out of the canvas bag and put it in the refrigerator. He carefully folded the bag and tucked it under his arm. Then he walked over to Dora and leaned down, his massive size dwarfing her tiny frame. Dora lifted her face to his, and ever so tenderly, he kissed her cheek.

As Mercedes watched, the sweet moment seemed suspended in time. The kiss was the most beautiful gesture she'd ever seen, and it brought tears to her eyes. She almost thought she saw a heavenly glow around the two elderly people. She could tell the kiss had nothing to do with romance. It was about a different kind of love.

"Is Elliott your doctor?" she asked after he'd left the apartment.

Dora chuckled. "No, Elliott isn't a medical doctor. He has a Ph.D. in social anthropology. He's a retired college professor, and he lives in Benton Harbor. He's such a good friend to me. Even though he's a very busy man, he comes over to Saint Joseph almost every day to check on me."

"Is he your boyfriend, then?"

Dora looked thoughtful. "I don't know that we think of our relationship in such terms. Elliott and I just love each other. He's the dearest friend I've ever had. I don't know what I've ever done to deserve a friend like Elliott Jordan."

"He seems very nice," Mercedes observed.

"He surely is," Dora murmured. "I can't imagine what I'd do if I didn't have Elliott in my life."

"How did the two of you meet each other?"

Dora seemed caught off guard by Mercedes' question, as if no one had ever asked her such a thing. "Oh, Elliott and

I go way back," she said. "Sometimes, it feels as if he's always been with me, although that isn't actually the case. Many years ago, he was my college professor. Since then, we've maintained a friendship."

Her blue eyes took on a faraway look. "A couple of years ago, when I knew it was time for me to leave the ashram, I was completely at loose ends. I had no idea where to go. Elliott suggested that I move here so that we could enjoy each other's company in our later years."

"Was it hard for you to leave the ashram?" Mercedes asked.

Dora nodded slowly. "Truthfully, I was very reluctant to leave. But..." She gestured toward the CD player and several of her statues. "I've brought the ashram with me into my new home. I've learned that the ashram has more to do with the state of the heart than with physical buildings."

She smiled blissfully. "And this new home of mine is so lovely. I'm so grateful to be here in Saint Joseph. Elliott occasionally takes me to Lake Michigan to spend a little time by the water. That's such a beautiful experience. There's a lookout park just across the street from here."

"Yes," Mercedes said. "I saw it."

"Sometimes, he drives me to downtown Saint Joseph," Dora continued. "And we take a walk along the bluff overlooking the lake. In recent years, we've enjoyed the antique shows and art fairs they hold there. And last winter, Elliott drove me out to see the Christmas lights on the bluff. The city puts up such an extravagant display. This area has always been Elliott's home. But it's all new to me. So, there's a lot for him to show me."

Then she looked down, her voice softening to almost a whisper. "Although I haven't been up for that sort of thing recently."

"Elliott is so kind to you," Mercedes noted.

Dora nodded in emphatic agreement. "I can tell you this, Mercedes. Elliott Jordan has the gentlest, most compassionate soul I've ever known a man to have."

Mercedes knew she was about to ask an intrusive question, but she was too curious to stop herself. "Since you and Elliott love each other so much, why haven't you gotten married?"

Dora drew in a long breath, fidgeting with the folds in her colorful skirt. "No one, other than my daughter Corina, has ever asked me that question, Mercedes." She gazed vacantly around the room, appearing to be lost in thought. "I suppose...." She hesitated, then started again. "I suppose it's been a matter of timing and circumstances."

She turned to face Mercedes. "When I first met Elliott, we were both single. We felt an instant attraction to each other. But it wasn't a romantic thing. It was a soul-to-soul type of connection."

She chuckled self-consciously. "Truthfully, I could've fallen in love with Elliott back then. He was so handsome and brilliant and wise. But he seemed so far above me, and I felt unworthy of his attention. The idea of him falling in love with me was beyond my wildest dreams.

"And, at the time, I felt constrained by societal prohibitions against being with someone outside of one's race. As a matter of fact, I was raised with the expectation that I would marry, not just within my own race, but within my own religious community."

She shook her head sadly. "I'm ashamed of the way I thought back then. It didn't take me long to realize those rules were meaningless. They were based on fear, not love. But Elliott had gone on to marry someone else. And then, I did as well."

"Is Elliott still married?" Mercedes asked. For a brief moment, she worried that Dora might be involved in some kind of love triangle.

"Oh no," Dora assured her. "His wife passed away during the time I was living at the ashram. So, he and I are both single. But what we have now seems perfect to me. I could never ask for anything more."

The idea that Dora and Elliott's love would never reach full fruition frustrated Mercedes. "You don't think the two of you will ever...?" Her voice trailed off when she realized she sounded pushy.

Dora responded in a kind but firm voice. "I've thought

about marrying Elliott. Of course, I have. Being that close to him would be lovely. But if he asked me to marry him now, I would have to say no. Because if he were to become my husband, I would risk saddling him with a mountain of medical bills. I'd never want to leave him with all that debt after I'm gone. I care too much about Elliott to do that to him."

Alarmed, Mercedes stared at Dora. "Are you sick?"

Dora smiled wanly. "Let's not talk about that right now. Let's just focus on the present moment, the moment that you and I are sharing."

As Mercedes surveyed Dora's face, she saw that the elderly woman looked utterly exhausted, dark half-moons underlining her weary eyes. "I really should go now," she said. "I think I've tired you out."

"I do feel a bit fatigued," Dora admitted. "Too much excitement for one day, I suppose. But I can hardly bear to see you go. My long-lost grandchild! May I be so presumptuous as to ask you to stop by and see me again?"

Mercedes didn't need to think before responding. "Of course! How can I stay away now? There's so much we haven't talked about yet." She cocked her head, looking at Dora questioningly. "Sometime, would you tell me the story about you and my grandfather? I'd like to know what happened between the two of you."

Dora nodded. "I'd be happy to do that. My love affair with Andrew is certainly a story worth telling. But I wouldn't know quite where or how to begin. How does one know when a story actually begins? Every moment, every day, every year always builds upon what happened the moment, the day, or the year before."

Suddenly, an idea struck Mercedes, and she spoke in an excited rush. "Dora, would you be willing to help me with a school assignment?"

Dora looked surprised. "Well, if I'm able to. What's the nature of the assignment?"

"I'm taking a course in geriatric nursing," Mercedes explained. "My professor told us that it's therapeutic for older people to reminisce about their lives. We have an assignment to spend time with a senior citizen and invite them to tell their life story. It's called doing a life review. Then we're supposed to write a paper about it."

She suddenly felt her face reddening. "I don't mean to imply that you're old."

"Of course, I'm old!" Dora chuckled. "I'm seventy-five. I think that qualifies as being a senior citizen by most people's standards."

"So," Mercedes said tentatively, "would you be willing to help?"

"I'm willing," Dora replied, "although I may not be your best candidate for the assignment. I haven't lived a very stable life. I've been all over the place, so to speak."

"But that's what will make your story interesting," Mercedes insisted.

"Then let's go ahead with it," Dora said. "Most of my days are behind me now. I guess if I'm going to tell my story, this is the time."

"Oh, thank you!" Mercedes exclaimed. "I was starting to worry about this assignment. I didn't have anyone to do it with. But then I met you, and it's all working out perfectly."

She stood up to leave. Dora stood up also, holding out her thin arms for a hug. "My little Sadie," she murmured. "It feels so wonderful to hold you again."

Mercedes allowed herself to soak in the warmth of the embrace, warmth that seemed to flow into an empty space in her heart. She was amazed at how connected she felt to Dora, at how well they seemed to know each other after such a short visit.

Then Dora stepped back, smiling. "I guess I'd better get prepared for this assignment. Going all the way back to the beginning will mean I'll have to do a lot of thinking. I'll get some things around so we can have some props." She seemed to have regained a bit of energy, and her blue eyes sparkled with excitement. "We'll have a wonderful time with this, won't we, Mercedes?"

"We sure will," Mercedes said. "Would it be okay if I came the same time next week? I'll need to go to South Bend to pick up Javi at his dad's place. But I can drive up here first."

"That would be just fine," Dora replied as she reached up to kiss Mercedes' cheek.

Mercedes had just closed the apartment door behind her when she heard Dora's cell phone ring. She stopped for a moment, pressing her ear to the door.

"Oh, Corina sweetheart," she heard Dora say. "You won't believe what a lovely surprise I had this afternoon." Then the conversation became muffled as Dora moved into another room.

Mercedes couldn't stop smiling as she headed toward the stairwell.

CHAPTER 3: DORA MILLER

The following Saturday, Mercedes entered the Harbor Lights lobby with considerably less trepidation than she'd experienced on her first visit. As she headed toward the stairwell leading to Dora's apartment, Audrey called to her from the reception desk. "You really made Mrs. Covington's day when you came to see her last week."

Mercedes paused, then altered her course, taking a few steps toward the desk. "How do you know that?" she asked.

Audrey smiled. "Mrs. Covington doesn't come downstairs very often. But I did see her sitting here in the lobby with a few other ladies the day after you visited, and all she could talk about was her long-lost granddaughter."

Mercedes chuckled as she pictured her sweet little grandmother engaged in animated conversation with her elderly friends. "Thanks for telling me that," she said as she headed back toward the stairwell.

Despite Audrey's reassuring words, butterflies danced in her stomach as she climbed the stairs to the second floor. She wondered whether this visit with Dora would feel as serendipitous as their first, or whether things would fall flat between them.

However, when Dora answered Mercedes' knock, her eager, bright-eyed greeting put Mercedes' mind at ease. The elderly woman was wearing an outfit similar to the one she'd worn the previous week, this time in shades of red, orange, and gold. Her long white hair was coiled into a tidy bun at the nape of her neck.

"It's so wonderful to see you again, Mercedes!" she exclaimed. "I've thought about our last visit all week long. And I've talked about it so much with Elliott that I'm afraid he's grown tired of hearing me prattle on and on."

As Mercedes seated herself on the sofa, she noticed a shabby suitcase made of cheap paperboard sitting on the floor beside the recliner. She wondered whether her grandmother had packed some of her belongings in preparation for a trip.

"So, how was your week?" Dora asked as she eased herself into her chair. "If I remember correctly, your son has been with his father. You must have missed him."

"Oh yes," Mercedes replied. "The apartment has been so quiet without Javi there. I'll be picking him up on my way home from here. I can't wait to see him again."

"And your schooling? How is that going?"

"I think I'm doing okay. I've had plenty of time to catch up on assignments with Javi gone."

"And your mother? How is she doing?"

Mercedes sighed, reluctant to delve into that gloomy topic again. "I saw her Thursday when I went over to the house to clean. She seems to be holding her own this week. As cranky as ever."

Dora folded her hands primly in her lap. "Mercedes, I think I owe you an apology. Last week, we talked at length about your mother. After you left, I realized I hadn't inquired about your father Joaquin. I hope that didn't imply that I thought of him as unimportant in your life."

The mention of her father caught Mercedes off guard, rendering her speechless. She stared at Dora in bewilderment.

"Are Denise and Joaquin no longer together?" Dora asked.

Mercedes shook her head, words still failing her.

"Do you still have a relationship with your father?"

Mercedes felt herself sinking into a pool of painful memories she'd buried years earlier. When she finally managed to speak, her words felt heavy. "My dad left when I was six."

"Oh!" Dora exclaimed. "I'm so sorry to hear that!"

The compassionate look on the elderly woman's face invited Mercedes to say more. She felt the door to the memories open wider, and she couldn't stop herself from plunging all the way in. "When I was little, my dad lived with my mom and me at my Grandma Norma's house. Some of the time, anyway. He and Mom fought a lot. She'd kick him out, and he'd go live with his friends for a while. Then they'd make up, and she'd let him move back in."

"That must've been hard on you," Dora noted. "All that coming and going. I seem to recall you were a daddy's girl when you were little. Whenever I saw you with your parents, you were always in your father's arms."

Mercedes nodded, her heart seizing with pain. She bent over slightly, shoulders hunched, trying to ward off the grief that threatened to overwhelm her. "Yes, it was awful sometimes. Mom would get so mad that she'd scream at my dad to get the hell out of her house. I always cried when I saw him walk out the door. But I always figured he'd come back. I knew I'd see him again."

She smiled, recalling fond memories. "When my daddy would walk back into the house a few days later, he'd call out, "Mijita!" And I'd come running and jump into his arms. He'd swing me around, and I'd giggle so hard that I could barely breathe.

"My dad's English wasn't very good, so he didn't actually talk much with me. But that was okay. He didn't need to talk to let me know how much he loved me."

She rocked slightly in her seat, the pain hitting hard again. "I remember what it felt like to snuggle up in his arms and lay my head against his shoulder. That always made me feel so safe. I remember what he smelled like. I can't describe it. It was just the smell of my daddy, and it was comforting to me.

"But one day, my Grandma Norma sat me down and told me my daddy wasn't coming home anymore."

"Oh my!" Dora exclaimed. "What happened?"

"Grandma told me he'd gone back to Mexico. A few years later, when I was old enough to understand, she explained the whole thing to me. She told me that my father had been an illegal immigrant. He'd come to Goshen because there were lots of jobs in the factories. Grandma told me he was a good worker. He sent money back to his family in Mexico, but he helped out my mom and grandma, too."

Dora nodded. "The few times I met Joaquin, I sensed he was a decent fellow. Do you know what prompted him to leave this country?"

Mercedes exhaled deeply, blowing her breath forcefully

through her lips. As she spoke, her body felt hot and shaky. "I can hardly stand to think about this. Grandma told me that one day when my parents were fighting, my mom called the police and filed a domestic violence report against my dad. When the police arrested him, they found out that he was in this country illegally. So, he ended up getting deported.

"My grandma felt terrible about the whole situation. She'd always liked my dad. She told me that my mom's allegations weren't true. She said Mom ended up regretting what she'd done. She'd called the police in a fit of rage, never expecting things to go as far as they did."

Teary-eyed, Mercedes looked up at Dora, who was shaking her head sadly, listening intently. She felt something burst open inside her, and she couldn't stop the words from pouring out. "I hate my mom for what she did to my dad. She's done a lot of terrible things in her life, but this was the worst. I cried so much when I finally understood that my daddy would never come back. I remember Grandma Norma holding me on her lap, rocking me, crying along with me. The two of us were just…wailing…in our grief."

"Oh my, oh my, oh my!" Dora suddenly seemed overwhelmed by the tragedy of Mercedes's story. Her frail hand shook as she lifted a tissue to dab at her eyes. She took a moment to draw several laborious breaths before adding, "Your grandmother was such a kind woman. When I was with Andrew, he introduced me to Norma. I sensed right away that she had a heart of gold."

Mercedes nodded, sniffling, staring down at the knees of her jeans. "Grandma Norma was very sweet. She's been gone for more than seven years, and I miss her like crazy. She felt so bad about my dad getting deported. She blamed herself for not stopping my mom from calling the police. So, she did a lot to try to keep me in contact with my father.

"About a month after he left, my dad wrote me a letter. He wasn't very literate in English, so the letter was hard to understand. But it was good to know he hadn't forgotten me.

"Grandma helped me write back to him. We sent a few more letters back and forth, two or three times a year. I always made sure to put one of my school pictures in with the letter so my dad wouldn't forget what I looked like.

"The summer when I was ten, Grandma Norma got me a passport, and she arranged for me to fly down to Mexico for a two-week visit with my dad. I know she was trying to do right by me. She was trying to make sure that I maintained a relationship with my father. But going to Mexico was the scariest thing that ever happened to me."

Mercedes raised her eyes to meet Dora's. "I wasn't scared because of my dad. It was because of other things. There are parts of this story I haven't told anyone."

Dora reached out to place a hand on Mercedes' knee, her face a mirror of her granddaughter's pain. "My dear, if you want to confide in me, I am more than willing to listen."

Mercedes hesitated, chewing on her lip. But the sincerity of Dora's words and the unbrokenness of her kindly gaze eased her discomfort. She leaned her elbow on the sofa's armrest, her head propped against her palm, her eyes downcast. "Grandma Norma was nervous about sending me off on my own. She arranged with the airline to have a flight attendant look after me. I guess children travel alone like that all the time. But I wasn't ready for it. I was so scared.

"I flew from Chicago to Houston, and then on to Veracruz, Mexico. At one point, the flight between Houston and Veracruz got rough. I started feeling sick to my stomach, and I threw up all over myself. I was so upset and so embarrassed that I couldn't stop crying. The flight attendant was nice to me and helped me clean up. But all I wanted was to go back home to Grandma Norma. Of course, I couldn't do that.

"My dad was there at the airport in Veracruz to pick me up. He was so excited to see me. He called out, "Mijita!" Then he picked me up and swung me around, just like he'd done when I was little.

"But after five years of not seeing him, my dad felt like a stranger to me. He wasn't the same person I'd known in Goshen. He looked a lot older, and he seemed broken down and worn out. When he tried to communicate with me, I could tell he hadn't spoken English in a long while. Honestly, I didn't feel very comfortable with him.

"After we left the airport, we had to take a ride in an old bus to my father's village. I think it took an hour or two to get there, but it seemed like forever. The route was winding and hilly, and I got sick from the bumpy ride. I thought I was going to throw up again. Thankfully, I didn't have anything left in my stomach.

"In the village, there were no paved streets, only narrow dirt roads. The stucco houses all looked the same to me, small and shabby and rundown. They were close together, practically on top of each other.

"I was shocked when I walked into my dad's house. It was so tiny, and they didn't have much furniture. My grandma's home was never fancy, but compared to my dad's place, it was a mansion."

"I can only imagine," Dora said. "The contrast must have been quite startling to you."

Mercedes nodded. "That's for sure. I'd had no idea how poor my father and his family were. I know he wanted me to feel welcome. But all in all, that visit was a disaster.

"My dad had gotten married when he moved back to Mexico, and he had three little children. His wife and children spoke no English at all. So, with my dad's English being so poor, it felt like I was cut off from everybody.

"I wasn't used to the food my dad's wife cooked, and I could hardly eat it. There was just one bedroom in the house, with only one bed. The two littlest children slept in the bed with their parents, while the oldest one slept on the floor. I ended up sleeping on the floor out in the front room. That was awful. I couldn't fall asleep at night, because of all the strange noises outside in the street. I was so scared and so homesick.

"My dad wanted me to meet his whole family: his parents, grandparents, brothers, and sisters. So, they had a big family gathering while I was there. I could tell nobody knew what to make of me, the little girl from America. I'd see them pointing at me and whispering. Several times, I overheard them calling me a *coconut*. I had no idea why. I was so embarrassed that I wanted to run away. But I had no place to run to.

"It was years later when I learned what the Mexicans meant by the term *coconut*. It refers to someone who is brown on the outside, but white on the inside. Somebody who looks Mexican, but acts white. I guess that's always been true about me."

Dora nodded in understanding. Mercedes paused, taking in her grandmother's kindly gaze before continuing.

"My father worked on a coffee plantation. Every morning, he rode to work in a big truck with a bunch of other men from the village. So, I was left in the care of his wife while he was gone.

"Those felt like the longest days of my life. I could tell my dad's wife resented me. I don't think she wanted to be reminded that her husband had had another life back in America.

"One day when she was fixing food for her children and me, I tried to help. I was trying to make her happy with me. I accidentally spilled a plate of rice and beans on the floor. She grabbed me by my shoulders and shook me, screaming at me in Spanish. Then, she sent me outside and wouldn't let me eat with her children, because I had wasted food.

"The first thing she did when my dad got home was to get in his face and scream at him. I knew she was complaining about me, giving him an earful. Even though I couldn't understand what she was saying, one thing was clear. She hated me and didn't want me there.

"I was so freaked out by that incident. Grandma Norma had never treated me that way. All I wanted to do was to go back home. Unfortunately, I had another week left to stay in Mexico. It felt like a year.

"I didn't want to stay in the house with my dad's wife all day, for fear I'd do something else to upset her. But I didn't want to go outdoors, either. I was pretty sure she'd been complaining about me to the neighbors, saying how bad and stupid I was. I was afraid everyone would make fun of me. So, I didn't know what to do with myself.

"And to top it all off, it was really hot there in Mexico, hotter than it ever got in Goshen. I couldn't handle it. I was so miserable.

"The day my dad took me back to the airport in Veracruz, he was sad to see me go. He broke down and cried. He knew the visit hadn't gone well, and he was sorry about that. He told me that someday, I would come back to Mexico to live with him and be part of his family, and that we would all be happy together.

"What he said scared me. It put a weird idea in my head. I was afraid the same thing would happen to me that had happened to him, that I'd be deported and have to stay in Mexico forever. Of course, I know now that something like that could never happen, because I was born in America and I'm an American citizen.

"I know my father didn't mean to frighten me. He was just having a hard time saying goodbye. But I don't think I've ever gotten over my fear of being deported to Mexico. The idea still bothers me.

"When I got home, Grandma Norma wanted to hear all about my trip. But I couldn't talk to her about it. She could tell it had been hard for me, and she felt bad. Over the years, she brought up the subject from time to time, apologizing to me, telling me she'd made a mistake in sending me off to Mexico on my own. 'I should've known it would be too much for a child,' she'd say.

"The first night after I came home from my trip, I lay awake in bed worrying about being deported to Mexico. Right then and there, I made a decision. In order to protect myself, I was going to live like I was completely white. To act as if the Mexican part of me didn't exist.

"I wasn't the only Hispanic kid in Goshen, not by a long shot. The last twenty or thirty years, there's been a large Hispanic population in the city. A number of children from Mexico and Central America went to school with me. But they all had Hispanic parents, with Spanish being the primary language in their homes. I was being raised in a white family, living a whole different kind of life. And I didn't know more than a few words of Spanish.

"Actually, I didn't even want to know Spanish. When I was attending Goshen High School, we were required to take a foreign language. Spanish was one option. But you know what I did? I took German instead. That was how much I tried to reject the Mexican side of me."

Mercedes raised her gaze and was surprised to see that her elderly companion was weeping silently.

"That's so sad," Dora whispered, shaking her head. "So tragic that such a beautiful child would feel she needed to reject a part of herself."

She wiped her eyes with a tissue, coughed a few times, then struggled to clear her throat. "Have you kept in touch with your father since your visit to Mexico?"

"No," Mercedes admitted. "I haven't had any contact with my dad for nineteen years. I have no idea where he is or what he's doing. Or if he's even alive. When I came back from Mexico, I forced myself to stop thinking about him. I put my dad in a little box in the back of my mind, and I closed the lid and went on with my life."

She was surprised to find that her own cheeks were wet with tears. Pulling a tissue from the box on the end table, she dabbed at her smeared mascara.

"Remembering all this is painful, isn't it?" Dora said softly.

Mercedes nodded, choking on a sob. "Javier keeps bugging me about us taking a trip to Mexico. He's from Mexico City. He wants our son to know his family and his culture. But I keep telling him no. I don't want Javi to go to Mexico."

"Why is that?" Dora asked.

"I'm afraid that Javier will want to keep him down there. I'm afraid that if Javier decides to move back to Mexico, he'll take Javi with him. And I'll lose my son forever."

The thought of that made her entire body tremble with anxiety. She folded her arms across her stomach and began rocking herself. "I could never live with losing my son. I told Javier that if he ever tries to take Javi out of the country, I'll go to court and fight him tooth and nail."

"Let's hope it never comes to that." Dora's calm, even tone was reassuring. "Perhaps you're letting your fear run away with you."

"Maybe so," Mercedes mumbled. "I get carried away sometimes."

She sat in silence for a moment, twisting a lock of her long black hair. "I should probably explain the whole situation to you. Javier and I are married. But we separated five months ago.

"We've always had a rocky relationship. During the height of the pandemic, things went from bad to worse. Javier was working from home most of the time. I was trying to complete my nursing courses online. At the same time, we were trying to help Javi with his virtual learning. The three of us were on top of each other in our apartment all day long."

Mercedes lowered her gaze, feeling ashamed of what she was divulging about herself. "I guess I drove Javier crazy with my messiness and disorganization. He was constantly on my case, telling me I needed to get my act together. I'd end up screaming at him. Sometimes, I'd get so upset that I'd throw things at him. He hates it when I act like that."

Shaking her head woefully, she added, "I can't really blame him. I know I can be a handful."

She glanced up at Dora, half-expecting to see a reproachful look on her grandmother's face. But Dora's expression remained serene. "What brought you to the point of separation?" she asked.

"Well," Mercedes continued, "one night in January, we had a huge fight. Javier usually stays calm while I yell. He says hurtful things to me, but in a quiet voice. When he starts yelling back at me, I know he's at the end of his rope. That night, things escalated to the point where one of our neighbors pounded on our door, threatening to call the police if we didn't quiet down. Javi got so upset that he cried and begged us to stop fighting. Both of us felt terrible about that. Javier ended up sleeping in Javi's room that night, just to make him feel secure.

"The next morning, Javier came to me and said, 'Mercedes, we need to talk.' So, we got our coffee and sat down at the table. 'This isn't working,' he told me.

"I didn't put up any argument. I knew he was right.

"He went on to talk about how it wasn't good for any of

us to live in such a volatile environment. 'I can't put my son through this any longer,' he said. 'I love you, Mercedes. But I think we need to take a break from each other.'

"That afternoon, he started looking for another place to live. He moved out a few days later."

"Was it hard to see him go?" Dora asked.

Mercedes nodded. "I cried a lot when he left. But it was also a relief. For the first time in years, I felt like I could relax and be myself, without worrying about him criticizing me all the time."

"From everything you've told me," Dora observed, "it seems that Javier is still a big part of your life."

"Yeah," Mercedes admitted. "We talk almost every day, and we text each other all the time. We still fight a lot, but we can't seem to let go of each other." She flashed Dora a grim smile. "And one of the things we fight about is going to Mexico."

"Does Javier know the story about you and your father?" Dora asked.

"A little bit of it," Mercedes replied. "Not everything I told you. Part of our whole Mexico argument is that he thinks I should visit my father again. He thinks I should get to know other family members in Mexico: my brothers, sisters, aunts, uncles, and cousins. He doesn't understand why I don't want to do that. He thinks I'm just being coldhearted."

Feeling drained and exhausted, she huddled in the corner of the sofa. After a few moments, she said, "I know it's not right to blame my dad for leaving me. It wasn't his fault. But when I was little, I didn't understand that. It felt like he'd abandoned me. Maybe that's why I don't trust Mexican men."

"Oh?" Dora said.

"But that's not fair. Because any time I need something, Javier is the first person I turn to. I can always count on him to come through for me. Financially, he takes good care of Javi and me."

"Perhaps someday," Dora suggested, "you will trust Javier with the whole story about you and your father. That might help him understand you."

"Maybe I will." Mercedes' eyes welled with tears again. "Thanks. It was so nice of you to listen to me."

"Oh, there's no need to thank me. It's the least I can do." Resting her hand on her heart, Dora drew several long breaths, her thin chest rising and falling with the effort. Then she spoke again. "Did you ever tell your mother about your difficulty in Mexico?"

Mercedes shook her head. "No. It never even crossed my mind to do that. She was partying so much at the time, and I knew better than to think she would care about what happened. I wouldn't tell her now, because she still wouldn't care. She'd just start talking ugly about my father."

"I guess none of that surprises me," Dora said. "I don't mean to speak badly of your mother. But when you were little, I could see that she was already heading into deep trouble with her drinking. I wanted so much to protect you. But I knew I was limited in what I could do."

Then she spoke in a hushed tone. "Mercedes, since you've confided in me, let me confide in you. Let me tell you something that no one else knows. Not a soul." She pointed toward the picture above the sofa. "The little girl in that painting is you."

Mercedes glanced over her shoulder at the picture, then stared at Dora in astonishment. "You're kidding me!"

"No," Dora said, "I'm telling you my heartfelt truth. When you were little, I wanted to make everything right for you, but I knew I couldn't. I felt so helpless. So, I painted this picture as a prayer of protection for you."

Dora's words sent an electric chill through Mercedes' body. For a few moments, she sat with her head bowed, trying to comprehend what Dora had told her.

Then, twisting herself around on the sofa, she gazed intently at the picture, wondering if Dora's painted prayer had indeed exerted an influence on her life. She studied the individual brush strokes in the little girl's face and hair, imagining the love that went into each stroke. A feeling she couldn't identify welled up inside her, overwhelming her. *Reconnecting with Dora can't be just a random event,* she thought. *Maybe it was our destiny to meet up again.*

She realized she needed to respond to Dora's revelation. "Thank you," was all she could manage to say.

Dora smiled, then looked down, self-consciously fingering the bangles on her wrist.

The two women shared a long moment of silence before Mercedes spoke again. "Maybe your prayer worked. I haven't gone down the same road my mom went down. Oh sure, when I was a teenager, I ran wild and nobody could stop me. I got into some trouble. But I've pulled myself out of that phase. And right now, I'm trying to get an education so I can make something of my life."

"My dear sweet Mercedes," Dora murmured. "I'm so happy for you. And so very proud of you."

Then Mercedes sat up straight, speaking with resolve. "I want you to know something, Dora. I don't drink, not at all. I don't use any drugs. I used to party, but when I started dating Javier, he didn't like it when I got drunk and crazy. The first time he took me to a club, I got a little out of hand. He was so angry with me. He told me he didn't want to be with a girl who made a fool of herself like that. We fought about it, and we even broke up for a few days. But in the end, I stopped doing drugs and I cut down on my drinking. And the minute I found out I was pregnant with Javi, I stopped drinking completely. I haven't had a drop of alcohol since then."

"Why is that?" Dora asked.

"It's for Javi's sake. I never want him to have the same impression of me that I have of my mother. Javier is glad I've made that decision."

"Does Javier drink?"

"I've known him to have a glass of wine or a cocktail," Mercedes replied. "But he's never been one to overdo it. He never drinks around me because he doesn't want to tempt me to drink. He knows that alcoholism runs in my family."

She paused. "Just recently, I learned that my grandpa had a problem with alcohol when he was younger. Did you know that?"

Pain flickered in Dora's eyes. "Yes. Andrew did struggle with addiction."

Mercedes sensed it was her grandmother's turn to feel the stirring of disquieting memories. She knew it wasn't the time to probe any deeper into her grandfather's problems.

After a moment of awkward silence, Dora spoke. "I guess I've asked you enough questions for today. You came here for help with your assignment." She pointed to the battered suitcase on the floor next to her chair. "Would you mind setting that on the coffee table?"

When Mercedes lifted the suitcase onto the table, Dora said, "You can go ahead and look inside."

Mercedes opened the suitcase's clasp and lifted the lid. She pulled out a long, plain, dark blue dress that looked as if it was made to fit a slender girl or woman. Then she pulled out a pair of thick black stockings, sturdy laced-up black shoes, and a white bonnet slightly yellowed with age. She looked at Dora, perplexed. "Is this a pioneer costume? Something from *Little House on the Prairie?"*

"No," Dora replied. "That's Amish clothing."

"Huh?"

"With growing up in Goshen, I'm sure you've seen Amish people."

Mercedes nodded, thinking of the horse-drawn buggies she'd often passed on northern Indiana highways. Many times, she'd wondered about the lives of Amish people, but had never known any personally.

"I was born and raised in the Amish community," Dora explained. "That clothing is what I wore as a teenage girl."

She chuckled at the stunned expression on Mercedes' face. "I can see that comes as a shock to you. I guess I should start my story by telling you about my childhood."

I was born in 1946, the fourth of Ezra and Martha Miller's six children. I was raised on a farm near the small town of Middlebury, Indiana, along with my sisters Rebecca, Sarah, and Katie and my brothers Daniel and Eli.

We were a typical Amish family for that time and place. I grew up with no modern conveniences in my home: no electricity, no telephone, no indoor plumbing. Our house was lit by kerosene lamps and heated by a woodburning stove. We did not own an automobile. Our transportation was the same as that of the Amish folk you see today: horse-drawn buggies. My father used horse-drawn implements to work his fields.

My Amish homelife was extraordinarily quiet compared to the average American household of that day. There were no voices emanating from a television set, no music blaring from a radio or record player. There was no ringing telephone, no sounds from electric appliances. Not even the hum of a refrigerator. Despite the fact that we were a large family, the soft-spoken demeanor of household members kept the noise level to a minimum.

I know that those in the broader world look upon Amish folk as oddities, with their unconventional lifestyle. But to a child growing up in the Amish community, those in the outer world are the peculiar ones. The Amish refer to them as "English."

You look baffled, Mercedes. I'm sure that when you speak of an English person, you are referring to someone who comes from the country of England. But when Amish people use the term "English," they are speaking about someone who is not Amish, someone whose primary language is English.

My first language was Pennsylvania Dutch, a variation of the German language. That is what was spoken in our home and community. So, to my young ears, the intonations of the English language sounded strange.

I didn't learn English until I started school. As an English speaker, it took me a long time to lose my Dutchy accent. I suppose I haven't lost it completely. My daughter teases me when she hears a slight Dutchy inflection in my speech, or when I inadvertently use a word from my childhood language.

I can't say I lacked anything during my growing up years. My siblings and I were well taken care of. Daily life was stable and predictable. We always had plenty of food, clean clothing, and the shelter of a warm home.

However, I never felt much affection from my mother and father as I was growing up. The rules of the church, which they regarded as the laws of God, came first and foremost in their lives. Those rules were strict, and the punishments for breaking them were harsh. Sadly, harshness seemed normal to me, as that was all I knew.

Amish girls are raised to keep a modest and plain appearance, to avoid calling attention to their feminine charms. As you can see from the clothing you pulled out of the suitcase, our dresses were as simple as they could possibly be. No printed fabrics. No lace or frills or ornamentation of any kind. Not even anything so fancy as buttons. We fastened our clothing with pins. We were never allowed to wear trousers, as they were viewed as men's clothing.

Wearing makeup or jewelry was forbidden in the Amish community. In accordance with the church's understanding of the scriptures, women's hair remained uncut. Worldly pleasures such as dancing, playing cards, and going to the movies were strictly prohibited.

Mercedes, your shocked expression tells me you could never imagine living like that. It must seem to you like a grim and repressive existence.

Of course, attending church on Sunday was a big part of my life. But our Amish congregation did not have a church building, as most religions do. Instead, we held our Sunday morning gatherings in the homes of church members. Each household in the congregation took their turn in hosting the service. Every time it was my family's turn to host the gathering, my mother, my sisters, and I would spend an entire day doing a deep cleaning of our home.

The church service consisted of an insufferably long sermon filled with grim warnings about sin, along with the singing of droning hymns. But putting up with that ordeal was worth it, because after the service, the congregation enjoyed the pleasure of a potluck dinner.

Let me tell you, Mercedes, those dinners were veritable feasts of the most delectable dishes you could imagine. By today's standards, Amish cooking is excessively high in fats and carbohydrates, contributing to obesity and other health problems. But in terms of taste, nothing can beat it.

As a child, I attended a one-room Amish school, where I learned reading, writing, and arithmetic. I learned a whole lot about the Bible, but little to nothing about history and science. Such subjects were considered unnecessary for life in an Amish community.

Even though I didn't want to, I was forced to stop my schooling after eighth grade, as Amish children were not allowed to pursue an education beyond that point. Instead, we were expected to return home and take our places in working on the farm.

Amish children grow up accustomed to hard work. I washed dishes, swept floors, and hung laundry on the clothesline. I fed chickens, gathered eggs, and milked cows. I pulled weeds in the garden and harvested vegetables. I helped my mother with cooking. I baked bread, pies, and cakes. I took part in canning vegetables, fruit, soup, and meat.

Yes, a lot was asked of children in my family. And we were expected to do our chores without complaining. Expressing anger or resentment was not allowed. Early on, I learned to push down the strong emotions that bubbled up inside me.

I suppose it was desperation that led me to find a way to release some of my pent-up feelings. When I was only five or six years old, I started to draw, and that habit stayed with me through my early teen years.

Some of my drawings were just for my own amusement, and I'd indulge myself any time I could get my hands on a pencil and a scrap of paper. I'd draw the animals in my father's barn, the flowers in my mother's garden, the trees in our yard. Sometimes, I'd sketch one of my parents or a sibling. But most importantly, I drew depictions of my feelings—the anger, the sadness, the fear—when I had no other way to express them.

I did all this in secret, of course. The Amish express their creativity through their cooking, quilt-making, flower gardening, and woodworking. But when I was growing up, my family didn't encourage what you would think of as the traditional visual arts: drawing, painting, sculpting. I didn't allow other family members to see my drawings, for fear that they would mock my creations. Or worse, that they would judge me.

So, I kept my drawings hidden under a corner of my mattress. But one day when I was fourteen, my older sister Rebecca found them and took them to my mother. When my mother saw the pictures of the flowers and animals, she was aggravated that I had wasted so much time drawing when I had better things to do.

But then, her aggravation turned to outrage when she saw the strange pictures portraying my emotions. She ripped them to shreds in front of me, telling me it was the devil who had made me do such a horrible thing. I had never seen my mother so worked up, and it terrified me.

As a punishment, she whipped me with a hickory switch, then sent me out to hoe in the vegetable garden. I had to work out there for hours in the scorching summer sun before she'd allow me to come back into the house. I was sobbing so hard that I could barely wield the hoe.

Right then, I didn't care whether I lived or died. Actually, I would've preferred death to the suffering and humiliation I was forced to endure that day.

That night, I cried myself to sleep, and the next day, I continued to cry while I completed my chores. But I made sure to stifle my sobs any time my mother came near me, for fear she'd heap more punishment upon me.

I suppose you could say I learned my lesson. It was a very long time before I mustered the nerve to draw again.

After that event, I had to plod through daily life without my emotional outlet—my coping skill, as people would call it today. Sometimes in moments of quiet desperation, I'd imagine that if I could will myself to stop breathing, my body would release my soul and it would float up to God. Then, I would be done with the pain of human existence.

I wish I could say that the punishment for my drawing was an isolated incident. Sadly, such occasions of being whipped and shamed were commonplace for my siblings and me. Just as you never trusted your mother with your troubles, I learned to hide myself and my true feelings from my parents. The less they knew about me, the less likely I was to be punished and humiliated.

I don't want to mislead you, Mercedes. There were moments of joy during my childhood. Granted, we had no entertainment like children have today. No television, no electronic devices. Nothing to read except for dry religious books that met the approval of our church.

However, we had our ways of having fun. We swung on our rope swing tied to the branch of the maple tree in our front yard. We played in our sandbox. We took delight in the barn cat's litter of kittens, or in the birth of a new calf. Sometimes, our mother would allow us to put on old clothes and splash around in the creek near our home. And we had a multitude of outdoor games that we played with other children in the schoolyard at recess.

Now, let me explain to you the practice of rumpschpringe, the "period of freedom," so to speak. The Amish know that, given their restrictive lifestyle, their young people will inevitably grow restless, craving adventure in the outside world. So, they allow for a time in which teenagers can sow their wild oats. Essentially, the adults turn their heads while their teens give full reign to their youthful inclinations. This is designed to get the foolishness out of a young person's system before he or she settles down, marries, and joins the church.

Mercedes, I know that after all I've said about the Amish lifestyle up to this point, hearing about this practice surprises you. Your Grandma Norma never would've given you permission to do some of the things I was allowed to do.

As I look back on my experience with my own rumpschpringe, I can see how dangerous that time can be for Amish youth. They inevitably encounter things in the English world they aren't prepared to handle. My period of rumpschpringe coincided with the early 1960s, a time when society was changing rapidly. It was a confusing enough time for English youth, and overwhelming for Amish young people heading out to get a taste of the world.

Initially, I wasn't inclined to embrace rumpschpringe, as I was a timid girl. If left to my own inclinations, I probably *wouldn't have done much running around at all.*

But my friend Mary had a more adventuresome spirit. One evening in the early summer of 1963, when I was seventeen, she persuaded me to go to a party held in the barn of a family from a neighboring church district. She and I drove there in her father's buggy.

When I stood in the doorway of that barn, I was frozen with fear. The activity inside seemed so loud to me, so frenzied. There were about a dozen Amish youth there, mostly young men, along with several Mennonites and a few English kids from the community. They were all drinking beer and smoking cigarettes. Because they were getting a little tipsy, their behavior was raucous and careless.

To top it off, one of the English kids had brought along a transistor radio. It was blaring loud music, the likes of which I'd never heard before. Some of the young people were dancing.

Let me tell you, Mercedes, I was scared to death. Mary had to take me by the arm and yank me inside. Otherwise, I would've turned and run, hiding in the buggy until she was ready to go home.

While Mary went to interact with the other young people, I stood by the door surveying the crowd, trying to calm my jittery nerves. I recognized all of the Amish youth, except for one young man whose good looks almost took my breath away. I figured he belonged to the same church district as the boy who was hosting the party.

I couldn't keep my eyes from following this handsome fellow as he moved around the barn, talking and laughing with others. Then, I heard someone address him as Ivan, and something clicked in my mind. This was Ivan Graber, a youth whose wild reputation extended far beyond the boundaries of his church district.

Many times, I'd overheard older men speak of Ivan's escapades, shaking their heads in contempt, a tinge of envy in their voices. Women would exchange shocked whispers about him, telling stories that left them feeling titillated. It was rumored that Ivan had a multitude of girlfriends, both in the Amish and English communities. Rumpschpringe or not, no Amish parents wanted their daughter getting involved with Ivan Graber.

I am not exaggerating, Mercedes, when I describe Ivan Graber's appearance as so striking that it would've stopped anyone in their tracks. He was tall and broad-shouldered, muscular from hard work on his father's farm. His dark eyes would gaze at you intently, taking you captive, casting a spell on you. He carried himself with confidence and pride, as if he knew he was irresistible to any woman, Amish or English.

There were only two other girls besides Mary and me at that party, which ensured that all four of us would receive an abundance of male attention. However, rather than exciting me, this prospect terrified me.

One inebriated Mennonite boy came stumbling over to talk to me, making me so nervous that I could hardly tell him my name. When he saw that he was not getting anywhere with me, he wandered away.

Then, to my astonishment, the dashingly handsome Ivan Graber came over to me. Although I had seen him drinking, he seemed perfectly in control of his faculties. He spoke to me in Pennsylvania Dutch. "Don't be nervous," he said. "I'll stick by you until you get your bearings."

He took my hand, a gesture so sweet, so reassuring, that my fear melted away right there on the spot. He made me feel protected.

I chuckle when I look back on that moment. That was Ivan's way of seducing a woman, making her feel safe and comfortable with him. He was good at it.

But at the time, I was too naïve to pick up on the game he was playing. I was powerless to resist his overtures.

"Come dance with me," he said.

"I don't know how," I mumbled, hanging my head in embarrassment.

Ivan put a finger under my chin and raised my face to meet his spell-binding eyes. "Just follow my lead," he said.

I guess that sums it all up, Mercedes. Soon, I was following Ivan's lead in any way you could think of. He was nineteen at the time, only two years older than me, but *lightyears ahead in terms of knowing the ways of the world.*

You're eager to hear what happened after that. I think it's best if I save that for our next visit.

People have often asked me how I feel about being raised Amish. They look upon it as a disadvantage. But I don't feel that way about my upbringing.

Granted, the rules were too rigid and unbending, the punishments for breaking them too severe. The lack of cultural and scientific progress in the Amish community is something I don't agree with. We live in an ever-evolving world. Staying stuck in the old ways isn't a healthy adaptation to the changes around us.

As with any culture, the Amish community has its strengths and weaknesses, aspects of both light and darkness. But all in all, I appreciate my Amish upbringing. I'm glad that was my beginning. I wouldn't have it any other way. Being raised Amish taught me devotion, discipline, resourcefulness, and self-control. It gave me a strong work ethic. These are values that have served me well in life.

Growing up in the simple lifestyle of the Amish also taught me to live in attunement with the rhythms of nature. It taught me to live in quietness, far from the chaos and maddening racket of the outside world. My early years in the Amish community carved out a quiet refuge in my soul, a stillness that I can return to again and again.

CHAPTER 4: DORA AND IVAN GRABER

Mercedes gripped the steering wheel of her car, her head throbbing, her shoulders aching with tension. The South Bend traffic inched along at a maddeningly slow pace, compounding her frustration by the minute.

Behind her in the back seat, Javi fretted, bouncing impatiently. "Hurry up, Mommy! You're going to make Daddy and me late for our trip!"

Javier and Javi had been anticipating this outing for weeks. They'd planned on taking the South Shore Line from South Bend to Chicago, where they would visit the zoo and the children's museum. Javi had been overjoyed at the prospect of his first train ride.

Just a few days earlier, during one of Mercedes' more agreeable phone conversations with her husband, he had invited her to come along on the Chicago trip. Ordinarily, she would have jumped at the opportunity. But she had declined, telling Javier she had plans to drive up to Saint Joseph to visit someone.

She could tell he was hurt by her refusal. "Who in Saint Joseph is so important that you have to go up there every weekend?" he'd asked her.

She'd hesitated, trying to think of the best way to tell him about Dora. "My grandpa's second wife," she'd finally said.

"June?" he'd asked, perplexed. "What's she doing in Saint Joseph? I thought she lived in Goshen."

"No," Mercedes had replied. "June is my grandpa's third wife. I'm visiting Dora. She was the wife between my Grandma Thelma and June."

That was all she'd told Javier. She hadn't been ready to reveal anything else about the inexplicable bond growing between her and her newly rediscovered grandmother.

"Hurry up, Mommy!" Javi called out again, kicking the back of her seat in his agitation.

"Shut up, Javi!" Mercedes snapped. "If you hadn't been messing around this morning when you were supposed to be getting ready, we'd be at your dad's place by now."

She instantly regretted her harsh words. Glancing over her shoulder, she saw the devastation on Javi's face. He had stopped his anxious bouncing and had curled himself into a ball of dejection.

Mercedes knew it wasn't fair to blame her son for the fact that they were behind schedule. Truthfully, she had lost track of time that morning when she'd gotten wrapped up in her social media accounts. When she finally realized how late it was, she had burst into Javi's bedroom and pulled him away from playing with his Legos.

After rushing him into the shower, she'd raced around trying to find clean clothes to pack for his weekend stay with his father. In the process, she'd stepped on one of the Legos, injuring her bare foot. This had thrown her off balance, and she'd banged her knee against Javi's dresser. The whole affair had left her screaming in pain.

After Javi was done with his shower, she'd decided that she needed one herself. By the time she'd finished drying her hair and applying her makeup, she'd known they were hopelessly behind schedule. And the frantic morning had left her and Javi completely at odds with each other.

The minute they'd jumped into the car, Mercedes' cell phone had started ringing. She'd figured it was Javier demanding to know where they were. She hadn't bothered to answer it, as doing so would've inevitably resulted in an exchange of angry words.

The car in front of her stopped suddenly. She'd been tailing it too closely and had to slam on the brakes to avoid a collision. "Goddammit!" she growled. "None of these dumbasses in South Bend know how to drive." She cringed at the sound of her own words. They were exactly like those that flew out of her mother's mouth.

She knew Javier would be furious with her for ruining the plans he'd so carefully made. And rightfully so. She had no excuse for her negligence. She dreaded the confrontation with him, knowing she would see the all too familiar judgmental look on his face.

Her phone rang for the umpteenth time. Tossing it to her son in the back seat, she barked, "For God's sake, talk to your father. Tell him we're on our way."

"Hi, Dad," she heard Javi say into the phone. "Mom said to tell you we're on our way." He paused, then said to Mercedes, "Dad wants to know how long it'll be."

"Maybe ten minutes," she snapped. "Depending on this stupid traffic."

When she finally pulled up at Javier's apartment building, she found him pacing in the parking lot. As always, he was impeccably dressed, wearing an expensive blue polo shirt, well-cut trousers, and a pair of loafers. But the fury on his handsome face marred his flawless appearance.

Javi jumped out of the car and ran to hug his father. Mercedes got out of the driver's seat, ready to offer a meek apology.

But before she could speak, Javier hissed, "Mercedes, you're an hour and a half late! You've ruined my day with my son. We've missed the train I'd planned on taking."

Javi looked up at Javier, his little face mirroring his father's anger. "Mom was messing around on her phone all morning."

Javier took his son by the hand, the two of them forming an outraged alliance against Mercedes. "I don't doubt that for a minute," he said, his voice dripping with sarcasm. "Mercedes, I asked you yesterday whether you wanted me to pick Javi up at your place this morning. You said no. You promised you'd have him here on time. Clearly, I was a fool to trust you. When are you going to grow up and act like a responsible adult?"

Javier's scathing judgement coupled with her pounding headache was too much for Mercedes to endure. The apology on the tip of her tongue vanished, and she erupted into a screaming fit laced with profanity.

Javier pointed a commanding finger at her, his tone righteously stern. "I will not allow you to behave this way in front of our son. Come, Javi, let's go inside. It's too late to start out for Chicago. We'll have to do that another weekend. Let's figure out something else we can do this afternoon."

His condescending tone enraged Mercedes all the more. "What makes you think you're so high and mighty?" she screamed. "You're no better than I am!"

Javier sighed in exasperation, shaking his head at the scene she was creating. "Mercedes, I don't have time to fight with you." Then he gave Javi a little nudge, and the two of them turned their backs on her and walked away.

Desolate, Mercedes stood by her car, tears streaming down her face as she watched her husband and son head toward the apartment building. She tried to tell herself that she hated Javier, that she didn't care what he thought of her. But being so coldly dismissed by him cut her deeply.

She got back into her car and sat there for a few minutes, trying to quell her sobbing before starting out on her drive to Michigan. But the more she tried to calm herself, the harder she cried. She finally gave up and drove with tears running down her cheeks and dripping off her chin.

After pulling into the Harbor Lights parking lot, she inspected her appearance in her rearview mirror. Her eyes were red and puffy, her make-up was smeared, and strands of her long hair were stuck to her wet cheeks. "Oh my God!" she muttered. "Could this day get any worse?"

She fished around in her purse for a tissue, but couldn't find one. Frantic, she checked the back seat, where she spotted a fast-food bag she had neglected to throw away. Inside it, she found a balled-up ketchup-stained napkin. She did her best to wipe her eyes and blow her nose with it, then combed through her tangled hair with her fingers.

When she entered the apartment building, she rushed toward the stairwell, keeping her head down, avoiding eye contact with Audrey at the reception desk. As she hurried up the stairs, she swore under her breath, berating herself for showing up at Dora's place in such a pitiful condition.

When Dora opened the door to her knock, a look of concern quickly replaced her welcoming smile. "Oh, my dear girl!" she exclaimed. "You're upset. Whatever is the matter?"

"I just dropped my son off at his dad's place," Mercedes sniffled. "And Javier and I got into a fight."

Dora placed an arm around Mercedes' waist and led her to the sofa, then sat down beside her and took her hand. "Would you like to tell me about it?"

Mercedes cringed at the thought of revealing to sweet, gentle Dora the shameful scene she'd created in front of her husband and son. But once again, the elderly woman's compassionate gaze made it impossible for her to hold back.

"Javier and I were starting to get along," she said, her tears flowing again. "Then today, I ruined everything. He and Javi were planning to travel to Chicago on the train. But I was late in dropping Javi off, and they missed their chance to go. Javier was so mad at me. He called me irresponsible. That set me off, and I screamed and swore at him."

Grateful for the box of tissues Dora offered, she took a handful to wipe her eyes and nose. "After the big fit I threw, I'm pretty sure Javier will go ahead and file the divorce papers."

"That isn't what you want, is it?" Dora said.

Mercedes shook her head. "No, not really. Things go good between Javier and me for a few days, then everything falls apart. I keep thinking we're going to get it right someday. But we've been together nine years, and the same thing happens over and over again."

Dora looked thoughtful. "Why do you suppose that is?"

Mercedes wiped her eyes again, sighing deeply. "Javier and I are complete opposites. We're like oil and water. We don't mix. He's serious and goal-oriented. He focuses on getting things done. I've never been one to take life too seriously. I believe in having fun."

She laughed bitterly. "I guess I'm just a screw-up. I know Javier thinks so."

"But you're going to nursing school," Dora observed, "and you're doing well." She gave Mercedes' hand an emphatic little pat. "That tells me a different story about you."

"It's nice of you to say that," Mercedes mumbled. "But I know Javier doesn't see me like that."

"Are you sure?" Dora asked. "He must certainly admire your educational endeavors."

Mercedes thought for a minute, twisting a lock of her hair. "He was behind me one hundred percent when I started nursing school. He's always told me that I'm smart. Here's something funny. You know how my family has always called me Sadie?"

"Yes," Dora replied.

"Well, Javier refuses to call me that. He calls me Mercedes. He says it's because I'm top of the line, like the automobile. The first time he said that, it made me so happy. After that, I never wanted anyone to call me Sadie again."

She hung her head, balling up the tissues in her hand. "But I can't seem to live up to my name with Javier. He wants to keep me on a pedestal, but I keep on disappointing him. And he gets so mad when I don't live up to his image of me. He'll say, 'Your better than this, Mercedes.' Then, he'll start taking cheap shots at my family. Every time I screw up, he blames it on their bad influence."

"Oh my!" Dora said. "I imagine that gets under your skin."

Mercedes nodded. "Our families are so different. We come from such different backgrounds."

"How so?" Dora asked.

"Javier comes from a rich family in Mexico City. They had cooks and maids doing the housework. A chauffeur drove him to school every day. Javier's father, uncles, and grandfather all held political office in their state. The family owns a chain of hotels in Mexico, Costa Rica, and Panama, along with a few other businesses.

"I wasn't raised with any religion, but Javier is very religious. His family is Catholic. Javier went to a private Catholic school in Mexico City. Then he went to a Jesuit University in Guadalajara. After that, he came to Notre Dame to get his master's degree.

"So, even though Javier and my father are both Mexican, they're from completely different worlds. My father was a poor worker on a coffee plantation. Javier came from the kind of family who would've owned the plantation."

"My goodness!" Dora exclaimed. "I had no idea Javier came from such a prestigious background! What kind of work does he do now?"

"He's an architect at a firm in South Bend," Mercedes responded. "He makes good money. That's why he's able to support Javi and me while he lives in his own place."

She smiled wryly. "Everyone says I should keep trying to make my marriage work. They say Javier is a catch, that he's worth hanging onto. Everyone except for my mom. She hates him. I'd been living with her and Grandma Norma up to the point when we got married, and Mom blames Javier for taking me away from her. I think she's afraid that he's better than us, and she wants to bring him down a notch. Behind his back, she calls him terrible names. She's even hateful to his face."

"Oh my!" Dora said. "It must be hurtful having your mother treat your husband so badly."

Mercedes nodded. "He hasn't done anything to deserve the way she treats him. He's always been polite to her. But I know he thinks she's disgusting, the way she lies around her dirty house cussing like a sailor and drinking herself to death. He tells me that I need to learn how to live a more dignified lifestyle. That's one of the reasons he wants me to spend time with his family in Mexico, so I can learn to live like an aristocratic Mexican.

"At first, Javier tried to win my mom over. He tried to improve her life. He fixed things around her house that were broken. He bought her a new microwave when her old one stopped working. He bought her a new cell phone and put her on our family plan. But even though he's done a lot for her, that never changes her mind about him.

"You know what he did for my mom a few years ago? He set up a Facebook account for her. She hardly ever gets out of the house, and he wanted her to have a way to stay in touch with friends. He sat with her for hours, explaining Facebook to her, being kind and patient.

"But she didn't appreciate it, and she's never done a thing with her account. And she has the audacity to keep on complaining that Javier never lifts a finger for her. He's finally given up on trying."

Mercedes rested her elbow on the arm of the sofa, leaning her cheek against her palm. Sighing deeply, she closed her eyes, sinking into the world of perpetual pain and frustration she lived in. "Mom wants me to leave Javier for good. She hounds me all the time about that. She keeps trying to set me up with her creepy next-door neighbor. And Javier thinks I should cut off contact with Mom because of her bad influence on Javi and me. But I don't have it in me to turn my back on her. I'm all that she has. So, I'm stuck between my husband and my mother."

"That seems to be true in several ways," Dora observed. "You live in Elkhart, halfway between Javier in South Bend and your mother in Goshen. And both of them are tugging on you emotionally, pulling you in two different directions. The strain of that must certainly wear on you."

"Yes," Mercedes sighed, grateful for Dora's understanding. "It really does."

"I'm curious," Dora said. "With such disparate backgrounds, how did you and Javier meet?"

Mercedes brought her hand to her mouth to cover an embarrassed smile. "That's a weird story. I'm ashamed of it, but I guess I'll tell you anyway. When I was in my late teens, I started running around and drinking lot. I couldn't wait for the day when I could legally drink in a bar. So, I started using a fake ID to get into clubs. On my twentieth birthday, I was sitting in a club in South Bend, having the time of my life, flirting with men and having them buy me drinks.

"I'd always dated white guys. I'd never wanted anything to do with Mexican men. But this Hispanic man came up to me in the bar, and he was unbelievably good-looking. I almost fell off my bar stool when he started talking to me. Right away, I could tell he was a classy guy, way above the other men in the club. He was dressed so nicely and was so well-mannered. Everything about him seemed perfect.

"He sat down on the stool next to me and introduced himself as Javier Maldonado. He said I reminded him of a Brazilian woman he knew, and he asked me where I was from.

"Because I'd had a lot to drink, I wasn't making good decisions. I started playing a game with him. I told him that I was from Brazil. I acted like I didn't know much English.

"Then, he started talking to me in Portuguese. Of course, I couldn't understand a word he was saying. I finally interrupted him and said that I was just kidding, that I was

American, born and raised in Indiana, not Brazil.

"Oh boy, he was upset with me. He didn't say another word. He just got up and walked away. I felt so bad about what I'd done. But there was something more to it than that. I'd felt some kind of vibe with Javier Maldonado, something I'd never felt with any other guy. I knew I'd blown an opportunity by not getting to know him.

"After a few minutes, I got up and went over to the table where he was sitting. I apologized for what I'd done. At first, he acted cold, as if he didn't want anything to do with me. But then, we introduced ourselves for real. He told me that he'd moved here from Mexico City, and that he was a graduate student at Notre Dame. I told him who I really was, that I had a Mexican dad and a white mother.

"We talked a little while, and he started warming up to me again. Then he asked me to dance. Out there on the dance floor, the chemistry between us was unbelievable. It felt like electricity was sizzling between the two of us.

"After that night, we started dating. We fell hard for each other. Javier treated me like a princess, sending me flowers, buying me gifts, taking me to fancy restaurants. I'd never experienced anything like that in my entire life. I thought I was living the dream.

"But wouldn't you know it, about four months into our relationship, I found out I was pregnant."

"Oh, my goodness!" Dora exclaimed. "That must've come as quite a shock to you."

"Yup," Mercedes said. "It was a real downer. Before we started having sex, Javier asked me about birth control. I told him I was on the pill. The truth was that I had a tendency to miss days here and there. I never thought that would matter. But as it turned out, it did.

"I was scared to death to tell Javier I was pregnant. I thought it would spoil everything between us. When I finally worked up the nerve to tell him, he was upset at first. Not mad, just caught off guard. But right away, he said he would step up and take responsibility.

"At first, I thought he meant he was going to give me money to pay for an abortion. He was horrified when I said something about making an appointment with a clinic. He told me he would never agree to have a woman terminate a pregnancy with his child. He said he was ready to do right by me, to marry me and take care of the baby and me.

"I couldn't believe it. Getting married was the farthest thing from my mind. I was just an immature kid. I didn't tell Javier I was twenty, not twenty-one, until we went to get our marriage license. He was so mad that I had lied to him.

"But we went ahead with our marriage. We had a beautiful wedding. Javier paid for the whole thing because my family didn't have the money for it."

Mercedes pulled out her phone to access her Facebook account. "Here's our wedding photo," she said, showing Dora a picture.

"Oh!" Dora exclaimed, clasping her hands together in delight. "You are so lovely in your wedding gown! And you're right about Javier. Looking at him does take a woman's breath away. The two of you look like celebrities."

Mercedes laughed. "We were hardly that." But she took another fond look at the picture before putting her phone away.

"Our marriage was rough from the start," she continued. "Early on, Javier accused me of being irresponsible. Before we started living together, he didn't know how messy and disorganized I am. He can't stand that about me. His family is very proper, and they do things just right. He expects me to behave like that, too. And that's not how I was raised. Not by a long shot.

"I really don't think Javier would've ever been interested in marrying me if I hadn't gotten pregnant. It wouldn't have taken him long to figure out that we didn't belong together.

"After Javi was born, things got even worse between us. I was trying my best to be a good mother, to be better than my mom had been. But it wasn't good enough for Javier. He thought I wasn't taking care of Javi well enough. I wasn't watching him closely enough. I wasn't feeding him the right food. I wasn't keeping him clean. I wasn't changing his diaper often enough. Javier was always checking up on me.

"Now that we're separated, it feels as if he's watching

every move I make with our son. Several times, he's threatened to take me to court to get full custody of Javi. He drives me crazy!

"And I know I drive him crazy, too. I have a problem with running my mouth when I get upset. I'm ashamed to say this, but I take after my mom in that way. Javier usually keeps his cool. But if I push him hard enough, he'll finally explode. We've had our screaming matches, that's for sure. He calls me an immature child. I call him a controlling jerk.

"When things are good between us, it's really good. We still have a lot of chemistry. That's never gone away. Our romantic life is wonderful. We don't have any problems in the bedroom."

Dora chuckled. Mercedes shot her an impish smile.

"But when things are bad, it really gets ugly," she continued. "Sometimes in the middle of a fight, Javier will bring up the night we met, when I was playing games with him about being Brazilian. He'll tell me that I've been untrustworthy from the very beginning of our relationship."

She pounded her fist on her thigh in frustration. "I just hate it when he judges me like that. Those are the times when I think I'll never be able to make it work with Javier. I think that I'd be better off being alone for the rest of my life than to be with someone who looks down on me."

"I know what it feels like to be judged," Dora said. "When I was a young woman, I went through a time where I faced scathing judgment from my family and condemnation from my church. It felt like everyone was looking down on me. That's a hard way to live. It becomes unbearable."

Dora mentioning her own life experiences jolted Mercedes, reminding her of the reason for her visit. "I'm sorry," she said. "We're supposed to be talking about you, aren't we? You were going to tell me more of your story."

"Oh, that's okay," Dora protested. "I don't want to rush you if you need more time to talk about what you're going through."

Mercedes shook her head. "No, I think I've said all I need to say for now."

"All right, then. We'll start where I left off last week." Dora got up from the sofa and walked across the tiny room to her bookcase. Mercedes noticed the weariness in the elderly woman's gait, and a wave of concern passed through her.

Dora pulled a photo album off one of the shelves. "At our last visit, I didn't have anything to show you except for the clothing. The Amish don't believe in having pictures taken of themselves, so I have no photographs from my childhood. But I will have a few pictures to show you today."

Last week, I told you about going to my first barn party. As you recall, I was standing by the door, too scared to join the fun, when Ivan Graber came over to talk to me.

As I listened to you describe your chemistry with Javier, it reminded me of how I felt when I first met Ivan. When he took my hand and led me out onto the dance floor, his touch almost made my skin sizzle. It was exciting, but also terrifying. I'd never before experienced that kind of attraction to a man.

Ivan taught me how to do a dance called the twist. Have you ever heard of it? It was all the craze back in the early 1960s. As I moved my body in ways I'd never moved before, I couldn't help but laugh at the sheer joy of being so free.

After we danced for a while, Ivan suggested that we go outside. We sat on the hood of his English friend's car, looking up at the starry night sky and talking.

It was getting chilly, and I started shivering. "Let me warm you up," Ivan said. He put his arm around me and pulled me close to him.

His doing that scared me to death, as I'd never been that close to a man before. But at the same time, I felt safe and protected with Ivan's arm encircling me.

We sat like that for a while. It was getting late, and I was starting to feel drowsy. I leaned my head against Ivan's shoulder. I felt him draw in a quick breath, as if my action had aroused something in him. He put his hand under my chin and turned my face to meet his. Then, he kissed me.

It was just one kiss. One sweet, tender kiss, the first that I'd ever received from a man. Then he drew back. "You should probably go," he said, "before I get carried away."

Just about that time, my friend Mary came out of the barn looking for me. She told me she was ready to leave. Ivan walked me over to the buggy. For a few moments, we stood there gazing at each other. The light of the summer moon illuminated his handsome features, making him seem like an otherworldly being.

"I'm sure we'll meet again soon," he said.

On the drive home, Mary giggled and clucked her tongue at me. "So, did you have a good time with Ivan Graber?" She kept pressing me to tell her everything that had happened.

But I didn't say a word to her. The enchanting night had deprived me of all reason, and I was convinced that I had fallen in love. I wanted to keep that sweet feeling all to myself.

It all happened that quickly, Mercedes. I'd spent less than two hours with Ivan Graber, and he had me under his spell.

Looking back, I know that Ivan didn't share the intensity of my feelings. I was only one in the long line of women he'd charmed and seduced.

A week later, I eagerly accepted Mary's invitation to go with her to another barn party, hoping I'd see Ivan there. Sure enough, I did. Toward the end of the night, he led me up to the hayloft, where we engaged in passionate kissing.

After that, he and I began going out together on a regular basis, once or twice a week. Truthfully, I didn't know whether he was dating other girls at the same time. He probably was. But I didn't let myself think about that possibility.

As I told you last week, I was soon following Ivan's lead anywhere he wanted to go, doing anything he wanted to do. Early on, he introduced me to his English friend Jeff, along with Jeff's girlfriend Diane.

I quickly understood why Ivan sought out English friends, as they provided us with transportation to places where we couldn't have gone in an Amish buggy. We went to bowling alleys and miniature golf courses and movie theatres. We went to drive-up restaurants where carhops brought us the hamburgers and milkshakes we ordered. I thought I was having the time of my life.

However, some of our date-time activities made me feel

uneasy. We went to all-night parties at the homes of strangers, where people guzzled beer, got rowdy, and broke out into fights. Couples would slip off into empty bedrooms to engage in intimate activities, as Ivan and I often did.

Once, we went to a horror movie, where I saw things happening on the screen that made me scream and cover my face. Ivan laughed at my reaction, telling me I needed to toughen up. He reminded me that I was on rumpschpringe, that it was my time to sample the whole range of worldly pleasures.

Of course, I wouldn't have gotten very far in the English world wearing my Amish garb. Ivan bought me a few pieces of English clothing so I could fit in when he took me places.

He and I developed a routine for our date nights. We'd first go to Diane's house, where I would change out of my Amish clothing into an English outfit. As you might imagine, I didn't know the first thing about English fashion. Diane helped me learn how to put a blouse together with a skirt or pair of slacks in a way that looked stylish. She helped me accessorize my outfits with things from her own wardrobe and collection of jewelry.

Diane was a sweet girl, and we quickly became close. The two of us were about the same size and had a similar complexion. When we'd go out together after Diane had fixed me up, we'd look like a pair: Diane and Dora, two peas in a pod. That was so much fun for me.

There was, however, the matter of my uncut hair. In the English world, I took off my Amish bonnet and unwound my bun, letting my hair hang loose. It was very long, reaching past my waist, and because of the curls, it was quite unruly.

One evening when I was changing clothes in Diane's bedroom, she pulled out a pair of scissors, telling me she was going to trim my hair. At first, I protested. I could easily change my clothing, going from Amish to English, then back to Amish at the end of the night. But I couldn't reattach hair that had been cut off.

Diane laughed, telling me she could trim off a foot of my hair, and I would still have plenty to wind back up into a bun. And that is what she did.

As I listened to the scritch-scritch of the scissors and watched the long strands fall to the floor, I cringed in fear, thinking about the severe punishment I could face for breaking church rules. But when I looked into Diane's mirror and saw the results of her handiwork, I was so delighted that my fear melted away. My hair hung loose around my shoulders, the curls framing my face. And for the first time in my life, I considered the idea that others might think of me as pretty.

I can tell you this, Mercedes. Ivan sure liked my new hairstyle. When he first saw it, he did a double-take. Then his face broke into a huge smile. "You look sexy," he whispered into my ear. That was the first time any man had ever said such a thing to me.

As you might imagine, that first kiss between Ivan and me had led to other activities, increasingly intimate in their nature. The night Diane cut my hair was the first night that he and I fully consummated our relationship.

I have to admit that was a confusing experience for me. My mother had never told me anything about intimacy with a man. In the Amish community, such matters were whispered about, but never discussed in an open and honest way. Part of me knew I was doing wrong. But again, Ivan had the right words to dispel my concerns.

Last week, I told you how people in the church enjoyed gossiping about Ivan. Well, my name was soon included in those salacious stories, and word that I was running around with Ivan Graber got back to my parents. It goes without saying that they were terribly unhappy with me. They sat me down and issued grim warnings about the perils of going down the wrong road. But because the church allowed for the tradition of rumpschpringe, they stopped short of exercising their full parental authority in forbidding me to keep company with Ivan.

So, for the rest of that summer and early fall, I followed Ivan's lead in embracing rumpschpringe with abandon, dispelling any thoughts about consequences that might lie ahead.

One night in October, Ivan and I were riding around with

Jeff and Diane. Jeff was driving with Diane beside him in the front passenger seat, while Ivan and I sat in the back. We were cruising through Goshen, something young people enjoyed doing at the time. Jeff and Ivan had both been drinking. They were laughing raucously and shouting out the windows at other drivers on the road.

To be honest, I wasn't enjoying the activity very much. I'd had my fill of Ivan and Jeff's unruly behavior. I was huddled in the corner of the back seat, thinking that I just wanted to go home.

All of a sudden, I heard the sound of screeching tires, followed by a loud crash and the feeling of the car careening out of control. Later, I learned that Jeff had run a red light going south through an intersection. The driver coming from the west had slammed into the side of the car where Diane and I were sitting.

Evidently, I was ejected from the car and lost consciousness, because I awoke to find myself lying on the pavement, bewildered by the commotion surrounding me: the screaming sirens, the flashing lights of police cars, the chorus of agitated voices. I had no idea why I was lying in the road. I attempted to get up, but felt so dizzy that I had to lie down again.

Someone shone a flashlight on me, running the beam over my body as if to assess the state I was in. A kind voice said, "Don't worry, miss, we're here to help you." Then I felt myself being lifted onto a stretcher and placed into the back of an ambulance.

I must've lost consciousness again, because the next thing I knew, I was lying on a bed in a room filled with bright lights and the voices of people I didn't know. "Where am I?" I asked, speaking in Pennsylvania Dutch. That was the language that came easiest to me when I was in a state of distress.

When I realized no one understood what I was saying, I had the presence of mind to repeat my question in English. A kind-faced woman in a nurse's uniform appeared at my side. "You're in the emergency room at Goshen General Hospital," she told me.

I'd never been in the hospital before. I'd never even set foot inside one to visit a sick friend or family member. The people in my Amish community rarely consulted doctors. We relied on our home remedies as much as possible.

"Why am I here?" I asked the nurse.

"You were in an accident," she explained.

I tried to get up. "I need to go home. My parents will be worried." But the minute I raised my head, I felt terribly dizzy, and I lay back down again.

"Lie still," the nurse said. "You've had a bad head injury."

Gradually, I became more alert and aware of what was going on around me. I remembered being in the car with Ivan, Jeff, and Diane, and I figured we must've been involved in a collision. I asked the nurse how the others were. "I'm not able to tell you that," she said.

A stream of medical professionals came in and out of the room. I couldn't keep track of them. I didn't understand what they were doing to me, or why they were doing it. But when they were finished with all the probing, checking, and testing, I was informed that I'd suffered a concussion, a scalp laceration, and various other cuts and bruises.

"You're lucky," one doctor told me. "It could've been much worse. You could've lost your baby, or even your own life."

His words bewildered me. "What baby?" I asked.

"Surely you know," he said. "You're pregnant."

I tell you, Mercedes, I was in no mental state to take in those words. They didn't seem real to me.

A few minutes later, Ivan walked into the room. I was relieved to see that he had suffered no visible injuries. He came to my bedside, whispering, "I'm so sorry, Dora. I'm so sorry." Then a nurse ushered him out.

I must've closed my eyes for a while. When I opened them again, I saw my parents standing there by my bed. I later learned that, at the scene of the accident, Ivan had informed the police where my family lived. Two of the officers had then gone out to our home to tell my parents the news of the accident.

I was so relieved to see my mother and father there.

Despite knowing how displeased they'd been with me in recent months, their presence was a comfort to me.

Amish people are generally not demonstrative with their emotions. But I could tell my parents were shaken up. My mother was biting her lip to keep back the tears, her plump body heaving with the sobs she was trying to suppress. My father held his big black hat in his hands, nervously rotating the brim around and around.

"Dora," he said, "you must realize what a dangerous road you've been going down. It has come to this."

I was expecting a long lecture from him. I would've welcomed it, actually, as I knew I deserved it.

But before my father could say anything more, the doctor walked into the room again. And he repeated to my parents what he'd told me: "Your daughter is fortunate. She could've sustained far more serious injuries in this accident. She could've lost her life. It's a miracle that she didn't lose the baby she's carrying."

I watched my parents' faces go slack from shock. My mother shot me an agonized look, whispering, "Oh Dora!" Then she covered her face with her hands, as if she couldn't bear the sight of me. My father abruptly turned his back on me, as if unwilling to be in the presence of someone who'd committed such a sordid transgression. He took my mother by the arm, and the two of them walked out of the room.

This time, the doctor's words registered in my muddled brain. Despite my dizziness, despite the pain that wracked my entire body, I felt the import of the momentous news. I was carrying Ivan's child.

I stayed in the hospital for two days. When it was time for me to be discharged, my parents hired an English driver to bring me home. The trip in the buggy would've been too arduous for me in my fragile condition. You look surprised, Mercedes. Hiring English drivers is a common practice in the Amish community when a trip is too long or too difficult to make in a buggy.

Despite her unhappiness with me, my mother, along with my sisters, provided me with tender care during my recovery at home. No one spoke of the pregnancy, although I'm sure my sisters had been told about it.

The day after I came home from the hospital, I was lying in my upstairs bedroom when I heard a knock on the front door. Then, I heard Ivan speaking with my father in the living room. Given everything that had happened, I was surprised that my father had allowed him in the house.

A few minutes later, I heard footsteps coming up the stairs, and Ivan walked into my room. My father followed close behind him, as if he didn't trust Ivan to be alone with me.

The usual confidence on Ivan's face had been replaced by strain. And I soon understood why. He informed me that my dear friend Diane had not survived the accident. She had died in the ambulance on the way to the hospital.

As my mind reeled from the shock of that news, my father said, "Dora, I believe you have some news of your own to tell this young man."

That was my cue. With my father standing there glaring at the two of us, I had no choice but to tell Ivan about my pregnancy. Tall, strong Ivan suddenly looked small and scared. He and I stared at each other in dismay, both of us knowing that our lives had been forever changed. Then, my father put a hand on Ivan's shoulder and ushered him out of the room.

Later, my father went over to the Graber farm to meet with Ivan's father. The two men must've had a day of reckoning. After their own discussion, they sat Ivan down and told him his reckless and carefree days were over. It was time for him to step up and marry me.

The following day, Ivan showed up at the house again, this time to offer me a halting proposal. I was still too dazed from my head injury, coupled with the shocking news about Diane's death, to know what I was doing when I agreed to marry him. Truthfully, though, I would've said yes even if I had been clearheaded. There would've been no other option for a pregnant Amish girl.

Mercedes, when you told me that Javier probably wouldn't have married you if you hadn't gotten pregnant, it made me think about my situation with Ivan. He'd run around with countless young women, with no intention of marrying any of them. There was nothing special about me. I just happened to be the girl who got pregnant, the girl whose angry father insisted that justice be done. I'm sure Ivan's proposal was dictated by circumstances, not by love.

It took me more than two weeks to gain the strength to be up and around and participating in family life again. So, during the lonely hours of my recovery, I had plenty of time to contemplate the change in direction my life had taken.

In my solitude, I shed tears for Diane, the sweet girl who'd been my closest friend the last few months of her life. I wanted to attend her funeral, to pay my respects to her family. But I knew that my parents would never allow that to happen.

I wondered if Diane's obituary had been in the newspaper. I assumed there had been some account of the horrific late-night accident in downtown Goshen. But I would never know, as our family never read the local paper.

The fact that I didn't get to say goodbye to Diane troubled me deeply. I had no way of coming to terms with my loss. No one in my family would've wanted to hear me talk about how much I was going to miss my English friend. Her death haunted me for a very long time.

It is only now that I realize the full import of my brief friendship with Diane. In her openhearted way, she taught me how to cope with the strangeness of the English world. Essentially, she held my hand as I waded into a new culture, coaching me when I felt lost and confused.

A few years ago, I persuaded Elliott to drive me down to Goshen, to the cemetery where Diane had been buried. There, I had the opportunity to stand by her grave and weep, thanking her for all she'd done for me.

This may seem odd to you, Mercedes. When I get dressed in the morning, I often ask myself, "What would Diane say about this outfit? Would she think this blouse goes with this skirt?" It's as if part of her is still with me.

Many times, I've asked myself the question, "Why did God take Diane in the bloom of her life, and not me? Why did she leave this world at such a young age, while I was spared to live on into my senior years?

Sometimes, I wonder whether that tragic accident offered me a portal for leaving my human life, an escape from having to cope with earthly troubles. But my soul must've declined that offer, saying, "No, let me stick it out. I need more experience in this lifetime. I have more lessons to learn."

And what a life it has been! Almost six decades have passed since the day of that accident. Granted, there have been times when I didn't think I could negotiate life's challenges, days when I looked back and wished it had been me instead of the English girl who'd died in that car crash. But none of us understand the wisdom of the cosmic plan. I tell myself it does no good to question.

However, it has occurred to me that one of the reasons I survived the accident was to bring into the world the child I was carrying. During the days of my recovery, I thought deeply about what it would mean to become a mother. After the initial shock of learning about my pregnancy, I was quite excited about the idea of having a child. I loved my unborn baby from the moment I learned of her existence.

Mercedes, you've probably figured out by this time that the baby I was carrying was my daughter Corina. I can tell you this: no matter what the ill-advised circumstances of her conception, Corina has been nothing but a blessing in my life. And she has proven to be a blessing to the world as well, with her outstanding career in the field of nursing. I've never doubted for a moment that she was meant to be here.

Of course, I've told Corina about the accident, and how I learned I was pregnant with her. She always says she and I survived that accident together. I believe our shared survival has helped forge the deep mother-daughter bond we enjoy so much.

As Ivan and I began discussing our plans for marriage, something came up that I hadn't foreseen. My husband-to-be informed me that he wanted to leave the Amish church. He told me that he'd been planning on going English for a *long time, and that he had no intention of living his entire life in the Amish community. He insisted that we start our married life in the English world.*

Even though I had partially entered the English world through my rumpschpringe escapades, I was in no way ready to completely walk away from the lifestyle I'd always known. Sure, I had often daydreamed about what it would be like to go English. But I'd never seriously entertained the idea. Such a possibility seemed far beyond the reach of a young Amish woman.

However, I once again gave in and followed Ivan's lead. My smooth-talking husband-to-be calmed my fears by pointing out how much I'd already learned about the English world. "We'll do this together," he kept saying. "You'll have me to lean on."

As you might imagine, Mercedes, both of our families were adamantly opposed to the idea of us leaving the Amish church. I recall my father's deep voice thundering at us, predicting that the wrath of God would fall upon us if we turned our backs on Him to follow the ways of the world. Whenever I wavered in the face of my family's fearful pleas and angry threats, Ivan reminded me that I now owed my loyalty to him, my future husband, instead of to my parents.

When our families realized they could have no impact on our decision, they shunned us. Shunning is the practice among the Amish when someone violates the rules of the church. Essentially, our families turned their backs on Ivan and me and had nothing more to do with us. The complete withdrawal of my parents' support was the most devastating thing I'd ever experienced. It was as if I'd ceased to be a person in their eyes.

Ivan and I got married at the county courthouse in Goshen in early November, just a week after we announced our decision to leave the Amish church. We really had no other option, as continuing to live in our parents' homes had become unbearable.

So, our marriage became a matter of desperation rather than an occasion to celebrate. I had no fancy dress like you had at your wedding. There were no flowers, no cake. Our only guest was Ivan's friend Dave, who served as a witness to the ceremony. Not even Jeff was there. He was still too distraught over Diane's death.

Here, look at the wedding picture that Dave took of us. I treasure this blurry little dog-eared photograph. It is the only item I have that marks the beginning of my life with Ivan. We look more terrified than happy, don't you think?

There was one way, however, in which good fortune proved to be on our side. The summer prior to our marriage, Ivan and his father had had a falling out over the lifestyle Ivan was choosing to lead. In rebellion against his father, Ivan had left the work on the family farm and had taken a job at a recreational vehicle factory in Middlebury. Thankfully, that job paid well enough for Ivan and me to rent a small one-story house on the outskirts of Middlebury.

It took a while to get adequate furnishings for our home. We started out with almost nothing. So, it was several months before our house began to feel comfortable. I felt so lost and insecure during those early weeks of my marriage. All I wanted to do was to run back to the comfort and familiarity of my parents' home. But I knew their door was no longer open to me.

The first three weeks of our marriage, Ivan rode to work with an English coworker. Then, he bought a car of his own. He already knew how to drive, as he'd often driven the vehicles of his English friends. I asked him to teach me how to drive, but he refused to do so. He told me there would never be a reason for me to get a driver's license.

I soon discovered that despite his turning his back on his upbringing, Ivan still wanted me to behave like an Amish wife. He insisted that I cook only Amish cuisine.

Once, I tried baking a chocolate cake from a recipe on the back of a cocoa powder container. After taking a bite, Ivan insisted that the cake was dry and refused to eat any more of it. The next day, he came home with an Amish cookbook he'd purchased at a gift shop in Middlebury. When he slammed it down on the kitchen counter, I knew what he expected of me.

Of course, he wouldn't begin to entertain the idea of me

working outside the home. He was quite clear about where my place was to be.

As it turned out, my husband claimed the right to all the freedom he wanted, while I was limited in what I was allowed to do. Women today would criticize that double standard, and rightly so. But I had no idea how to stand up to Ivan. So, as I'd always done, I accepted my lot in life.

In the early months of our marriage, I came to understand that Ivan and I really didn't know each other. I often felt as if I was living with a stranger. Without family and community support, we found ourselves terribly alone in the English world.

Perhaps it's more accurate to say that I felt alone. Ivan had his friends and the people he worked with. My only English friend had been Diane, and she was gone.

Several times, I brought up to Ivan the idea of joining one of the many Mennonite churches in the community. I'm sure we would've been warmly welcomed by them. Mennonites are like first cousins to the Amish, and there are similarities between the cultures. I'd known of other people who'd left the Amish church and had ended up joining the Mennonites. That provided a way for them to ease into the English world.

Perhaps if we'd had a church community to support us, Ivan and I would've been able to find our way as a couple. But my husband had no interest in joining a church of any kind.

Of course, much of my attention was focused on my rapidly progressing pregnancy. At the time of our wedding in November, I was just beginning to show. Over the next few months, my belly grew by leaps and bounds. As the few articles of English clothing that I owned quickly became too tight, I had to return to wearing my Amish dresses.

The changes in my body bewildered me. I desperately wished I could talk with my mother about what was happening, and that I could consult with the midwife who tended to the pregnant women in my Amish community. I knew English women went to doctors when they were pregnant, and that they delivered their babies in hospitals.

But I had no idea how to obtain such a doctor.

One afternoon in January, I set out for the walk down our long driveway to our mailbox by the road. At that point, I could no longer button my winter coat because of my protruding belly.

Coincidentally, my neighbor lady was out at her mailbox, which was right next to ours. I had previously seen this woman from a distance, but had never mustered the courage to speak to her. She was a heavy-set English woman in her late fifties or early sixties, with a round cheerful face and short gray hair.

As she turned to head back to her house, she saw me approaching the mailboxes, and she stopped to speak to me. "I'm Irene," she said, holding out her hand to shake mine. "My husband Virgil and I saw you and your husband moving in a couple of months ago. It's so nice to have young people living next door."

"I'm Dora," I said. Then, I stood there tongue-tied, not knowing what else to say to the kindly lady.

Irene glanced down at my bulging belly. "Is this your first child?" she asked.

I nodded.

"When are you due?"

I felt my face reddening with embarrassment. "I don't really know."

Irene looked perplexed. "What does your doctor say?"

"I don't have one," I mumbled.

Irene gazed at me for a few moments, deep in thought. She seemed to be putting the pieces together, trying to make sense of the pregnant teenager who was living an English lifestyle but wearing an Amish dress. "Come inside with me," she finally said. "We'll get you set up with a doctor."

I followed her into her modest ranch house, which was similar to the home Ivan and I were renting. But unlike our place, it was packed full of comfortable furniture and cluttered with an abundance of houseplants, knickknacks, and family photos. It looked as if Irene and her husband had lived there for decades.

She led me to her kitchen, where she picked up her phone book and started searching through the yellow pages. "My niece had a baby a year ago," she said. "She went to an obstetrician in Middlebury. Let's see if we can get you in with him."

When she found the number she was looking for, she offered to make the call right then and there. "I need to talk to my husband first," I told her. I knew Ivan would be upset with me if I made arrangements for prenatal care without his permission.

When Ivan came home from work that afternoon, I told him about my conversation with Irene and showed him the phone number of the obstetrician.

At the time, we did not yet have a telephone in our house. Ivan told me he'd make the call from his workplace. He ended up setting an appointment for late in the afternoon so that he could drive me to the clinic after he got off work.

I was so happy when the doctor announced that my baby was thriving and developing normally. I had loved my child from the moment I knew of her existence. But when I heard her heartbeat there in the doctor's office, I was overcome by a more powerful kind of love. She was no longer just an idea of a baby. I was carrying a real flesh-and-blood child.

"When is my baby due?" I asked the doctor.

"In about three months," he told me.

After that, I felt less lonely during my long solitary days in the house. I talked with my baby when I didn't have anyone else to talk to. I viewed my unborn child as my little companion.

A week after my encounter with my neighbor Irene, she came over to check on me. When I invited her in, she glanced around my sparsely furnished home, a worried look on her face.

"I don't mean to intrude," she said. "I just wanted to know whether you were able to get in with the doctor."

"Yes," I told her. "I had my first appointment yesterday."

She breathed a sigh of relief. "I'm so glad that worked out for you." Then, she held out the large paper bag she was carrying. "My niece is about your size. I thought maybe you could use her maternity clothing. She won't be needing it anymore."

I thanked Irene, and she left. When I pulled out the contents of the bag, I gasped in awe. It was a veritable treasure trove of the prettiest maternity outfits I could ever imagine, clothing I never would've known how to pick out in a store.

I couldn't wait to show my husband what Irene had brought me. However, he was less than pleased. "We're not a charity case," he growled at me. "I'm fully capable of providing for us."

I have to hand it to Ivan. He truly was a good provider. Week by week, he brought home items for furnishing our home: a kitchen table, a sofa, a dresser for our bedroom, a crib for the baby. He knew how to find good values at discount prices. Sadly, I never took part in deciding what to purchase. Ivan handled all that on his own.

One day, he walked into the house with a television set. I was taken aback, unsure whether I wanted that strange device in my home. Ivan told me to give it a chance, that I'd enjoy watching TV after I got used to it.

As it turned out, watching the lives of other people on the screen helped to ease my boredom and loneliness. I'd get up in the morning looking forward to watching my favorite shows. The behavior of English people never ceased to bewilder me. However, watching television did provide me with an education in the ways of people in the broader world.

Yes, in some regards, I have to give Ivan credit for being a good family man. He worked hard and provided us with everything we needed. He paid all our bills and kept up our home and property. However, in other ways, he lived as freely as he had before we were married. He couldn't seem to give up the habit of running around with his friends every Friday and Saturday night.

I suspected that he was having extramarital affairs. I knew that my husband was strikingly handsome, and that it was difficult for any woman to resist his charms. He often came home with the scent of women's perfume on his shirt.

Once, I found a tube of lipstick that had rolled under the front seat of our car. But whenever I questioned Ivan about such things, he readily came up with a convincing explanation.

Mercedes, you wonder why I was so tolerant of Ivan's misbehavior. I guess it was because I understood his precarious position in the English world. Without having one foot planted in the structure of the Amish community, Ivan didn't know how to handle the freedoms English life afforded him. He didn't fully know how to recognize danger, how to back away from something that was going to be harmful in the long run. Yes, I was discouraged when he would come home drunk after a night out with his friends. But I'd tell myself that as he grew older, he'd give up such nonsense.

Furthermore, I simply didn't know how to stand up to my husband. An Amish girl is raised to be subservient to men. As a wife, she is expected to submit to her husband's will, to respect his authority as head of the household. I had no idea how to put my foot down, even in the face of Ivan's most egregious behavior.

Yes, I was restricted as a young wife, while my husband did whatever he wanted to do. However, there was one freedom that I persuaded Ivan to allow me. I was keenly aware that my Amish schooling had left me woefully unprepared for life in the English world. I felt terribly self-conscious about my limited education. So, after much pleading on my part, Ivan grudgingly allowed me to work on getting my high school equivalency diploma.

I began my studies three months after we married, and I passed my final test about two years later. This endeavor opened up a new world to me. I was amazed at how much information had passed me by while I lived in the isolation of the Amish community.

Of course, I had to put my studies on hold when my child was born. In April 1964, our daughter Corina entered this world, a beautiful, well-developed nine-pound baby. She came quickly and easily, as if she was fully prepared to take on life outside the womb.

When she was first placed in my arms, I experienced a love I didn't think it was possible to feel. I could hardly comprehend my overflowing emotions. From the look on your face, Mercedes, I can see that you felt the same way when your son was born.

Corina was such an exquisite little creature. She looked a lot like her father, inheriting his dark hair and complexion. Even at a few months of age, her big brown eyes sparkled with her zest for life.

While I'd always considered myself to be ordinary at best, Corina was extraordinary. She was everything I wasn't. I could hardly believe I had given birth to her.

Growing up, I had watched many Amish women take care of their babies. I was familiar with the simple, home-sewn garments in which newborns were clothed. In the weeks before Corina was born, I realized I had no idea how to dress an English baby.

My neighbor Irene must have sensed how clueless I was about such things. She came over frequently during the last weeks of my pregnancy, bringing gifts of diapers, sleepers, and receiving blankets.

"My husband and I were never blessed with children," she told me. "So, I can't help being excited about your little one. Virgil tells me I'm a silly old woman, being so tickled about a baby before it's even here."

After Corina was born, Irene fell head over heels in love with her. She came over several times a week to see her. "Babies change so fast at this age," she said. "I don't want to miss anything."

And almost every time she came, she brought along something cute for my baby girl to wear. "I saw this when Virgil and I were out shopping," she'd say. "I knew Corina would look adorable in it."

When Corina was two months old, I persuaded Ivan to start letting me go to the grocery store with him, just so I could take my little one out in public. People would gush over her, saying what a beautiful baby she was. Whenever I carried around my child all decked out in the fancy outfits Irene bought her, she was like my personal ornament. Having her in my arms made me feel beautiful myself.

Here's a picture of Corina I had taken at a photo shoot in a department store. She was six months old, and had just learned to sit up on her own. Isn't she adorable? All these years later, seeing this picture still takes my breath away.

I have pages and pages of Corina's baby pictures in this album. You can go ahead and look. Shortly after she was born, I persuaded Ivan to buy me a camera so that I could capture her childhood in photos. No doubt, I went overboard.

So, when my marriage was lonely, when I had no family to lean on, I had the companionship of my baby girl. I loved her so dearly that I could hardly let her out of my arms.

That didn't mean Corina was a timid or clingy child. No, not at all. Early on, she showed signs of being intelligent and inquisitive, eager to explore the world around her. In many ways, she took after her father. In addition to his height, his complexion, and his facial features, she inherited his boldness and self-assurance.

But unlike Ivan, Corina has never been reckless. She's always been as steady as a rock. Her adventures have never been impulsive, and her risks have been well-calculated. At times when I haven't known what to do, she has stepped up to take charge.

When Corina was little, I tended to think of her as opposite of me, having characteristics I always wanted but never possessed. Sometimes, however, I questioned that assumption. Was it possible that nature had endowed me with personality traits similar to those of Corina? Had those qualities failed to sprout and grow in the barren soil of my childhood? Had they been driven underground by the harsh rules of the Amish community? Could I hope to someday have a sparkling personality like my daughter's?

In May 1967, three years after Corina was born, my son Wesley made his entrance into the world. I had expected my second delivery to be even easier than my first, but Wesley took a long time in coming. I was surprised at how small he was, weighing in at not quite seven pounds.

He looked very different from his sister, with his fair skin and soft blonde curls. When he looked at me, his big blue eyes seemed to search my soul. While I thought of Corina *as sparkling, I thought of Wesley as angelic. Here is a picture of him as a newborn. Isn't he precious?*

Sometimes, I think I've never really known my son. To be sure, I've wanted to. But there's always been something mystical about him, something just out of reach of my understanding. His temperament was so unlike Corina's that one could hardly believe they were brother and sister.

From infancy on, Wesley was quiet and contented. He demanded very little from me, and could entertain himself in solitude for hours. He didn't seem unhappy or withdrawn. He was simply at peace in his own little world.

When he was a toddler, I would sit and watch Wesley as he played, trying to imagine what was going on in his little mind. But inevitably, Corina would come to claim my attention.

I don't mean to suggest that her attention stealing was malicious. It was just that, in her mind, she and I were the primary pair. From the beginning of her life, it had been just the two of us, as Ivan had never figured very strongly into her relationship picture. And she viewed her little brother as a latecomer on the scene.

I tried so hard to give Wesley the attention he deserved. I tried to be evenhanded between him and his sister. However, being fair seemed impossible, because Corina demanded so much and Wesley needed so little. Sometimes, I'd scoop Wesley up and hold him to my heart, hoping to forge a bond between us. But I never felt I could truly reach him.

You're probably wondering whether being a father slowed down Ivan's running around. Unfortunately, it didn't. I came to dread the weekend, knowing that my husband would be gone Friday and Saturday nights until the early hours of the morning.

Mercedes, I can tell you're angry about the way Ivan treated me. Looking back, I realize that I was angry, too, although I never allowed myself to admit that. I wasn't raised to have any sense of self-worth or personal rights. I had witnessed many instances of Amish men mistreating and disrespecting their wives, denying them any say in important matters. But the Amish community didn't view that dynamic as being wrong. It was seen as the natural order of things.

As strong of a woman as you are, you never would've put up with Ivan's nonsense. You would've packed up the children and left him. But I didn't see any way to do that. Where would I have gone? I had no means of supporting myself and my children. I had no access to Ivan's bank account. I didn't even know how to drive a car. I had to depend on my husband for everything.

More than that, I still had very little confidence in negotiating the English world. In the late 1960s, when I was the mother of two young children, there was so much turmoil and unrest in society: the defiance of the so-called establishment, the civil rights movement, the protests against the Viet Nam war, the assassination of public figures. It all scared me to death. If I would've stayed in the Amish community, I would've been sheltered from all that.

In many ways, Corina was the one to lead me into the English world. At age five, she started kindergarten in the public-school system, and before I knew it, she was in first grade. She rode the school bus just like any other child. In the grocery store, she'd tell me what to buy to pack in her lunchbox, pointing out the food the other children were bringing. When we shopped for clothing, she'd show me how to pick out things similar to what other little girls were wearing.

Here is her first-grade school photo. She looks like any other little girl in her class. You could never tell her parents had been raised Amish.

Then, there were the events at her school that I needed to attend: the Christmas concert, the spring musical, the parent-teacher conferences. The first time I entered her school building, I did so with a great deal of trepidation, feeling clueless and unworthy. But Corina took me by the hand and confidently led me inside.

Yes, Corina was an English child, through and through. She spoke the English language perfectly, without the Dutchy accent Ivan and I were unable to shake. I never attempted to teach her Pennsylvania Dutch, although she did pick up quite a bit of it from listening to Ivan and me converse in that language.

As you can tell, Corina was a precocious child, far more capable than other little ones her age. By the time she was six, she was functioning as my partner in the household when her father was gone.

No, fatherhood didn't put a halt to Ivan's wild ways. But something else happened that brought him up short. On a Friday night in April 1971, he had gone out with his friends as always, leaving me anxiously waiting for him to come home. But he failed to show up at two or three o'clock in the morning like he usually did. The hours passed, with me becoming increasingly frantic with worry. When dawn came, he still wasn't home.

Around 9:00 A.M., I received a phone call from the county jail. It was my husband. He told me that a fight had broken out in the bar where he'd been drinking with his friends, and that he'd been arrested for disorderly conduct.

"Don't worry," he told me. "My friend Dave will pick me up and bring me home." Then he added in a strangely solicitous tone, "I just wanted to let you know that I'm safe. I figured you were pretty scared when I didn't come home last night."

I was shocked to hear that Ivan had been involved in a fight. As foolhardy as he was, I'd never known him to be violent. I told myself that he was probably just a by-stander, that he was in the wrong place at the wrong time when the police came to break up the scuffle.

When Ivan walked into the house several hours later, shame was written all over his face. His clothing was dirty, his shirt was torn, and one eye was blackened. I could tell that being jailed like a common criminal had humiliated him. The consequences of his lifestyle had finally caught up with him.

He slumped down at the kitchen table, his head in his hands. "Dora," he said, "I need to talk to you."

I sat down with him, and he began speaking in the language of our childhood. "I want you to know that I'm done with all this nonsense. I don't want to live like this anymore."

Perhaps I was gullible, Mercedes, but I believed him. The conviction in his voice and the earnest look in his eyes made me know he was speaking from his heart. I'd always known that the values he'd learned from his parents were somewhere inside him, and that they were strong enough to lead him back to doing right.

Then my husband said something I never expected to hear from him. "I've been thinking about this for quite some time, Dora. I want us to go back to being Amish. Living in the English world has caused so much trouble for me, and for you as well. I want us to live in a community where our children are safe from worldly influences, where they will grow up learning to live godly lives."

Mercedes, I think my head must've been spinning in circles as I listened to Ivan talk. I just couldn't picture him wanting to give up the modern lifestyle we'd grown accustomed to. Still, I went along with his idea, as docile as I'd always been.

The two of us talked for a long time about how difficult it would be to reenter the Amish community. We would have many broken relationships to mend. We would have to face condemnation from our families, our bishop, our congregation. There would be a great deal of doubt about the sincerity of our intention to renounce the ways of the world. And for many years, other people would look askance at us.

Yes, Ivan realized all this, and he still wanted to face the challenges and return to the Amish community. When it seemed as if we'd settled on a course of action, Ivan looked at me with tenderness in his eyes. For the very first time, I sensed that our marriage meant something to him.

He got up and walked over to seven-year-old Corina, who was occupied with her crayons and coloring book at the other end of the table. He bent down and kissed the top of her head. Corina looked up at him with wary eyes, as if she was skeptical of the change he was proposing.

I suddenly realized that I'd been so caught up in the discussion with Ivan that I hadn't noticed our daughter sitting *there listening to every word we were saying. She wouldn't have understood all of the Pennsylvania Dutch we were speaking, but she certainly would've picked up the gist of the conversation.*

Then Ivan went into the living room where Wesley, who was not quite four, was quietly playing with his set of plastic farm animals. Ivan picked him up and squeezed him tightly. Wesley squirmed, trying to get down, as if he was uncomfortable with his father's attention.

"Son," Ivan said, "I'm going to be a better father to you. I promise." In that moment, my heart swelled with joy as I envisioned the future for our little family.

However, in the next moment, Ivan said something that burst my bubble of hope. "I've been telling the guys that I'm done partying with them, that I'm going to be a family man now. They're all bummed out about that. So, I promised them one last night."

"Oh Ivan," I protested, "do you have to go?"

"Just one more time," he assured me. "I won't even be out late. I'll probably be home by midnight."

Then he went to bed and slept until late in the afternoon. That evening after supper, he kissed me goodbye with a tenderness I hadn't felt from him since the very first time he kissed me.

"This is my last night out, Dora," he said. "Then I'll be all yours. You can count on it." And out the door he went.

Once again, I went to bed alone that night. I told myself this would be the last time I'd have to wonder when my husband was coming home. Comforted by that thought, I fell asleep.

Around two o'clock in the morning, I awoke with a start, drenched in perspiration, my heart pounding wildly. I sensed something was terribly wrong. Something dark and ominous was about to enter my life. I'd never had such a premonition before, nor have I since then.

I jumped out of bed and went to check on the children. They were both fine, sleeping soundly. But the reassurance of their safety did nothing to dispel the terror that held me in its grip. I went out to the living room and began pacing the floor, desperately praying for Ivan to come home.

Suddenly, I saw headlights pulling into our driveway. Thinking it had to be my husband, I rushed to the door and flung it open. But instead of Ivan, I saw two police officers coming up the walk.

"Are you Mrs. Ivan Graber?" one of them asked.

"Yes," I said, my heart in my throat. "Did you come to tell me that my husband is in jail again?"

"Mrs. Graber," the other officer said, "may we come inside?"

I nodded, and the two of them stepped into the house. "You'll need to sit down," the first officer said. "We have some unfortunate news for you."

I sank down onto the sofa. The officers sat down with me and proceeded to tell me a story so horrifying that I couldn't take it in. Unbeknownst to me, Ivan had had a longstanding feud with a man by the name of Jack Conway, a patron of the bar Ivan and his friends frequented. On Friday night, Mr. Conway had accused Ivan of making a pass at his girlfriend. He'd thrown a punch at him, and Ivan had swung back. Evidently, Ivan had gotten the best of Mr. Conway before their fight had been broken up by the police.

Mr. Conway had gone back to the bar on Saturday night, ready to settle the score. He had assaulted Ivan, and in the course of their scuffle, he'd pulled out a knife.

"Where is my husband now?" I asked.

One of the officers reached over and placed a hand on my shoulder. "Mrs. Graber, I'm afraid your husband didn't make it."

"What do you mean?" I cried out.

"Your husband didn't survive the attack. One of his stab wounds was fatal. Jack Conway has been arrested for his murder."

The officer's words paralyzed me. I couldn't move. I couldn't speak. I couldn't even think.

"Is there someone we can call for you?" the officer asked.

"No," I whispered, "I'm all alone."

Just then, I heard Corina's bedroom door creak open. She came padding down the hallway in her little nightgown.

"What's wrong, Mommy?" she asked.

I got up, and Corina took my hand. Together, we went to get the still-sleeping Wesley out of his bed. Then I sank to the floor. Holding my children close to me, I cried and cried.

That's all the farther I can go today, Mercedes. Telling this story has taken an emotional toll on me. I see by your tears that it has moved you as well. Thank you for your kindness in listening to me.

You may have rightly guessed that, after Ivan's death, I never did return to the Amish church. If Ivan had survived, we probably would've stayed married for life. And right now, I'd be an Amish wife, living with Ivan on a farm in the Amish community near Middlebury. It may surprise you to know that I cherish that thought. No doubt, we would've had more children. I might've ended up as a mother of eight or ten.

However, I don't think that was meant to be my path in life. Perhaps Ivan and I were never destined to be lifelong traveling companions.

But right now, I need to shed tears for my first husband. He and I almost had an opportunity to make things right in our marriage, to find our way forward together. That opportunity was snatched from us. And all I can do is grieve.

CHAPTER 5: DORA, CORINA, AND WESLEY

The warm summer breeze wafted through the open car window, caressing Mercedes' face and playing with her hair. Once again, Saturday afternoon found her heading north toward the city of Saint Joseph. Although she was trapped in a stream of slow-moving traffic, she was managing to maintain a perfect sense of calm.

She smiled to herself, remembering how she'd reacted to frustrating circumstances while driving in South Bend just a week earlier. She'd sworn, pounded on the steering wheel, and shouted at other drivers. She wondered at the change in herself.

When she'd informed Javier that she was going to Michigan to visit Dora again, he hadn't been surprised. "I figured you'd see her this weekend," he'd said.

His accepting attitude had encouraged Mercedes to drop her defenses and be more open with him. "Dora is helping me with a school assignment," she'd explained. "She's telling me her life story."

"Wow," Javier had said, "that must be interesting." Then he'd added, "Just be careful driving up there. I heard there's an art festival going on in downtown Saint Joseph, so there will be lots of people coming into the city."

As Mercedes inched forward in the traffic, she thought about her last visit with Dora, and a melancholy feeling washed over her. The story about Dora's first marriage had haunted her all week.

She'd even had a dream about the heartbreaking saga, with characters so vivid that she couldn't get them out of her mind. Beautiful, free-spirited Corina demanding to be the center of her mother's attention. Sweet, solitary Wesley content to occupy a quiet corner of the room. Handsome Ivan, his proud, confident demeanor suddenly deflated by the weight of shame and remorse. And timid, vulnerable Dora, struggling with all her might to do right by her family, to make the best of an ill-advised marriage.

As Mercedes pondered the disastrous ending of Dora and Ivan's marriage, her melancholy deepened. She wanted to go back in time to help the two young people, to set them on the right track, to warn them away from the tragedy that was about to befall them. She wished she could teach Ivan how to be more sensitive and considerate. She wished she could coach Dora to stand up for herself.

Dora and Ivan. Dora and Ivan. The names rang a sorrowful note in her heart, bringing tears to her eyes. *Dora and Ivan.*

Suddenly, she realized that the faces in her inner vision had changed to those of Mercedes and Javier. *Mercedes and Javier.* Their struggle wasn't quite like that of Dora and Ivan. Yet, it was just as real, generating its own kind of pain.

Then a third face popped into her mind's eye: little Javi, gazing imploringly at the parents on either side of him. As Mercedes watched the trio in her imagination, grief welled inside her and a sob escaped her throat.

"Are Javier and I doomed to fail like Dora and Ivan?" she whispered to herself. She contemplated the similarities between the two relationships. Both couples had been caught off guard by an unplanned pregnancy. Both couples had responded to the situation by getting married before they were ready to handle that commitment. Perhaps such a hurried arrangement was always destined for failure.

But then, she recognized the differences. Javier had never treated her like Ivan had treated Dora. Sure, it seemed as if he was relentlessly critical of her. But he had never manipulated or taken advantage of her. He had never cheated on her. He had never limited her freedom. He had always encouraged her to achieve and to be her best. And he had never deprived her of his attention and affection.

She knew herself to be impulsive and undisciplined, quick to unleash her temper on her husband. But she had a backbone. She knew her rights as a woman. She never let anyone run over her.

Dora and Ivan had never experienced a strong emotional bond with each other. They had stayed together out of duty. But with Mercedes and Javier, there was chemistry, sizzling passion that prevailed over chilly resentment, unrelenting passion that kept them connected no matter what happened between them.

Perhaps, Mercedes thought, *the differences in the two stories might outweigh their similarities. It might make a difference in their endings.*

"How are you, my dear?" Dora asked as she welcomed Mercedes into her apartment. "You look especially lovely today."

Mercedes took a seat on the sofa, smoothing her brightly patterned maxi skirt, then folding her hands with their freshly painted nails. "I hope I look better than I did last week," she said with an embarrassed smile. "I was a mess."

Dora seated herself in her recliner, gazing at Mercedes with tender eyes. "But you seem sad, sweetheart. I sense you have something on your mind."

"Well," Mercedes admitted, "on the way over here, I was thinking a lot. I guess I was sad, and maybe a little worried."

When she saw Dora's brow furrow with concern, she quickly added, "Oh, it wasn't about my life." She hesitated, then said, "I've been worried about you."

Dora brushed a wisp of hair from her face, smiling self-consciously. "Sweetie, you don't need to worry a bit about me. I'm well taken care of here."

"That's not what I mean," Mercedes said. "I know this might sound weird, but I've been worried about the young you. When you stopped your story last week, you had just become a widow. It seemed like your world was spinning out of control. I can't imagine how hard it must've been to pick yourself up and face life on your own."

Dora sighed, nodding slowly, a faraway look in her eyes. "Yes, Mercedes, it was hard. For a while, there was nothing in my world but overwhelming sorrow and deep despair. I had no idea what lay ahead for my children and me."

Mercedes noticed that her grandmother's face had turned pale, and that her hands were trembling in her lap. "Dora," she said, "you don't need to tell me things that are too painful for you. I don't want to put you through that."

Dora smiled wanly. "Thank you, my dear. I appreciate your sensitivity. But if I leave things out, I won't be giving you a complete picture. Maybe it will do me good to share some details I've never shared with anyone else."

As you might expect, hearing the news of Ivan's death sent me into a state of extreme shock. When I look back, much of that time is a blur to me. I'm sure a lot of things happened that I wasn't fully aware of.

One of the police officers must've gone to my neighbor Irene's house and asked her to come over. I remember her walking into my home in the early hours of the morning and enfolding me in her arms. She stayed with my children while the officers took me to the morgue at Goshen General Hospital. I was told I needed to identify Ivan's body, to verify that it was my husband who'd been killed in the bar fight.

Forgive me for my difficulty here, Mercedes. This is a part of the story that's hard for me to get through. As the coroner walked me over to a table where a body lay covered with a sheet, I could still make myself believe there might have been a mistake. Surely, I would find it to be some other man's body.

Then the coroner pulled the sheet back, just enough to uncover the face. There was no mistake. It was Ivan, lying there so cold and still.

Thankfully, there were no injuries to his face, other than traces of the black eye he'd sustained the night before. I never saw the stab wound to his torso that had cost him his life. I'm glad I have no such details to recall.

The officers asked me where Ivan's parents lived. They said they needed to inform them of their son's passing. I gave them the location of the Graber farm.

I leaned over to kiss Ivan's forehead. Then I felt myself falling. The officers caught me. I can't recall what happened right after that.

I do remember lying in bed with my children snuggled up on either side of me, both of them whimpering in fear. Irene was there. She made breakfast for the children and offered me some. Of course, I was unable to eat anything.

Later, a second woman, Irene's sister, showed up at the house. For the next few days, those two women took care of everything in my home: the cooking, the laundry, the care of the children. Irene even called Corina's school to inform the principal of Ivan's death, telling him that Corina would be absent for a few days.

Even though it felt as if my life had come crashing down around me, I knew I had to pull myself together to explain to the children what had happened. I wasn't able to talk coherently with them until late Sunday afternoon.

However, even before I told Corina that her father was gone, she'd already picked up on the fact that something terrible had happened to him. I explained to her that someone had hurt him, and that he'd died. As Wesley was not quite four, it was much more difficult to make him understand that his father was never coming home again.

Of course, I needed to plan a funeral. I'd had no experience with anything like that, and in my muddled state of mind, I had no idea how to go about it.

Thankfully, I had help. After Ivan's body had been released from the morgue, it had been taken to a mortuary in Middlebury. The undertaker kindly guided me through the process of making arrangements. At his suggestion, I decided to hold a service there at the funeral home so that Ivan's friends could pay their respects.

Throughout the seven-and-a-half years of being married to Ivan, I had felt so isolated as an Amish woman living in the English world. But at my husband's funeral, I was surprised at how far our ties had reached into the English community.

In addition to Ivan's friends, dozens of his coworkers attended his funeral. The owner of the company he worked for was also there. Corina's schoolteacher and principal came to pay their respects, along with the parents of some of her friends.

Of course, Irene and her husband Virgil were there, never leaving my side. Some of our other neighbors came as well. Overall, the show of support touched me deeply.

Lying there in the casket, my husband was as strikingly

handsome as he'd ever been in life. As I gazed at his face, I saw a sweetness, a softness that I'd never seen before. A tender feeling washed over me. I knew that my husband was at peace, that despite his misguided earthly life, his soul had gone to its true home.

After the service, my dear little Corina stood alone at the casket for a long time, staring somberly at her father as if trying to commit every detail about him to memory. I held Wesley up so he could see his father and say goodbye to him. He didn't want to look and buried his face against my shoulder.

I chose to hold a graveside service as well, for family and friends from the Amish community. It was conducted by the bishop from the Graber family's church district.

We buried Ivan in the family plot where his grandparents had been laid to rest. I thought it only fitting that he be buried with his Amish family members, as it had been his intention to return to them.

I didn't have the opportunity to hold an in-depth conversation with Moses and Miriam Graber about their son's tragic death. I regret that such communication never took place, that we were unable to support one another in our shared grief. The two of them looked so worn down and defeated as they stood at their son's graveside. I could only imagine their anguish when the police officers delivered the heart-wrenching news. They had been so worried about the direction Ivan's life had taken. That day, their worst fears had been realized.

However, I was able to tell them that just before their son died, he had made the decision to give up his worldly life and return to the Amish church. I hope that gave them some peace of mind.

My parents were there with me at the graveside service. Afterwards, my mother pulled me into her arms, sobbing, "Dora, Dora, come back to us."

My father struggled to keep his composure. "Dora, you must surely know that for the safety of yourself and your children, you must come back home."

At that moment, I felt so fragile and so broken that

heeding my parents' advice seemed like the only thing I could do. Returning to the familiar safety and security of the Amish community seemed far more appealing than braving life on my own in the English world. My children and I could live in my parents' home for years to come, where I would never have to worry about a roof over our heads or food on the table.

However, I said nothing to my parents. I just nodded in agreement to what they were urging me to do.

"Put your affairs in order," my father instructed. "Then let us know when you're ready."

But as I tucked my children into bed that night, my daughter had something to say on the matter. I hadn't realized that Corina had overheard my conversation with my parents. She must've been right there at my side, her sharp little mind tuned in to pick up everything she could of the Pennsylvania Dutch we were speaking.

"Mama," she said, "I don't want to be Amish."

I was taken aback by her sudden declaration. "Why not?" I asked.

"Because the kids at school would make fun of me," she said.

"But if you were Amish, you wouldn't be going to that school," I told her.

She stared at me, horrified. "You mean I wouldn't get to see my friends?"

"You'd make some new friends at the Amish school," I said.

She shook her head emphatically. "No, Mama!" Then she buried her head under the covers, wailing, "No, Mama, no, no, no!"

I was so shaken up that I went out to the living room where I sat alone in the darkness, just thinking things through. I remembered how, when it came to leaving the Amish church, I'd felt caught between loyalty to my parents and loyalty to my future husband.

Now, I felt caught between my parents' pleas and the wishes of my daughter. And I knew in my heart that I had to choose the wellbeing of my child. I knew it would be unfair to abruptly pull Corina out of the life she'd always known and subject her to a culture to which she wasn't accustomed. I knew that my free-spirited daughter would be miserable living under the restrictions of the Amish church. I knew it would be a crime to limit her brilliant intellect to only eight years of Amish schooling.

Corina likes to tell her friends and coworkers about her Amish roots. She teases them, telling them how close she came to being raised Amish. People are always shocked when she says those things, as Corina comes across as an educated and worldly-wise person. She enjoys seeing such reactions.

I sometimes think that Wesley could've thrived in the Amish community. He probably would've been happy with farm life. The Amish have been known for their willingness to help when other people face hardships. Sizable groups of them often show up at the sites of natural disasters in various parts of this country. Perhaps my son's Amish heritage comes through in his work for the International Red Cross.

Over the weeks following her father's death, Corina tried to maintain her usual buoyant attitude. But from time to time, I'd find her huddled alone in her bedroom, tears in her eyes, looking as if the weight of the world had fallen onto her little shoulders. When I'd sit down to talk with her, she'd bring up a few more questions about her father's death.

"What are we going to do now, Mama?" she asked me time and again.

"We'll figure it out," I kept telling her.

Corina still has clear memories of her father. Every now and then, she and I have conversations about him. Early on, she came to understand that his reckless behavior led to his untimely death. I think that's why my daughter has always been careful in the life choices she's made.

Wesley responded to his father's death in a totally different way. He'd always been such a quiet little boy, and had been slow in developing language skills. I always suspected it wasn't that my son didn't know how to talk. He *just felt little need for verbal communication. In the month before Ivan's death, Wesley had finally come to the point where he would carry on a full conversation with me.*

But after his father's passing, my son stopped talking. That was the only way I could tell that the loss of his father had made an impact on him. He would say a word or two in response to my questions. Mostly, he'd just nod or shake his head. Sometimes, he wouldn't respond at all.

His big blue eyes always seemed to be staring out into space. It broke my heart to know that my little boy had no way of expressing his feelings about the loss of his father.

Four months after Ivan's death, our neighbors' golden retriever gave birth to a litter of puppies. Virgil brought one over to the house, asking me whether my children might enjoy having a puppy to raise.

My first inclination was to say no. As you might suspect, I had my hands full, and I was reluctant to take on another responsibility. But when Wesley saw the puppy, his eyes lit up in a way I'd never seen before. He came running to claim his new pet. I knew I couldn't refuse to take on something that would mean so much to him.

Later that very day, I overheard Wesley talking to his puppy, chatting away as if nothing traumatic had ever happened to him. Soon, he was talking with his sister and me as well, although never as much as he did with the dog.

Nowadays, people talk about therapy dogs and emotional support animals. Those terms weren't in use when Wesley was growing up. But that golden retriever pup healed my little boy's broken heart. The dog, whom he named Bob, was his constant companion for the next seven years.

Even when he was old enough to understand, it was difficult to engage Wesley in any conversation about his father. Sadly, he has no memory of his father today. I've seen pain flicker in his eyes when Corina and I talk about Ivan. However, unlike his sister, who always probes for details so she can understand the big picture, he never asks questions about his father.

A week after Ivan's funeral, I wrote a letter to my parents informing them that I'd decided to remain in the English world.

They were terribly upset, as I knew they would be. Their return letter was filled with sorrow and anger, accusing me of turning my back on my upbringing, my family, my community, and my God. They predicted that my decision would lead me down a path of sin and misery, ending in the eternal damnation of my soul.

You're wincing, Mercedes. My parents' words must sound terribly harsh to you. Yes, their response hurt me. It cut me to the core. But it didn't surprise me.

Over the years, I made efforts to visit my parents from time to time. I wanted my children to know their grandparents. But those visits were difficult. The air between my parents and me was always charged with tension, making it impossible for them to form a bond with Corina and Wesley.

I made sure to avoid visits during mealtimes, as someone who has left the Amish church isn't welcome to eat at the same table as the rest of the family. My children and I would've had to sit at a table off to the side. I didn't want to put Corina and Wesley through such a humiliating ordeal.

Inevitably, I'd be in tears as I drove away from a visit with my family. This would upset my children, who didn't understand the dynamics involved. The visits became less frequent as the years passed. My life drifted farther and farther away from those of my parents and siblings.

As it turned out, I was the only one of my parents' children who left the Amish church. The rest of my family remained firmly entrenched in the Amish community. My parents have now been gone for almost forty years. Three of my siblings have also passed. My remaining two siblings are surrounded by their own children and grandchildren, and I doubt that they give me much thought. That's okay. But I do think a great deal about them.

As you might imagine, facing life as a single mother was a daunting task. I had no idea how I was going to keep body and soul together without the husband on whom I'd been dependent for more than seven years. But help came to me in surprising ways.

In the early days after Ivan's death, my neighbor Irene frequently came over to check on the children and me. The day after I received the letter from my parents, she found me in tears. We sat down to talk, and I told her how I'd lost the support of my Amish family because of my decision to remain in the English world.

Her tears flowed along with mine. "Your dear little children need grandparents," she said. "Especially after losing their father. Virgil and I will be Grandpa and Grandma for Corina and Wesley."

And that is exactly what they did. I'd go farther than that and say they became like parents to me.

The day after that conversation took place, Irene drove me to the grocery store and paid the whole bill, just to make sure my children and I had enough food in the house.

Several days later, she took me to the bank to look into accessing the money from Ivan's account. To my surprise, I discovered that Ivan had stashed away far more money than I'd ever suspected.

Over the following weeks, Virgil took it upon himself to teach me how to drive Ivan's car. Then, he led me through the process of getting my drivers' license. He also schooled me on the basics of auto maintenance, such as when to take the car in for an oil change.

For the first year or so, Ivan's friends Dave and Jeff came over every week to do yard work for me, cutting the grass, raking leaves, and shoveling snow. I'm sure they felt guilty about Ivan's death, as they'd been involved in the same reckless lifestyle. I think both of them sobered up and matured after their friend met such a tragic end.

Unbeknownst to me, Ivan had a small life insurance policy through his employer. Additionally, his coworkers took up a collection for me, amounting to several thousand dollars. Altogether, it was enough for the children and me to live on while I got my bearings.

One day about three months after Ivan's death, I heard the sound of a car pulling into my driveway. I looked out the window and saw Moses Graber getting out of the passenger seat. His English driver remained in the car, waiting for him to complete his errand.

When I opened my front door, Moses was standing there on my doorstep, tall, dignified, and austere in his dark Amish suit and black hat. He handed me an envelope.

"This would've been my son's share of inheritance from the farm," he told me. "I thought it was only right that you should have it for the upbringing of his children. Put it in your bank account to keep it safe."

I was flabbergasted. I thanked him profusely for his kindness.

"God bless you, Dora," he said. Before he turned to leave, I saw tears in his eyes.

Still stunned, I watched the car pull out of my driveway. Then I opened the envelope and found a check for twenty thousand dollars.

Mercedes, that incident still touches me. In holding with Amish tradition, Moses Graber could easily have justified keeping his back turned on me. But he transcended the harsh rules of shunning and chose love instead.

I will forever be grateful to Ivan's father, but not just for the money. The gesture itself meant almost more to me. I still get tearful when I think about it.

That's not to say the money wasn't a godsend. It helped to keep the wolf away from the door while I figured out how to move forward with my life.

After a year of deliberating, I decided that I wanted to go to college. Even though it had taken me two years to get my GED, mastering the required subject matter had come fairly easily to me. I figured I could do equally well in college.

When I talked about the matter with Irene, she looked a little dubious. "What do you want to study?" she asked.

"I'm not sure yet," I admitted. "I've thought about being a nurse or a teacher. Something I could do to support my children."

"Well, if that's what you want," she said, "give it a try."

So, when Wesley started first grade, I enrolled at Goshen College, a private Mennonite school about ten miles from my home.

The minute I stepped foot inside a college classroom, I knew I was in over my head. I was twenty-seven at the time. Being surrounded by students considerably younger than me, who all seemed so intelligent, so worldly-wise, and so sure of themselves, created enormous anxiety for me. In order not to stand out as the misfit I believed myself to be, I tried to keep as low a profile as possible.

I lasted at Goshen College for only one semester. While I managed to pass all my classes, I just couldn't muster the courage to take on any more.

I felt utterly discouraged, and I castigated myself terribly. I told myself that I was a failure, that I'd never be able to do right by my children, that I would never amount to anything in life.

However, when I was done berating myself, a more reasoned voice in my mind began to speak. It told me that preparing myself for a profession would be a long, expensive ordeal. It would quickly use up the inheritance money Moses Graber had given me for the children. It didn't seem right to use those funds for my own education. If anything, I needed to put the money away for my children's education.

So, I let go of the idea of getting a college degree. Mercedes, you might think I gave up too easily. I wonder about that sometimes. But looking back, I see that I made the best decision I could at the time.

Corina had been enthused about the idea of me going to college. I was afraid to tell her that I'd dropped out, as I didn't want her to view her mother as a failure. But when I broke the news to her, she said, "That's okay, Mama. I'll just have to pick up where you left off."

Her words stunned me. They seemed too precocious for a nine-year-old. As it turned out, they were prescient. Years later, when Corina started nursing school, I was so happy to help fund her education with her father's inheritance money.

So, leaving the dream of college behind me, I went to work at the same recreational vehicle factory that had employed my late husband. I sewed seat covers for the motor homes the company manufactured. As I'd had many years of experience with my mother's old treadle sewing machine, I found I was able to excel at my job.

Being praised by my supervisor for turning out quality products in a timely manner was a gratifying experience. I was quite proud of myself. Not only was I earning money to support my children, I was making a contribution to the company I worked for. For the first time ever, I felt as if I'd found a measure of success in the English world.

I stayed with that company for twenty-three years. They treated me well. Looking back, I have so much gratitude for that place. My work there provided me with steadiness and stability during the ups and down in other parts of my life.

Let me assure you that I don't view my time at college as counting for nothing. Something very important came out of that brief journey. One of the classes I took was an introductory sociology course, taught by a handsome young African American professor just a few years older than me.

You guessed it, Mercedes. That young professor was Dr. Elliott Jordan.

I always sat in the back of his classroom, trying to be as inconspicuous as possible, keeping my head down to hide the fact that I was perpetually close to tears. One day, as I trailed behind the other students filing out of the classroom at the end of the hour, Professor Jordan stopped me. "Is everything okay, Miss Graber?" he asked.

I halted in my tracks, startled by his question. As the class was large, consisting of fifty students or more, I was surprised that he even knew my name.

He repeated his inquiry. "You seem troubled. Are you having difficulty here at the college?"

The kindness in his voice unleashed my tears. "I don't think I belong here," I choked out between sobs.

He hesitated a moment, pain flickering in his eyes. "I understand that feeling," he said. I knew he was referring to his own experience of being a black man on a predominantly white campus.

"Tell me why you feel that way," he said.

We ended up sitting there in his classroom for a full hour as my story spilled out of me. I actually missed my next class, but I didn't care. Talking with Professor Jordan seemed far more important than listening to a world history lecture.

I told him about my Amish upbringing, my early marriage, my difficulties in entering the English world, my husband's untimely death, and my struggles as a single mother.

Professor Jordan listened with rapt attention, in a way that no one had ever listened to me before. I felt undeserving of his compassion.

In addition to teaching my sociology class, Professor Jordan taught cultural anthropology, the field in which he'd earned his doctorate degree. My transition from the Amish culture into the English world seemed to interest him. As I thanked him for his kindness at the end of our talk, I could tell an idea was brewing in his mind.

"I know you are a busy woman, Miss Graber," he said, "but do you think you could find the time to meet with me again? I'm preparing to write an article for a professional journal. Your experience in adapting to a new culture would provide me with valuable information."

I readily agreed to his request. At the time of our first talk, the semester was nearing an end. So, we continued meeting for several months after I'd dropped out of college.

That is how my friendship with Elliott developed. By the time his article was finished and ready to publish, I felt as if he knew me better than anyone else had ever known me.

Truthfully, I could've talked with Professor Jordan forever. He was so intelligent, so well-educated. I'd never before been close to someone like that. He asked me questions that no one else had ever asked me, questions that seemed to get to the heart of who I was.

In addition to discussing what I'd been through, he talked with me about the struggles of other minority groups in this country. I came to understand what it was like for him as a *black man living in white America.*

I know you've had your own challenges, Mercedes. You know what it feels like to be an outsider, both here in the United States and in Mexico.

However, I felt a connection with Elliott that went far beyond our shared difficulties with mainstream culture. At the time, I had no frame of reference for such an experience. Now, I would describe it as a soul connection.

My feelings for Elliott confused me. Frankly, they terrified me. Coming from my repressive Amish background, feeling such a deep tenderness toward a man seemed wrong. Entertaining that beautiful feeling seemed self-indulgent and dangerous.

Believe me, Mercedes, I had to work very hard to push that feeling down. The thought of never seeing Elliott again filled me with great sorrow.

On the day of our last meeting, I could tell Elliott was also having difficulty with the idea of us parting ways. "I guess this is it," he said sadly.

He reached out to take my hand. That was one of the sweetest experiences of my lifetime.

"Let's stay in touch," he said.

I nodded, the tears streaming down my face.

Back in the 1970s, people didn't have access to one another through email or texting or social media. What Elliott and I exchanged with each other was our mailing addresses. Our way of staying in contact would be through letter writing.

For many years, we exchanged one or two letters annually. That is how I learned about his leaving Goshen College and taking a position at a school in southwestern Michigan. That is how I learned of his marriage to Deborah, a faculty member at the same college. And that is how I learned of the birth of their son.

Although our letters were infrequent, the nature of my communication with Elliott was on a different plane than what I shared with anyone else. It was as though he spoke to a part of me that I didn't even know existed. Over the years, he helped me understand myself on a deeper and deeper level. What a gift he gave me!

The years of Corina and Wesley's childhood rolled by quickly. As they had promised, Virgil and Irene played the role of grandparents to my children.

It was wonderful having them next door to us. As Virgil and Irene never had children of their own, they took delight in helping me raise my mine.

They provided childcare while I worked, for several hours every day after school and during the summer months. Irene decorated beautiful cakes for Corina and Wesley on their birthdays. She and Virgil spoiled them with presents at Christmastime. Virgil set up Easter egg hunts for them. Every year at Halloween, Irene sewed them the costumes of their choosing, and Virgil took them trick-or-treating.

I owe Irene and Virgil more gratitude than I could ever express. They helped my children enjoy typical childhood pleasures. Given my awkwardness with the mainstream culture, I never could've managed all that on my own.

Both Corina and Wesley look back on those years with great fondness. Whenever we reminisce about good times from the past, my children always bring up memories of Grandma Irene and Grandpa Virgil.

In school, Corina did very well, getting good grades with little effort. I never had to prompt her to complete her schoolwork. She took care of that on her own and needed no help from me. She demanded to be her own person, motivating herself to reach her goals, never feeling bound by anyone's expectation of her.

She ended up being popular with her peers, although she didn't seem to care what they thought of her. Often, she'd reject a fashion trend, wearing what she pleased. Then, other girls would start following her example. Without intending to, she ended up being a leader and a trendsetter.

Wesley was an indifferent student who preferred to focus his attention on what truly interested him. He had a heart for nature and animals, and he loved being outdoors. He maintained friendships with a few other quiet little boys, but was never popular in school like his sister was.

When my son was around six or seven, I discovered that he had inherited my artistic abilities. I wanted to encourage his talent, rather than squelch it like my parents had done with mine.

Thankfully, our shared love of creativity provided a way for me to build a connection with my son. I'd sit beside him while he drew pictures of rivers and mountains and animals in the jungle. I would pick up a pencil and draw something of my own. If I would attempt to engage him in conversation, he wouldn't respond. So, we'd sit side by side, drawing in silence.

Despite all my efforts, I've never felt that I've done right by Wesley. That breaks my heart. I'm so thankful he had the grandfatherly figure of Virgil living next door. Next to his beloved dog Bob, Virgil was my son's best friend.

In the fall of 1975, when Wesley was eight, Virgil got him involved in a local 4-H club. And, with Virgil's supervision, Wesley began raising a newborn goat.

As you might imagine, that goat was everything to my son. He spent hours and hours with him. When I couldn't find Wesley at dinnertime, I'd know where to look. He'd always be in Virgil's barn, hanging out with the goat. It would take considerable coaxing to get him to come inside, wash up, and sit down to dinner with Corina and me.

In July of 1976, Virgil helped Wesley enter his goat in the Elkhart County 4-H fair. The two of them spent all day at the fairgrounds from Monday to Friday. Wesley was so proud when his goat won a blue ribbon.

However, things fell apart for Wesley when someone offered to buy his goat. That upset him terribly. Virgil explained to him that raising farm animals was a business, that he could take the money from the sale and use it to raise more goats. Still, my son couldn't face the loss, and he cried inconsolably.

To cheer Wesley up, Virgil took him and Corina to the fair on Saturday, allowing them to spend the whole day enjoying carnival rides and stuffing themselves with corndogs, elephant ears, and cotton candy.

At the last minute, Irene and I decided to go with them. While Virgil escorted the children around the fairgrounds, Irene and I browsed through the various exhibits: sewing, knitting, quilting, and baked goods.

The day was hot, and as Irene was a heavy-set woman, she quickly became exhausted. So, we stopped to rest under a tent where people were watching a troupe of square dancers perform.

We were only looking for a place to sit down and catch our breath. However, I quickly became entranced by the delightful activity in front of me: the ever-changing patterns formed by the dancers, the lively swinging and twirling, the women's colorful, full-skirted costumes.

My thoughts rushed back to the night at the barn party when Ivan taught me how to do the twist. I smiled to myself, remembering how fun it had been to feel so carefree. In the years since Ivan's death, all my time had been consumed with working and taking care of my children. I'd rarely done anything fun. I'd never even taken the time to read a book for my own pleasure.

"Virgil and I used to square dance," Irene commented. "That was before we got too old and too fat."

"I've never square danced," I told her. "But I wish I could. It looks like so much fun."

"Then why don't you?" Irene said. "You're still a young woman. It's time for you to get out and do something for yourself. Virgil and I can look after the kids while you're dancing."

Believe it or not, Mercedes, that is exactly what happened. That moment of sitting there with Irene under the square dancers' tent proved to be a pivotal one. It set my life on a whole new trajectory.

But that is a chapter of my story best saved for next week.

CHAPTER 6: MICHAEL MITCHELL AND DODI-GIRL

"He's playing that damn music again," Mercedes muttered as she climbed the steps to Javier's third floor apartment. Javi trailed behind her, carrying a backpack stuffed with clothing and toys he'd brought for spending the weekend with his father.

On the drive over, Mercedes had had such a nice time with her son. They'd talked about the books Javi had checked out of the library for his summer reading program, a few of which he'd brought along to read at his dad's place. He was just about to turn nine, and would be entering fourth grade in the fall.

"What are you looking forward to doing in fourth grade?" Mercedes had asked him.

"Spelling," Javi had said emphatically.

"Of course," Mercedes had chuckled. For the past year, Javi had been obsessed with spelling bees, and was determined to someday participate in the national spelling bee.

"Tell me all the big words you know, Mom," he'd said, "and let me see if I can spell them."

As she couldn't readily think of any such words, she'd looked at highway signs for cues. "Close your eyes," she'd told him, so he couldn't see the words she was looking at. And he'd correctly spelled "construction," "interstate," "northbound," and "Michigan."

"How did you get so smart?" she'd asked him.

"That's just the way I am," he'd said proudly. "I know a lot of things. Ask me about the state capitols."

Mercedes had listed off every state she could think of, and Javi had rattled off the capitol city with hardly a moment's thought. She'd disagreed with him at times, insisting that the capitol of Illinois was Chicago and the capitol of New York was New York City.

Javi had held his ground. "No, Mom. The most famous city in the state isn't always the capitol. The capitol of Illinois is Springfield and the capital of New York is Albany."

So, she'd readily given in when he insisted that the capitol of Missouri was Jefferson City, not Saint Louis. "I've never heard of Jefferson City, Missouri," she'd said.

"Well, Mom," he'd shot back, "it's a real place."

The way he said that had struck her funny, and they'd both laughed. Afterwards, she'd indulged in satisfying thoughts about what a bright child she had. She'd even gone so far as to give herself credit for his intelligence.

Now, as she approached Javier's apartment, she deeply resented having her mellow mood broken by her husband's annoying preference in music.

The music wasn't loud. The strains of Mexican opera emanating from the apartment were barely audible in the stairwell. Javier was too well-mannered to impose on his neighbors by playing his music at top volume. What bothered Mercedes was knowing that listening to the classical music of his native country was Javier's way of staying connected with his aristocratic Mexican heritage. She hated that.

She knew her husband harbored a deep reverence for the old traditions from his country of origin, and it made her feel distant from him. Javier inhabited a world about which she knew little, and to which she could never belong. She sometimes wished she could destroy that world so that he would be forced to live in hers.

Scowling, she knocked on the apartment door. *Just keep your damn mouth shut, Mercedes,* she cautioned herself. *You don't need to pick a fight with him.*

Javier opened the door smiling broadly, clearly in a cheerful mood. "Beautiful Mercedes," he said, his Spanish accent more pronounced than usual. "It's so nice to see you."

As Mercedes entered the apartment, Javi brushed past her to hug his father. Then he ran to his bedroom to drop off his backpack.

Javier stepped over to his stereo system and turned up the volume. Then he reached for Mercedes' hand. "Dance with me, mi amor," he said, drawing her into his arms.

121

Mercedes closed her eyes, swaying to the music, allowing herself to follow Javier's lead. He pulled her closer, and she felt herself softening, melting, floating on a dream.

Damn it, she thought, *why does he have this effect on me? I wish we could stop fighting and make this work.*

Just as quickly as those thoughts entered her mind, her actions belied her heart's desire. She stiffened and pulled back. "This music is getting on my nerves," she said. "You play it every time I come over."

Javier dropped his arms and stepped away from her, his handsome face clouded with pain. "Why do you always have to ruin things, Mercedes? Every time we start getting along, you push me away. Why can't we just enjoy being with each other?"

Mercedes hung her head, hating herself. "I don't know. I don't know why I do that. I'm sorry, Javier."

She held out her arms, ready to dance again. But Javier shook his head and turned away. "I'm not in the mood anymore."

Walking over to the doorway of Javi's bedroom, he called out to his son, "Guess what! The books I ordered for you came this morning."

"What books?" Mercedes asked, but Javier paid her no attention.

Javi came bounding out of his room. "Really, Dad? Let me see."

Javier pointed to a package on his kitchen table. Javi grabbed it, then sat down on the sofa tear it open.

Javier sat down next to him. "This one is about the Mayan civilization," he said, pointing to one of the books in Javi's hands. "And the other one is about the Aztecs. Son, this is the history of our people. Can you believe it? Which one should we look at first?"

"Which one came first?" Javi asked.

"The Mayans," Javier replied. "Their civilization dates back to four thousand years ago. The Aztec empire only goes back to about seven hundred years ago."

The two of them began pouring over the books. Javi asked intelligent questions, and Javier always had a ready answer. Mercedes knew he was drawing from the history courses he'd taken during his college years in Mexico.

"I'm going to read both of these books all the way through this weekend," Javi chortled. "Do you think they'll count for my summer reading program?"

"I'm sure they will," Javier replied. He pulled his son close and kissed the top of his head.

Mercedes stood by the doorway watching them, feeling left out and alone. "I'm going now," she said, wanting some kind of acknowledgement from her husband.

Javier glanced up at her. The hurt she'd seen in his eyes minutes earlier was now masked by cold indifference. "Are you going to see Dora?" he asked.

Mercedes nodded.

"Bye, Mom," Javi said, not taking his eyes off his new books.

Without another word, Mercedes turned and left the apartment, closing the door softly behind her. Slowly, she made her way down the stairs and out to her car, wondering how her mood had so quickly changed from joy to desolation.

As she drove to Saint Joseph, she did an uncharacteristic search of the feelings and motivations lying in the depths of her heart. "I'm afraid," she said to herself. "When it comes down to it, I'm scared to death of being close to Javier."

After knocking on Dora's apartment door, Mercedes waited a full two minutes for a response. *Something must be wrong,* she thought. *Maybe I should go downstairs and ask about Dora at the front desk.* But just as she was turning to leave, she heard the whisper of shuffling footsteps.

When Dora finally opened the door, her appearance shocked Mercedes. The elderly woman looked thinner than Mercedes had remembered, the outline of her bony shoulders visible under the pink satin bathrobe she was wearing. Her long hair was disheveled and hanging down her back.

"Oh, my dear, forgive me, forgive me!" she exclaimed in a breathless voice.

"Were you not expecting me?" Mercedes asked. "Did I come at the wrong time?"

"Oh no," Dora replied. "I knew you were coming. It's just that.... Well, it's been a difficult morning."

Through the slightly open bedroom door, Mercedes caught a glimpse of an unmade bed. She knew Dora had been lying down.

"Should I come another time?" she asked. "Maybe you need to rest."

"No," Dora said. "Please stay. I don't want to miss a moment of the precious time I have with you. Just give me a minute to brush out my hair." She disappeared into the bedroom, closing the door behind her.

Mercedes seated herself on the sofa, then glanced around the apartment. She noticed the dirty dishes piled on the kitchen countertop, which struck her as out of character for neat and tidy Dora. The bookshelves were dusty, and the carpet looked as if it hadn't been swept in a while.

A crumpled paper bag sat on the coffee table, its top tightly rolled to protect whatever contents it held. Mercedes wondered whether the bag had something to do with the story to come.

Five minutes later, Dora emerged from her bedroom, her long hair coiled into a bun. Steadying herself with one hand on the arm of her recliner, she made a sweeping gesture with her other hand. "I'm afraid this place is a mess. I just haven't had it in me to keep up with it. Corina has arranged to have a cleaning service come in to help. Someone will be here on Monday." Then, with a heavy sigh, she eased herself into her chair.

Mercedes wondered what to do in the face of Dora's undeniably increased frailty. "I probably shouldn't stay too long today," she said. "I'm afraid you're not up for talking."

"Oh, please don't rush off," Dora protested. "With a glass of water and my lozenges, I'll do just fine."

She pulled a packet of lozenges from the pocket of her robe and laid it on the table beside her. Mercedes went to the kitchen to get her a glass of water.

"Thank you, sweetie," Dora said as Mercedes handed

her the glass. "I haven't even asked how you are today. You look a little distracted. I hope you're not upset with the way things are here."

"No," Mercedes said as she settled back onto the sofa. "I just came from Javier's place. We got into it a little bit. Nothing big, but it bummed me out."

"Was he unkind to you?" Dora asked.

"No," Mercedes admitted. "He didn't do anything. It was actually me having an attitude with him."

Dora's questioning expression invited Mercedes to say more. "It's all so stupid, really. When Javi and I got to Javier's apartment, he was playing Mexican opera music on his stereo."

"Oh, that sounds beautiful!" Dora exclaimed.

"It is," Mercedes said. "But I hate it. And I had to go and make an issue of it."

"What makes you hate that music?" Dora asked.

"Opera was part of Javier's life growing up in his wealthy Mexican family," Mercedes explained. "He thinks everything about that life is so perfect, better than anything we have here in this country. It's as if he's still living in that world."

She went on to tell Dora about the books Javier had bought for Javi. "He's trying to instill cultural pride in our son," she said. She immediately felt embarrassed when she heard the sarcasm in her voice.

"Tell me why that bothers you," Dora said.

"It makes me feel like an outsider," Mercedes blurted out. "It's like Javier and Javi have their own little club, and I'm not part of it. Javi and I do fine on our own. But the minute Javier is in the picture, it's as if he puts a claim on our son. As if he's trying to make him into something that I'll never be. I end up feeling like I'm not good enough for either one of them."

She shook her head in frustration. "Like today, when they were looking at the books together, talking about their great heritage. And I stood there feeling like an idiot."

Dora looked puzzled. "Why not join in with them? Aren't the Mayans and the Aztecs part of your heritage, too? Why not let Javier share his wealth of information with you as well? It's certainly worth knowing about. Those cultures made a great contribution to civilization in the western hemisphere. You deserve to feel proud of that heritage."

Mercedes stared at Dora, a dawning awareness creeping over her. "I never thought about it that way. I guess I thought that history didn't apply to me because I was raised in a white family here in the United States."

Dora reached over to pat Mercedes' knee. "That wonderful genetic endowment is in your blood, my dear."

Mercedes nodded slowly, taking in Dora's words. "How do you know about these things?" she asked.

"Well...." Dora smiled sheepishly. "I can't claim to be a well-read person. But I do enjoy learning about the world as much as I possibly can."

She pointed to her bookshelves. "Take a look at that coloring book, the one under the box of colored pencils."

Mercedes retrieved the book from the shelf, then sat down to leaf through the pages. In it, she found maps of countries, continents, and the entire planet. Some of the pages had been colored, while others still awaited the touch of Dora's pencils.

"Corina gave this to me," Dora explained. "She ordered it off the internet. I know it's meant for school children, but I enjoy it so much. I color in it almost every day. Just a little at a time, until my eyes give out. When I color a map of a country, I try to commit a few facts about it to my memory."

Mercedes looked through the pages to find a map of Mexico. "Here's where I went to visit my father." She held up the book to show Dora, pointing to a rural area near the city of Veracruz.

Dora peered intently at the map. "Isn't that something?" She took off her glasses to rub her eyes, as if to clear her vision. "How about the ancestors from your mother's side? Do you know where they came from?"

"I don't have details," Mercedes replied. "I think my Grandma Thelma said something about her family coming from England or Ireland."

She turned the pages to find a map of the British Isles. "Now, you've got me interested. Someday, I'll have to do research on my family tree, both sides of it." She paused, then looked up at Dora. "Where do your people come from?"

Dora replied without hesitation. "Corina looked into that for me. She did some genealogical research and printed off articles she found on the internet. Basically, my Amish ancestors came from Germany and Switzerland. They had a hard time of it in Europe. They had to keep moving from place to place, as some countries didn't appreciate the presence of their religious group. When William Penn set up his colony in the late 1600s, my ancestors came over to Pennsylvania to find religious freedom. As you probably know, there is still a large settlement of Amish people living in Pennsylvania."

"That's fascinating," Mercedes murmured.

Dora reached out to clasp Mercedes hand. "Isn't it amazing, sweetie, how our lives have streamed from different corners of this earth, bringing us together to enjoy this precious moment. I am so humbled by the beautiful diversity on this planet, with all the different races and ethnic groups contributing something wonderful to the whole."

Then she sat back, a weary look crossing her face. "Every time I turn on the news, I hear about so much suffering in the world. So much pain and injustice. I tell myself we should be past all this, that we should be working together for the good of all. But we're not at that point yet."

She folded her hands together as if in prayer. "I wish I could see everything set right before I leave this planet. Sadly, I don't think that's going to happen. I just have to trust the divine intelligence to work things out in its own timing."

Mercedes could hardly fathom what her grandmother was saying. Her thoughts had never run along such lines.

"All I can do," Dora continued, "is to live in peace with those around me. I'd like to think that's my own little way of helping the planet move toward healing."

"You've got a point," Mercedes said. "I don't think I'm doing a very good job of that. Especially when I keep on fighting with my husband."

"Why do you suppose," Dora asked, "that you and Javier can't seem to give up the struggle?"

"I was actually thinking about that on the way over here," Mercedes replied. "The way I see it, it all boils down to me being afraid to love him. I know Javier loves me. He tells me that all the time. But I'm afraid that if I let him know how I feel about him, I'll end up getting hurt. So, I just keep fighting to keep him at a distance."

Dora looked a little startled by Mercedes' revelation. "You are wise, my dear. You are so wise to figure that out. Many people spend their entire lifetime embroiled in conflict, and they never come to understand that it all boils down to fear."

With a trembling hand, she lifted her glass for a sip of water, then struggled to release a lozenge from its wrapper. "I know what it's like to be afraid of loving someone. There was once a man in my life who loved me dearly, but I was unable to reciprocate his feelings. I guess that's a good place to pick up my story."

Mercedes, I debated whether I should include this particular chapter in my life review. Compared to the nearly eighteen years I spent living with my parents and the seven-and-a-half years I was married to Ivan, my time with Michael Mitchell was short, barely a year in duration. It is only now that I recognize the significance of the months we spent together. Michael supported me through a transition in my life, helping me venture out of my limited little world to discover new aspects of myself. He deserves more recognition in my life story than I've ever given him.

When I ended my story last week, my neighbor Irene and I were sitting under a tent at the county fair, watching a troupe of square dancers perform. Irene was encouraging me to follow through on my interest in learning how to dance.

The idea made me smile. I told myself that someday, I would take square dance lessons. But in my mind, I pushed that event off into the distant future.

Irene knew full well that I would never pursue my desire without a nudge from her. After the performance was over, she said, "Let's go talk to one of the dancers to see how we can get you signed up."

I froze in my tracks. "Not now!" I whispered.

She took my arm to propel me forward. "There's no time like the present."

She guided me up to the stage where she addressed one of the female dancers. "This young lady wants to learn how to dance. Can you tell her how she might get involved?"

The woman's face brightened. "Oh, of course. Our caller holds classes for newcomers every September. That would be a perfect time for you to join us."

The thought of starting lessons so soon flooded me with anxiety. "I don't have a partner," I protested, hoping that would disqualify me.

"That's okay," the woman assured me. "Single ladies come to the class all the time. You'll find somebody to dance with. Let me give you a flyer."

She reached for one on a nearby table. Irene took it from her hand. Waving it in front of my face, she said, "I'll call. That way, I'll make sure you get signed up."

Six weeks later, on a Saturday evening in early September, I reluctantly drove to the park pavilion in Elkhart where the square dance lessons were to be held. I don't think I ever felt so out of place as I did when I entered that building. Even though I was wearing blue jeans like most of the other woman in the class, I still felt conspicuous. In my mind, I was back to being the Amish girl in a long dress and bonnet, standing out as an oddity in a crowd of English people.

Thankfully, the caller, a kindly man named Wayne, did his best to welcome everyone and make them feel at ease. My fears began melting away as I got caught up in the enjoyment of learning beginner-level dance steps. Wayne patiently went over and over the simple patterns, making sure that every student was able to master them.

I soon realized I was picking up the steps faster than most of the other students, which gave me a boost of confidence. I'd had no idea that I'd be good at square dancing. In fact, I had expected to struggle. It didn't seem likely that someone from an Amish background would excel at an activity that involved moving to the beat of lively music.

The woman at the fair had predicted there would be plenty of single men available to pair up with ladies who'd come to the class alone. That was indeed the case. In my estimation, those fellows were a sorry-looking lot, socially awkward, shabbily dressed men all fifteen to twenty years older than me. During breaks in the lesson, they sat in a cluster on one side of the room, talking with no one but each other. In any other circumstance, I would've steered clear of such men. However, I did appreciate and accept their offers to dance with me.

About halfway through the evening, when I was partnered with one of those fellows, he attempted to lead me through a step I had not yet learned, a twirl under his raised arm. His rough jerking motion threw me off balance, and I fell to the floor.

The other students gasped, and Wayne immediately halted the lesson. Lying there on the floor, I felt mortified. I told myself this was the inevitable result of me coming to a place where I didn't belong. I vowed to leave the class and never return.

As I struggled to sit up, I felt a touch on my shoulder. Then, I saw a hand reaching out to help me. As I took the hand and allowed it to pull me to my feet, I saw that it belonged to one of the single men I had not yet danced with.

Up to that point in the evening, the faces of all those men had blurred together in my mind, and I could hardly tell one from the other. But when I looked into the eyes of my helper, I noticed that they were an unforgettable shade of blue, twinkling with kind humor.

The owner of those spectacular blue eyes was a small man with a wiry build and rumpled sandy hair. His face was deeply tanned and weathered, and he appeared to be around fifty. Yet, he had a boyish look about him. I couldn't help but smile at him.

"That was quite a spill you took," he said. Then he spoke to the man whose rough actions had caused me to lose my balance. "Goddammit, Fred, when are you going to learn to treat a lady like a lady?"

Wayne announced that it was time for a break. Before he dismissed the class, he gave a two-minute lecture about respecting newcomers and not pushing them through steps he hadn't yet taught. "The last thing we want is someone getting hurt," he cautioned.

Then, he invited the class to partake of the cookies and soft drinks on the refreshment table. I limped over to a chair on the sidelines where I sat down to catch my breath. Moments later, the blue-eyed man was there in front of me holding out a paper cup filled with cola. "I thought you might like something to drink," he said.

I accepted his offering with appreciation.

He sat down next to me. "Feeling any better?"

Something about his presence made me feel lighthearted. I smiled at him. "I'm fine. Just a little shaken up."

"I'm Michael Mitchell," he said. He repeated his name rapidly in a silly voice, emphasizing the alliteration. "Michael Mitchell, Michael Mitchell. Try saying that ten times in a row." Then he laughed. "Make it simple. Just call me Mike."

I hadn't yet learned the names of more than three or four people in the class. But I knew there was one name I would never forget: Michael Mitchell, the man with the magnificent blue eyes.

"I'm Dora," I said.

"Pleased to meet you, Dora," he said with a theatric gesture of his hand. "You're new here, and you're already a good dancer. At least when some jerk isn't throwing you around like a sack of feed. Me, I've been taking square dance lessons for three years, and I still can't get the hang of it." He mocked himself by crossing his eyes and making a goofy face. "Guess I'm just a slow learner."

Then Wayne called for the students to find a partner and form squares on the dance floor again. Michael held out his hand. "How about dancing with me this round, Dora? I'll keep all the morons away from you."

Taking his hand, I couldn't help but giggle.

"Poor kid," he said to the other dancers in our square. "She's stuck with me for the rest of the night."

Michael Mitchell spoke the truth when he said he wasn't a good dancer. As a first-timer, I quickly surpassed him in learning steps and patterns that stumped him again and again. However, he entertained his fellow dancers by cracking jokes and mocking his own shortcomings. By the end of the evening, I was having so much fun that I'd almost forgotten about my humiliating fall.

I could hardly wait for the next Saturday to roll around, as I expected to have an even better time at my second lesson.

Sadly, when I arrived for the class, my hopes were quickly dashed. We students we were told that Wayne was out sick, and that a substitute teacher would be taking his place. The substitute was an inexperienced caller who fumbled through the lesson and succeeded in doing little more than confusing the dancers.

On top of that, there were far more women than men who'd come without a partner that evening. I ended up sitting on the sidelines much of the time, growing increasingly despondent.

After his kindly attention to me the first night, I half-expected Michael Mitchell to come to my rescue again. But he was busy dividing his attention among all the single women, making sure each of them had at least a little time on the dance floor. I noticed he was choosing partners least likely to be chosen by anyone else: the timid, the overweight, the elderly. They all accepted his offer with gratitude, gazing at him with adoring eyes.

My old feelings of not belonging settled in again, pulling me downward into a pit of despair. Tears began trickling down my cheeks. At breaktime, I decided it would be best if I went home, as I didn't want to make a weeping spectacle of myself.

I slipped out the back entrance of the pavilion, hoping to escape notice. However, I encountered a group of men standing there by the door, smoking cigarettes. Among them was Michael Mitchell.

"Leaving already, Dora?" he asked.

"Yes," I said, attempting to brush past him.

"You haven't danced with me tonight."

"You haven't asked me." I was surprised by the hint of bitterness in my voice, and I hoped Mike hadn't noticed it.

"Well, I'm asking you now." Mike took one last drag on his cigarette, then tossed the butt on the ground. He held out his hand. *"Dance with me one time before you leave, Dora."*

"I really need to go," I protested.

He contorted his boyish face into an exaggerated pout. *"Please? Pretty please?"*

I couldn't help but laugh through my tears. *"Okay,"* I relented. I allowed him to take my hand and lead me back into the building.

When we entered the light of the room, Mike fixed his kind blue eyes on my tear-stained face. *"You're having a rough time of it tonight, aren't you, kiddo?"*

I nodded, desperately willing my tears not to start again.

"I thought so," he said. *"It's hard to see such a pretty girl looking so sad. I wanted to get around to you earlier, but...."* He gestured around the room. *"I had to do my duty."*

The squares of dancers were forming again, and Mike attempted to lead me out onto the floor. But unbidden tears started coursing down my cheeks again. *"I'm sorry,"* I said. *"I can't do this."*

Mike shrugged. *"Well, we're not going to get anywhere with the lesson tonight without Wayne being here. And you know what, kiddo? It seems to me that you need to talk more than you need to dance."*

He led me off the dance floor and out the back door again, where we sat in the darkness at a picnic table.

"I might be a lousy dancer," he said, *"but I'd like to think I'm a decent human being. I've got some good shoulders to cry on. So, tell me what's going on with you."*

"I don't belong here." Hearing myself say that, I realized those words had turned into a tired old refrain in my mind. *"I don't belong"* had become the story of my life.

"Dora, that's hogwash!" Mike huffed. *"You belong here just as much as anyone else does. Maybe more than some of the others. You came here wanting to learn. You're giving*

it your best. A lot of fools who come to this class don't give two hoots about learning, and they don't even try. All they want to do is stand around and bullshit. That really frustrates Wayne. He'd just as soon they go home and stop cluttering up the place. So, get that idea out of your head. You belong here. Okay? Now, tell me what's really going on."

Much the same as I'd done with Elliott years earlier, I opened up to Mike about my personal life. I did not, however, mention my Amish upbringing. I only told him that my husband had been killed, and that I was struggling under the load of being a single parent.

"Wow!" Mike exclaimed, shaking his head in disbelief. "I never would've guessed that. Someone as nice as you are doesn't deserve getting such a bum hand in life. You've had to be incredibly strong to get through all that."

"I don't feel like a strong person," I said. "I don't have any confidence in being around other people. I haven't gotten out much since my husband died."

"I understand," Mike said. "I went through a divorce fifteen years ago. My wife left me for another man. It took me the better part of ten years to get over it. I didn't do much besides go to work and hole up in my house. I finally told myself I had to get out and get on with my life."

He gestured toward the pavilion, where the sounds of the dance music and the shuffle of feet emanated from the building. "That's why I come here, just to keep myself from turning into a hermit. You'll get through this, Dora. Just hang in there and give it some time. You'll be okay."

I sat beside him in silence, soaking up his reassuring presence. Strangely, I felt the urge to snuggle up to him and lay my head on his shoulder, like a child seeking comfort from a loving parent. Of course, I didn't.

Then Mike stood up and held out his hand. "Ready to dance again?"

"I am," I said, confident that my flow of tears had been turned off for the night.

Mike stuck with me as my dance partner for the rest of the evening. As we were parting ways to go home, he squeezed my hand. "You're a good kid," he said.

"I'm not always sure of that," I told him. "I never measure up to who I think I should be."

"You are a good person," he insisted. "I have an instinct about these things. I wouldn't trust most of the people here any farther than I could spit. Some of them would just as soon stab you in the back as to look at you. But you're not like that. You're cut from a different cloth."

His words jolted me. "Little does he know what kind of cloth I'm cut from," I thought. I chuckled at the reaction I imagined he would have if he ever found out I was raised Amish.

"What?" he asked.

"You said I was cut from a different cloth. That's probably because of how I grew up."

He raised an eyebrow. "Now you've got me hooked. You have to tell me about that sometime."

Then he caught me off guard by taking my face in his hands. They felt rough and workworn, but gentle and comforting. His magnificent blue eyes gazed intently into mine. "Dora, I want you to know that if you need a friend, I'm here."

Mercedes, you look put off by Mike's behavior. I can imagine what you're thinking. Nowadays, a man is called out for touching a woman in such a way. Behavior like that is seen as intrusive and patronizing. Back in the seventies, the awareness of such matters wasn't as it is now.

But yes, Mike often treated me as if I were a child. Looking back, I can see that was somewhat detrimental to me, as it undermined my own strength.

When I answered my ringing telephone the following evening, I was shocked to hear Michael Mitchell's voice on the other end of the line. "I hope you don't mind that I called," he said.

"How did you get my number?" I blurted out. Then I caught myself, knowing I must've come across as rude.

After a moment of awkward silence, Mike spoke again, sounding chastened. "From the sign-in sheet at the dance class."

Mercedes, you're wondering whether Mike was stalking me. I can see how you'd think that. But back then, we weren't as protective of our privacy as we are now. I can assure you that Michael Mitchell never had any sinister intentions toward me.

"You've been on my mind," he explained. "I had a feeling that I should check up on you. I knew you were shy, and that you probably wouldn't reach out to me. I hope I'm not interrupting anything important."

"I'm fine," I told him. "I'm just winding down for the evening, getting ready for work tomorrow."

Feeling more at ease with his call, I sat down at the kitchen table with the phone in hand. We settled into a lighthearted conversation, each of us divulging a little more about our life.

I learned that Mike had three grown children and two grandchildren. He informed me that he worked as a meter reader for a local utility company.

"I'm not getting rich off my job," he told me. "But I'm a simple guy. My work keeps a roof over my head, gas in my car, and food in my belly. I can't ask for more than that. All in all, I'm a lucky man."

He told me he'd dated a few women after his divorce, but that he'd never been serious about any of them. "I guess I just haven't been ready to risk getting my heart broken again," he said.

Our conversation eventually led us to the point where I revealed to him that I had grown up Amish.

"Well, knock me over with a feather!" he exclaimed. "I never would've taken you for Amish, not in a million years. I've crossed paths with a few Amish fellows in my time. I have a lot of respect for the Amish. They're good, honest people." He paused, then added, "But I can see how you would want to break out of that and experience more of life."

I admitted to Mike that I'd almost gone back to the Amish community after my husband's death, but that I'd decided to stay in the English world for the sake of my children.

"I'm glad you did," he said. "Otherwise, I never would've met you. And we wouldn't be having this nice little chat."

Mike and I must've talked for an hour. When I told him that I needed to check on the children, he said, "Oh, I'm sorry. I shouldn't have kept you so long. It was nice talking with you, kiddo. I'll see you next Saturday, I hope."

"Of course," I said.

That night, I was too stirred up to fall asleep until the early hours of the morning. I wondered whether Michael Mitchell would be calling again, whether he was going to make a habit of checking up on me. It worried me a little. I didn't want him to think I had an interest in anything beyond a friendship with him, although I had to admit that I truly enjoyed spending time with that goodhearted fellow.

After our rather intimate telephone conversation, I wondered how Mike would behave toward me at the next square dance class. Would he assume that the two of us would be partners for the evening? I fretted a great deal over the matter.

I needn't have worried. When I walked into the pavilion on Saturday night, Mike came over and enveloped me in a warm embrace. "How are you doing, kiddo?" he asked.

He was my partner for the first dance of the evening. When it ended, he said, "I'm not going to monopolize you, even though I'd like to. You should have a chance to dance with people who know what they're doing." With that, he walked away.

I was almost sorry to see him go. I watched him offer his hand to an elderly woman who'd been sitting alone on the sidelines, and I thought again about what a nice guy he was.

At breaktime, I found Mike at my side again. "You're looking good out there, kiddo," he said. He flashed me a cheesy smile, giving me a thumbs-up gesture. "Are you thirsty? Want something to drink?"

I nodded. He was off in a flash, returning half a minute later to offer me a cup of punch. Then he sat beside me until Wayne called the class back into session. "Dance with me?" he asked.

I accepted his outstretched hand. "Sure."

As he had before, Mike entertained me and the rest of

the dancers in our square with his silly banter. Afterwards, he moved on to another partner, and I walked back to the chairs on the sideline.

A heavyset middle-aged woman scooted over to sit next to me. "Are you going out with Michael Mitchell?" she asked.

I stared at her, startled. "Oh, no! We're just friends."

She smirked, as if she didn't believe me. "Well, maybe you should. There are a lot of women here who wouldn't mind dating him. He's a nice guy. You could do a lot worse."

The class ran overtime that evening. Mindful of how late it was getting, I left immediately after it was over. As I headed toward my car, I heard the sound of footsteps behind me. I turned around and saw Michael Mitchell running to catch up with me.

"Why are you being antisocial, Dora?" he asked. "You should stick around and chat a little bit. Get to know people."

"I have to get home to my children," I said. "My neighbors are watching them, and I don't want to keep them waiting."

Mike stood there with his hands in his pockets, awkwardly shifting his weight from one foot to another. "So, your neighbors are your babysitters?"

"They're more like grandparents," I explained. "Their house is like a second home to my children."

"Do you...do you suppose they'd keep the kids another night?"

"They're always happy to have my children," I said.

He looked at the ground, chuckling nervously. "Would you like to get together sometime? You told me you don't get out much. I thought maybe you and I could do something fun."

My heart leaped into my throat. I couldn't quite tell whether Michael Mitchell was asking me on a date, or whether he was just offering to help me expand my experiences in the community. I hoped it was the latter. I hadn't been on a date since my rumpschpringe years, when I'd run around with Ivan and his friends. The thought of dating as a grown woman terrified me.

Sure, I'd joked with women at work about the guys we thought were good-looking. Many times, my coworkers had *offered to introduce me to men or to set me up on blind dates. But I'd always declined, coming up with one excuse after another.*

Truthfully, I had no confidence in relating to the opposite sex. I'd always thought of myself as a shy, plain little woman that no man would ever be interested in.

So, my first inclination was to decline Mike's offer. However, since he and I seemed to be striking up such a warm friendship, I didn't want to spoil what we had going. I also didn't want to make things awkward between us at upcoming classes. For a few seconds, my mind raced through the pros and cons of saying yes or no.

Suddenly, I remembered Mike telling me that he'd never been serious about the women he'd dated after his divorce. With relief, I concluded that if we did spend time together, it would certainly be a casual thing.

So, I smiled at him and said, "Sure!"

"We could go out to dinner," he said. "We'll figure out what to do afterwards."

As I drove home, I tried to push away the lurking fear that Mike wanted me to be his girlfriend. "Surely," I told myself, "a man of his age would not expect such a thing from a thirty-year-old woman."

On Monday after work, when I went to Irene's home to pick up the children, I informed her of my plans with Mike for the following Friday evening. "It's not a date," I assured her.

She threw back her head and laughed heartily. "It most certainly is a date," she said. "Dora, it's about time you went out with a man."

Before I left to meet Mike on Friday evening, I told my children I was going to have dinner with a friend. They happily went to spend the night at Irene and Virgil's house, where they knew they'd be spoiled with games, movies, and treats.

Mike had suggested that we meet at an Italian restaurant in Elkhart. When I arrived at that location, I discovered that the place was a shabby little establishment. While I was secretly disappointed with my surroundings, I was also relieved that I didn't have to worry about handling myself in a fancy restaurant.

It took only a minute or two for us to settle into an easy conversation. I must admit to wincing at Mike's ineptness in eating his spaghetti. After embarrassing mishaps, which were numerous, he'd make his trademark cross-eyed silly face, mocking his own lack of grace.

"I live just a mile from here," he informed me after we finished eating. "I'd like to show you my place." I agreed to his request and followed him there in my car.

As we drove down the long dirt lane leading to his property, I wasn't surprised by what I saw. Mike lived in an ancient mobile home perched on a quarter-acre clearing surrounded by woods. A ramshackle garage and several broken-down sheds stood near the trailer.

Mike parked alongside the lane, and I pulled up behind him. He jumped out of his car, gesturing with a flourish. "Welcome to my humble abode."

When we walked into the trailer, I was pleased to see that Mike kept his home clean and tidy. But everything appeared old and outdated. All the furnishings looked shabby: the battered cabinets, ancient refrigerator, and cracked linoleum in the kitchen; the worn carpet and threadbare couch in the living room.

"This is where I hang my hat," he said. "Nothing much to it. The trailer isn't great. But I love the woods. Someday, I plan to haul this heap of junk away and build a cabin on this spot. I'm working on drawing up the plans."

I could easily picture Mike living in a little cabin in the woods. It would suit him perfectly.

"Want to take a tour of my property?" he asked.

He grabbed a flashlight from a kitchen drawer, and I followed him out the front door into the evening's waning light. It was early October, and the first hints of color had just appeared in the trees. As we walked down the long lane we'd just driven up, Mike reached over and took my hand.

I breathed deeply, inhaling the cool fresh air. As I exhaled, it felt as if I was releasing a load of stress that had been building up inside me for years. I glanced over at the man whose hand I was holding, whose blue eyes twinkled in his weathered face, and I decided I was quite happy with the moment.

"You have a beautiful piece of property," I told him. "You're really lucky."

"Yes, I am," he replied. "My home isn't worth anything, but the nature is priceless."

As we strolled down the lane, Mike used his flashlight beam to point out a dozen species of trees on his property. He picked up a dry leaf from the ground. "Have you ever smelled sassafras?"

I shook my head. He crumbled the edge of the leaf and held it under my nose.

"Mm," I said as I inhaled the fragrance. "That's wonderful!"

"Have you ever had sassafras tea?" he asked.

"No," I admitted. "I haven't."

"It's made from the tree root. I'll make it for you sometime."

"Sounds good," I said. It occurred to me that Mike's promise of future tea meant that he expected our friendship to continue. The thought pleased me.

Then, we veered off the lane into the darkness of the woods. Using the beam of his flashlight, he showed me a fallen tree that looked as if it had been on the ground for quite some time. "I come out here and sit when I need to do some deep thinking," he told me. "You'd be surprised what answers come to you out here in the quiet of nature."

On the way back to the lane, he pointed the flashlight beam on a deer path running through the woods. "Every year during deer hunting season, a few morons come stomping around here looking for something to shoot. I'm not going to have that kind of mayhem on my property."

He shone his beam on the "No Trespassing" sign alongside the lane. "They completely ignore that sign. So, I pull my shotgun out of my bedroom closet and fire off a few warning shots. They skedaddle right out of here."

We reached the end of the lane and turned around. As we headed back toward his house, a squirrel scampered across our path. Mike then described the menagerie of creatures that made their home on his wooded acreage. In addition to the deer and squirrel, he listed rabbits, chipmunks, raccoons, and countless varieties of birds.

"Ugh," I said when he mentioned being visited by the occasional skunk.

"Skunks don't bother me," he chuckled. "We have a mutual respect society. I leave them alone, and they leave me alone."

Before we went back into his trailer, Mike led me over to one of his ramshackle wooden sheds. He pointed his flashlight beam at a place where a board had been broken off at the bottom, leaving a hole large enough for a critter to crawl through.

"This is where my possum friend lives," he chuckled. "I keep threatening to charge him rent, but he doesn't listen. And I end up bringing him my table scraps every day. I guess he takes me for a sucker."

When we went back inside the trailer, I wondered what would happen next. I was just about to grab my purse and say it was time for me to leave when Mike suggested that we watch a movie. Knowing I didn't need to get home to my children, I decided it would be okay to stay for a while.

We sat together on the sagging couch. Mike flipped through the channels on his ancient black-and-white television set and found an old John Wayne western. I had no interest in the movie and had difficulty keeping my eyes open. When Mike saw me nodding off, he put his arm around me and pulled me close to him.

I must've fallen asleep in seconds, because the next thing I knew, Mike was gently shaking me, telling me the movie was over. I looked up to find myself gazing into his magnificent blue eyes.

"How're you doing, Dodi-girl?" he asked, christening me with the first endearing nickname I'd ever had. Ever so gently, he brushed my lips with a kiss. In my groggy state, the tender gesture seemed dreamlike.

"I'm sorry," he said. "I should've asked first."

But I lifted my lips to meet his for another kiss, and then another and another. Mike brushed the hair off my face and ran his workworn fingers over the contours of my cheeks. "I'd better send you home, Dodi-girl," he said. "It would be way too easy for me to get carried away, and I don't think that would be good for you."

Reluctantly, I got up, and Mike walked me out through the darkness to my car. He wrapped his arms around me one last time. But instead of kissing me, he held me close, pressing his cheek against mine. "If I could," he whispered, "I'd make all the hurt inside you go away."

When I went to bed that night, I could still feel the comforting sensation of Mike's arms around me. I slept soundly for ten hours straight and didn't wake up until the children came bounding into the house the next morning.

My relationship with Michael Mitchell kept rolling forward, even though I wasn't sure I wanted it to. But I didn't do anything to stop it, either.

Others in the square dance class soon picked up on the fact that Mike and I were dating. Mike stopped making his rounds of the single ladies in the class, and I became his only partner. His being taken out of commission irked some of the other women, many of whom would've loved to be in my shoes.

By the end of November, we'd finished our lessons and had moved on to attend the square dances held at different locations in the community. Mike was familiar with all the venues, as he'd been involved with square dancing for three years. The Saturday night dance in South Bend ended up being our favorite. It became the highlight of my week.

Of course, I had to acquire the traditional square dance garb. Mike took me to a square dance store in South Bend, where he bought me skirts, blouses, a crinoline, and a pair of dance shoes. He bought shirts for himself that matched my outfits.

Wearing such flamboyant costumes was a new experience for me. Even after I'd put away my Amish clothing, my English attire had always been subdued. I had never attempted to make a fashion statement, or to stand out in any way.

Mercedes, I'm almost embarrassed to tell you how much those frilly, colorful dance costumes delighted me. Wearing them prompted me to make other changes to my appearance. I decided to go to the salon to get my hair done. Corina insisted on going with me so that she could consult with the stylist about what to do with my drab hair. I started wearing a little makeup, the way Diane had taught me years earlier. Now, my daughter served as my coach.

The first time Mike saw me with makeup, he looked troubled. "You don't need all that, Dodi-girl," he said. "In my opinion, you're more beautiful without it. But you go ahead and do what you want to do."

Corina was impressed with my new venture. Even though she insisted that my square dance costumes were ridiculous, she was happy to see me excited about something. "I wouldn't be caught dead in a square dance outfit," she told me. "But it's good for you, Mom."

The first night Mike and I went to the South Bend dance, I learned there was a second type of activity associated with a square dance venue: round dancing, a partner dance that borrowed steps from ballroom dancing.

The first time I watched couples gliding across the floor in a round dance, I was enamored with the activity. I begged Mike to attend lessons with me, which were held an hour before the dance started.

Mike was hesitant. He'd never attempted round dancing before, claiming the steps were far above what he could master. But he gave in to my pleas.

While I enjoyed square dancing, I adored round dancing, which, in my estimation, was a more elegant form of dance. Mike and I learned steps in the waltz, the fox trot, the swing, the cha cha, and the tango. Actually, I learned the steps and pulled Mike along with me.

Dancing made me feel younger than I'd felt in a long time. When I'd been married to Ivan, I'd felt like a sad old woman. Now, I felt like a free-spirited teenager.

In addition to our night out dancing, Mike and I began spending time together about once a week, sometimes on a Friday evening, sometimes on a Sunday afternoon. He understood that I didn't want to leave my children more often than that.

I'd talk to Mike on the phone every night after the children had gone to bed, just so I could hear his friendly voice. Afterwards, I'd sleep better, knowing there was someone out there who cared about me.

Mercedes, I craved something from Mike. I can't say I had romantic feelings for him. I don't believe I ever did. But he possessed an abundance of tenderness that he offered me freely, and being with him soothed my soul. I could be myself with no pretentions, basking in the affection of a man who adored me.

I don't think I completely understood my feelings for Mike back then. I told myself he was my best friend, but in my mind, I refused to grant him the status of boyfriend. I can see by your expression, Mercedes, that you've figured something out. Mike was the loving father figure that I lacked during my childhood. I couldn't stop myself from clinging to him.

Being with Mike was so easy, and I always felt lighthearted in his company. In addition to being a kind and thoughtful man, he was an unrelenting comedian. If laughter is the best medicine, then I received regular doses of that good potion when I was around Mike. I learned to be silly with him, something new for the girl who'd been serious-minded all her life.

Mike and I enjoyed cuddling and kissing, but for the first two months of our relationship, our physical contact went no further than that. I never planned on being sexual with him.

It had been a very long time since I'd been intimate with a man. Ivan had lost interest in sex with me after Wesley was born, and I'd known he was getting his needs met elsewhere. After his death, I'd reconciled myself to the idea of being celibate for the rest of my life.

One Friday evening in November, I drove to Mike's house so exhausted that I was on the verge of tears. On top of putting in extra hours at work, I'd attended parent-teacher conferences at my children's school that week. And I'd been up late night after night, trying to catch up on a backload of laundry.

As always, Mike was there to comfort me. "Someday," he told me, "some man is going to come along and make your life a whole lot easier." I had the sense he wanted that man to be him. In my state of utter fatigue, the idea sounded good to me.

He made me a cup of the promised sassafras tea, which I sipped while he rubbed my feet. Then he massaged my shoulders, which led to hugging and kissing. And I realized I wanted more from him.

"Are you sure this is okay, Dodi-girl?" he asked as our passionate kissing began leading to more intimate activities.

"Yes," I said, "I'm absolutely sure."

What can I say, Mercedes, except that Mike was a delightful lover? All I had previously known was Ivan's self-serving inclinations. Mike was the man who introduced me to the pleasures of intimacy, pleasures that I didn't know existed. After my initial sexual encounter with him, there was no stopping me. I wanted more and more of him, and I could hardly leave the man alone.

Of course, my passion pleased him, but I believe it also misled him. "You're a dangerous woman, Dodi-girl," he'd often say. "You're making me fall for you."

Sometimes after our lovemaking, I'd lie there and watch him as he got out of bed and pulled on his ill-fitting trousers and the out-of-style shirt he'd bought at a thrift store. The way my lover dressed, the way he wore his hair, even the way he moved reminded me of someone from my father's generation. And I'd have difficulty looking at the man with whom I'd just shared amazing intimacy.

"Dora, what are you doing with this old guy?" I'd ask myself. But I'd immediately dismiss the question, as I knew I was not yet done with Michael Mitchell. I wasn't ready to go back to a life that didn't include him.

Did I think of Mike as someone I would marry? No, I did not. But Mike was a lover, in every way you can consider that word. He spoiled me, coddled me, catered to my every desire. It was an intoxicating experience for me.

To be honest, Mike shared my reservations about our age difference. At moments when we were at our closest, I could tell his whole heart and soul wanted to plunge ahead into a lasting relationship with me. That's when I'd see a shadow cross his face, and he would mention his concern about how young I was.

One Sunday afternoon in early December, as I drove down the lane to Mike's trailer, he startled me when he suddenly appeared at the edge of the woods. His ragged old coat and stocking cap were covered in freshly fallen snow, so I knew he'd been out in the elements for a while. He came over to my car. I rolled down the window to talk with him.

"I just needed to spend a little time out there," he said, pointing toward the spot in the woods where he sat to meditate. His face was reddened by the cold. But his blue eyes had a strange glow about them, as if he'd just had a supernatural experience.

When we entered his trailer, he shed his snowy clothing, then sat me down to talk. "Dodi-girl, you know I've been worried about our age difference," he said. "When I was out there sitting on the log, something came to me, clear as day. This might sound weird, but I caught a little glimpse of the future. I know there will come a time when I'll need to hand you off to another man. But it's my job to love you now."

His words saddened me, and I could think of no response to his revelation.

"Let me love you now," he reiterated, pulling me to my feet and into his arms.

Then, we ate some chili he'd cooked, bantering in our usual lighthearted manner. "Eat up, Dodi-girl," he said. "I want it all gone. I don't think the possum likes spicy food."

Afterwards, we made love, enjoying the beauty of the moment, not knowing what would lie ahead for us.

From time to time, Mike would inquire as to when I planned to introduce him to Corina and Wesley. "I love kids," he kept telling me.

I did my best to avoid that topic. Despite the fact that I was now deep into the relationship with Mike, I knew it wasn't going to be permanent, and I didn't want to create complications for my children.

However, in mid-December, Corina demanded to know where I was going with my friend all the time. I finally confessed to the children that I was dating someone. Wesley didn't seem to understand the concept of dating and had no interested in talking about the subject.

Corina, however, was incensed. "You have a right to date, Mom," she said. "But you have no right to keep secrets like this. You tell me I need to be honest with you, but you haven't been honest with me."

Chastened, I apologized to her and yielded to her demand to meet the man who'd been taking up so much of my time. Her anger then turned into excitement as she plied me with questions about Mike. I knew she was spinning a fairytale romance in her mind, imagining me with a handsome, charming man who would someday be her stepfather.

When Mike came to our home several days later, Corina was there at my side, ready to welcome him. I can't say I was surprised to see the disappointment on her face when she first laid eyes on the scruffy older man with the disheveled clothing and rumpled hair. While she politely responded to his inquiries about her school, her friends, and her hobbies, she showed little interest in getting to know him better. She quickly excused herself from the conversation, saying she had homework to do.

Then, I called Wesley out of his room to meet Mike. I fully expected him to be indifferent to the stranger who had entered our home. But his reaction floored me. My son looked at Mike as if he recognized something in him, as if he was meeting a kindred spirit. When Mike asked him questions, Wesley responded readily.

Before long, Mike and Wesley were sitting on the living room floor playing with Wesley's Hot Wheels cars, discussing the different makes and models. Then they went on to play with Wesley's collection of dinosaurs. My son listened with wide-eyed interest as Mike described the critters that lived in his woods. He was especially enchanted by the idea of the possum living under Mike's shed.

As Mike and I said goodbye at the end of his visit, I saw tears of joy in his eyes. "I just love that little fellow," he whispered to me.

So, Mike and I developed a new routine. On Friday night, he and I went on a date. On Saturday night, we danced together. And on Sunday afternoon, he came to my house to spend time with the children and me.

Even though Wesley knew the schedule, he kept pestering me with, "When's Mike coming over?"

As do many older men, Mike had the habit of calling younger males "son," even when they were unrelated to him. Wesley looked at Mike curiously the first time he used that term with him. Then, he smiled broadly. I knew Mike had touched some deep longing inside my child.

I could also tell that Mike was becoming increasingly invested in taking on the role of Wesley's father. I found that unnerving. Something was happening outside of my control, something that I never meant to happen.

But Mike's relationship with Corina was not as affectionate. At twelve-and-a-half, my daughter was several inches taller than me. Sometimes when she talked to me, she'd use a bossy tone. While I took that with a grain of salt, the behavior irked Mike to no end.

Over and over, he'd tell me that I allowed Corina to wield too much power in the family. "You're the parent and she's the child," he'd lecture me.

He'd even say such things in front of Corina. That infuriated her. I knew she thought Mike was trying to diminish her influence in our family life, and she wasn't about to let that happen.

I tried to explain to Mike how, from the time Corina had been a toddler, she'd been my little partner. I told him how she'd clarified aspects of the English world for me when my Amish background had left me at a disadvantage. I described to him how bravely she'd stepped up to share the load after her father died.

"That's the only dynamic she's ever known," I told him.

His response was, "Well, things need to change." And I knew that in spite of his support and gentleness with me, he had no real understanding of what the children and I been through as a family.

When Mike would bark at Corina for overstepping her bounds, she'd look at him with hatred in her eyes. "This isn't going to work," I'd tell myself. And I'd fear that the inevitable end to my relationship was soon to come.

But there was my son to consider. He dearly loved his surrogate father, and Mike never presumed to reprimand him in any way. I knew that my breaking up with Mike would devastate Wesley.

Early on, Corina adapted to Mike's visits by absenting herself from the family circle. She'd arrange to go to a friend's house, or would spend the entire afternoon in her room. Thus, Wesley, Mike, and I were left to enjoy peaceful times together. That arrangement worked, even though I knew it was untenable in the long run.

As the holiday season approached, I sent a Christmas card with an enclosed letter to my friend Elliott. I informed him of the bold new changes in my life: my venture into dancing and my relationship with Mike.

A week later, I received a card from Elliott. Enclosed with his letter was a picture of him and his new wife. I was startled to see that she was white. Six months earlier, when he'd written to me about getting married, I'd assumed that he had chosen a spouse from his own race.

As I stared at the photo of Elliott and his Caucasian wife, I was flooded with feelings that almost made me double over in pain. When Mike called me that evening, he could tell I was distracted. He pressed to know what was wrong. I convinced him that I was overly tired.

That night, I lay in bed trying to make sense of my feelings about Elliott's photo. I could come to only one conclusion: I was jealous.

"If Elliott was going to marry a white woman," I whispered to myself, "why couldn't it have been me?"

I immediately felt ashamed of myself. I had no reason to believe that I'd ever be deserving of Elliott's romantic attention. He was so intelligent, so wise, so dignified, so handsome. So far above me. What would he ever see in a plain, uneducated little woman so lacking in confidence and knowledge of the world?

"You're being ridiculous," I told myself. Still, tears rolled down my face and soaked my pillow as I allowed myself to feel how much I longed for my dear friend.

Despite my efforts to shake off those feelings, the pain lingered for a full week. While I couldn't imagine a long-term relationship with Mike, I knew that, given the opportunity, I would've married Elliott without giving it a second thought. Admitting all that to myself was unsettling, to say the least.

Looking back on that time makes me so grateful that I now have Elliott in my life on a daily basis. We weren't ready to be together then. But we are now.

In the letter Elliott sent with his Christmas card, he asked me one simple question about my relationship with Mike: "Do you love him?"

That question pierced my heart. As I'd never been able to be anything but honest with Elliott, I wrote back to him the very next day, saying: "I love the way Mike loves me."

Mercedes, that's the most accurate way I can sum up my dynamic with Mike. I loved being loved, but I was unable to give back what I received. I'm ashamed of that. Some might say that I used Mike, and they would be right.

Mike never saw the letter from Elliott. I whisked it away the moment it arrived. But I left his card and photo in a basket on my kitchen counter, along with the other holiday cards I'd received.

The following Sunday afternoon, when Mike came over for his weekly visit, he sat down at my kitchen table to look through my cards. When he found the picture of Elliott and his wife, he barked, "Who the hell is this?"

I knew right away that he was offended by the sight of a mixed-race couple. "They're my friends," I told him.

He tossed the photo back into the basket. "I didn't know you had friends like that."

I turned away to hide my reddened face, pretending to stir a pot of soup on the stove. The subject of Elliott and his wife was so fraught that I couldn't find a single word to say about it. Sadly, I realized there were lengths to which Mike's kindheartedness didn't extend. That chilled me.

On the afternoon of Christmas day, Mike came over to my house to share family time with the children and me. He brought the gift of a board game for Corina and Wesley. That didn't impress Corina, but Wesley was delighted.

Then my son presented Mike with a gift he'd made for him: a cartoon drawing of Mike's possum wearing a Santa Claus hat.

Mike was so tickled with that drawing. He and Wesley laughed uproariously over it. Then Mike picked Wesley up, tussling with him and swinging him around, telling him he'd put that picture on his refrigerator and keep it there forever.

I was ashamed of the fact that I had nothing for Mike other than a tin of cookies I'd baked for him. But he had something for me. Look inside this paper bag, Mercedes. This simple holiday candle is what Mike gave me on the one and only Christmas we spent together.

"It's not much," he told me apologetically. "I wish I could give you the world, but I can't."

I knew the gift was inexpensive, but I'd never received anything given to me with such love. The candle is more than forty years old now. It's chipped, and the holly leaves are broken and falling off. Several times, I've been on the verge of throwing it out. But I always hesitate, and then I tuck it away again. It is my only memento of my relationship with Michael Mitchell.

By three months after we started dating, Mike had assumed the role of my partner in life. Clearly, he saw the children and me as his responsibility. I knew that taking on the extra load was a lot for him. But his manly pride obligated him to carry out his perceived duty.

When my car broke down, I called Mike. He dropped what he was doing and came right over. As he poked around under the hood, he told me what parts needed to be purchased, offering to save me a mechanic's fee by installing them himself.

When my landlord failed to respond to my complaint of a leaky kitchen faucet, Mike showed up at my house with his tools and proceeded to fix the sink himself.

When Wesley fell and hit his head, Mike came to the emergency room to be with us while Wesley got his scalp laceration stitched. Afterwards, he carried my son to the car. Then he spent the night at my house, sleeping on the couch, just to make sure Wesley was going to be okay.

With Mike coming to my home with increasing frequency, it wasn't long before Virgil and Irene had the opportunity to meet him. They all chatted amiably together, as if they'd been lifelong friends. Mike praised Virgil and Irene for everything they'd done for the children and me.

"Well," Virgil said, "we're getting older. We're not going to be around forever. It's good to see that Dora has someone else to look after her."

I found that conversation unsettling. It was as if my neighbors had passed their torch to Mike. I wondered whether they expected me to be under Mike's watch and care for the rest of my life.

One Sunday in late February, Mike informed me he couldn't come to my house, as his grandchildren were spending the day with him. He invited me to bring my children over to play with them.

Corina turned up her nose when she saw Mike's shabby mobile home. However, she was charmed by his four-year-old granddaughter. She took the little girl under her wing, reading her stories and braiding her long hair.

As it was a balmy late winter day with a hint of spring in the air, Mike, his seven-year-old grandson, and nine-year-old Wesley went out to the front yard to play football. I watched them from a lawn chair.

Mike proved himself to be nothing but a grownup kid as

he playfully tackled and wrestled the boys. Recently melted snow had left the yard soggy, and all three of them were soon covered in mud. I could tell Wesley was exhilarated by his romp in the yard. He repeatedly doubled over with laughter at Mike's silly antics.

Corina eventually wandered out of the mobile home to see what I was doing. She stood with her arms crossed over her chest, shaking her head as she watched Mike entertain the boys by making himself look foolish.

"Mom," she said, "why on earth are you dating that dork? You know he's not your type."

"So, what is my type?" I asked, suspecting that my soon-to-be-teenage daughter knew more about such matters than I did.

Corina furrowed her brow. "I don't know, Mom. I haven't figured that out yet."

As I drove the children home that evening, Wesley said, "That was so much fun, Mom. When can we go back there again?"

"Soon," I promised him.

So, as winter turned to spring, Wesley and I made frequent visits to Mike's trailer. More often than not, Corina declined going with us. Wesley loved tagging along with Mike as he puttered around his property, and Mike included him in whatever task he was doing.

One day when we were there, Wesley burst into the trailer, excitedly informing me that he'd caught a glimpse of the possum eating the table scraps Mike had put out for him. At home the following week, I had a hard time convincing my son that we couldn't save our leftovers to take to the critter living under Mike's shed.

On a Sunday in April, Mike rented a large van, and he and I, along with my children and his grandchildren, drove all the way to Toledo, Ohio, to visit the zoo. We had more fun than you can imagine on that outing, and we functioned so effectively as a family unit that it frightened me. Corina sat in the back with Mike's granddaughter, entertaining the little girl with nursery songs and clapping games. Wesley and Mike's grandson sat in the seat behind Mike and me, tussling and poking at each other. Mike had to remind them repeatedly to settle down.

Poor Wesley ate too much cotton candy at the zoo and got sick on the way home. Mike stopped at a rest area and escorted Wesley to the men's room, taking care of him as if he were his own child.

Late that evening, Mike called me for our ritual of saying goodnight to each other. I sensed an unusual seriousness in his tone.

"I know I don't have any right to ask this question, Dodi-girl," he said. "But if I don't, I'll regret it."

"What?" I said, a knot of dread forming in my stomach.

"Where is this thing going between the two of us?"

I froze for a few seconds. "I-I don't know," I finally stammered.

"I mean, can you see us together long term? I know you're young and beautiful, and I'm an old man. But we get along so well, and when we're with the kids, we seem like a family. It feels right to me."

I wondered whether he'd forgotten the epiphany he'd had in the woods just a few months earlier, when he'd foreseen the day that he'd have to let me go.

"I haven't thought much about it," I mumbled.

I knew I wasn't being honest with Mike. I knew that despite my addiction to his affection and wonderful caretaking, I would never consider committing to spending a lifetime with him.

"You know, I'm falling in love with you," he continued. "No, that's not true. I already have. I love you, Dodi-girl."

I stood there clutching the phone, tongue-tied, imagining the shadow of hurt feelings passing across Mike's face as he waited for a response that didn't come.

"I'm sorry for putting you on the spot," he said. "This is all so new for you, and you don't know what you want yet. I know you're not ready to love me back right now. But I love you, and that's enough for me."

"Let's just take it slow," I said, trying to rescue the moment. "Let's see where it goes."

"Okay," he said. But I think we both knew that my failure to respond to his declaration of love was a permanent answer to his question.

Even though we continued our relationship, it lost some of its lightheartedness. Pain had crept between us.

Several weeks later, when my period failed to arrive on time, I began to worry. My cycles had always been regular, and the cessation of menstruating could mean only one thing. When I broke the news to Mike during a Wednesday evening phone conversation, his initial shock quickly turned to excitement.

"I don't want you to worry, Dodi-girl," he told me. "I'm here for you, every step of the way."

The following Sunday afternoon, he came to my house with a large rolled-up sheet of paper in his hand. He spread it out on my kitchen table to show me the plans he'd drawn up for the cabin he wanted to build.

"I've made some changes," he announced. "I've added a second story." Pointing out details with his pencil, he said, "Corina and Wesley can have the upstairs bedrooms. We'll put the new baby downstairs with us."

Mercedes, I was ready to go along with those plans. I thought my destiny had revealed itself, that I was meant to marry Michael Mitchell and raise a child with him.

But two weeks later, I again had to break news to Mike. My period, which was two months late by that time, had finally come. It was an extra-heavy period, and I wondered whether it was actually a miscarriage.

I can never be sure that I didn't carry Michael Mitchell's baby for six weeks. The thought saddens me. I wish I could've known that child.

Mike broke down in tears when he heard my news. I knew he was weeping for more than the anticipated baby. He was grieving over the loss of something that could've strengthened our ties as a couple and a family.

Then he pulled himself together and said, "We'll just have to keep carrying on, Dodi-girl."

We tried to go on with our shared life. We kept on dancing together. But there was no more talk about the cabin.

As Mike and I continued with our round dance lessons, other students began making comments about our mismatched abilities. "You're a lot better dancer than Mike is," one man told me. "You carry all the weight. Without you, he couldn't make it through a single step."

One Saturday evening, my round dance teacher took me aside and said, "Dora, you know that Mike is holding you back. With your talent, you could reach the highest levels of round dancing. Have you ever considered finding a different partner?"

Her words triggered a swell of mixed emotions inside me. I could feel my face turning red. My teacher quickly apologized, saying, "I'm sorry for overstepping my bounds. I didn't mean to cause problems for you and your boyfriend."

Then one day in early summer, a woman in my class turned my life in a new direction by making an offhanded comment: "Since you guys like round dancing so much, you should try taking ballroom lessons."

My ears perked up at her suggestion. "Where could we do that?" I asked.

"There are two studios here in South Bend," she informed me. "Arthur Murray's and Tony O'Reilly's. I've taken lessons at Tony O'Reilly's. I loved it. Tony recently brought in a really good teacher from New York City."

Thrilled with the idea, I turned to Mike. "Can we try that?"

Mike looked glum and muttered something under his breath. Clearly, he had no interest in pursuing ballroom dancing. But for my sake, he reluctantly agreed to go. We decided to check out Tony O'Reilly's studio.

Mercedes, looking back at that moment makes me feel ashamed. I took advantage of Mike. I knew he was so afraid of losing me that he was willing to cater to my every desire.

When I called the studio to ask about the cost of the lessons, I was shocked to learn how expensive they were. I proposed to Mike that we split the cost. He agreed to that. However, he ended up refusing my half, paying the full amount on his own.

157

The first time we set foot in Tony O'Reilly's studio, Mike was put off by the glitzy ambiance. He was ready to turn around and walk out, but I persuaded him to stay. To my delight, I learned that we were to be taught by the studio's celebrated new instructor, Vincent Perez.

To say that I was in awe of Vincent is a vast understatement. I idolized him. He was of Puerto Rican descent, a man of medium height with alluring dark eyes and olive skin. He appeared to be in his mid-forties, and his black hair was touched with gray at the temples. Despite the fact that he was slightly overweight, all of his movements were fluid and graceful, and he always looked exotic in his dance tuxedos.

Vincent came from New York City, that mysterious place so far from my sheltered upbringing. In my mind, Vincent's worldly wisdom was beyond anything I could hope to understand. I wanted him to impart it all to me. I hung onto every word he said.

You're smiling, Mercedes. You know that I had a schoolgirl crush on Vincent. Because he was so adept at charming the ladies, I doubt that any of his female students were able to escape falling for him.

I think Mike mistrusted Vincent to the same degree that I adored him. For that reason, he had great difficulty in learning anything from our instructor. Over and over, he failed to comprehend what Vincent was trying to teach him.

So, Vincent would demonstrate the steps for Mike by taking me into his arms, and together, we would glide across the dance floor. I'd catch our reflection in the full-length mirrors that lined the walls of the studio. The image of the two of us took my breath away. It was like a little girl's fairytale dream come true.

The more I danced under Vincent's tutelage, the more the ingrained rigidity from my childhood melted away. With something akin to spiritual devotion, I surrendered myself to dancing. It began to feel like a calling, something I was born to do.

I wanted to become the most accomplished dancer I could possibly be. When I learned there were levels to be reached in ballroom dancing—bronze, silver, and gold—I was determined to pass each one. Thus, I studied every aspect of dancing with the discipline and dedication of an Olympic athlete.

It was utterly impossible for Mike to keep up with me. More and more, he sat on the sidelines while our teacher worked with me alone. He would look so lost and out of place, his tousled hair and shabby clothing contrasting sharply with Vincent's polished appearance.

Vincent praised me profusely, and I loved pleasing him. When I would master a challenging step, he'd flash his dazzling smile and say, "Fantastic," or, "Marvelous," in his charming Spanish accent. And I would feel brilliant.

Vincent couldn't seem to remember that my name was Dora. He always called me Dori. I didn't mind that. Dora seemed like such a plain and ordinary name. Dori sounded more glamorous, like the image I was trying to cultivate. Soon, I stopped correcting Vincent when he mispronounced my name, and after a while, everyone in the studio knew me as Dori.

At the studio, I could pretend that I didn't carry the baggage of being raised Amish, or of being the widow of a man who'd been killed in a bar fight. No one asked me personal questions, so I didn't have to divulge anything about my life. After just a few steps of a waltz or a tango, my past would melt away, and I would float off into a land of enchantment.

Just as square dancing had brought a change to my appearance, so did ballroom dancing. While most of the students were ordinary-looking, I kept my eye on the way the female teachers dressed. Their look was rather provocative, to say the least, with short skirts, flashy jewelry, and lots of makeup.

When I started emulating that style, the other ladies at the studio complemented me, telling me I looked cute. I picked up on cues that the men considered me attractive. I knew Mike was concerned, but he said little about the matter.

Corina showed mixed reactions to my changed appearance. At times, she was coach and cheerleader for my new look. But when she was angry with me, she'd throw some pretty unflattering names at me, which cut me to the core. I'd wonder what kind of example I was setting for her.

Only a handful of the students at Tony O'Reilly's studio were serious about dancing. Just a few of us were intent on moving up through the levels and preparing ourselves for competitive performance. The rest were unexceptional students who came primarily for the social life.

Of course, Tony O'Reilly was intent on running a profitable business. Thus, he and his instructors did their best to cater to each student. Even though the teachers might've preferred to spend their time with the more promising dancers, they paid quality attention to every person who paid for their pricy lessons.

Mike and I had our lesson on Tuesday evening. On Thursday evening, we attended the dance party, which was the big weekly event at the studio. Mike didn't enjoy the party at all, but he always gave in to my pleas to go. He questioned whether it was right to leave Corina and Wesley so many times during the week.

I didn't always want to burden Irene and Virgil with the care of the children. I reasoned that it was okay to leave thirteen-year-old Corina in charge while I was gone on Tuesday and Thursday evenings.

Still, I used Mike's concern as an excuse to stay home on Saturday nights instead of going to the square dance with him. The truth was that I had become bored with square dancing. Nothing could match the thrill of ballroom dancing.

Tony O'Reilly and the instructors at the studio did everything they could to create a scintillating atmosphere at their Thursday night parties. The studio was always decorated with sparkling lights and other showy ornamentation. About once a month, the staff put on a theme party, at which the instructors and some of the students wore costumes.

Mike thought those theme parties were a bunch of nonsense. I admit to growing impatient with all the distracting superficiality. All I wanted to do was dance.

The instructors always made a point of being even-handed in asking their students to dance with them at the party. Having the opportunity to dance with Vincent three or four times during the course of the evening made it worth putting up with all the bedazzled silliness.

Mercedes, I hate to admit this, but I often wished Mike wasn't there with me at the studio. I wanted him to leave me alone in my dream world with my teacher. I think he sensed that.

There at the studio, the differences between us were magnified. There, we were worlds apart. I had taken flight, soaring through the advanced levels, while Mike was still plodding along, earthbound, barely at a beginner's level.

Oh, Mike didn't create any problems for me at the studio. He didn't behave like a jealous boyfriend, and he didn't monopolize my time. He was proud of my success, and he encouraged me to dance with more accomplished partners.

"You're amazing, Dodi-girl," he'd tell me. "Almost too good to be true."

While he spent much of his time at the party standing outside smoking cigarettes with other men, he always came in to sit with me at break time, dutifully bringing me refreshments. I knew the other students wondered about the oddity of our relationship: the talented young woman paired with the stodgy older man.

Despite my charming dance teacher's efforts to maintain the appearance of congeniality with all his students, Vincent couldn't hide his disdain for Mike. Perhaps it was because Mike was so down-to-earth and unpretentious, while Vincent was all about the show.

"You shouldn't be dancing with that boyfriend of yours," he scolded me as we waltzed together one Thursday evening. "You've got so much potential, and Mike's never going to get anywhere. Not in dancing. Not in life. He's holding you back."

He led me in an advanced step, then said, "Where's your

confidence, Dori? You don't need to settle for a guy like that."

Vincent's comment cut me to the core. After the waltz ended, I rushed out the door so I could have time alone to regain my emotional equilibrium. It was a clear summer night, and as I gazed up at the vast expanse of the starry sky, I wondered whether Vincent's observations were true. Was I keeping myself down by clinging to the security of my relationship with Mike? Did I need to let go so I could explore my potential to the fullest?

Ever mindful of my wellbeing, Mike came out to join me. "Is everything all right, Dodi-girl?" he asked.

I nodded, avoiding eye contact with him. When he put his arm around me, I couldn't make myself snuggle up to him the way I usually did. He dropped his arm and stepped away. "I'll leave you alone," he said.

As he turned and headed back toward the door, he added, "Don't worry, I'll stop bothering you." It was the first time he'd ever addressed me with sarcasm in his voice.

When I went back inside, I sat down next to Mike, trying to mend the rift between us. But he didn't speak to me, and I could think of nothing to say to him.

Then, I saw Vincent strutting across the dance floor toward me. Somehow, I knew what was going to happen. I knew I was on the verge of something significant, another turning point in my life. My heart ached with sorrow for what I was leaving behind, yet every cell in my body trembled in anticipation of what was to come.

Giving Mike an unmistakably dirty look, Vincent extended his hand to me. "Dance with me, Dori," he said in a voice of charming desperation. He fixed his dark eyes imploringly on mine, as if beseeching his beloved for a favor.

Mercedes, that look undid me. It melted me. I couldn't help but surrender to Vincent's charisma.

Out of the corner of my eye, I saw the devastation on Mike's face. As Vincent led me onto the dance floor, Mike got up and headed toward the door. He didn't come back inside for the rest of the evening.

Vincent led me in a very sensual cha cha. I threw myself

into it, doing steps I didn't even know I could do. We put on quite a show, which earned applause from the other teachers and students.

Afterwards, Vincent told me he wanted to talk with me, and we went to Tony O'Reilly's office to converse in private. Vincent appeared regal and authoritative as he sat behind Tony's massive desk, while I perched nervously on the edge of my seat.

"Dori, I'd like to see you take more lessons," he said. You're doing fantastic, and if you double up on lessons, you'll be all the way through the gold level in no time at all."

My mind reeled at his request. I knew that assuming Mike would pay for any more lessons was out of the question. "I can't afford that," I protested.

Vincent seemed to understood what I was getting at. "We can't count on Mike paying, can we? It's best to have him out of the picture." He leaned back in Tony's desk chair, striking a dramatic pose. "Here's what I'm willing to do. I'll cut the cost of your lessons in half so that you can take twice as many for the price you're paying now."

I stared at him in disbelief. "Really? You'd do that for me?"

"Yes." He flashed me his charming smile. "I wouldn't do this for just anybody. But I believe in you, Dori. I believe in you more than you believe in yourself."

Then Vincent proceeded to inform me of an upcoming competition he was preparing to enter, and he asked me if I would like to be his partner.

I was so stunned that I was incapable of responding. Me, the shy little Amish girl, dancing in a ballroom competition with the sensational Vincent Perez? How could that be possible?

Vincent didn't seem to need an answer, because he'd already decided that I would accept his proposition. "I know you think you're not ready for this, Dori," he said. "But you are. There is no one else in this studio I'd rather have as my partner. You and I are going to work hard together, and we're going to be spectacular."

Instead of going to Mike's house the following Sunday, I spent the afternoon in the studio with Vincent. Mercedes, I'm sad to say that I never again drove down the long lane to that shabby little trailer in the woods. I knew Vincent disapproved of me spending time with Mike. I didn't want to do anything to displease my beloved teacher, the man who was grooming me to become the studio's next dance diva.

Mike knew I was pulling away. He stopped calling me at bedtime. I stopped going to the square dance altogether, as Vincent told me I was wasting my energy on that ridiculous activity.

Strangely, Mike kept coming to the Thursday evening dance parties. He and I now drove there in separate vehicles, as I'd started going early to practice with Vincent.

I think Mike figured that was the only time he was going to see me. He never made any attempts to dance with me, and he no longer took it upon himself to supply me with refreshments at break time. Occasionally, he'd catch my eye and smile at me from across the room, lifting a hand in greeting.

Enamored by my close association with Vincent, I was blind to what I was losing: a relationship with a man who loved me more than anyone else had ever loved me.

One Thursday evening in early September, I stayed late after the party to get in another half hour of practice with Vincent. When I walked out into the parking lot, I saw Mike and several other men with their heads under the open hood of a car, apparently trying to determine why the vehicle wouldn't start.

Mike turned around when he heard the sound of my footsteps. When he saw that it was me, he walked over to join me at my car.

"How are you doing, Dodi-girl?" he said. "Getting ready for your big competition?"

"How did you know about that?" I asked.

He shrugged. "Word gets around. Everybody at the studio is talking about you being Vincent's new partner. You're making a lot of the ladies jealous."

Then he looked down at the pavement, pushing a stone around with the toe of one worn shoe. When he looked up at me again, I could see that his marvelous blue eyes were clouded with pain.

In my heart, I felt an enormous surge of everything that I wanted to say to Mike. But for the life of me, Mercedes, I couldn't get the words out of my mouth. Instead, tears began pouring from my eyes.

"I miss you, Dodi-girl," Mike said, a sob catching in his throat.

"I'm so sorry, Mike," I blurted out. "I'm so sorry."

"That's okay." He held out his arms and drew me into an embrace. "You're moving forward, and that's what you need to do. You're soaring, and this old man has no right to hold you down."

I began to sob. Mike held me tenderly, caressing my back. "It's okay, Dodi-girl. We both knew this day had to come."

Then he released me and stepped back. "Go, Dodi-girl. Go with Vincent. I just hope to God he treats you right."

As he turned away, he said, "I should've known better than to open up my heart like this. But it was wonderful loving you. It was truly wonderful."

Then he stopped and looked at me again, his face contorted in agony. "The kids," he whispered. "Give my love to the kids. Tell my boy Wesley that he'll always be in my heart." And with that, he walked away.

Mercedes, that's the last time I ever saw Michael Mitchell. He never returned to the studio after that night. Some of the women whispered about how badly I'd treated him, and they gave me the cold shoulder. But by then, I was so securely tucked under Vincent's wing that no one dared to do anything to blatantly offend me.

Years later, when I was married to your grandfather, I saw Mike's obituary in the newspaper. He had died from lung cancer. At the time, I was too focused on the problems in my marriage to consider my feelings about his death.

Now, I wish I could've done something to ease Mike's

suffering at the end. I wish I could've given back to him even a fraction of what he'd given to me.

Mercedes, if my sole objective as a young woman had been to be loved by a man, I would've found fulfillment in my relationship with Mike. I would've had to look no further, because Mike was uniquely gifted with the ability to love a woman with his whole heart.

But love wasn't all I needed. Despite all my sentimental musings, I know that if I would've stayed with Mike, I would've settled into a mode of depending on him to meet my every need. And he would've been willing to do that. I would've ended up living my entire life in the little cabin in the woods he wanted to build for me.

Before long, I would've felt confined. A simple, earthy lifestyle suited Michael Mitchell, but it wasn't in the cards for me. I needed to move on, to do the exploring my soul longed to do, to discover other aspects of my being.

Still, during difficult periods of my life, I've dreamed about Mike. In those dreams, he is still loving me, taking care of me, making me feel secure in the warmth of his embrace. After all these years, I still crave his affection.

I never properly thanked Mike for what he did for me. But I imagine that when I leave this human form and pass on to the next phase of my soul's existence, I'll run into Mike. I'll thank him then. Of that, you can be sure.

CHAPTER 7: VINCENT AND DORI PEREZ

Late Thursday night of the following week, Mercedes' phone rang just as she was crawling into bed. It was Javier.

The two of them had talked at length on Monday evening, two days after her visit with Dora. Mercedes had explained the insight she'd discussed with her grandmother, that picking fights had been her way of protecting herself from getting close.

Javier had listened intently and had seemed to understand. They'd ended the call on an affectionate note, both expressing hope that they could make the marriage work. Since then, they'd touched base several times, and their brief conversations had gone well.

So, Mercedes was pleased to hear from her husband again. She curled up in bed, phone to her ear. "Hello, Javier," she cooed.

"I'm calling to see how you are, mi amor," Javier said, his voice soft and gentle. "And to talk about plans for the weekend. I think this would be a good Saturday to take Javi to Chicago." He paused. "I'd love to make it a family outing and have you come along. Unless you're planning to see Dora again."

Mercedes drew in a sharp breath, knowing the conversation was about to take an unpleasant turn. "Javier," she said, "Javi can't stay with you this weekend. He wants to go to his friend's birthday party."

She braced herself for what was to come, and wasn't surprised when Javier's tone changed to one of judgmental authority. "Why didn't I know about this party?" he asked.

"I just found out myself," Mercedes said defensively.

"When did you find out?"

"Tuesday."

"That was two days ago. Why didn't you let me know right away?"

Mercedes clenched her jaw to keep from snapping at him. "I was busy. I had to study for an exam."

"But we talked on Tuesday night. Why didn't you bring it

up then? I'm Javi's father. I should have a say in decisions like this."

"I just didn't think about it," she said. "I'm sorry."

"Well," Javier huffed, "I believe Javi spending time with his father is more important than a child's birthday party."

"In most cases, I'd agree with you," Mercedes said. "But Javi is dead set on going to this one."

"Why?"

"Because this little boy doesn't have many friends. He has a disability. Javi says he gets bullied in school. He says there probably won't be many kids at the party, and he doesn't want to let his friend down."

There was a long silence on the other end of the line. Mercedes knew Javier was torn between insisting on his rights as a father and supporting his son's inclination toward kindness.

"Okay," he finally said. "But you should've discussed this with me right away. This is inexcusable, Mercedes. I keep hoping you'll behave like an adult someday. Clearly, that's never going to happen."

Boiling rage welled inside Mercedes like hot lava in her veins. She could feel the urge to yell building up in her throat, the curse words on the tip of her tongue. She wanted to pummel Javier with insults and accusations, then hurl her phone against the bedroom wall.

Suddenly, a picture of Dora's gentle face floated into her inner vision. The image said nothing, just gazed at her silently and lovingly.

Mercedes closed her eyes and took a deep breath. When she opened her mouth to respond to her husband's insult, she was surprised to hear herself speaking in a calm and even tone. "Javier, I really am sorry. You're right, I should've talked with you sooner, before you started making plans. I know I'm not perfect. I'm disorganized and scatterbrained. I'm hotheaded, and sometimes I act like a brat. I know I can be hard to deal with. But I'm trying to be a better person, and I don't deserve the way you talk to me. It makes me feel like trash. Like a great big pile of garbage. I deserve more respect from you."

Speaking those words seemed to crack open a hard shell that had surrounded her heart for as long as she could remember. Tears of relief poured from her eyes. For a few moments, all she could do was sob.

"But I love you, Javier," she choked out. "I love you." And she realized she hadn't said those words in a very long time.

There was another lengthy silence on the other end of the line. Mercedes had no idea how her husband would respond. But in that moment, she wasn't concerned. She had spoken her true feelings, and that was all that mattered.

Then Javier spoke, his voice thick with emotion. "I'm so sorry, Mercedes. I never knew I was making you feel so bad. I always thought you weren't listening to me when I was upset with you, so I'd scold you all the harder. Yes, you deserve my respect. Above all things, you deserve my respect. And I love you too, Mercedes. My love for you is more than I can ever put into words. From now on, I will do my best to treat you the way you deserve to be treated."

He hesitated. "If you're going to Saint Joseph to see Dora on Saturday, why don't you stop by on your way there? It'll be a time for just the two of us. I think we need that."

After dropping Javi off at his friend's party early Saturday afternoon, Mercedes drove to her husband's apartment.

Javier answered her knock on the door, and without a word, drew her into his arms for a long embrace. Then, he led her over to the sofa, where they sat together in silence. Mercedes reached for his hand, intertwining her fingers through his, allowing herself to breathe deeply and peacefully in his presence.

Then, something strange began to happen, something outside of her volition. The layers of defense surrounding her heart seemed to melt away. The process felt strange, almost terrifying, leaving her feeling unbearably vulnerable.

But she allowed it to happen. She and Javier sat in sweet stillness, feeling the love pulsing between their palms.

When Mercedes entered Dora's apartment several hours later, the elderly woman greeted her with an impish smile, as if she couldn't wait to reveal a delightful secret.

Mercedes was relieved to find Dora looking so much better than she had the previous week. She was wearing a long silk skirt patterned with bright splashes of pink, turquoise, and gold. Stunning gold hoop earrings added a glamourous touch to her outfit. A sparkling barrette held her gray hair together at the nape of her neck, creating a cascade of curls that ran down her back.

Mercedes thought she saw a hint of blush on Dora's cheeks and lips, and wondered whether she'd put on makeup for the occasion. "You look beautiful!" she exclaimed.

"Thank you," Dora murmured, self-consciously fingering the gold bangles encircling her wrist. "My doctor put me on a new medication that has helped me feel much better. I am so grateful."

Mercedes wondered whether she should take the opportunity to probe into the status of her grandmother's health. But Dora didn't seem to want to dwell on that subject. She gestured eagerly toward the three large storage tubs sitting on the living room floor.

"What do you have here?" Mercedes asked, catching Dora's mood of excitement.

Dora's eyes sparkled. "Something I thought you might find interesting. I had Elliott pull these tubs out of my closet this morning. They're too heavy for me to handle. Go ahead, open them and look inside."

Mercedes removed the lid of the tub closest to her and pulled out a dazzling scarlet gown accented with black lace. "Oh my God, this is gorgeous!" she exclaimed. "Is this yours?"

"Yes," Dora replied. "It was one of my dance costumes. I wore it for tango exhibitions."

Mercedes examined the exotic gown, admiring the exquisite details. She tried to imagine young Dora wearing it as she glided across the dance floor with her partner.

"There's more," Dora said, her face beaming. "Keep looking."

Mercedes pulled out one gown after another, laying them

out so she could see them in detail. Soon, all the furniture in the room was draped with the brilliantly colored costumes: gowns with long flowing skirts; tiny, short-skirted costumes with spaghetti straps; gowns fashioned from satin and velvet, fur and feathers, rhinestones and sequins.

Dora picked up the various garments that Mercedes set aside, lovingly caressing the fabric, running her fingers over the fancy trim, gazing at them as she held them out in front of her.

"These take up so much space in my small apartment," she said. "But I can't bear to part with them. Everywhere I've moved, I've dragged these big tubs along with me. I've gotten rid of many of my possessions, but never my dance costumes."

"You must've been a fantastic dancer," Mercedes said.

Dora sighed, a faraway look in her eyes. "Yes. Vincent and I had an extraordinary partnership. Together, we were brilliant."

Last week, I told you the story of how my obsession with ballroom dancing led to the end of my relationship with Michael Mitchell. As Mike and I began drifting apart, my bewildered son kept asking me when we were going to see him again. I had to keep coming up with excuses. Finally, after the night at the studio when Mike and I acknowledged our parting of ways, I admitted to the children that we had broken up.

"Good!" Corina huffed.

But Wesley stared at me in shock. "What does it mean to break up?" he asked.

I cast about for an explanation, then resorted to a tired old cliché. "It means that Mike and I don't love each other anymore."

"That's not true!" Wesley protested. "Mike loves us. I know he does."

"Yes," I agreed. "But we decided we weren't suited for each other."

"You decided that!" Wesley hissed, anger glinting in his eyes. As he turned away from me, I heard him mutter, "Mike

was supposed to be my dad."

As you recall, Mercedes, Wesley had no memory of Ivan at that time. Michael Mitchell was the only father figure he'd ever known. While our neighbor Virgil was a grandfather to my son, Mike was a dad, perfectly suited for such a role. It didn't surprise me that the loss of him devastated Wesley. I can't begin to tell you how guilty I felt about that.

I also told you last week about Vincent asking me to be his partner in a dance competition. He decided that we would enter the waltz category. The two of us spent countless hours together practicing for the event. I danced fanatically and compulsively, trying to numb the pain of my breakup with Mike, trying to obliterate the guilt about the heartbreak I'd inflicted on my son.

During our long hours together, Vincent and I learned more about each other's personal life. Vincent had never known anything of my history prior to my relationship with Mike. One day, he asked me whether I'd ever been married. I told him that I was a widowed mother of two, and that my husband had been killed in a bar fight.

I watched Vincent's eyes widen with interest as I divulged that information. It seemed as if that terrible detail about my past added intrigue to his image of me.

I learned that Vincent's day job was selling cars at a local dealership. I figured he was good at it, with his confident manner and his power of persuasion. However, he spent every free hour at the studio, working the job he truly loved.

Vincent told me his late father, who was Puerto Rican, was also a dancer, and that his father's elderly mother still lived in Puerto Rico. Vincent had been born in Puerto Rico but raised in New York City, where he'd lived until he came to South Bend to take the job at Tony O'Reilly's studio.

Vincent was single, but admitted to having been married before. I never knew how many times, as he tended to be vague about such details. I deduced that part of his reason for moving to the Midwest was to distance himself from some relationship that had gone wrong.

"I put the past behind me and keep moving forward," he

told me. As positive as that sounded, I wondered whether that was his way of hiding things he didn't want me, or anyone else, to know about.

Vincent and Tony O'Reilly were the best of friends. Tony relied on Vincent for advice in running his business. Vincent brought with him an air of big-city glamour that would otherwise have been missing from the studio. Tony appreciated that, as it gave him an edge over the local competition. To my surprise, I learned that Tony allowed Vincent to live in a small apartment above the studio.

Despite the euphoria that dancing brought me, I felt guilty about spending so much time away from my children. To make up for that, I started taking Corina to the studio with me. Wesley had no interest in going along with us, opting instead to spend those hours at Virgil and Irene's house.

The first time Corina set foot in the studio, she looked around, taking in the glitzy ambience. "I have to give you credit, Mom," she said. "This is a lot better than your square dancing."

When I introduced her to Vincent, the two of them hit it off immediately. Corina asked him many questions about dancing, and he was so kind as to lead her in a few beginner steps. Of course, he praised her, telling her that someday, she was going to be as brilliant a dancer as her mother was.

I'm not sure that was the best thing to tell my daughter, as she's never wanted to follow in anyone's footsteps. She's always been determined to chart her own course in life. After several trips to the studio, she lost any desire to go back. Still, she maintained a positive attitude about my dancing, never complaining about me being gone so much.

Vincent and I ended up taking second place in our category at the competition. I felt terrible afterwards, thinking I'd let my partner down. With tears in my eyes, I apologized to him for the mistakes I'd made.

He looked at me sternly. "Listen to me, Dori. Don't apologize. You should never say you're sorry when you've done your best. You worked hard, and you did a marvelous job. It just takes time for dance partners to develop chemistry with each other. We'll get there. We'll dazzle the world. There are many first-place trophies in our future. I can guarantee you that."

I stood there pondering my teacher's words, overwhelmed by his presumption that we would have an ongoing partnership.

Then Vincent said, somewhat irritably, "And for heaven's sake, Dori, out of thirty entries in the waltz category, taking second place is pretty damn good. I get tired of your negativity. You should be celebrating, not complaining."

I took those words to heart and walked away from that conversation with a smile on my face.

Mercedes, I've already admitted to you that I was infatuated with Vincent. But I knew that every single one of his female students felt exactly the same way about him.

Vincent had a way of making any woman he danced with feel like a queen. At our Thursday evening parties, each of us women would patiently await our turn to dance with our beloved teacher. We'd beam with pleasure when he'd grace us with his dazzling presence. But we all knew we were enjoying a fantasy. Vincent was above us, out of our realm.

However, because Vincent was spending extra time practicing with me, I soon began to hear resentful comments about him playing favorites. Then the rumor began to fly that Vincent had chased off Michael Mitchell so that he and I could be together. Gossip about a budding relationship between us added intrigue to studio life.

All of this talk confused me, as nothing romantic had ever transpired between Vincent and me. I seemed to be the last person to know that Vincent considered me to be, not only his dance partner, but his girlfriend. I started noticing that between dances, he was often sitting next to me, his arm resting across the back of my chair. Occasionally, I'd feel his hand caressing my shoulder, or his fingers running through a strand of my hair.

Vincent was generous with his complements to all the ladies. He used praise to motivate his students, rather than *berating them for their weaknesses. That made him an effective and extraordinarily popular teacher.*

But while Vincent was affirmative with everyone, he literally showered me with praise. He'd tell me what a gifted dancer I was, what a hard worker, what a quick learner, what a beautiful performer. He'd tell me it was a supreme pleasure to work with me. The line between his regard for me as a dance partner and his feelings for me as a woman seemed blurry, to say the least.

In any case, I was intoxicated with the attention I was receiving from this most desirable of men. I was living out a fairytale, a story about a handsome prince and a peasant girl. Slowly but surely, I moved into the niche of being Vincent's girlfriend, knowing that all the other women in the studio wished they were me.

Remember when I told you that, instead of loving Mike, I loved the way he loved me? Now, I can see a similar dynamic in my relationship with Vincent. I was enamored with his image rather than being attracted to the person he really was. I was in love with the status that being with him afforded me.

Oddly, it took a long time for my supposed romance with Vincent to move beyond the confines of the studio. Even then, it was limited to going out with other couples for drinks after studio parties.

As an Amish girl, I'd been raised to abstain from alcohol. Although I'd drank during rumpschpringe, I'd quickly become disenchanted with alcohol because of my experience with Ivan's overindulgence.

Fortunately, Vincent was not the problem drinker my husband had been. When we went out with other couples, he limited himself to one or two drinks. Far too sophisticated for beer, he ordered cocktails with exotic-sounding names for himself and me.

I'd sit there coyly sipping a drink I didn't particularly enjoy, growing bored while I listened to Vincent and his friends talk about nothing much at all. Imitating the other women, I learned to giggle and cling seductively to my man.

The fellows in the studio crowd enjoyed teasing Vincent about the sizzling sexual activity he must be enjoying with his much younger girlfriend. They made suggestive comments that left me feeling uncomfortable. You're wincing Mercedes. I'm glad to know that if you found yourself in such a situation, you wouldn't put up with it for a minute.

My daughter tells me that I've suffered from something called "learned helplessness." I was raised to be a docile and submissive female. I had never learned how to stand up for myself in the face of mistreatment. It's hard to look back and see how vulnerable and defenseless I was in my younger years.

But to tell you the truth, outside of the flirtation and posturing with the studio crowd, there was nothing at all happening in my relationship with Vincent. I began to feel impatient, and a bit worried.

When Vincent and I would go out for drinks with his friends, the two of us would travel together in his car. Afterwards, he'd drive me back to where I'd left my car in the studio parking lot. One Thursday night, instead of just dropping me off, he surprised me by getting out of his car and walking me over to my vehicle. Then, he took me into his arms and planted a lingering kiss on my lips.

I tried not to notice that kissing Vincent wasn't nearly as thrilling as dancing with him. I had a strong suspicion that the whole scene had been staged for the benefit of the people who were milling around in the parking lot.

As he kissed me a second time, he ran his hands over my body in a way that he'd never done before. Deep down, I knew it wasn't my sexual appeal that animated him in that moment. It was the presence of onlookers.

Several weeks later, on a night when my children were with Virgil and Irene, Vincent finally invited me to his apartment above the studio. I assumed that meant he was ready for physical intimacy.

I'd been looking forward to that step in our relationship with both anticipation and dread. Lovemaking with Mike had always felt easy and natural. But I imagined that with Vincent, it would be a completely different matter. The thought of having sex with such a worldly-wise man was as frightening as losing my virginity, and I wondered whether I'd be good enough for him.

Mercedes, I don't think I've ever been so shocked as when I stepped inside Vincent's apartment. I must've stood still for a full minute trying to take everything in. I had imagined my dance instructor to be living in a place as stylish as his personal appearance. In reality, his living quarters were exactly the opposite of that.

There was no glamour, no reflection of Vincent's personality in the apartment, just a few pieces of shabby furniture and overwhelming clutter. Remains of carryout meals littered the kitchen table and countertops, and a stale odor permeated the entire place.

Vincent offered me a drink. When he opened the refrigerator, I saw that it held little more than a bottle of wine and half-empty containers of condiments.

We took our drinks to the dimly lit living room and sat several feet apart on the grungy sofa to watch television. After half an hour, Vincent yawned and stretched out his arm to encircle my shoulders. I snuggled up to him, trying desperately to breathe romance into the moment.

"I'm tired," he said. "Let's go to bed."

He got up, and I followed him into his bedroom, only to receive another shock. The mess in Vincent's sleeping quarters far surpassed the dismal state of the living room and kitchen. It looked as if a whirlwind had hit the room. Clothing had been flung across the furniture, some items landing in piles on the floor. Messy stacks of paper on an old desk had spilled over onto the chair, and then onto the floor. General rubbish filled up the rest of the floor space, so that I literally had to wade through things to get to the bed.

I recognized pieces of Vincent's dance wardrobe among the mess: tuxedo trousers, a tie, a cummerbund. When I saw several suits in a drycleaner's bag draped across the headboard, I reassured myself that at least Vincent wasn't dressing himself from the piles on the floor. Still, I couldn't imagine how he managed to emerge from the mess sporting his million-dollar look.

Vincent swept a pile of dirty laundry off the bed and threw back the covers. Without a word, he began undressing, tossing his clothing on the floor as he stripped.

Not knowing what else to do, I followed suit, removing my own clothing while choking back tears of disappointment. I'd envisioned my first sexual encounter with my new boyfriend to be much more of an event than this.

There we stood, eyeing each other's naked bodies in the dim light of the room. "You're gorgeous," Vincent said rather offhandedly.

"So are you," I lied, finding it difficult to look at his pudgy middle-aged physique.

Vincent got into bed. "Well, climb on in," he grunted. Obligingly, I crawled under the covers and lay next to him. The sheets smelled musty, as if they hadn't been laundered in months.

As I'd grown accustomed to the lean physiques of my former lovers, Ivan and Mike, I felt disoriented when Vincent took me in his arms and pulled me close to his fleshy body. He began kissing me, somewhat mechanically. I had the odd feeling that it was more out of obligation than desire.

Then we made love. Well, sort of. It was, quite frankly, a disappointing experience.

"Sorry, Dori," Vincent said. "I'm really tired. I'll make it up to you later." Then he rolled over and began snoring within seconds.

I lay with my back to him, curled up in a tight ball, clutching the covers to my chest. I willed myself not to cry, but I couldn't hold back the tears that spilled from my eyes and soaked my musty pillow. "What in the world am I doing here?" I asked myself.

I thought about the comfort of Mike's arms and began to sob. Knowing that my companion, whose loud snoring reverberated throughout the small room, would never hear me, I whispered Mike's name, beseeching him to come to my rescue as he'd done so many times before. Too distraught to sleep, I lay there for hours, feeling totally lost in the bed of my new lover.

Mercedes, you look like you feel sorry for me. It really was a pitiful moment. I actually contemplated slipping out of bed, getting dressed, and leaving Vincent's apartment without waking him.

But I knew that if I ended my relationship with him in such a manner, I would also be ending our dance partnership. I would never be able to step foot in the studio again. I had far too much invested in dancing to ruin everything I had accomplished.

I must've fallen asleep in the early hours of the morning, because my memory of waking up in that apartment is so vivid. I opened my eyes to see Vincent sitting at his desk sorting through a stack of papers. He was shirtless, his belly bulging over the waistband of a pair of ragged sweatpants. His face was unshaven, and the sleek black hair that was usually swept back in a debonair style now hung in strands over his forehead.

The unexpected sight dismayed me, but at the same time, it amused me. I had to bite my lip to keep from laughing. "Oh my God!" I thought. "My celebrity dance teacher's alter ego is an aging slob!"

When Vincent saw that I was awake, he flashed me his charming smile. "Good morning, sexy," he said. "Want some breakfast?"

I got out of bed and followed him into the kitchen. There on the table were two cups of carryout coffee, along with a bag of donuts. I figured he'd gone out to get the food while I was still sleeping.

After we ate, he led me back into the bedroom, and before I knew it, we were making love again. Once again, I had the feeling he was delivering what he thought he owed me. Passion on his part was markedly absent. As young people would say today, he just wasn't into it.

However, this time our encounter was more successful, somewhat redeeming the disappointment of the previous night.

Afterwards, as we lay side by side in the bed, Vincent asked in a teasing tone, "Are you my woman now?"

The question struck me as odd. It sounded as if he wanted me to agree that I was his property.

"What do you think?" I asked, rising up on my elbow and leaning over to kiss him. I couldn't bring myself to utter a straightforward acknowledgement of this new state of affairs.

Nevertheless, I knew that a bond of sorts had been forged between us. Like it or not, I had entered Vincent's world on a deeper level. Much as I'd done when I was married to Ivan, I determined to make the best of a situation that was far from optimal.

Mercedes, as I tell you all this, I suddenly understand the context for Vincent's question. In attempting to forge a romantic bond with me, he was trying to ensure the permanence of our dance partnership. In his mid-forties, his career was on the wane, while I, at thirty-one, still had years of growth ahead of me as a dancer. There would always be the possibility of him losing me to a more youthful partner. Knowing me as he did, he probably figured that adding the element of romance to our relationship would keep me tied to him for years to come.

Vincent and I continued our halfhearted dating habits. However, the vast majority of our time together was spent in the studio. In that environment, our relationship sparkled. It was now clear to everyone that we were a couple, the most dazzling dance couple in the studio. We were the envy of all, setting the bar to which others could only hope to measure up.

Vincent stopped charging me for lessons, as I'd crossed the line from being his student to being his partner. Much to his amazement, I quickly caught up to his level of skill. I completed the silver level in all of the dances he taught, and rapidly mastered steps in the gold level. We spent countless hours practicing advanced routines in preparation for future exhibitions and competitions.

Despite our lackluster romance, dancing with Vincent enthralled me, mesmerizing me to the point where I'd lose track of time. The hours would fly by, and I'd be unaware of

180

the fact that I was growing tired. When we'd stop for the night, long after everyone else had left the studio, I'd rush home and fall into bed, sleeping only a few hours before getting up for work the next morning.

People frequently commented on the chemistry between Vincent and me. During our exhibition dances, we'd strike sensual poses that left the audience gasping. Yes, while dancing together, Vincent and I were on fire, hungry lovers yearning for a passionate union. But the spark between us extinguished itself once we left the dance floor.

In fact, off the dance floor, we were quite content to stay in our separate worlds. Truthfully, I had little desire to spend time with Vincent away from the studio. From this vantage point, Mercedes, I can see that he and I shared nothing at all in common except for our love of dancing.

However, as much as I hated Vincent's little apartment, I did spend the occasional night there, desperately trying to convince myself that there was more to our relationship than dancing.

I'll never forget the first dance competition in which Vincent and I were awarded a first-place trophy. Although my partner was used to having crowds of people adore him, bowing to a wildly applauding audience was a heady experience for me.

The two of us were billed as "Vincent Perez and Dori Graber," and we performed the tango. Mercedes, I wore that stunning red dress, the first one you pulled out of the tub. At that time, my hair was dyed black, and I had darkened my pale skin with the help of a tanning bed. If it hadn't been for my blue eyes, I would've looked almost as Hispanic as Vincent.

As we left the dance floor amidst applause and whistles of admiration, I realized I was now seen in the same exotic light as was Vincent. No one could've possibly guessed that I'd lived my early life as a fair-skinned, sandy-haired Amish girl.

Back in the dressing room, Vincent hugged me, his eyes glistening with tears. Then he said the most heartfelt words

I'd ever heard him speak. "Dori, I've been dancing for more than thirty years. I've had many partners, but none of them quite suited me. There were always problems. Most of them were prima donnas, hard to get along with. And some of them just didn't click with me. Now, when I'm getting to be an old man, you come along, my perfect partner. You learn so quickly, and you don't give me any trouble. You're gorgeous and showy. We move together like a dream, as if we were made for each other. I just wish I would've found you years ago."

I don't recall how I responded to Vincent's impassioned speech, but I do remember how I felt. At that moment, my life seemed complete. My every wish had come true. I had soared high into the sky, landing on a cloud of euphoria. I imagined I would stay there forever.

One Thursday night in March, I walked into the studio to find it draped in new decorations: hearts, doves, roses, lace, all in sparkling white. I assumed we were having another theme party. Although I was puzzled as to why I hadn't been told about it, I didn't give the matter much thought.

I sensed an undercurrent of excitement among the studio crowd. People were whispering and giving each other knowing looks, and Vincent's mood seemed unusually ebullient. When I asked him what was going on, he smiled but said nothing.

Toward the end of the evening, Tony O'Reilly called for a break in the dancing. He delivered a short speech about the importance of the studio family and the lasting relationships forged among the members.

Then, he turned the floor over to Vincent. And with a crowd of eager onlookers, Vincent strolled over to me, got down on one knee, presented me with a ring, and asked me to marry him.

The other teachers and students burst into noisy cheering and whistling. But after a few minutes, the commotion quieted down, and an expectant hush fell over the room. I realized I was on center stage, that I had an audience awaiting my response to Vincent's proposal.

What could I say but, "Yes?" Even though a quiet little voice in the recesses of my mind whispered, "Dora, this isn't right," I could say nothing but, "Yes." I couldn't ruin the party. The grand occasion allowed no room for doubt or hesitation.

So, I beamed at my dance partner and said, "Yes, Vincent, I will marry you."

The crowd burst into cheering again, and the champagne corks popped. Tony O'Reilly called for an engagement waltz. For a few minutes, Vincent and I had the dance floor to ourselves, while our audience gushed over our beauty and brilliance.

Only later did I recognize the significance of the timing of this event. The holiday parties were over, and the last excitement we'd seen in the studio had been on Valentine's Day. It was late March, the weather was dreary, and attendance at the Thursday night party had been falling off. What better way to liven things up than to throw an engagement party for the dance king?

For years, I wondered whether Vincent would've ever proposed to me without the opportunity to make a spectacle of the occasion. I hate to say this, Mercedes, but I don't believe Vincent had the capacity to feel deeply about anyone else. As you might've deduced, he was enamored with his own image, self-absorbed to the point of narcissism.

However, I can now see the thread of sincerity in his proposal. He wasn't in love with me, but he truly wanted me in his life. As I mentioned earlier, his motivation was simple. As an aging dancer, he'd found a younger partner who refreshed and enhanced his image. By marrying me, he could ensure that I wouldn't wander away with an up-and-coming star. Marriage would solidify the bond of our dance partnership.

The morning after the engagement party, I awoke with a sober realization: if I was indeed going to marry Vincent, I had to step out of my fantasy world and take care of business. And the first item on my list of things to do was to break the news of my engagement to Corina and Wesley.

Only a few months earlier, I had informed them of my breakup with Michael Mitchell. How was I to explain the fact that I was already planning a marriage to someone else?

I spent all that day trying to muster my courage, rehearsing a speech in my mind. The following morning, as the children and I were eating breakfast, I finally broached the subject.

"I have something I need to talk about," I told them. My mouth felt so dry that I almost choked on my words, and I didn't think I could continue.

"Well, spit it out," Corina said impatiently.

When I didn't immediately respond, she eyed me suspiciously. "You're dating someone again, aren't you?"

I nodded.

"It's Vincent, isn't it? You're dating Vincent."

"How did you know?" I asked, dumbfounded.

She crossed her arms over her chest and gave me a smug smile. "I could tell by the way you guys acted around each other."

When Corina had spent time with Vincent and me at the studio, I hadn't given her any indication that he was anything more to me than my dance instructor. But I knew my daughter had observed the sensual way we'd danced together. I wondered what impression that had left in her mind.

"Are you going to marry Vincent?" she asked.

"I-I think so," I stammered.

I averted my eyes from Corina's demanding stare and glanced at Wesley. His face was contorted in distress. My placid son, who usually hid his feelings so well, was unable to conceal them this time.

"Wesley," I said, my heart seizing with pain. "Are you upset with me?"

My son pushed away from the table, ran into the living room, flopped down on the sofa, and buried his face in his arms. I followed him and sat on the floor next to the sofa, calling his name, begging him to talk to me. When he refused to respond, I tried to gather him into my arms, but his little body was stiff and unyielding.

Tears poured down my face as I told Wesley how much I loved him, how much I wanted him to be happy. But I knew he didn't believe a word I was saying.

Suddenly, he sat up and screamed at the top of his lungs, "You were supposed to marry Mike!" Then he curled himself into a ball, sobbing as if his heart had been shattered into a million pieces. I knew that something inside of him had broken, that he no longer trusted his mother to do right by him.

"Maybe you'll like Vincent," I said.

"No, I won't," Wesley sobbed. "I hate him! I hate him!"

I finally gave up and walked away, mercilessly berating myself for the pain I'd inflicted on my innocent child.

"How can it be," I asked myself, "that my decision to marry Vincent makes some people so happy and others so miserable?" At that point, Mercedes, I hadn't fully considered what would make me happy. I hadn't learned to do that yet.

A month before Vincent proposed to me, Tony O'Reilly had hired a new instructor, a young man named Shane. Without a doubt, Shane was an accomplished dancer. But his personality proved to be detrimental to studio life. He was the proverbial "bull in a china shop," perpetually doing or saying things that offended students and other teachers. Soon, Tony and Vincent were having conversations about what to do with Shane.

Shane loved finding ways to get under Vincent's skin. He'd approach me when I was sitting next to Vincent and would ask me to dance. Then he'd take my hand and strut out onto the dance floor, where he'd lead me in steps more acrobatic than a man Vincent's age would be able to do. In front of everyone, he'd make a point of teaching me new steps, as if he was now my instructor.

To be shown up like that infuriated Vincent. I knew that losing his dance partner to someone more capable would be a humiliation he'd never overcome. Shane also knew that about Vincent. He loved poking that sore spot.

One Thursday evening a few weeks after the

engagement party, Shane sat down next to me while Vincent was dancing with one of his students. As usual, Vincent was playing the role of prince charming.

Shane shook his head, smirking. "Vincent makes himself out to be such a lady's man. You know who he really is, don't you, Dori?"

"Of course, I do," I said defensively. "He's my fiancé."

Shane threw back his head and laughed. "You mean you've never wondered why Vincent takes all those young men upstairs to his apartment?"

His words confused me. You have to remember, Mercedes, how naïve I was back then. I understood little to nothing about same-sex relationships. Deep down, I'd always known that Vincent wasn't attracted to me in the same way Michael Mitchell had been, or even in the way Ivan had been in the early years of our marriage. But I'd allowed my thoughts to go no farther than that.

Apparently, someone had overheard what Shane said to me and reported it to Tony. Several days later, I heard that Shane had been fired. He was never allowed to set foot in the studio again. As close as Tony and Vincent were, I knew Tony would protect his friend's reputation at all costs.

Shortly after our engagement, I suggested to Vincent that he needed to spend some time with my children before we got married.

"I already met your daughter," he said. "We got along just fine."

"Yes," I said, "but I also have a son. You need to get to know him, too."

Vincent kept putting me off, saying he didn't have time in his schedule to drive all the way over to my place in Middlebury. Even though I was equally busy, I agreed to bring the children to South Bend. I wasn't about to let them see the state of Vincent's apartment, so we agreed to have dinner in a restaurant.

Corina handled herself well during that visit, as I knew she would. She asked Vincent polite questions, not only about dancing, but about his job at the car dealership.

Whenever he'd ask her a question, she'd elaborate at length, filling up any uneasy breaks in the conversation.

Unsurprisingly, my son passed that hour at the dinner table in almost complete silence. When he failed to answer any of Vincent's questions with more than an indifferent monosyllable, Corina jumped in and spoke for him.

On the drive home, I asked the children what they thought of Vincent.

"He's cool," Corina said. "I like him."

Wesley remained silent. I didn't push him for a response, as I wasn't ready to hear his true opinion. I convinced myself that the visit had gone well, and I allowed myself to be optimistic about our future as a family.

After Vincent met my children, I tried to persuade him to introduce me to his family. He wasn't enthusiastic about the idea and tended to be evasive whenever I brought the matter up. I never did meet his two adult children, as he had little contact with them at that point in time. He had several brothers living in New York City, whom I never met. But I did have the pleasure of meeting his sister Isabella, who lived several hours away in Chicago.

How I adored Isabella! When we first met, she charmed me instantly, much in the same way Vincent had charmed me. Isabella was ten years younger than Vincent, only a few years older than me. She was plump and very beautiful, with lively dark eyes and a cascade of black curls that hung to her waist. And she had a big, warm, colorful personality.

Isabella talked nonstop, constantly entertaining her audience with her over-the-top stories. I never grew tired of listening to her. Whenever I was in her company, her lighthearted humor melted away my worries. She took me under her wing, affectionately referring to me as the little sister she'd never had. I took to that role eagerly, as I'd never been the subject of much interest in the eyes of my biological siblings.

Isabella showered me with a great deal of loving attention, far more than Vincent did. Early on, she informed me that she usually didn't approve of her older brother's *choices in women, but that she liked me. She told me I was much classier than Vincent's previous wives and girlfriends, head and shoulders above them. Confronting her brother with her fists raised in a mock threat, she informed him that she'd beat him to within an inch of his life if he didn't make things work with me.*

If I had any doubts about marrying Vincent, they were overshadowed by my enthusiasm for becoming Isabella's sister-in-law.

Three months after our engagement, Vincent and I were married in a romantic June wedding. And where do you supposed the ceremony was held? At Tony O'Reilly's studio, of course. Our wedding became yet another occasion for studio fanfare.

Sadly, I didn't have much input into planning my special day, as Vincent and Tony made most of the arrangements. Isabella was eager to help. Her influence made the occasion a magnificent affair, with lavish flowers, an ornate cake, and my expensive wedding gown. What a contrast to my first wedding, a simple ceremony in the county courthouse!

Mercedes, let me show you some of the pictures in our wedding album. I imagine you've never seen a bride in a dress like this. It might seem a little risqué, but it suits a dance queen, don't you think? All my studio friends raved about my gown.

My children were in the wedding party. Look at this picture of Corina as a bridesmaid. Isn't she gorgeous? She was the product of Isabella's artful care, and she rivaled me for the center of attention. She loved every minute of it.

Here she is, posing with Tony O'Reilly. He gushed over her, telling her she'd make a beautiful dancer, predicting that she'd be the future star of his studio. She batted her eyes at him and promised to sign up for lessons, something she had no intention of doing.

Here's a picture of my little Wesley. He looks so forlorn in his tuxedo. Poor thing, he endured the wedding with such patience.

On that unforgettable day, I negotiated the final step in

the transformation of my persona by taking on an exotic name that befitted my new life. I was now Dori Perez, living in a world that young Dora Miller couldn't have imagined in her wildest dreams.

After the wedding, I put my children in the care of Virgil and Irene, and Vincent and I flew to Puerto Rico for our honeymoon. Going to Puerto Rico had been my idea. I was convinced that if we wanted to make our marriage a success, I needed to understand my husband's culture. I was fully prepared to incorporate aspects of it into our married life.

Mercedes, that's how serious I was about making my marriage work. If Vincent had been willing to put in the same effort, things probably would've turned out differently.

While Vincent's parents were both deceased, his elderly grandmother was still living in a small village a short distance from Puerto Rico's capitol of San Juan. So, the first stop on our honeymoon trip was a visit with her.

Vincent's "abuela" was a diminutive, sharp-tongued woman in her nineties. She spoke no English, so Vincent translated the limited conversations between her and me. I'd never heard Vincent speak Spanish before, and I enjoyed the thrill of hearing my new husband converse in a language that I associated with romance. We stayed in his grandmother's tiny house for two days.

As we were saying our goodbyes, Vincent's grandmother took a long look at me, then turned to her grandson and delivered a scolding monologue. I was afraid she was telling him that she didn't approve of me. After we left her home, I asked him what she'd said.

Vincent, still looking chastened from the scolding, grinned sheepishly at me. "She told me you're a good woman, the best I've ever had. She said I need to grow up, settle down with you, and become a good husband."

I give Vincent's grandmother credit for my lovely honeymoon, because her lecture seemed to yield results. As Vincent showed me the sights of Puerto Rico, his affection seemed more genuine.

We first went to San Juan, where we visited old churches and a centuries-old fortress built to protect the city. The next day, we drove an hour outside San Juan to enjoy the mountains and waterfalls in the El Yunque National Forest. Our last few days were spent driving along the shoreline of the island, enjoying the magnificent blue waters and stopping to explore quaint little villages.

At night, my husband made love to me with a depth of feeling he'd never shown before. All in all, it was a spectacular trip, a once-in-a-lifetime experience. I can still recall the details as vividly as if they happened yesterday.

As we boarded our plane to return home, my heart was filled with hope. I believed we had crossed a threshold into a new level of intimacy. I fully expected the fairytale to continue.

Mercedes, you ask where Vincent and I lived after our honeymoon. That's where my story takes a difficult turn.

During the three short months between our engagement and our wedding, when I was scrambling to make plans for married life, Vincent was reluctant to discuss the matter of housing. I knew the children and I couldn't move into his tiny upstairs apartment, and I doubted that he'd want to move to my home in Middlebury.

I proposed various options, but Vincent repeatedly diverted our conversations away from such topics. I began to realize that he wanted the image of being married, but that he didn't want to face the tough issues that came with merging his life with someone else's. Deep down, I knew he didn't want to give up his apartment above the studio.

Finally, he agreed to my idea of renting a place in Elkhart, which would put us halfway between his work in South Bend and my work in Middlebury. So, a month prior to our wedding, I informed my landlord that I was giving up the home I'd rented from him for fifteen years, and I signed a lease on a house in Elkhart.

Corina was excited about the move. She was fourteen at the time, and had just finished up her last year of middle school. My adventuresome daughter was eager to leave

Middlebury behind and start her freshman year at a larger school in Elkhart.

But as you might imagine, it was very difficult for Wesley to leave the only home he'd ever known. Even though I promised him that he could still visit Virgil and Irene, the thought of not having them next door was more than he could bear. And of course, our move came right on the heels of his losing his relationship with Michael Mitchell.

It goes without saying that Virgil and Irene were devastated to see my children and me leave. My decision to move to Elkhart crushed their hearts. Looking back, that chapter of my life seems like a time when I behaved selfishly, a time when I made choices that hurt others so badly. I've had to work hard on forgiving myself for that.

After our honeymoon, I expected my new husband to help my children and me pack up our belongings and move into our new home. To my dismay, Vincent managed to make himself scarce during that time, leaving it up to Corina, Wesley, and me to load all of our furniture onto the moving van. He seemed quite happy to continue spending his nights in his old apartment.

The first night the children and I spent in our new home, I slept alone in the bed I'd purchased for my husband and me. The following day, I did something I'd never done before. I confronted Vincent at the studio.

"What's going on?" I asked him. "I see less of you now than I did before we got married."

"I don't know what you're talking about, Dori," he snapped. "Anyway, now is not the time or place to discuss our personal business."

But I pressed on. "Forgive me for being so presumptuous, but don't a husband and wife generally live together in the same house? Why did you ask me to marry you if you didn't intend to share a life with me? It looks as if I've uprooted my children for no reason at all."

I could tell Vincent didn't appreciate my tone of voice. His jaw clenched and his eyes glinted with anger. "These things take a while, Dori. In case you haven't noticed, I'm working two jobs. I haven't had time to move my things."

I knew I was pushing the limits with him, but I couldn't contain my anger. "If you don't want to move, then I'll move. I'll pack up my things again, and my children and I will move right back to Middlebury." With that, I turned my back on my new husband and marched out the door.

Mercedes, I'd never stood up to Vincent before. As you can imagine, his dominant personality demanded to be in charge at all times. Just as I'd followed his lead in the dance, I'd allowed him to direct me in other aspects of my life. I can only imagine the look on his face when I walked away from him.

For the sake of my children, I did my best to keep my composure when I got home. But Corina had an uncanny way of sensing when something was troubling me. "Mom, why aren't you at the studio with Vincent tonight?" she asked.

"I have things to do around here," I told her.

My daughter knew full well that household chores had never before kept me from dancing. She shot me a haughty look. "When is this husband of yours going to move in with us?"

"He will eventually," I said. "He hasn't had the chance yet."

She rolled her eyes as if she didn't believe me.

As soon as the children were in bed for the night, I went to my room and allowed my pent-up feelings to release in frustrated sobs. I must've cried myself to sleep, because the next thing I knew, the ringing telephone woke me up. It was Vincent.

"Dori," he said, "did you realize you forgot to give me a key to our house?"

"What?" I mumbled in my state of sleepy confusion.

"I'm coming over tonight. Leave the front door unlocked, and I'll be there shortly."

True to his word, my husband climbed into bed with me half an hour later. He reached for me and drew me into his arms. "I'm sorry, Dori," he said. "I've been acting like a jerk. I'll make it up to you, I promise."

The next moment, he was snoring loudly. I extricated myself from his embrace and rolled over. Even though his noisy snoring kept me awake, I lay there smiling, once again filled with hope.

The following weekend, with the help of some of his studio friends, Vincent moved his belongings into our home. Some of them, anyway. He made the point of telling me there wasn't enough room in our house for all of his things. He declined to tell me what he did with the rest. Months later, I found out that he'd never completely given up his apartment above the studio.

And so, our married life began. During the day, Vincent and I went our separate ways to work, and at night, we tried to bring our disparate lives together.

Actually, I was the one who tried. Vincent's response to family life was to distance himself from it. He was seldom home in the evenings, as he taught at the studio five nights a week. He turned one of our upstairs bedrooms into what he called his personal office. It ended up being his hideaway, where he napped, ate, read magazines, and watched television. He rarely acknowledged my children. Clearly, he had no intention of taking on the role of stepparent.

Early on, I tried orchestrating family dinners, envisioning the four of us chatting about our days over homecooked meals. However, Vincent found innumerable reasons not to be present at dinnertime. His meals tended to be takeout food at odd hours of the night.

I'm sure Wesley was relieved that he didn't have to contend with his stepfather. He acted as if Vincent didn't even live in our home. But Corina didn't adjust well to this new phase of our family life. I believe that after initially forming a promising connection with Vincent, she felt deeply hurt by his later indifference toward her. She'd been looking forward to having him as a father figure. I can understand her anger when Vincent failed her in that role.

However, Corina's anger created difficulty for me, as she began baiting Vincent at every opportunity, hurling sarcastic comments at him. I made every effort to block her attacks, steering her away from encounters with him whenever I could.

So, instead of longing to have my husband at home with me, I began to feel relieved when he was gone. The sweet intimacy of our honeymoon quickly dissipated, and I knew it would never return.

Before we moved to Elkhart, I had promised Wesley that he could spend at least one weekend a month with Virgil and Irene. Sadly, that arrangement was over before it even started. Virgil suffered a stroke three weeks after we left. He never recovered his health, and passed away a few months later.

Wesley took Virgil's death very hard. I tried to talk with him about it, but my son had little to say. He only withdrew further into himself.

Of course, we brought Wesley's dog Bob with us when we moved to our new home. I hoped that having the ongoing relationship with his beloved pet would help Wesley adjust to the change. However, one month after Virgil passed away, Bob was hit by a car when he ran into traffic.

We rushed him to a veterinary clinic, hoping to save his life. But his injuries were too extensive. The veterinarian told us our best option was to humanely euthanize him in order to spare him the suffering involved with a prolonged death.

Wesley held Bob in his arms while the doctor administered the lethal injection. My son's face was an expressionless mask that covered his unspeakable pain.

As we walked out of the clinic after that tragic ordeal, he said only one thing to me: "This never would've happened if we would've stayed in Middlebury."

After that, Wesley stopped communicating with me altogether, much as he'd done as a toddler after his father died. I knew that multiple traumas in such a short span of time were more than his sensitive nature could bear.

Mercedes, I simply didn't know what to do for my son. There had always been a part of Wesley that I couldn't reach, and after all those losses, it seemed as if I couldn't *reach any part of him. Knowing how I failed my son during that time is one of the reasons why I feel I've never been a good mother to him.*

Several months after school started in the fall, I checked in with Wesley's sixth grade teacher to see how he was doing. She seemed surprised by my concerns. "He's one of the quiet children in my classroom," she said. "But he's made a few friends. He does his schoolwork. So, I can't say I have any complaints about him."

I was relieved to hear that Wesley was adjusting well to at least one aspect of his new life.

Of course, Vincent and I continued with our dance partnership. We spent countless hours at the studio perfecting our routines. There, all was well between my husband and me.

In that way, we were fortunate. The world of competitive dancing can be rigorous and cutthroat. I've watched dance couples engage in bitter power struggles as they strive for higher levels of achievement, blaming each other for failures. I've seen partnerships dissolve because of this.

But Vincent and I didn't struggle with each other. We worked together with amazing ease. Sometimes, he would look at me tenderly and say, "Dori, you're fantastic. You're the best partner I've ever had."

He always said "partner," not "wife." Still, the compliment was gratifying, and at those moments, it didn't matter to me that the rest of our shared life offered no satisfaction.

What was there to do but to keep on dancing? Dancing became more of a compulsion than ever. I was afraid to stop. I was terrified of what would happen if I did.

Mercedes, you're wondering what Elliott had to say about that phase of my life. That's a good question. He and I were talking about that this morning when he came to help me pull the tubs out of my closet.

The truth is that Elliott and I didn't have much communication during my years of marriage to Vincent. I didn't know how to explain to him the peculiar arrangement

I was in. I was afraid he would ask me questions I didn't want to think about. I was afraid he'd know that I wasn't being true to myself.

As I mentioned several weeks ago, my efforts to stay in contact with my parents diminished over the years. However, I believed they needed to know that I had remarried, and that I had moved from Middlebury to Elkhart.

When I told Vincent of my intention to visit my parents, he let me know he wanted no part of my plan. "Dori, you've already told me you don't get along with your parents," he said. "Why do you insist on revisiting the past? From my experience, it never does any good to stir up an old can of worms."

I probably should've listened to him. I can't imagine why I thought introducing Vincent to my mother and father would be a good idea. I suppose the longing for acceptance by one's parents never dies.

I continued to pester Vincent about the idea until he grudgingly relented. Late one Sunday afternoon, after we'd spent several hours practicing in the studio, he and I drove over to my family's farm near Middlebury.

From the moment Vincent and I stepped across my parents' threshold, things went wrong. Since the Amish have no telephones, I was unable to call ahead and inform them we were coming. So, our visit caught them off guard, and they were absolutely shocked to see us.

I'd go so far as to say my parents didn't recognize me at first, with my makeup, my dyed hair, and my foreign-looking husband in tow.

"Mom and Dad," I said, "I want you to meet my new husband. He and I got married a few months ago." But instead of greeting us with welcoming smiles, my parents' faces hardened into expressions of disapproval.

Vincent stared around their home, astonished by the old-fashioned furnishings: the kerosene lamps, the woodburning stove, my mother's treadle sewing machine. I realized I hadn't adequately prepared him for what to expect in an Amish house.

My parents were just about to sit down to their Sunday supper. To their credit, they rose above their practice of shunning and invited us to join them.

My father delivered a longwinded prayer before the meal, including a petition for the Holy Spirit to convict all those who'd strayed from the path of righteousness. As we began to eat, my mother mentioned that they'd been to a church service that morning. She fixed her sad eyes on me and asked where Vincent and I were attending church.

I desperately did not want to tell my parents that instead of worshipping in a house of God that day, my husband and I had been in the studio, engaged in the most sinful activity of dancing.

"Vincent and I just moved to Elkhart," I mumbled. "We're not quite settled yet, and we haven't found a church."

Vincent shot me an incredulous look, as if he couldn't fathom where that response had come from. Although he'd been raised Catholic, he didn't actively practice that religion, and he and I had never even entertained the idea of attending church together.

I'm sure my mother picked up on the truth behind my implausible excuse. Tears sprang to her eyes, and her face remained downcast for the rest of the meal.

From that point on, references to my parents' religious beliefs dominated our dinner conversation, along with inferences that my husband and I were falling short of doing God's will. All that talk must've seemed like a foreign language to Vincent. From time to time, he'd shoot me a look that said, "Is this for real?"

Finally, he'd listened to enough innuendos about his character, and he spoke up to my father. "This is a free country, Mr. Miller," he said. "We're all entitled to live the way we want to. You have no right to judge me, and if you don't mind, sir, I'd like you to keep your negative opinions of me to yourself."

You're laughing, Mercedes. It's funny now, but back then, it was absolutely terrifying. I don't believe anyone had ever spoken like that to my domineering father, and the outraged expression on his face was awful to see. The four of us endured the rest of the meal in cold silence. Vincent and I excused ourselves at the earliest opportunity, telling my parents we had things to do that evening.

As we said our goodbyes, my father sulked in the background, while my mother clung to me, pleading, "Come back to the fold, Dora. It's never too late."

I nearly ran from my parents' house, vowing with each step to never return. Without a word to each other, Vincent and I got into the car and headed for home. I squeezed my eyes shut, holding my breath, trying to ward off the pain that threatened to consume me. When I finally dared to sneak a peek at my husband, I saw that his jaw was clenched in anger.

"Did you know this was going to happen, Dori?" he asked.

"No," I mumbled, turning to stare out the window.

"I don't understand why you insist on bringing such complications into our life," he said. "I did what you asked this one time, but I hope you know I'm never doing it again. Whatever craziness happened during your childhood, it's over and done with, and we're not going to revisit it. Okay?"

"Don't worry," I said. "I'm never going back there again."

After recovering from my disconcerting visit with my parents, my relationship with Vincent settled back into its former pattern: long hours of practicing dance routines in the studio while living separate lives outside the studio. I couldn't help but be troubled by the emptiness in my marriage. Time and again, I tried to do something to remedy the situation.

First, I suggested to Vincent that we consider looking for a home to buy, instead of just renting. He brushed me off with, "When would I have the time to go house-hunting?"

Next, I tried to interest him in planning a family vacation. "If you want to take your children somewhere," he said, "go right ahead. I don't have a problem with it."

My last desperate attempt at building a family life was suggesting that he and I spend one evening a week playing games and watching movies with my children. He shot me an incredulous look. "Where on earth do you come up with these ideas, Dori? Don't you have enough to do with your job and dancing?"

At that point, I knew deep down that nothing in my marriage was ever going to change. Instead of dwelling on that fact, I saved myself from despair by placing my focus back on dancing. When I finally decided to accept the status quo, to stop expecting anything more from Vincent than being my dance partner, our life flowed smoothly.

Vincent and I continued to star in exhibitions and competitions, creating a name for ourselves in the local circles of semi-professional ballroom dancing. We were now billed as "Vincent and Dori Perez," and were well-known in dance clubs within a three-hundred-mile radius of Tony O'Reilly's studio.

We were photographed by the press more times than I could count, in dramatic poses with Vincent gazing adoringly at me. We were held up as an example of the perfect married dancing couple. Women I didn't know would approach me and tell me, with sighs of envy, how lucky I was to have a husband who could dance.

Despite Vincent's lack of effort, my sister-in-law Isabella helped to hold our family together during those years. She loved her niece and nephew, and they adored her in return. While my children barely tolerated Vincent's aloof presence, things were different when Isabella was around. Even Wesley would light up when I'd tell him she was coming to visit. Isabella made the children and me feel like our family life was worth something.

When Vincent and I traveled to dance events, Isabella would often accompany us with my children in tow. I'd see her in the audience proudly cheering our performance, with Corina and Wesley sitting on either side of her.

She loved helping me choose my dance costumes. Many of the beautiful gowns in these tubs are ones she picked out. She was able to envision outfits I couldn't have come up with on my own. I believe I was as well known for my costumes as I was for my dancing.

Our life rolled along like this for almost four years. Vincent's fiftieth birthday came and went, while I entered my mid-thirties. Sometimes, I'd ask myself, "What will happen to us after the dancing is done?" But I'd never allow myself to dwell on that foreboding thought. I would just focus my mind on the next dance competition.

As the years passed, Vincent was gone from home for longer periods of time. Sometimes, he wouldn't come home all night long. I figured he was spending the night at his old apartment above the studio.

From time to time, I'd wonder what he was doing there, and with whom. This might sound cold, Mercedes, but I couldn't bring myself to care. Any semblance of intimacy between my husband and me had long passed. And homelife was more peaceful without his presence there.

Several times, I heard rumors about Vincent's close relationships with young men at the studio. I finally confronted him about it, not because I cared, but because I thought he might be concerned about what others were saying.

His face turned white, and he was silent for a long while. "Dori," he finally said, "it isn't what you think it is."

"What is it, then?" I asked.

He made no reply. I never knew the full truth about the matter. Frankly, I didn't want to know.

One fateful evening in March of 1982, I received a telephone call from the studio. It was Tony O'Reilly. The minute I heard his voice, I knew something was terribly wrong.

Tony informed me that Vincent was in the emergency room. He'd injured his knee while giving a dance lesson. At that moment, I knew with a deep certainty that my days as one-half of a celebrated ballroom dance couple were over. I could feel the house of cards I'd been living in come tumbling down around me.

More than thirty years of dancing had taken a toll on Vincent's body. I'd known from the beginning that he was dancing on borrowed time. He suffered chronic pain in his back and in all his joints, but he rarely complained about it. He stubbornly refused to allow pain to stand between him and what he loved.

In that agonizing telephone conversation, Tony told me my husband had twisted his knee in such a way that it had given out, and he'd fallen to the floor. I shuddered, trying not to picture that scene, as I knew it must've been terribly humiliating to Vincent.

I immediately dropped what I was doing and rushed to the hospital to be with my injured husband. I couldn't bear to look at his face, as I didn't want to see the devastation there. Although he didn't say it, I'm sure Vincent knew the impact of his injury on his dancing career.

After x-rays were taken of Vincent's knee, we learned that the ligaments had been badly torn, requiring surgery. Then, there were complications, and Vincent was forced to take a leave of absence from his sales job. Of course, he wasn't able to go to the studio.

As he couldn't make it up the stairs to the privacy of our bedroom or his office, there was nothing he could do but to spend six weeks lying in the recliner in our living room with his leg elevated.

I've never seen an individual more frustrated with his life circumstances. My poor husband was trapped in an utterly wretched state of existence. While he'd formerly coped with family life by withdrawing from it, he could no longer do so, as his recliner was positioned in the middle of the family's pattern of traffic.

I could tell the children were getting on his nerves. He spent his days morosely watching television or thumbing through magazines. He drank far more alcohol than he'd ever previously consumed, and he ate continuously.

Piles of garbage accumulated around Vincent's chair: dirty dishes, bottles, cans, junk food wrappers, discarded magazines and newspapers. I tried to clean up the mess, but this irritated my already irritable husband, so I backed off and allowed the piles to grow.

With his increased eating and drinking and the loss of the exercise of dancing, Vincent rapidly put on weight. I had difficulty looking at his bloated face and flabby body, and I could tell he was disgusted with himself.

The children weren't used to Vincent's presence in the home. Corina couldn't stand to witness the deterioration of the dance king, and her jabs at him became more vicious. I tried to stop her. But by that time, she was a senior in high school, almost eighteen years old. She was her own person, and her behavior had long been out of the reach of my influence.

Then Vincent did something he'd never done before. He started yelling back at my daughter, his frustrated bellows resounding throughout our home. To my dismay, even Wesley joined in the fray, coming to his sister's defense.

The children whined to me about what Vincent was or was not doing. They complained that he monopolized the television and ate all the good snacks in the house. They demanded to know why they had to clean their rooms when their stepfather wasn't made to clean up his mess.

During those days, keeping peace in the household preoccupied my every waking moment. I thought of creative ways to keep Corina away from Vincent. Even if it went against my motherly instincts, I agreed to all her requests to go places with her friends, just to get her out of the house.

I didn't even consider going to the studio without Vincent. In the face of his disability, it would've been cruel to flaunt the fact that I could still dance. Furthermore, I was afraid to leave him home alone, undefended against my children's attacks.

After the six longest weeks of my life, Vincent's surgeon gave him clearance to return to his day job. Thankfully, that eased some of the tension in the household. But he was still forbidden to dance. I don't know what the doctor told Vincent, but he informed me in a private consultation that my husband would never dance again.

Vincent had grown accustomed to sleeping in the recliner, so even after he was back on his feet, he returned to the chair at night. He never slept in our bed with me again.

We were worlds apart, two strangers sharing living quarters, no longer held together by the bond of the dance.

I tried to ignore the cloud of doom that hung over our household. I tried hard to maintain an optimistic attitude in the face of a dying relationship.

On a Tuesday afternoon in May, I came home from work to find Vincent already home, propping up his still sore leg in the recliner. "How was your day?" I asked as I passed through the living room.

"Funny you should ask." The tone of Vincent's voice stopped me in my tracks. He adjusted the recliner to the upright position, as if preparing for a serious conversation. I sat down on the sofa to listen to what he had to say.

"I had lunch with Tony O'Reilly today," he informed me. "We had a good talk."

"About what?" I asked.

"Well, he brought up the fact that he's getting older and needs to slow down. He said he wants to cut back on some of his responsibilities at the studio." Vincent paused and took a deep breath. "He asked me if I wanted to manage the studio. He offered me a fulltime job."

"Wow!" I exclaimed. "What did you say?"

Vincent smiled. I realized it was the first time I'd seen him smile since the day of his injury. "I said yes, of course. You know I'd jump at the chance to get out of the business of selling cars. This is the perfect opportunity for me."

Right then, I was so thrilled for my husband that I clapped my hands and squealed like a little girl. "Oh, that's wonderful, Vincent! Even if you can't teach, you can be around what you love. I think this will be perfect for you."

For a fleeting moment, I allowed myself to believe that my husband and I were on the threshold of a new beginning. But that fragile thought was extinguished the instant it lit up my mind.

"Dora." Vincent dropped his head, his voice sounding heavy. A sense of foreboding crept over me. Never before had I heard him call me Dora.

"Dora," he repeated, "I can't do this anymore."

He lifted his face to meet my gaze. As I looked into his

tired eyes, I could see what I'd been trying so hard not to see: that our marriage sucked the life out of him. And I knew it was doing the same to me.

Tears sprang to my eyes, but I could offer no protest. I couldn't come up with any objections. I couldn't identify even one reason why we should stay together. We'd had a great dance partnership, but that was all. And it was over.

I opened my mouth and uttered the most truthful words I'd said in a long time: "I can't do it either, Vincent."

A heavy silence hung in the air between us. Finally, Vincent spoke. "I never meant to hurt you, Dora. I'm just not cut out for being a husband."

We both knew what he meant. Neither of us needed to spell it out. Vincent preferred being with a man over being with a woman.

"Where are you planning to go?" I asked, knowing the answer before the words even left my mouth.

"Back to my apartment above the studio," he said. "I'll be leaving this weekend."

I imagined Vincent moving back into his messy little hideaway, the place he'd never fully left. It was as if our shared home was eager to eject him, while his old apartment stood ready to welcome him back with open arms.

I sighed deeply, then nodded. "Okay."

True to his word, Vincent moved out the following Saturday. As I didn't want the children present during that process, I allowed Corina to drive herself and Wesley over to Middlebury to spend the day with Irene.

Several of Vincent's friends from the studio came to do the heavy lifting and carrying for him. I didn't want to experience the pain of watching my husband of four years exit my life. So, as soon as the movers arrived, I left the house.

I took a long stroll around our neighborhood, trying to wrap my mind around the enormous change taking place in my world. When I walked back into my house an hour later, my husband and his belongings were gone.

I spent the rest of that day cleaning my home from top to bottom, throwing out the clutter Vincent had left behind. I rearranged furniture and reorganized cupboards and closets. In my mind, I was cleaning out the old, making room for whatever the future would bring me. Once again, it was time to start over.

Mercedes, you ask me whether I was sad. Of course, I was. Tears rolled down my face while I swept and scrubbed. But to tell you the truth, I'd already faced the worst of my grief several months earlier when I'd lost my dance partner.

I didn't see Vincent until three months later when we met in court for the finalization of our divorce. It was a simple matter, as there was nothing to contest, and Vincent and I held no malice toward each other.

I was relieved to see that Vincent looked much healthier than he had on the day he'd left. He'd lost most of the weight he'd put on, and he'd recaptured his old sparkle and swagger. When I watched him approach me in the courthouse corridor, I could see the man who'd swept me off my feet the day I'd first entered Tony O'Reilly's studio.

My former husband flashed me his dazzling smile, kissed me on the cheek, and said, "Dori, you look fabulous."

After the brief hearing, we said our goodbyes. Vincent didn't seem sad, and I doubted that he missed my presence in the new world he'd created for himself. "Dori, you're a wonderful woman," he said, giving me one of his hallmark adoring gazes. "You'll make some man a fantastic wife someday. But we both know I'm not the one for you."

"Thank you for the dance, Vincent," I said. "We had a short run, but it was great while it lasted."

"It was my pleasure," he replied, bowing theatrically.

As Vincent walked away, I smiled to myself, thinking that I could easily become infatuated with that charming fellow all over again.

I thought I'd run into Vincent again someday. But I never saw or heard from him again. I imagine he's gone by now. If he were still living, he'd be around ninety.

A few years ago, when a hurricane struck Vincent's birthplace of Puerto Rico and devastated the island, I thought about his relatives living there. I prayed for them, hoping they were spared the worst.

You're wondering whether I regret the time I spent with Vincent. That's a complicated question. I do regret some of the choices I made during that chapter of my life. I pursued my own interests without paying enough attention to the needs of others. I am not proud of that. Still, I wouldn't have missed my dancing years for anything in the world.

Was the marriage a mistake? No doubt it was. But my dance partnership with Vincent was one of the most exquisite experiences of my lifetime. Vincent taught me how to express my feminine grace and charm. How tragic it would've been if I'd gone my whole life without discovering that aspect of myself! I'll always be grateful to him.

Mercedes, I know you don't have a very high opinion of Vincent. You're angry with him for deceiving me about his sexual preferences. But any anger I've ever felt about Vincent's dishonesty has since turned to sadness. I'm sad that he felt deception was needed in the first place. I'm sad that he had to hide who he was, that he couldn't live openly and honestly as a gay man.

If I'd had more understanding of the matter back then, I would've gladly remained loyal to Vincent as his dance partner, without burdening our beautiful arrangement with the pretense of romance and marriage. I would've spared myself and my children so much pain.

To this day, I miss dancing. As you can see, I can't bear to part with my costumes. I often dream about dancing, gliding across the floor in Vincent's arms, moving in perfect harmony with him.

But last night, I dreamed I was dancing with Elliott. We danced so lightly that my feet barely touched the floor.

No, sweet Mercedes, you don't need to help me put the costumes away. I'll fold them up after you leave, and Elliott will put them back into the closet for me. This may be the last time I take them out, and I'll want to tuck them away with extra loving care.

CHAPTER 8: DORA MILLER ONCE AGAIN

"Why are you so scared, Mom?" Javi asked as he stood with Mercedes on the front porch of his grandmother's new residence.

Mercedes looked down at her son, smiling grimly. "I'm afraid your grandma isn't going to like what I have to tell her."

"Well, that's nothing new," Javi observed. "Grandma never likes anything anybody says to her."

Earlier that week, Mercedes had gone through the tortuous ordeal of moving Denise out of her lifelong home and putting her into the care of her stepmother June. The process hadn't gone well. There had been much yelling, blaming, and accusing on Denise's part. At the end of the day, Mercedes had left in tears, worrying about whether her mother would adjust to the change.

Taking a deep breath, she knocked on the door. When she received no answer, she knocked again. Finally, she heard a groggy voice mumble, "Who's there?"

"It's me, Mom," she called. Then she opened the door and went inside.

Denise looked much the same as she had at her old home, stretched out in a recliner, her massive abdomen rising and falling with her labored breathing. Only this time, she was lying in a new chair. June had refused to allow the old recliner in her home. "I don't know what kind of infestation that thing might hold," she'd said. "It's not coming into my house."

So, Mercedes had bought her mother a new recliner with money Javier had given her. Denise had complained bitterly about the chair at first. But, by all appearances, she'd grown quite comfortable in it.

"It's about time you came to check on me," she whined to Mercedes. "It seemed like you dumped me here and then ran off and forgot about me."

Mercedes chose to ignore her mother's negativity. "Javi's here to see you, too," she announced. She turned to call out to the porch, where Javi was waiting with his father. "Come in and say hi to Grandma, sweetie."

Denise broke into a smile when her grandson entered the room. "There's my baby boy!" she chortled. Then she glanced at Mercedes, the scowl returning to her face. "It's about time you brought him over. I thought you were trying to keep him from me, or something."

"Hi, Grandma," Javi said cheerfully. He walked over to the chair and wrapped his arms around her bulky body.

"Careful there," Denise chortled. "You're gonna squeeze your grandma to death." She grabbed Javi's face between her swollen hands and covered it with noisy kisses. "Goodness sake, ain't you just gettin' to be a handsome little devil. When all the girls come chasin' after you, just remember your heart belongs to your grandma."

Denise released her hold on her grandson, then turned an accusing eye on her daughter. "What you been so busy with that you couldn't come by to see me?"

"I'm in school, Mom," Mercedes replied. "I've told you that a hundred times. Don't you remember?"

"Oh," Denise muttered. "You still doin' that?"

"Yes," Mercedes said. "I have another year to go, and I don't plan on dropping out." She paused, dreading what she had to say next. "Mom, I have some news to tell you."

"Well, don't just stand there," Denise demanded irritably. "Spit it out."

"I know you're not going to like this. But Javier and I are back together."

Denise's face darkened. "What the hell are you doing, girl? I thought you were done messin' around with that son-of-a-bitch. You told me you were gonna try going out with Jared."

Mercedes laughed. "Mom! I never told you anything like that! I've never wanted to go out with Jared. The only man I'm interested in is my husband."

Denise closed her eyes and shook her head slowly, as if appalled by her daughter's terrible judgement. "Sadie, Sadie, Sadie. Why'd you have to go and bring him back into your life again? You know the man ain't nothin' but trouble."

Mercedes felt the old familiar anger welling inside her, and it took every ounce of her willpower to keep from lashing out at her mother. "Mom," she said, forcing herself to speak calmly. "Javier is a better man than you think he is. We've come a long way in working through our problems. We're happy with each other. And Javi's happy, too. It's good for him to have his mom and dad back together."

Denise shot Javi an incredulous look, as if expecting him to validate her ugly opinion of his father. "Yes, Grandma," he sang out. "It's good to have Mom and Dad together. It's the absolute best."

The dismay on her mother's face made it hard for Mercedes to continue, but she plunged ahead. "Mom, Javier is here, too. He wants to talk with you."

As if on cue, Javier walked through the open door from where he'd been waiting on the porch. Mercedes moved aside as he stepped up to his mother-in-law's chair. Ignoring Denise's scowl, he took her puffy hand in the two of his.

"Miss Covington," he said graciously, as if he hadn't just heard her nasty tirade against him. "I know this may not be the news you want to hear, but Mercedes and I have decided to live together again. I want you to know that I love your daughter very much, and that I intend to be the man she needs me to be. I'm committed to doing right by her and our son."

Still holding Denise's hand, he looked her straight in the eye. The scene between her husband and her mother seemed surreal to Mercedes, as if she was in an audience watching a stage play. Handsome Javier, with a look of determination on his chiseled features, gazing down at the bloated face of his invalid mother-in-law. Denise staring up at him in openmouthed bewilderment.

Mercedes held her breath as the seconds ticked by, wondering what was going to happen next.

"I'm going to do right by Mercedes," Javier repeated. "And by you, too. You're the mother of the woman I love, and I want to do right by you."

Mercedes watched expressions pass over her mother's face that she'd never seen before. First came stunned disbelief. Then came the look of a fearful child terrified of abandonment and desperate for security. She knew Javier's words had touched a vulnerable spot in her mother's heart, a spot Denise kept guarded with her hateful attitude.

My husband is a wonderful man, Mercedes thought. *He's the best of the best.* She saw that her mother was still clutching Javier's hand, as if to draw strength from the man she now viewed as her protector.

Denise's eyes had softened. "I guess we can try to put our differences aside and be a family," she said, her voice husky with emotion.

Mercedes exhaled slowly, tears streaming down her cheeks.

As they left the house, Javier put his arm around Mercedes' shoulders, and she encircled his waist with her arm. When they reached their cars parked along the curb, Javier kissed his wife passionately before opening her car door for her. "Run along now, mi amor," he said. "You don't want to keep Dora waiting."

Taking Javi by the hand, he headed toward his own car. Mercedes watched her husband drive away toward the home she now shared with him. Then, with a smile on her face, she set out on the trip to Saint Joseph.

As Mercedes stepped into the lobby of the Harbor Lights apartment building, she tried to shake off the dreamy state that had enveloped her on her drive to Michigan. Witnessing the encounter between Javier and her mother had drained an enormous amount of tension from her body, leaving her feeling as light as air. She was still playing that incredible scene over and over in her mind, trying to take in everything that had happened.

But her reverie was broken when she opened the door to the stairwell and saw Dr. Elliott Jordan coming down the stairs. He was carrying a large musical instrument case. Mercedes stopped and held the door for him.

"Hello, Miss Maldonado," he said in his sonorous voice. "It's nice to see you again."

"It's good to see you, too, Dr. Jordan," Mercedes said. She suddenly felt intimidated in the presence of the gracious gentleman who played such an important role in her grandmother's life.

The two of them stepped out of the stairwell into the lobby. "How's Dora today?" Mercedes asked.

Elliott furrowed his brow, lifting a hand to stroke his white beard. After a long pause, he said, "Miss Maldonado, come sit with me for a few minutes." He gestured toward the chairs surrounding the small table on the other side of the lobby.

When they had seated themselves, Elliott gazed at Mercedes somberly, as if hesitant to broach a difficult subject.

"Is something wrong with Dora?" Mercedes asked, her heart in her throat.

"Nothing more than the fact that she's growing steadily weaker," Elliott replied.

A wave of fear passed through Mercedes. For the first time, she allowed herself to fully face the possibility that her days with her recently discovered grandmother were numbered. "I've picked up on the fact that she's not well," she said. "But she's never talked about her health, and it seems as if she doesn't want to."

Elliott sat with his eyes downcast for a few moments, as if in deep thought. "I hesitate to break Dora's confidence," he finally said. "She loves you so much, and I'm sure she doesn't want to waste any of the precious time she has with you by dwelling on her difficulties. But I think you should know what's happening so that you'll be prepared."

Mercedes drew in a sharp breath. "What's happening?" She dreaded hearing the answer to her question.

Elliott glanced around the lobby. "Did Dora tell you about the Coronavirus outbreak here in this facility?"

"No," Mercedes said. "We've never talked about that."

"Then I suppose you never heard that she was one of those who got sick."

Mercedes gazed at him in horror. "No! I had no idea!"

"It was in the early days of the pandemic," Elliott explained, "before people fully understood what was happening. Dora was helping out a sick friend in a nearby apartment, not knowing, of course, what the nature of the illness was. And she ended up getting sicker than the person she was helping."

"Oh no!" Mercedes exclaimed. "Did she have a hard time?"

Elliott's eyes clouded with pain. "Yes, Miss Maldonado, she did. Your grandmother had a pre-existing condition, a mild case of cardiomyopathy. Before the virus, it wasn't causing her many problems. It just slowed her down a bit."

He ran a hand over the top of his curly white hair, sighing deeply. "I didn't think she was going to make it. I thought I was about to lose the dearest friend I've ever had. She was in the hospital for a month, much of that time in the ICU on a ventilator."

Elliott's revelation sent Mercedes' thoughts into a tailspin. She leaned forward, burying her face in her hands, trying to ward off the image of her grandmother in such a dire condition.

She felt Elliott's hand on her shoulder. "I'm sorry," he said. "Perhaps I shouldn't have told you."

Mercedes raised her head. "That's okay. I guess I shouldn't be surprised. So many senior citizens have been affected by this virus." After a moment's pause, she asked, "Were her children able to be there for her?"

"Her son was out of the country," Elliott replied. "He was unable to fly home because of the pandemic. But he did his best to stay in touch with his mother by telephone."

He chuckled. "But with Corina, it was a different matter. She took a leave from her job when she heard her mother was sick, and she spent six weeks up here in Michigan. Being a nurse, she insisted on providing care for her mother while she was in the hospital. Of course, that was against hospital protocol. But she got around that. Nothing stops Corina when she has her mind set on something. So, she put on her protective gear and was there at her mother's bedside day after day, monitoring her status, talking to her, encouraging her. I think her daughter's presence had a lot to do with Dora's recovery."

He raised his eyes to the heavens, bringing his hands together in a gesture of prayer. "Thank God, she came through. She won that battle. And she and I have been blessed with one more wonderful year together."

He shifted in his chair to fully face Mercedes. "But I don't think she's going to win this time. The virus took a toll on her lungs and her already weakened heart. Her doctor has now diagnosed her with congestive heart failure. The condition takes her energy bit by bit. She has her good days, and it's tempting at those times to think she's getting better. But overall, she's in decline."

Mercedes nodded sadly. "Thanks for telling me the truth, even though it was hard to hear. It explains so much. Will Corina be coming back to take care of her mother again?"

Elliott smiled. "Bless her heart, it's almost as if she never left. She stays in daily contact with her mother. About twice a week, I get a call from her, wanting to know my assessment of her mother's condition. And every month, she flies up from Florida to spend a few days with Dora."

"She's an awesome daughter," Mercedes murmured. She wondered whether she would ever come to the point of providing such loving care to her own mother.

Elliott nodded emphatically. "Yes, Corina is absolutely devoted to her mother. Seeing that does me so much good."

He reached over to take Mercedes' hand. "And you are such a kind young woman yourself, coming to see your grandmother every week. I know Dora gets lonely. She's hardly able to leave her apartment anymore. I try to spend as much time as I can with her, but I'm limited in what I can do. Your visits mean the world to her."

He rose to his feet, picking up his instrument case. "I'd prefer that you don't mention our conversation to Dora. As I said before, she doesn't want to waste the precious time she has left by dwelling on her difficulties. Go on up and have a wonderful visit with her. Don't bother to knock. Dora is settled comfortably in her chair, and it's best if she doesn't get up to answer the door. Just go in. She's expecting you."

When Mercedes reached Dora's apartment, she felt

uneasy about walking in unannounced. So, she tapped on the door, calling, "It's Mercedes," before she opened it and stepped inside.

She found Dora seated in her recliner, her legs elevated and covered with a colorful blanket. Although the elderly woman appeared frail and tired, her smile was bright and welcoming.

After seating herself, Mercedes glanced around the apartment. She was taken aback when her gaze fell on the wheelchair parked beside the sofa.

Dora seemed to read the concern on her face. Not waiting for a question, she quickly explained. "It was such a nice day yesterday. Elliott wheeled me out to see the lake one last time."

"It's only July," Mercedes blurted out. "You'll have plenty of nice days yet this summer and into the fall."

Dora smiled, but said nothing. Mercedes instantly regretted what she'd said, realizing the phrase "one last time" had nothing to do with the seasons.

But Dora quickly moved on from that painful moment. "How are you, my dear?" she asked. "Did you just come from Javier's place?"

"No," Mercedes replied. "I just came from my mom's house. But Javier was there, too."

"I'm guessing from the peaceful look on your face that things went better than they usually do with your mother."

Mercedes nodded. "Yes, they did. I actually think a miracle happened today."

"Oh?" Dora said, her posture perking up a bit.

"Do you remember when I told you about feeling pulled between my mom and Javier? It was really stressful. I was so confused about what I should do. But that feeling is gone now. It seems as if we're all coming together as a family."

Dora clasped her hands together enthusiastically. "Oh, Mercedes, I'm so happy for you! That truly is a miracle! Yes, sometimes we do struggle and struggle with a problem that seems intractable. Then, it suddenly vanishes."

She paused, then said, "I take it that you and Javier are officially back together?"

"Yes," Mercedes replied, "we are. Javier gave up the lease on his apartment and moved back in with Javi and me. We've started looking for a bigger place where we can be more comfortable. In a year or so, we'll start looking for a house to buy."

A broad smile spread over Dora's face. "My dear granddaughter, I'm so thrilled for you. From the beginning, I sensed it was important for you and Javier to work through whatever problems were keeping you apart. I believe the kind of love the two of you share is rare. It isn't easy to come by. I searched for years for love like that."

Mercedes nodded thoughtfully. After a few moments, she spoke hesitantly. "My whole life, I've done whatever I've wanted to do. I've insisted on having everything my way. I've fought everyone I thought was trying to control me. I thought it would kill me to give up my freedom."

She chuckled self-consciously. "But I think I might be changing. It seems as if I'm ready to cooperate with Javier instead of fighting with him. Maybe I'm growing up. Do you think so?"

"It could be," Dora said. "We all have some maturing to do, albeit in different ways. After Vincent left me, I was forced to do a lot of growing up."

Mercedes leaned forward with interest. "Is this the day when you tell me the story about you and Grandpa? I can't wait to hear it."

Dora shook her head. "No, after Vincent and I divorced, a few years passed before I met your grandfather. They were important years that deserve their own chapter in this life review. The story about my marriage to Andrew will need to wait until next week. We'll make it a special occasion.

As I've already told you, Mercedes, I cried a river of tears the day Vincent moved out. I had to grieve, even though I knew our parting of ways was best for both of us. But after I stopped weeping, I began to think. My children were gone until late that evening, and there was no commotion in the household to distract me from listening to my innermost thoughts.

I considered the fact that I was now thirty-six, and had twice fallen into marriages with men I didn't really love. I realized my feelings for Vincent had been nothing more than childish infatuation. I told myself it was time to grow up and take charge of my life, that it was time to make my own decisions instead of blindly following others.

I thought about my job. I'd been stuck in the company's sewing department for eight years, doing the same thing day after day, never considering the possibility that I might be capable of doing something else.

I even thought about God. I hadn't pondered spiritual matters since I'd stopped following the strict religion of my childhood. I felt questions stirring inside me. I wondered about the purpose of my life, and whether I was doing what I was meant to do.

But most of all, I thought about my children, who had just turned eighteen and fifteen. Corina was now a legal adult, and Wesley wasn't far behind her. That reality hit me hard. I knew that for the past five years, I hadn't given them my best, as I'd been so preoccupied with dancing. Pangs of remorse stabbed my heart. I knew I'd missed out on some precious times with them.

Now, my preoccupation was gone, and I told myself that nothing stood in the way of my relationships with my children. I resolved to become a devoted mother to them, to make the best of the years they remained in my household.

However, when my children came home that evening, my fantasies about motherhood were quickly dashed. Wesley went straight to his room, avoiding me as he usually did. He stayed there for the rest of the evening, coming out only to get a snack from the kitchen.

The next morning, he gruffly informed me that he was going to spend the day with a new friend, David Yoder. He left the house without even asking my permission.

Corina spent the day writing a paper for school. Early that evening, I found her primping in front of the bathroom mirror, getting ready to go out with friends.

In a moment of weakness, I blurted, "Everyone else is

leaving me. Are you going to leave me, too?"

She rolled her eyes as she brushed her hair. "Mom," she scolded, "I'm never going to abandon you, if that's what you're worried about. You should know me better than that."

Mercedes, those were words flippantly spoken by a teenage girl. But over the years, I've come to realize that Corina really meant what she said to me that day. No matter where in the world my daughter might be, I always know I can count on her. We now live hundreds of miles apart, but I know that Corina will be at my side the moment I need her.

Sometimes, I think Corina came into my life to serve as a guide and protector for me. That might seem like an odd thing for a mother to say about her daughter. But ever since Corina was a little girl, she's made it her business to look out for me. I am humbled by the gift of her presence in my life.

In the weeks following Vincent's departure, I sadly discovered that pouring my energy into my children was not going to fill the void in my life.

I learned that Wesley's new friend David Yoder was the son of a Mennonite minister in Elkhart. The Yoders were wonderful people. I had no reason to mistrust them. They welcomed my fatherless son into their family circle, and Reverend Yoder became a mentor to him.

To my astonishment, Wesley began attending church with the Yoder family. When my children were younger, they had occasionally attended church with Virgil and Irene, but neither of them had shown a true interest in religious activities. Now, Wesley insisted on going to church every Sunday morning. He also became involved in the church's youth group.

How could I possibly object to such a development, when my son had lost every father and grandfather figure he'd ever known in his life? I knew it would be wrong of me to stand in the way of Wesley's relationship with the Yoder family. So, I relinquished him to their influence, while quietly dealing with my regrets and sense of inadequacy.

I turned my attention to Corina, but soon discovered that

she wasn't inclined to sit still for much mothering. When she and I were together, she enjoyed having my undivided attention. But the truth is that she didn't spend much time with me. She was focused on her own life, clearly on the fast track to independent adulthood.

Shortly before her high school graduation that June, she announced her plan to attend nursing school in the fall. I panicked when I heard her say that. I pictured her moving out of my home and onto a college campus, perhaps even going to an out-of-state school.

As usual, my perceptive daughter picked up on my feelings before I even voiced them. "Stop worrying, Mom," she scolded. "I'm not running away from you. I'll be living at home and commuting to a school in South Bend. I know you still need me here."

Mercedes, this is where I drew on the money Moses Graber had given me after Ivan died. With it, I paid a large portion of Corina's tuition. I was so happy to be able to provide assistance in her educational endeavors. However, I'm sure she would've found a way to make it through nursing school without my help. She was that independent and that determined.

The more I realized my children didn't need me, the further I slid into despair. I searched for other ways to fill the emptiness in my life. For a few months after Vincent left, Isabella and I stayed in contact, trying to pretend we were still sisters-in-law. We talked on the phone, and she came to visit a few times. "I'm still here for you," she'd tell me.

However, I grew weary of listening to her berate her brother for ruining his relationship with the best woman he'd ever had. Such conversations left me feeling deeply depressed. I loved Isabella, but our shared pain was the only thing holding us together. The last time she hugged me and said, "Let's stay in touch," I knew we wouldn't.

I tried dancing at the other ballroom studio in South Bend, Tony O'Reilly's competition. But I ended up shuffling around the floor with partners who didn't possess one tenth of Vincent's talent. The activity was tortuous, and only served to twist the knife in my wounded heart. I had to face the fact that the magic of the dance had taken wing and flown from my life. I finally packed up my dance costumes and shoved them deep into the back of my bedroom closet.

My personal appearance, which had once been of utmost importance to me, now became a matter of indifference. I didn't have the heart to dress in my Dori Perez clothing anymore. Those provocative outfits belonged to an era now past. I began wearing less and less makeup, until I was wearing none at all. I'd gaze at my plain, washed-out reflection in the mirror, thinking, "What on earth has happened to me?"

One day, Corina said to me, "Good Lord, Mom, why don't you fix yourself up a little bit? Maybe you overdid it when you were with Vincent, but you don't have to go to the other extreme."

At my divorce hearing, I changed my last name back to Miller. It seemed as if the name Perez had nothing to do with me anymore. Going back to being Dora Miller was like going back to a home base, a place from which to launch the next chapter of my life.

It often felt as if I'd actually stepped back into young Dora's bleak existence. I'd lie in my bed staring at the ceiling, wondering how all the color had drained out of my life so quickly.

I did, however, have the presence of mind to do one constructive thing. After several years of having little contact with Elliott, I reached out to tell him about my divorce and the end of my dancing career.

He promptly sent back the kindest letter I have ever received. "Dora, I know this must be a terribly difficult time in your life," he wrote. "Please remember there are better times ahead. Good things will certainly come to such a wonderful person as you."

As I held that beautiful letter in my hands, it seemed as if a shaft of light penetrated the darkness surrounding me. For the first time in months, I felt a flicker of hope, genuine hope, and I realized I was smiling.

I folded the letter and placed it in my dresser drawer. Over the next few weeks, I took it out and read it daily, pondering on what good things were about to enter my life. Strangely, I didn't doubt Elliott's words.

Mercedes, you say that Elliott was like a spirit guide to me. That's an interesting observation. Although I know he's fully human, he seems to have played that role in my life. He was always there in the background, quiet and unobtrusive, but ready to respond when I reached out for help. It is only in recent years that he has stepped out of the shadows to become a visible presence in my daily life.

That fall, Corina started nursing school and Wesley started his sophomore year of high school. Both were so caught up in their activities that it seemed as if I never saw them for more than a few minutes at a time. My heart was achingly empty. "I can't go on living this way," I told myself time and again.

Then one day at work, I saw a job opening posted on the bulletin board in our breakroom. It was for an assistant in the human resources department. The company was trying to fill the position from within the organization before advertising in the broader community.

When I saw that posting, a light flashed on in my mind. I remembered Elliott's words, and I instantly knew the position was meant for me. That very day, I filled out an application.

As it turned out, even though I had no employment experience outside of the company's sewing department, my excellent work record proved to be in my favor. Also, because I'd been with the company for so many years, they knew I had a feel for how the business was run. They decided that I could easily be trained to fill the position.

Mercedes, that new job did so much for me. Although it wasn't nearly as thrilling a venture as dancing had been, it gave me a new challenge. It kept me moving forward in life.

It also helped me grow into a more sophisticated woman. My position involved traveling to conferences and trainings. I began interfacing with the company's management. I gave up the jeans and tee shirts I'd worn in the sewing department and began wearing business attire, the new costume for that era of my life.

One morning when I was getting ready for work, Corina checked out my appearance and said, "Mom, I think you're finally getting your act together."

Was working in human resources one of my hopes and dreams? No, I can't say it was. But it was an invaluable experience for me. It gave me a new kind of confidence in myself. Despite the fact that I had only one semester of college on my resume, mingling with professional people made me feel as if I had a career instead of just a job. Just as dancing had done, my new position brought out an aspect of myself that I hadn't known existed.

A month after I started my new position, I wrote to Elliott to tell him about it. He promptly wrote back to congratulate me. "I always knew you were capable of something like this, Dora," he said. "You will discover more and more of your capabilities in the years to come."

Although I had my ups and down, the next few years of my life were relatively quiet. Truly, I needed a break from pain and drama. Corina decided to complete a four-year nursing program, and she continued with her education while still living at home. Wesley was doing well in high school, still involved with the Yoder family and their church. Neither of my children gave me much of anything to worry about.

I developed several close female friends, Jeanette and Valerie. Having someone to socialize with helped ease my loneliness when my children were involved in their own pursuits.

My father passed away in 1983, and my mother died the following year. I was dutifully present during their final days, respectfully interfacing with my siblings while keeping myself at a safe emotional distance.

It was hard to acknowledge that my parents' earthly lives had ended without them coming to the point of accepting me. But I had already made peace with that sad reality. I trust that somewhere in our souls' journeys, the rift between my parents and me will heal. I trust that we will come to a place of mutual understanding.

A greater loss for me was when my former neighbor Irene passed away. When I learned that my one-time surrogate mother was in failing health, I spent as much time as I possibly could with her. Before her death, I was able to tell her how much I loved her, and to express my abundance of gratitude for everything she'd done for my children and me.

I'll never forget our final exchange of words, when she was hours away from death. "Irene, you've been such a blessing to me," I told her.

She opened her eyes for the last time and whispered, "And you to me."

Mercedes, you're crying. You understand what a sweet parting that was. Irene has often come to me in dreams, and the presence of her spirit is a comfort to me. I imagine that when I cross over to the other side, she will be one of the souls waiting there to welcome me.

But then, something happened that turned my world upside down again. In the spring of 1985, a month prior to Wesley's high school graduation, he came to me and said, "Mom, I need to talk to you."

I can't tell you how much this took me by surprise. Never in all his life had my son requested to have a serious conversation with me. I'd always been the one to pursue communication with him, and my attempts had rarely met with success.

So, I braced myself for the worst. Was Wesley about to tell me that he'd failed a class and couldn't graduate? That he'd had a brush with the law? That he'd gotten some girl pregnant?

We sat down at the kitchen table. I could tell right away that he expected opposition from me. He had a strange look of determination in his eyes.

"What is it, Wesley?" I asked.

He was silent for a long time, and I wondered whether he'd changed his mind about talking to me. Finally, he said,

"I've figured something out, Mom. I know what I want to do with my life."

I exhaled deeply, relieved that my worst fears weren't about to be confirmed. *"So, what is your plan?"* I asked, expecting to hear a teenager's pipedream.

"I'm going into the Peace Corps."

I jumped up from the table, as shocked as if he'd told me that he was planning a life of selling illegal drugs. *"How on earth did you come up with such an idea?"* I said, my voice rising in consternation. *"Who in the world put such a thought in your head?"*

"Mom," he said with uncharacteristic maturity, *"if you want to talk with me about this, you need to calm down."*

I sat down at the table again, my heart pounding. *"How did you come up with this plan?"* I asked, trying hard to control my agitation.

"I've been meeting with my guidance counselor at school," he said. *"He was trying to talk me into going to college. I told him I wasn't interested in college, that I just wanted to do something where I could help people. We discussed different things. When he mentioned going into the Peace Corps, I knew that was exactly what I wanted to do."*

He gazed at me intently. As I looked into his big blue eyes, it seemed as if I was looking into his soul. For the first time, I could see who my son really was. Truthfully, I wasn't ready for that.

"You know how you know something on a deep level?" he said. *"You don't know how you know it, but you know it for sure?"*

My mind raced back to such profound moments in my own life. *"Yes,"* I replied. *"I know what you're talking about."*

"Well, that's the way I feel about going into the Peace Corps. It's the right thing to do. I feel that deep inside of me."

I knew right then I could never dissuade my son from his plan, but I wasn't ready to give up the argument. *"Wesley,"* I said, *"you just turned eighteen. Why don't you wait a few years? Get a job somewhere around here and give yourself time to figure things out."*

Anger flashed in his eyes. "Mom, I'm not a child. You can't make decisions for me anymore."

Those words shot through me like bullets, riddling me with guilt. He and I both knew that many decisions I'd made in the past had not been good for him. He no longer trusted me in that regard. He was ready to take charge of his own life.

Tears of remorse welled in my eyes. "I can't help but wonder whether you are going into the Peace Corps just to get away from home," I said. "I know your childhood has been rough. I know that growing up without a father hasn't been easy. And I know I haven't always been a good mother."

My son shook his head, dismissing my words. "Mom, don't even go there. This isn't about you. It's just time for me to get on with my life, and you need to get on with yours. Don't waste your time worrying about me."

Then a suspicion hit me. "Wesley, were the Yoders in on this decision?"

He pondered my question for a minute. "Yes and no," he said. "I made the decision after talking with my guidance counselor. Then, I went to talk it over with Reverend Yoder."

He looked at me pointedly. "Reverend Yoder was supportive of my decision. He said he was proud of me. And he wrote a letter of recommendation for me."

I was aghast that so much had happened without me knowing about it. Had I really been that far out of the loop when it came to my son's life? "Wesley, why didn't you tell me about all this?" I asked him.

His response was prompt and succinct. "I was afraid you'd try to stop me."

I sat there at the table with my head in my hands, trying to quell a flood of emotions. "Okay, Wesley," I finally said. "When is this going to happen?"

"In July," he replied. "My guidance counselor already helped me sign up for it."

And that was that. Wesley's decision was locked in, his plan well underway. I walked away from that conversation stunned and shaken. Protesting thoughts churned in my *mind, but I knew it was pointless to express them. As Wesley had said, this wasn't about me. It was about his life.*

Thankfully, in the coming months, Wesley allowed me to participate in preparations for his departure. He informed me that after three months of training, his first assignment would be in Malawi, a country in Africa. We went shopping for the recommended clothing, and I accompanied him to get the necessary vaccinations. I knew he was indulging me, but I was grateful that he allowed moments of mother and son closeness.

On a Saturday morning in late July, Corina and I drove Wesley to the South Bend Regional Airport. Reverend Yoder and his wife also came to see Wesley off. They told him how touched they were by his decision to enter a life of service. They hugged him, as proud of him as if he were their own son. Then Reverend Yoder had us all hold hands, and he led us in a prayer of protection for Wesley.

In that moment, I both loved and resented the Yoders. I loved them for helping my son find his way when he had no other significant source of guidance. I resented them for making me feel like an inadequate mother, and for helping my son leave me.

Wesley looked so small and vulnerable as he boarded his plane. He'd always been slight of build, never achieving Corina's height or her robust persona. He hardly looked full grown.

We stood there watching Wesley's plane taxi down the runway, lift off, and soar away. He was on the first leg of his journey, bound for the Peace Corps training center. Corina had her arm around my shoulders, lending me support. "You'll be all right, Mom," she kept saying. "You still have me."

Mercedes, if I'd known my son would never again come back home to live, I couldn't have borne the sorrow of watching him leave that day. After fifteen years of service with the Peace Corps in various part of the world, Wesley took an administrative position with the International Red Cross. While he comes back to the states to visit every couple of years, the world is now Wesley's home.

When Vincent and the children and I had all lived together, the house had felt crowded and cluttered. Now, with two of the four occupants gone, the place seemed empty and melancholy. My soul ached with the heaviness of yet another loss, the most wrenching loss of my life.

Mercedes, I think that when a person's heart is laid bare from pain, it changes your priorities. It shifts your focus, bringing new questions into your awareness. Day after day, night after night, one such question haunted me. How could my son, at eighteen, know his life purpose so clearly, when I, at thirty-nine, still didn't know who I was?

Every time I'd drift into thoughts about the meaning of my life, I'd reflect back on what I was taught during my growing up years. I knew the harsh religion of my childhood would never be enough for me. It would never satisfy the longing in my soul.

I couldn't rid myself of the idea that there was something about spirituality that had eluded me. One Sunday morning, I slipped into the back pew of Reverend Yoder's church, the place my son had loved so much. I wanted to discover what it was that Wesley had found so compelling.

But whatever had spoken to Wesley didn't speak to me. I stayed for half an hour before slipping out again. I knew that whatever I was searching for wasn't there.

I repeated the same experiment with several other churches, and experienced the same results. The yearning of my heart remained unfulfilled.

One evening when I was having dinner with my friends Valerie and Jeanette, Valerie began telling Jeanette and me about the wonderful experience she was having with her yoga class. "I'm hooked on yoga," she gushed. "Everybody should try it sometime." Turning to me, she said, "Dora, why don't you try it? You're always so stressed out. Yoga would help you a lot."

Valerie's words struck me as profoundly as if they'd come directly from God. I didn't think twice before responding. "Let me know when the next class is," I said. "I'll go with you."

Mercedes, that was the beginning of a new journey for

me. As Valerie had predicted, I fell in love with yoga. It felt exactly like what I needed at that point in my life. Then, someone in the class convinced me to try Tai Chi, and someone at the Tai Chi class recommended a drumming circle.

The hunger in my soul carried me from one such activity to another. Within a few months, I was deeply immersed in the world of alternative spirituality. I read books, I listened to tapes, I started meditating. I joined a chanting group. I went on vision quests. I received energy healings. I was hooked on what those experiences brought me, a connection with a realm of reality I'd never known before.

The inner stillness brought about by these activities tapped into the best of my upbringing, the quietness and simplicity of the Amish lifestyle. It felt like going home, to the true home inside myself.

Of course, I wrote to Elliott about all of this. He seemed intrigued by my pursuits, although he never showed an inclination to follow a similar path. "It's good to hear you've found something that speaks to your heart," he told me.

A year after Wesley left for the Peace Corps, Corina graduated from nursing school. She passed her boards on the first try, then easily landed a job in a hospital in South Bend. I knew she was ready to move on with her life. However, she was hesitant to leave home, fearing that I wouldn't be able to cope with being alone.

"It's okay," I told her. "You have a right to live your own life." So, she and a nursing school friend rented an apartment close to the hospital where they both worked.

It seemed foolish for me to live alone in a four-bedroom home, spending money to pay for unneeded space. I decided it was time to move out and find an apartment of my own. I chose to stay in Elkhart, as I had developed friends and connections in that city.

Mercedes, that was the first time in my entire life that I'd lived alone. It felt strange to set up a home just for myself. However, I rented a two-bedroom apartment, just in case Wesley decided to come back home.

Let me assure you that Wesley didn't completely shut me out of his life after he left for the Peace Corps. He sent me dutiful letters once a month, describing his activities, promising me that he was safe. I always knew he wasn't telling me everything, that he was omitting any information that would worry me. He remained almost as guarded with me as he'd always been.

I suppose the decision to rent a two-bedroom apartment was based on wishful thinking, because Wesley's monthly letters reflected no inclination to abandon his mission. So, while waiting for him to occupy the second bedroom, I turned that space into a meditation room.

After I finished arranging and decorating my apartment, I was pleased with the beautiful little sanctuary I'd created. While there were the inevitable moments of loneliness, my solitude provided me with ample time to meditate and reflect. I was able to focus on who I was and what I wanted out of life.

I took on a new identity, that of a spiritual seeker. I found a social niche among other likeminded individuals, people with whom I shared a worldview, a vocabulary, a style of dress.

Once again, I experienced a metamorphosis in my personal appearance. The glitzy outfits of my dance queen days were long gone. Now, when I wasn't at work, my signature look was bohemian. I let my hair grow long. I began wearing clothing and jewelry made by artisans in other countries: colorful maxi skirts, shawls and caftans, strings of beads and dangling earrings.

I felt more authentic with that look than I'd ever felt in my Dori Perez clothing. As you can see, Mercedes, I've hung onto that style all these years. Sometimes, I think that with my long hair and long skirts, I've reverted back to a version of my childhood appearance. The thought amuses me. I guess life sometimes leads us in a full circle.

Despite the success in my career endeavors, despite the joy of my spiritual quest, there was still an unfulfilled desire in my heart: the longing to experience true love. I knew my marriages to Ivan and Vincent hadn't begun to tap the potential of what an intimate relationship could hold. I wanted to surrender my whole heart into a relationship with a man. I wanted a soulmate.

As my fortieth birthday came and went, I began to feel desperate. I could vividly imagine my ideal partner, and could envision our life together. I prayed to have that partner enter my life. I meditated on my image of him, hoping to make him magically appear.

But the search for love wasn't the same as practicing relentlessly to master a dance routine. It wasn't the same as striving for and reaching a professional goal. I couldn't materialize a soulmate through concerted effort and sheer willpower. How was I going to find this lover of mine?

My attempts at dating disappointed me time and again. I soon discovered that while the eccentricities of men in my social circle were initially intriguing, they often masked deep-seated problems that I found intolerable. In no time at all, I found myself in a pattern of moving from one unsatisfying relationship to another.

Each time I'd start dating a new man, I would hope that I'd finally found a lifelong partner. But when the relationships didn't work out, I'd end up feeling bitter and ashamed. I knew I was giving away something of myself to men I had no business being with.

After several years, I was thoroughly jaded with the dating scene, and had almost accepted the idea that I would remain single for the rest of my life.

One Saturday afternoon in August of 1988, I took my friend Jeanette on an outing to Amish Acres in Nappanee. I know you're familiar with Nappanee, Mercedes. It's a small town southwest of Goshen, where you grew up.

Amish Acres, which highlighted the culture of the Amish community, was a popular tourist attraction in those days. It included a barn restaurant that served Amish cuisine, a living history museum, gifts shops, a theatre, and old-fashioned hayrides. Every August, it hosted an arts and crafts festival that drew visitors from all over the country.

I had been talking with Jeanette about my Amish upbringing. Because she was so intrigued, I decided to take her to Amish Acres for a "show-and-tell" of sorts. We timed our visit so that we could also attend the arts and crafts festival, a three-day event that started on Friday and ran through Sunday afternoon.

Jeanette and I ate dinner at the barn restaurant, then browsed through the museum and looked at displays of Amish quilts. After that, we strolled around the grounds where the festival was held, going from booth to booth looking at what the vendors had to offer. All the while, we could hear the strains of music in the background, as various groups had been scheduled to perform throughout the weekend.

At one point when Jeanette went off in search of a restroom, I sat down to wait for her under a tent where a band was playing. Instantly, their genre of music caught my attention. It wasn't the usual country/folksy sound typical of groups playing at such festivals. This was something I would describe as New Age or alternative music. I'd been exposed to such music during my spiritual pursuits and had always felt drawn to it.

I sat there perfectly still, allowing the music to carry me into a sweet trance. When Jeanette came back from the restroom, I told her I wanted to stay and listen for a while.

I found my attention focused on one particular member of the four-man group. Initially, he played the guitar, his fingers doing a delicate dance on the strings. Those fingers riveted me. It seemed as if the musical notes they created rode on a wave that traveled directly to my heart.

It might sound silly, Mercedes, but that was truly a magical moment. Despite my many transcendent experiences in my spiritual explorations, I'd never known anything so enchanting. Each moment seemed to stretch into eternity. I didn't want to move a muscle for fear of breaking the spell.

Then my gaze left those magical fingers and traveled up to the guitar player's face. He was a rather ordinary-looking man, medium height, slim, bearded, balding, somewhere in his forties. A keen intelligence shone in his dark brown eyes. But there was also something haunting about those eyes, something that tugged at my heart.

As I watched the man play, one word came to my mind: perfection. I couldn't stop staring at him. At one point, his eyes met mine, and he smiled ever so slightly. That fraction of a second took my breath away.

I looked for a wedding ring on his left hand. His ring finger was bare.

Jeanette kept nudging me, whispering, "Are you ready to go?" I repeatedly shushed her, saying, "Not yet."

At the end of the second song, the guitar player put down his instrument and walked a few steps to the back of the stage to pick up a flute. I noticed that he had a pronounced limp. But even that imperfection seemed perfect.

When he began playing the flute, I realized he was an accomplished musician on more than one instrument. The evocative strains of the flute brought me to tears. It was if the man was telling me something, revealing to me the longings of his heart.

Jeanette finally gave up on me and walked away to look at the crafts in a nearby booth. I hardly noticed her absence. I was hardly aware of anything around me.

All too soon, the performance was over. Apparently, the guitar-and-flute player was the spokesman for the group, as he addressed the small crowd in attendance. "Thank you so much for listening to us. Come back and see us again. We'll be here tomorrow afternoon from two to three."

Of course, he was addressing the entire audience. But the way I received those words, they were meant specifically for me. The man had issued me a personal invitation.

"You really had a thing for that guitar player, didn't you?" Jeanette observed as we left the grounds.

I just smiled at her.

You guessed it, Mercedes. That man was your grandfather. I know you're eager to hear the rest of the story. I hate to disappoint you. But I am so tired, so very tired. Next week, I'll tell you more. Perhaps I'll be feeling better by then.

CHAPTER 9: ANDREW AND DORA COVINGTON

"Why are you up so early, mi amor?" Javier asked as he walked into the kitchen. He was still in his pajamas, his hair rumpled from a long night's sleep. "I thought you liked to sleep in on Saturday mornings."

Mercedes looked up from her seat at the kitchen table. "I need to get this paper done," she said, gesturing toward her laptop computer. "It's due on Monday. I knew we were going to look at apartments this morning, and I promised Dora that I'd visit her this afternoon. I wanted tomorrow to be family time with you and Javi. So, I decided to get up early and get my assignment done, so that it's off my mind."

Javier smiled broadly. "What are you working on?"

Mercedes knew he was impressed with her efforts to organize her time. "I'm writing my paper about doing the life review with Dora," she replied.

Javier walked to the counter to pour himself a cup of coffee. "Want a refill?" he asked.

Mercedes slid her empty mug toward him. "Yes, please."

Javier poured the coffee, then leaned down to kiss her bare shoulder. "Am I bothering you?" he said playfully.

"Yes!" Mercedes giggled. "Now get out of here so I can get this done!"

Chuckling, Javier left the kitchen, and Mercedes returned her gaze to the document on her computer. She scrolled up to the top of her work and reread what she had written. "I guess it's okay," she said to herself. "It's the best I can do."

But she still needed to compose a few closing sentences. It seemed impossible to put into words the profundity of her experience with Dora. "Although I'm finished with my assignment," she finally wrote, "my relationship with my step-grandmother isn't over. I haven't heard all of her story yet. I'm so drawn in that I can't possibly stop listening now. I think the most important part is yet to come."

Suddenly, the words began to flow from her fingertips on the keyboard. "Doing a life review is supposed to be therapeutic to the elderly person who tells their story. I hope the process has been helpful to Dora. But I can say one thing for sure. It has been far more helpful to me. Getting to know my long-lost grandmother has changed me in a way that nothing else in my life has ever changed me. I'll keep on listening to her until the day comes when she can no longer speak."

She clicked "save," then sent the completed assignment to her instructor.

Late that afternoon, Mercedes pulled into the Harbor Lights parking lot just as dark, low-hanging clouds began spitting out a chilly rain. Pulling her jacket hood over her head, she sprinted from her car to the entrance of the building, then rushed up the stairs to the second floor.

When Dora opened her apartment door, Mercedes was relieved to see that her grandmother was up and around again. But there was no denying the fact that Dora's every move was made with the greatest effort.

The elderly woman wore a long multi-tiered skirt, the likes of which Mercedes had never seen before. The colorful cotton fabric was faded, threadbare in spots. The waistband was bunched up and pinned around Dora's frail body, suggesting that she was much thinner than the initial wearer of the garment. Still, the original grandeur of the skirt was apparent.

A deep-purple velvet shawl covered Dora's shoulders. Her long white braid contrasted beautifully with the dark fabric.

Although it was only four o'clock, the overcast skies bathed the tiny apartment in shadows suggestive of twilight. The darkened living room was illuminated only by a burning taper candle wedged into a wine bottle on the coffee table.

Mercedes took off her wet jacket and hung it over a chair in the kitchen. As she seated herself on the sofa, she noticed how comforting the apartment's once-strange ambience now felt to her. The faint drone of the music and the musky scent of the incense embraced her lovingly, while the unusual pictures and figurines surrounded her with their reassuring presences. She slipped off her shoes and settled into a cross-legged position. *I could stay here forever,* she thought.

"Your apartment feels so peaceful," she said to Dora. "It's the most peaceful place I've ever been. It's so calm and sweet."

A radiant smile lit up Dora's face. "My dear, you're sensing the vibrations. That's what happens when you embrace life for what it is, a divine gift. If you approach every activity of daily life as sacred, it creates a sacred atmosphere in your living space."

She gestured around the room with a graceful sweep of her hand. "This special feeling has been created by the sacred music, the chanting, the prayers, the loving conversations, the peaceful interactions. When we conduct our lives in such a way, we create our own heaven on earth."

Dora's words took Mercedes' breath away. Her mind was so overwhelmed by their beauty that she found nothing to say for the next few minutes. Dora eased herself into her recliner and sat with Mercedes in a silence completely devoid of awkwardness.

"Your skirt is so lovely," Mercedes finally commented. "I've never seen anything like it. Where did you get it?"

"I bought this skirt in a boutique many years ago," Dora replied. "Back in the 1980s. I wore it the first evening your grandfather and I spent together. I knew today would be the time to tell the story you've been waiting so patiently to hear, and I thought wearing this skirt would add something special to the occasion."

"It's beautiful," Mercedes murmured, awed by the significance of the garment.

"You know, dear," Dora said, "I've never told anyone the entire story of my relationship with your grandfather. Even Elliott knows only parts of it. I just haven't been able to bear the pain of talking about it. My love affair with Andrew ended on such a sorrowful note."

She brushed a wisp of fluffy hair off her face, then turned to Mercedes with a tearful smile. "But since you brought me his letter, the story now has a different ending. Yes, the story is now complete, and I can tell it."

Then a shadow crossed her face. "But I must caution you, my dear. While the story has its beautiful parts, there are parts that will seem ugly to you, things you'd prefer not to know about your grandfather. You may have difficulty listening to it at times."

"Please don't leave anything out for my sake," Mercedes said hurriedly. "Because that's the way relationships go, the good and the bad together."

"Yes," Dora agreed. "People often have to struggle before they can live harmoniously with each other. Some couples are never fortunate enough to reach that place of peace. Andrew and I were unable to find that state of sustained harmony in our earthly lives. But now, in spirit, we're perfect lovers."

The elderly woman was suddenly overtaken by a coughing spell that racked her frail body. "Can I get you anything?" Mercedes asked, concerned.

"I think a cup of tea would keep my throat lubricated while I talk," Dora replied. "And please, fix one for yourself as well." She pointed to two ceramic mugs sitting on her bookshelves. "Let's use those. You can heat up water in the tea kettle on the stove. The mugs are old, and they're not safe to use in the microwave."

When Mercedes brought the steaming mugs of tea to the living room, she sat one of them on the table next to Dora's chair. Then she resumed her seat on the sofa.

"These mugs hold a special memory for me," Dora said. "Andrew served tea in them the first evening I spent at his apartment."

Mercedes looked closely at the mug in her hand. She imagined her grandfather holding the same mug decades earlier, drinking tea in the company of the woman who would become his lover. The rim of the mug was chipped, and she could see where the handle had been broken off and glued back on. Clearly, the object held so much value for Dora that she hadn't been able to part with it.

For several minutes, the two women sat in quiet contemplation of the flickering candle flame. The melting wax dripped slowly down the sides of the bottle, adding another layer to the drippings from previous burnings.

"The last time I burned this candle was more than thirty years ago." Dora's voice sounded wistful. "It was one evening during the early months of our marriage, when Andrew and I shared a night of beautiful intimacy. What a lovely memory that is!"

Mercedes, you ask whether I went back to Amish Acres to listen to that band again. Yes, I did. I couldn't stop myself.

I went alone, though, as I didn't want anyone else to know about my silly scheme. I could hardly even admit to myself what I was doing. But here's the truth. I was hoping to orchestrate a moment when the guitar player and I would have an opportunity to talk.

I arrived at the band's venue precisely at two o'clock on Sunday afternoon, ready to take in their entire performance. The audience was larger than it had been the previous day, filling nearly all the chairs under the tent. I was not able to sit in the front row as I had hoped. So, there was no eye-contact with the guitar player, no exchange of smiles. I was so disappointed that I could hardly appreciate the music.

However, I was not ready to give up. After the performance, people from the audience crowded around the stage talking to the bandmembers. I joined the crowd, but stayed in the back, patiently awaiting my turn. I didn't want others around when I finally had my moment with the guitar player.

Sadly, by the time I reached the stage, the only bandmember still talking to the crowd was the keyboard player. The other bandmembers were busy loading up their equipment. The guitar player was occupied with something at the back of the stage, his back turned to me.

I tried to make the best of the moment by chatting pleasantly with the keyboard player. I told him how much I'd enjoyed the music and thanked him for being at the festival.

And that was that. "I guess this wasn't meant to be," I told myself, swallowing my disappointment.

Just as I was about to walk away, the guitar player turned around in a flash, as if he'd been struck by something. He broke into a wide smile when he saw me. "Wait!" he called.

I wasn't sure whether he was talking to me or to the keyboard player, but I stopped in my tracks. "Tell her about our upcoming concerts," he said to his bandmate.

I listened obligingly as the keyboard player rattled off information about three or four of the band's upcoming performances. I watched for a moment as the two men prepared to hoist a heavy speaker off the stage. Just as I was ready to leave again, the guitar player looked over his shoulder and said, "Do you have time to stick around for a minute or two?"

"Sure," I said.

In that moment, it seemed as if the encounter I'd envisioned was becoming a reality. The brief transaction seemed serendipitous, as if every nuance had been orchestrated by a higher intelligence. I was so overcome with emotion that my body was trembling from head to toe. I thought my knees were going to buckle, so I sat down in a front-row chair. I closed my eyes, trying to calm myself.

Several minutes later, I heard footsteps approaching, a markedly uneven gait. I opened my eyes to see the guitar player limping toward me. He seated himself several chairs away, turning his body to face mine. "I'm glad you came back," he said.

I recalled my impression from the previous day, that his invitation to the crowd had been personally addressed to me. A surreal feeling crept over me. It seemed as if the guitar player and I were communicating on two different levels, one through an ordinary exchange of words, the other on a wavelength I couldn't begin to fathom.

"I enjoyed your music so much," I said. I wondered whether he was picking up on my unspoken communication, that I'd come back to the festival in the hopes of seeing him.

The guitar player smiled. "Our music doesn't always have broad appeal. People at places like this usually expect to hear a country band."

I wrinkled my nose, and he laughed. "How did you become interested in alternative music?" he asked.

"The past couple of years, I've been involved in spiritual pursuits," I told him. "Yoga, tai chi, drumming, chanting. That's how I've been exposed to this music."

The man looked startled. "I can't believe I haven't run into you before." He held out his hand. "I guess we should introduce ourselves. I'm Andrew Covington."

Mercedes, when I took your grandfather's hand, I thought the electric current passing between our palms was going to scorch my skin. I could barely even utter the words, "I'm Dora Miller."

Just then, one of his bandmates called out, "Hey, Andy," apparently needing his help with something.

Andrew hurriedly rose to his feet. "Can I get your phone number?" He patted his pockets, as if looking for something to write with.

I helped him out by opening my purse, pulling out a pen and a small notebook, and jotting down my number for him. Smiling, he slid the piece of paper into the pocket of his jeans and limped away.

The rest of that day, I felt both elated and disoriented as I tried to take in everything I'd experienced in my surreal encounter with Andrew Covington.

By the next morning, I had talked myself down to a state of normalcy. "You were being silly," I scolded myself. "He's not going to call. He'll probably lose your number. Or he'll just forget about you."

As one week passed without a call, and then two, I became increasingly convinced that I would never hear from Andrew Covington again.

Then, on a Friday evening almost three weeks after my outing to Amish Acres, my telephone rang. Back in those days, I had no caller ID, no way to screen calls. I figured it was Corina. She called me almost every night to tell me dramatic stories about her shift at the hospital. So, I took my time in getting to the telephone, knowing she would let it ring until I picked up.

When I answered the call, I was startled to hear a male voice asking, "Is this Dora Miller?"

"Yes," I replied.

"This is Andrew Covington."

I was so surprised to hear from him that all I could say was, "Oh!"

"I meant to call sooner," he said. "But there's been a lot going on in my life. Things are just now starting to settle down."

"I understand," I said. "Life can get crazy sometimes." Then I realized I knew nothing at all about his life, other than the fact that he played in a band.

As if he could read my thoughts over the telephone line, Andrew began to explain. "My ex-wife is having problems with our daughter. Denise is going through some kind of teenage rebellion. She's a handful for her mother, and the two of them get into some pretty heated fights. Norma calls me when things get out of hand. Recently, I've had to go over to her place two or three nights a week to help calm Denise down."

Mercedes, you look a little shaken by what I just said, although you're not surprised. You already knew that your mother was a rebellious teenager.

But Andrew's revelation caught me off guard. "Wow," I thought. "This guy has some serious complications in his life." I wasn't sure I even wanted to continue our conversation.

However, I was too polite to cut him off. "How many children do you have?" I asked him.

"Just one," he said fondly. "Just my little Denise." He paused, then asked, "How about you?"

"I have two," I replied. Then I told him about Wesley being in the Peace Corps and Corina starting her nursing career.

"That's awesome!" he exclaimed. "You must be a proud mother."

From there, we launched into an easy conversation. While I knew little about Andrew Covington, it also seemed as if I'd known him forever.

We talked about his music. Then I asked him what he did for a living. He told me was a computer programmer, that he set up financial records for a company in Elkhart.

"The GI Bill paid for my schooling," he explained. "Prior to my time in Viet Nam, I was a construction worker. When I came back home with an injury, I wasn't able-bodied enough to go back to my old line of work. I felt totally lost. The GI Bill helped me establish a new career. I can't say that I love my work, not like I love my music. But it's a good job, and I'm thankful for it."

"I understand," I said. "I work in human resources. It's a great job, but I'm not passionate about it."

"What are you passionate about?" he asked.

I thought for a moment. "My children, of course. And my spiritual journey."

"That's amazing!" he exclaimed. "I could answer exactly the same. I can't believe how in sync we are."

His observation sent an electric chill through my body. I didn't know how to respond without sounding too eager. "It's strange, isn't it?" was all I managed to say.

Shortly thereafter, Andrew ended our conversation. "I really enjoy talking with you, Dora," he said. "But I promised Norma that I'd call her. Listen, are you busy this weekend? My band has a gig tomorrow night, but I'm free on Sunday. Would you like to get together and continue our conversation?"

Mercedes, I have to admit that I said yes with a bit of trepidation. I sensed there were some overwhelming issues in Andrew Covington's life. But the longer I talked with him, the more I felt drawn to him. The pull was irresistible.

So, I agreed to meet him in McNaughton Park by the Saint Joseph River in Elkhart. "I think we could talk easier in a secluded environment like that," he told me. "Sometimes, I get a little edgy being in public. It's funny. I'm okay on the stage playing with my band. But I get freaked out in places like restaurants."

"The park will be fine with me," I assured him.

Sunday was a beautiful late-August day with a hint of fall in the air. McNaughton Park was just a half-mile from my apartment, so I decided to walk instead of drive. As I approached our designated meeting spot, I saw Andrew *sitting at a picnic table with his back to me, gazing at the river.*

When I was about twenty feet away from him, I called out his name. He jumped as if he'd been shot, then whirled around to see who was approaching. The startled look on his face relaxed into a wide smile when he saw me.

"Sorry about that," he said. "You took me by surprise. I was waiting for the sound of a car pulling up."

"I don't live that far from here," I told him. "There wasn't any point in driving."

He patted the bench beside him. "Come have a seat."

We sat together looking out over the water, making small talk about the grandeur of the scene. "Nature keeps me sane," Andrew said. "It calms me down more than any pill anyone could ever give me."

I didn't know what to say in response to that disclosure. So, after several moments of silence, I asked, "How is your daughter? Is everything okay between her and her mother?"

Andrew shrugged. "For the moment, I guess. But I never know when things will blow up again."

"That must be really hard," I said. "Some guys would just walk away from it all."

Andrew winced. "I did that once. I can't do it again."

"What do you mean?" I asked.

He hung his head, speaking bluntly. "Denise was born in 1972. My beautiful baby was my pride and joy. She was a daddy's girl. She actually preferred me over her mother. Whenever she had her crying spells, Norma would be at her wits' end. She'd hand Denise over to me, and I'd be the one to settle her down.

"But when Denise was a year old, I left for Viet Nam. That was really hard on Norma. I know she felt abandoned, having to take care of our child on her own."

He swallowed hard, as if choking back strong emotions. "When I came back home in 1975, my little girl didn't know me. She was afraid of me. And things weren't the same between Norma and me. I felt like an intruder in their home.

"On top of all that, my mother got sick with cancer and died six months after I came home. When I was growing up,

my dad was a no-good drunk. He terrorized our household. My mom was the one who held the family together. Losing her was more than I could handle. I guess I got swallowed up in my grief, and I wasn't there for Norma like she needed me to be. She started to lose patience with me. We gave the marriage a few years, but things just didn't work out."

He fell silent. I knew that the phrase, "things didn't work out," could cover a lot of ground. But I sensed it was not the time to pry. "How long have you been divorced?" I asked.

"Nine years," he said. "I can't live with Norma and Denise, but I try to be there for them. That's the least I can do."

He turned to face me fully. "Look, Dora, I don't want you to get the wrong idea about Norma and me. I've dated a few women since my divorce, and they always get hung up on the idea that I'm still involved with my ex-wife. I'm not. Norma and I were high school sweethearts. We were kids when we got married, too young to know what we were doing. I doubt that our marriage would've stood a chance, Viet Nam or not. I have no romantic feelings for Norma anymore. It's just that...." His voice trailed off.

I finished the thought for him. "You feel responsible for her and your child. You can't let go of that obligation, even if you're involved with someone else."

He looked at me with gratitude in his eyes. "Yes. Thank you for understanding that. I think you're the first woman who has ever understood."

He exhaled slowly, as if deeply relieved. "I wanted to get that off my chest so it doesn't become an issue later on. And there's something else I want to get out in the open, in case things go a little farther between us. I have a prosthetic leg. I lost my leg in Viet Nam."

Caught off guard by that news, I must've recoiled slightly. Andrew looked dejected. "Some women are put off by that. A missing leg isn't exactly a turn-on."

I spoke hesitantly, wanting to choose my words carefully. "I think a missing limb has nothing to do with who you really are. I am not a superficial woman. What matters to me is what's in a man's heart."

As Andrew and I gazed at each other, a wave of deep

empathy flowed between us, enveloping the two of us in a warm glow. I was certain he felt it as much as I did.

"I knew that about you," he said so softly I could hardly hear him. "I knew that about you the moment I first saw you in the crowd at the festival."

I sensed there was something else that burdened Andrew's soul, something he couldn't so readily bring forward. A question popped out of my mouth before I knew what I was saying. "What was it like in Viet Nam?"

Andrew's face darkened, and he looked away from me. "That's something I don't talk about with anyone. Not ever. Okay?" The gruffness in his voice broke the spell between us.

Feeling stung, I pulled back from him. "Okay."

He averted his gaze, staring at the river again. "Sorry, Dora. I didn't mean to be so harsh."

Still, I was a little put off, and was about to tell Andrew that I needed to get going. He must've sensed that, as he turned back to face me, smiling again, ready to give me his full attention. "I've told you so much about me. Now, I want to hear more about you."

He listened intently as I told him the story of my Amish upbringing. "It stands to reason that I would meet an Amish girl at Amish Acres," he chuckled.

I went on to tell him about my first marriage ending in my husband's tragic death. I told him about my years of being a single mother, then my marriage to Vincent.

Andrew winced when I talked about my dancing career. "I'd never make a dance partner," he said. "Not with this bum leg."

"My dancing years are behind me," I assured him. "I've accepted that fact. I'm not looking for anyone to fill Vincent's shoes."

"You know," Andrew observed, "you've been through a few battles of your own. You're sitting here with me so beautiful, so serene, so composed. I never would've guessed you've had such a challenging life. Dora Miller, you are an amazing woman."

I felt myself blushing. "Thank you, Andrew. But let me

remind you that I have the same daily struggles that everyone else has."

We went on to talk about my yoga class and my meditation group. When I brought up the subject of my drumming circle, Andrew said, "I used to be into drumming big time. But I've drifted away the past few years. That's probably why I never met you there."

He cocked his head, giving me a long look. "Maybe our paths weren't meant to cross until now."

He picked up an acorn that had fallen on the picnic table and rolled it around between his fingers. "I used to be into all that stuff you just talked about. Maybe it would do me good to get back into it."

I almost said, "We could do it together." But I stopped myself when I realized how presumptuous that would sound. I longed to touch Andrew in some way, to satisfy the growing desire I felt for him. I didn't fully understand that desire. It went far beyond physical attraction.

Bringing myself back to a more grounded state of mind, I said, "I need to leave in a few minutes. I'm going out to dinner with my daughter this evening."

Before we parted ways, Andrew asked if he could give me a hug. I surrendered myself to the warmth of his arms, feeling our two essences melt together into one. He must've held me for a full minute. I didn't want him to let go. I thought for sure he was going to kiss me, but he didn't.

"Dora, it's so wonderful to meet a woman like you," he said after finally releasing his embrace. "I think we have a lot more to say to each other. I'll call you soon. This time, I won't wait three weeks. I promise."

On my walk home, mixed emotions churned inside me. One part of me was singing at the top of her lungs that Andrew Covington was the man I'd been searching for, the partner I'd envisioned for so long. Surely, the intensity of our attraction had to signify something. I'd never felt this way about any other man I'd dated.

But a skeptical voice chimed in with a note of caution. "You're letting your feelings run away with you, Dora. This man has issues. He's already told you about them. He's tied up with an ex-wife and a troubled teenager. He comes with baggage from the war. Take it slow. Don't lose your head over him."

Dinner with Corina that evening provided a distraction from my runaway thoughts. Instead of revealing to her that I'd met a potential love interest, I asked her if she'd been dating anyone.

She rolled her eyes. "Mom, you know I don't have time for men right now. I like my freedom. I'm not ready to get bogged down in relationship problems."

She looked at me pointedly. "Have you ever heard that saying, 'It takes a really good man to be better than no man at all?'"

Her words sobered me. I realized my thoughts and feelings about Andrew Covington had drifted far out into fantasyland. Still, when I went to bed that night, I couldn't rid my mind of the idea that I had found my soulmate.

True to his word, Andrew called me three days later. This time, our discussion turned to his history of drinking. "I want to be honest with you," he said. "I want to get all the cards out on the table. If this thing between us goes anywhere, I don't want you to be blindsided by any surprises."

He disclosed to me that prior to going to Viet Nam, he hadn't been much of a drinker, but that after he'd come back home, he'd spiraled down into full-blown alcoholism.

"I've been through that," I told him. "My first husband had a drinking problem. He couldn't stay out of the bars."

"I wasn't into the bar scene," Andrew said. "I was too much of a loner for that. I drank at home. And it created problems in my marriage."

"Was that the reason for your divorce?" I asked.

"It was a big part of it," he admitted.

I knew I was about to trigger a touchy issue, but plunged ahead. "Was the drinking because of what happened to you in Viet Nam?"

"Yup," he replied without hesitation. "It was the PTSD. A lot of Viet Nam vets ended up like me, drinking to calm our

nerves and to drown out memories. Also, there was the pain from my injury. I have chronic pain in my wounded leg, the part of it that's still there."

He paused, then said, "Dora, I'm telling you this because I want to be honest with you. But I don't want you to worry. I went to treatment after my divorce, and I haven't touched a drop of alcohol since then. I don't ever intend to. I have no desire for it."

"What do you do about the pain?" I asked.

"I'm on medication," he said. "Nothing illegal. Everything is above board, prescribed by a doctor."

At the end of our conversation, Andrew suggested that we get together that weekend. Remembering how he was sometimes ill at ease in public places, I considered inviting him to my apartment.

But before I could issue that invitation, Andrew said, "Why don't you come to my place Saturday? I can cook for you. I know my way around the kitchen."

He told me he lived in a large Victorian home on the north side of Elkhart that had been divided into multiple apartments. "I was lucky to get one of the downstairs apartments," he said. "The landlord took pity on a war veteran with a bum leg."

When I stepped into Andrew's apartment on Saturday evening, I couldn't help but contrast the moment with my initial exposure to Vincent's living quarters. The place was small but clean and tidy, with charming Victorian architectural features. The orderly environment matched my style of living and instantly made me feel comfortable. The pictures and decorative objects reflected Andrew's love of nature and his mystical inclinations.

"I love your place!" I gushed, ecstatic to discover that we shared similar tastes. I tried to stop myself from once again jumping to the conclusion that I'd found the man of my dreams. But my heart leaped far ahead of my reason.

Andrew had prepared lasagna and a green salad, all of which was quite delicious. After we ate, he made tea in these mugs we're using right now, and we went to sit on his *sofa. He lit a candle like the one you and I are enjoying, creating a lovely ambiance in the room.*

We sat together in the flickering candlelight, facing each other as we talked. As the time passed, we slipped into the intimate conversation of kindred spirits. It felt as if I'd been searching for Andrew all of my life, and I sensed he felt the same about me.

At one point, Andrew reached over and took my hand, and we gazed deeply into each other's eyes. I knew his mind was forming the same question that was on my mind: is this the beginning of something special?

Suddenly, he winced and pulled his hand away. For an instant, I felt rejected. Then he said, "Dora, I want to make passionate love to you. But I'm scared to death. My attraction to you is so powerful. It overwhelms me. I don't know what to do with that feeling. I don't know where this is going."

I bit my lip to keep my own emotions from gushing out, as I felt so drawn to Andrew that I thought I would burst. Never before had I considered engaging in physical intimacy at such an early point in a relationship. But my desire had exploded through the gates of my self-control.

Then Andrew pulled me to him, and we began kissing as if we were devouring the essence of each other. As our passion became more heated, he once again pulled back. "Dora," he said, "I'm nervous about you seeing my leg. It's not a pretty sight."

"Don't worry about that," I murmured as I pulled him back to me.

When we moved to the bedroom and began removing our clothing, I found the sight of Andrew's leg to be disturbing indeed. The limb was missing from just below the knee. The thigh muscles appeared wasted, and a massive scar ran from hip to knee.

I couldn't keep the tears from running down my face. My empathy for him in that moment was so great that I couldn't help but feel the agony he'd endured when he was injured.

When Andrew saw my tears, he covered his leg with the sheet in embarrassment. But I pulled the sheet back and

247

gently caressed his thigh. "This is part of you," I said, "and I accept it."

He drew me into his arms, and we began to make love in the sweetest of ways. There was none of the awkwardness that often accompanies the first encounter of new lovers. Physically and emotionally, we seemed to be in perfect harmony.

That night, I experienced a depth of feeling I didn't know was possible to reach. As Andrew and I surrendered ourselves to each other, it seemed as if our souls merged and soared to the heights of heaven. My imagination had become a reality, a reality far more amazing than anything in my daydreams.

After our lovemaking, we lay in each other's arms in a state of perfect bliss. I knew with certainly that I'd found the man I'd been searching for. I knew I had fallen deeply, deeply in love with Andrew Covington.

When it was time for me to leave, Andrew held me tightly, as if he couldn't bear to let me go. He kissed me one last time, then whispered in my ear, "I'll call you."

As I drove home, I wept tears of joy. I thanked God again and again for bringing Andrew into my life. The long wait had finally paid off. My true love had arrived at last.

I didn't doubt Andrew's promise to call me. It was inconceivable to think that he wouldn't. I fully expected to hear from him the following day.

But he didn't call me on Sunday, nor on Monday or Tuesday. I began to feel uneasy. By Wednesday evening, my insides were knotted with anxiety. I could no longer wait to hear the reassuring sound of my new lover's voice. I decided to call him.

Then I realized I didn't have Andrew's number. He'd asked for mine, but had never offered me his. He'd never invited me to call him. So, I turned to the telephone directory, hoping he hadn't opted for an unlisted number. To my relief, his name and number were in the book.

When he answered my call, the ominous chill in his voice filled me with dread.

"Andrew," I said, "this is Dora."

"Oh," was his gruff reply.

I waited for him to say, "How are you?" or, "I'm glad you called." But he didn't, and a heavy silence hung between us.

"Are you okay?" I finally asked.

After another long pause, Andrew said in the same cold, flat voice, "I'm sorry, Dora. I can't do this."

My heart leaped into my throat. "Can't do what?" I asked.

"This. Me and you. I can't bring a woman into my life right now."

I was stunned. I'd thought he'd already brought me into his life. I'd assumed that issue had been settled the night we made love. "Why not?" I asked.

"If you must know," he said, "my daughter has been raising hell this week. I don't know what in the world is going on with her. Last night, she was out all night. Her mother had no idea where she was. I was on the phone with Norma all night long, and I didn't get a wink of sleep. Around six this morning, the police brought Denise home. It turns out that she was drinking with some kids, and they started vandalizing property. She has a hearing in juvenile court next week."

"I'm really sorry, Andrew," I said. "I know this is hard on you."

"It's all my fault," he said bitterly.

"How could that be?" I protested. "You aren't forcing your daughter to do what she's been doing."

"Well, that's the way I feel about it," he snapped. "Don't I have a right to feel what I feel? You women are always concerned about your feelings. You never consider what a man goes through."

"I'm sorry," I said. "I didn't mean to upset you."

"Look, Dora," he said, his voice softening. "I can't bring someone else into this mess right now. It wouldn't be fair to Norma and Denise, and it wouldn't be fair to you. I'm sorry if you think I led you on."

I felt my body growing cold and weak, and I began to shake so badly that I could hardly hang onto the telephone receiver. "Andrew, I can't believe this," I choked out. "How can you throw all this away after the beautiful night we shared?"

"Don't make this difficult, Dora," he said, the anger returning to his voice.

"Okay," I whispered. I hung up the phone, then stumbled to my bedroom and threw myself across my bed, wanting to die.

The next two days, Thursday and Friday, I called in sick to work because I was too emotionally distraught to face anyone. I had never neglected my work responsibilities like that before. But I knew that if I showed up at my office, I wouldn't be able to do anything but sit at my desk and sob.

For those two long days at home, I didn't talk to anyone. I didn't answer my telephone. I didn't change out of my pajamas. For the most part, I lay in bed weeping. I longed for sleep to give me a reprieve from my suffering. But every time I managed to doze off for a few minutes, I'd wake up abruptly, my entire body racked with grief.

I felt so sick that I was unable to choke down anything more than a few sips of water. From time to time, I'd get up and vomit, until I had nothing left in me to bring up.

I simply couldn't comprehend how two lovers could come together in such perfection, only to have one of them cruelly tear himself away. It felt as if something had been ripped from my solar plexus, leaving behind a burning hole.

I berated God for playing such a horrible trick on me. "How could you do this?" I cried out. "How could you lead me to the door of paradise, then drop me into the abyss of despair?"

By Friday evening, the intensity of my grief had subsided, and I began to think about rejoining the land of the living. I got up and showered. Afterwards, I stood in front of the bathroom mirror gazing at my washed-out appearance.

"Dora, this quest to find a soulmate is nothing but foolishness," I scolded myself. "You got caught up in a little girl's magical thinking. See where it got you? You're an absolute mess. You can never afford to do this again."

I put on a clean pair of pajamas. Then, weak from hunger, I raided the refrigerator for leftovers. I felt stronger after I ate. I reminded myself that prior to meeting Andrew, I had been leading a satisfying life as a single woman, and that I could do so again. I told myself that I had the strength to stand up and move forward into my future, leaving this devastating disappointment behind me.

Mercedes, I've never forgotten how I felt at that moment. It was one of those times when I had to delve deep into my own resources to discover what was there. It was one of those times when I had to lean on myself and be my own friend. That was a precious experience.

I sat down to watch television, snuggled under a warm, comforting blanket. Around ten o'clock, when I was thoroughly exhausted and finally relaxed enough to get a good night's sleep, I was startled by a knock on my door.

"Who in the world could that be?" I wondered. I got up to answer the door. And there stood Andrew Covington, his face twisted in pain. I stared at him, not knowing whether I wanted to slam the door in his face or rush into his arms for a joyful reunion. I did neither.

"Dora," he asked, "can we talk?"

"I guess so," I said.

Mercedes, you think I was foolish to agree to that. You would've told him to get lost, or something harsher than that. Perhaps I was foolish. In spite of what he'd just put me through, I invited Andrew into my home.

But I kept my distance from him. I curled up in my chair again and pulled my blanket around me, protecting myself. I had nothing to say to him, not even words of anger. I had cried myself completely empty. I had finally managed to crawl out of my hole of despair and had reclaimed my composure. I didn't want Andrew to stir me up again.

He sat on my sofa looking dejected and ashamed. I waited for him to say what was on his mind, and was flabbergasted when the first words out of his mouth were, "My God, Dora, you're so beautiful."

There I sat in my ragged pajamas, my hair still damp from my shower, my eyes red and puffy from hours of crying.

Feeling anything but beautiful, I wanted to pull the blanket over my face.

"Dora," Andrew continued, "the minute you hung up the phone Wednesday night, I regretted what I said to you. I knew I'd been an idiot, but I didn't know how to undo the damage I'd done. I tried to call you earlier tonight. When you didn't answer the phone, I figured you didn't want to talk to me. And it hit me full force how stupid I'd been."

He looked at me pleadingly, as if seeking reassurance. I had none to give him.

He leaned forward, elbows on his knees, staring at the floor. "Dora, I know you're the perfect woman for me. I'm extremely attracted to you, physically, emotionally, and spiritually. But truthfully, I have no confidence that I can be the man you need me to be."

I listened quietly. Apparently, Andrew wanted to be back in my life again. A wave of exhaustion washed over me. I leaned my head on the arm of my chair, as I had no energy to hold it up.

My silence must've made Andrew nervous. "Dora, let me explain," he said.

"Go ahead," I mumbled, not meeting his gaze.

In a halting voice, Andrew proceeded to inform me that he was prone to bouts of deep depression. He told me that some of his previous girlfriends had left him because they weren't able to cope with his moods. And I realized that when Andrew had coldly pushed me away, it was the depression speaking. Now, everything made sense.

"It wouldn't be easy being with me," he said. "When the pain in my leg flares up, I'm not good for much of anything. And it looks like the problems with Denise aren't going away anytime soon. That would put a constant strain on us. But I know I can't walk away from you without at least giving this relationship a chance. If you tell me that you never want to see me again, I'll understand. But I hope you want to try as much as I do."

I struggled to find what I wanted to say. But before my mind could formulate a verbal response, I felt my body get out of my chair, cross the room, and sit down next to Andrew on the sofa. He reached for my hand, and I laid my weary head on his shoulder.

We sat together without speaking, silently consenting to begin a life together. We both knew it wouldn't be easy, but neither of us could truly fathom how difficult it was going to be.

So began my relationship with your grandfather, Mercedes. So began the rocky road of fiery passion and searing pain.

After our relationship recovered from that early upheaval, I discovered that my initial assumption about Andrew was correct. He and I truly were soulmates. We seemed to be perfectly in tune with one another, with an uncanny understanding of each other's thoughts and feelings, desires and motivations. Even our eating and sleeping habits seemed to be in sync.

We saw each other every weekday evening after work. We spent our weekends together. Whereas my relationship with Vincent had been all about the outward show, my love affair with Andrew was a preciously private matter. We withdrew from the world into a cave of shared solitude.

Yes, Mercedes, your grandfather and I were inseparable. Except for when his dark moods drove us apart.

I soon discovered that life with Andrew was defined by cycles. We had our periods of intense passion, when we basked in the bliss of our intimacy, when our love affair filled our every need. Then, I would feel Andrew cooling and withdrawing, sinking into a testy depression. I learned that if I tried to be close to him when he was in such a state, I would be met with a chilly rebuff.

The first time that happened, I thought Andrew was trying to end our relationship. Bewildered, I asked him if he was breaking up with me.

"No," he snapped. "Everything will be fine if you give me some space for a while."

So, that's what I learned to do. I actually became quite adept at backing off at the first signs of his dark mood. "He warned me about this," I'd remind myself.

Then, I'd busy myself with something else. I'd tackle a project in my apartment. I'd go out with one of my girlfriends or do something with Corina.

A few days later, after his dark mood had lifted, Andrew would eagerly pursue me again, as if reuniting with a long-lost lover.

Part of me understood the cycles, and I tried to flow gracefully with the ups and downs in our relationship. Another part of me invariably felt startled and hurt by my lover's rebuff. Even though I'd tell myself not to feel rejected, I always would. However, when Andrew would initiate intimacy again, the heat of our passion would melt away any resentment I'd accumulated during our time apart.

Each time he came back to me, hungry for love, Andrew would apologize for his behavior. I'd be seduced into believing his dark moods would never again come between us. But the cycle rolled on and on.

We had a particularly difficult time as we moved into the cold, dark days of winter. Andrew would sink into depressions that lasted up to a week at a time.

His episodes sometimes coincided with flare-ups of pain in his leg. But more often, they were triggered by news of his daughter's misbehavior. My efforts to comfort him at those times were completely ineffective. When he was embroiled in drama with Norma and Denise, it seemed as if I was invisible to him.

Thankfully, there was one thing that worked fairly well in bringing Andrew out of a bad mood. That was his music. His band played at various venues once or twice a month, and they got together to practice between performances. Andrew would always come home in a much better frame of mind after spending time with his bandmates.

Mercedes, you ask whether Andrew ever introduced me to Norma and Denise. Yes, he did. We hadn't been together for more than a few weeks before Andrew said he wanted me to meet his ex-wife and daughter. He drove me over to their home in Goshen, the house you grew up in.

The first time I saw the three of them together, I instantly understood their family dynamics. I knew right away that I didn't need to worry about competing with Norma for Andrew's affection. I actually liked her. Just as you described her, I found Norma to be a kind, loving person. I could tell she was under enormous strain in trying to deal with Denise. The poor woman looked as if she hadn't had a good night's sleep in ten years. While she desperately needed her ex-husband's help in managing their unruly daughter, she clearly had no romantic interest in him.

At one point in the visit, she pulled me aside. "I hope things work out between you and Andrew," she said. "I think you'll be good for him."

No, it wasn't Andrew's former wife who was my rival for his affection and attention. It was his daughter.

It may surprise you to know, Mercedes, that your mother was quite beautiful as a young woman. Like you, she had a tall, willowy figure and a mane of long hair. Only her hair was blonde instead of dark like yours.

But lovely as she was, there was something wild, almost feral, in Denise's eyes. That unnerved me, and I feared the girl was headed for deep trouble. I don't think Andrew ever recognized that look. He only saw his precious baby girl.

Whenever his daughter was agitated, which was virtually all the time, Andrew would plead, cajole, appease, and coddle her. He'd end up giving her anything she wanted just to calm her down. I could see that Denise easily overran her worn-out mother, and that she was highly skilled at manipulating her father. But I could never tell Andrew that. He did not want my opinion about his child.

One weekend during our first autumn together, Andrew and I went on a day trip to South Haven, a small Lake Michigan town just north of here. As we were strolling through a tourist boutique, I pointed out some jewelry I was interested in. He shrugged me off, then pointed to a shirt. "Don't you think Denise would look pretty in that? I think I'll get it for her."

That might seem like a little thing to get upset about, Mercedes, but it shook me. I wanted Andrew to be thinking about me in those terms, not his sixteen-year-old daughter. At that moment, I realized he would never get over his obsession with Denise. He would always feel he owed her something, because of having gone off to war in the early years of her life.

After we'd dated for two months, I introduced Andrew to Corina. She was polite to him, and the two of them seemed to like each other well enough. However, I could tell Corina was holding herself back. She wasn't willing to invest in my new relationship until she was sure it was going to last.

When the spring of 1989 arrived, Andrew's ups and downs smoothed out for a while. He remained in exceptionally good moods for long periods of time. Since we weren't suffering the setbacks of his depressive episodes, our love deepened. It seemed as if the clouds had finally parted, allowing the sunlight to illuminate our blessed union.

Mercedes, I was so profoundly in love with your grandfather. I am forever grateful for having tasted the sweetness of such an exquisite experience.

When his leg could tolerate the strain of the activity, Andrew and I enjoyed taking walks together. One Saturday afternoon in May, we went for a stroll in McNaughton Park, where we'd met for our first date. A bright blue sky and temperatures in the seventies made for a perfect day, and our hearts were brimming over with affection for each other.

We sat down to rest at the picnic table where we'd had our first long conversation. Andrew gazed at me for a few moments, as if trying to work up the nerve to tell me something. Then he turned away, looking out over the river.

We sat in silence for two or three minutes before he began speaking in a voice breaking with emotion. "Dora, I love you more than I can possibly express. I never thought I'd muster the courage to ask you this question, but I know with all my heart that I want to. Will you marry me?"

The day was so perfect and the moment was so precious, there was only one word to be uttered. That word was, "Yes."

In the back of my mind, I remembered acquiescing to two previous marriage proposals, agreeing to ill-advised partnerships that couldn't weather the test of time. But unlike my feelings for Ivan and Vincent, my love for Andrew was a mature love, a deep-down, all-encompassing heart-and-soul kind of love.

Still, in the recesses of my mind, I recognized a flicker of uncertainty. However, Andrew's confidence gave me confidence, and I said, "Of course I'll marry you."

That night, Andrew stayed with me at my apartment, and our lovemaking soared to new heights of ecstasy. I was one with my lover. I couldn't imagine a life without him.

Our plans for married life evolved quickly. Collaborating with Andrew was easy, as we agreed on almost every detail. We considered having him move into my apartment, as his place was too small for two people.

However, we decided that starting our life together in a new residence would be symbolic of a new beginning. So, we pooled our savings to put a down-payment on a two-bedroom bungalow on the northwest side of Elkhart, located on a wooded lot on the Saint Joseph River.

Finding that house seemed serendipitous. The first time we saw it, we both knew it was meant for us.

I remembered how Andrew had told me on our first date that nature kept him sane. I hoped that living near the water, surrounded by woods, would be therapeutic for him.

Mercedes, I'll never forget your grandfather's exhilaration the day we finalized the purchase of our home. After signing the last of the documents, we strolled hand-in-hand around the perimeter of our new property.

Andrew talked excitedly about all his ideas for enhancing the landscaping. "This would be a perfect spot for a bed of daylilies." "What do you think about putting a retaining wall over there?" "We need to do something with shade-loving plants here on the north side." "I can picture a row of arborvitaes here." "How about sunflowers along that fence?"

Then he pulled me into his arms and held me tightly. "I can't believe it, Dora. I can't believe something this good is happening to me. I'm going to be living with the love of my life on this awesome piece of property, our own little paradise."

Releasing me, he gazed at the scenery around us. "It almost makes up for everything bad I've ever been through." His face darkened ever so slightly. "How could I possibly deserve this?"

"You deserve it," I assured him. "We both do. We've both waited a long time for something like this to happen."

I tried to dismiss Andrew's words of doubt. Later, however, they came back to haunt me. Mercedes, I've come to realize that your grandfather's feelings of unworthiness played a major role in the breakup of our relationship.

We got married in August 1989, just a few weeks after we purchased the house. Now that we had a place to live, neither of us felt there was any reason to wait. We held the ceremony on our patio in our beautiful backyard.

Our wedding was far from the ostentatious event I'd had when I married Vincent. It was just a small private affair with a few friends and family members in attendance. Andrew and I exchanged heartfelt vows we'd written ourselves.

I was so pleased to have Corina there. Wesley was still stationed in Africa at the time. He hadn't yet come home since first leaving the states. I'd been hoping he could make it to my wedding, but he sent his best wishes instead.

Andrew's brother came from Ohio. That was the first and only time I met him. As Andrew was estranged from his father at the time, he didn't want him at the wedding.

I agreed to Andrew's suggestion of inviting Norma and Denise, although I secretly feared Denise would act up and ruin the day. Thankfully, she refrained from making a scene.

For several months after our wedding, my new husband and I floated along on a cloud of bliss. We busied ourselves with one project after another, fixing up our home and landscaping our property.

Andrew's carpentry skills proved to be an enormous asset. He knew exactly how to tackle renovation projects in parts of the house that needed repair. The two of us worked side by side, in tune with one another, sharing the enjoyment of our task.

I was so pleased with that house. After leaving my childhood home, I'd only lived in rented space, which had always felt like it belonged to someone else. My love nest with Andrew truly was home. I couldn't imagine anywhere in the world I would rather be.

Of course, I wrote to Elliott to tell him about my marriage. "It's the real thing this time," I promised him. "I am truly in love with this man."

You look sad, Mercedes. You know that such perfection could never last. In the late fall, when the weather turned cold and the days darkened, so did Andrew's mood. It seemed as if a black cloud had descended upon our beautiful love affair. Before I knew it, we were back in the grip of that dreadful cycle.

With being married and sharing a residence, it wasn't as easy to distance myself from Andrew's moods. During the times when my husband was walled off in the cave of his gloom, my sorrow and loneliness felt unbearable.

I never doubted that Andrew loved me, and that he was committed to our marriage. But it seemed as if his dark moods were becoming increasingly nasty. I had difficulty making sense of this, and couldn't understand how my loving husband could be so ugly at times.

As I'm sure you know by now, Mercedes, I'm not much of a fighter by nature. I try to make the best of adversity, and I rarely confront anyone unless circumstances are quite compelling.

So, when faced with the challenge of Andrew's ever-darkening moods, my first thought was to question whether I might be doing something to cause them. One day, after he'd just emerged from a dark mood and we'd reunited in lovemaking, I broached the subject.

"Andrew," I whispered as I lay in his arms, "what am I doing wrong?"

"What do you mean?" he asked.

"Sometimes you get so angry with me."

He abruptly pulled away. "It's not you, Dora," he said. "Don't make this about you. That just makes it harder for me."

"What is it, then?" I persisted. "Talk to me. Tell me what's bothering you."

Andrew rolled over and sat on the edge of the bed, his back to me. "I know from experience that talking doesn't help. These things just happen. I can't explain it. So please leave it alone, Dora. Okay?"

After that, I tried very hard not to take the ugly episodes personally. I told myself that if I learned to go with the flow, I would be fine.

I'd seen women at work in relationships similar to mine. Some of them had come to talk to me in my capacity as human resources assistant. So, I was well aware of the toll a spouse's mental instability could take on a person.

However, I still refused to acknowledge that my husband's behavior was, at times, nothing short of abusive. It took me a long time to fully admit that Andrew's mood swings and angry outbursts were eroding my spirit.

I told no one what was going on in my home. None of my friends knew, and I tried very hard to keep Corina from picking up on what was happening. I took great pains to hide the secret from my coworkers. I was afraid I would hear words of advice that I had sometimes offered to others: leave this relationship before it destroys you.

I had no desire to face another divorce. Aside from the ugly incidents, Andrew and I still seemed perfectly suited for each other. So, I worked at becoming even more adept at picking up signs of an approaching storm. I'd scurry out of Andrew's way at the first indication of tension or surliness, and would place no demands on him at those times. I convinced myself that I could make my marriage work if I managed things just right. I failed to see that I was doing nothing less than walking on those proverbial eggshells.

Invariably when his dark mood passed, Andrew would reach for me again, desperately needing intimacy. But as the cycle rolled on and on, it became increasingly difficult for me to let down my guard and open my wounded heart. I'd have no time to build up trust before our relationship would be ambushed by another sinister mood.

One day, after taking the brunt of an angry outburst that came without warning, I understood why Andrew and Norma were unable to stay married. I knew why his former girlfriends had walked out on him. But I was determined not to follow in their footsteps. I loved Andrew too much to abandon him.

Another day, when my husband was in the throes of depression, I made the mistake of suggesting that he might benefit from taking psychiatric medication. He turned on me in a fury. "You have no right to talk to me like that," he snarled. "I'm not one of your problem employees."

The intensity of his reaction sent me flying from the room. I never raised that delicate subject again.

After that, "I'm not one of your problem employees," became Andrew's go-to phrase anytime I came close to confronting him.

One evening in the summer of 1990, Corina showed up at my house unannounced. That struck me as odd. Since my marriage to Andrew, she'd never popped into my home like she'd done when I lived alone in my apartment.

"Mom, we need to talk," she said.

The two of us went out to sit at the table on our patio. I sensed she was highly anxious about what she needed to tell me. "You're not going to like this," she said.

"Go ahead," I told her, knowing I was about to face something unpleasant.

She began speaking hesitantly. "My roommate Sarah and I have been looking for jobs in different places around the country. Just to see what we could come up with. We weren't totally serious about it. But we've both lived here in Indiana all our lives, and we thought it would be nice to see other parts of the United States."

She took a deep breath, then said in a rush. "We found a hospital in rural Georgia where they have a shortage of nurses. *We put in our applications, and both of us were offered jobs. We figured we could have a little adventure while doing some good in an underprivileged area. So, we're moving in two weeks."*

I was so stunned that I couldn't speak. My mind rushed back to five years earlier, when my son had presented me with a similar speech. I must've sat there motionless for a full minute, trying to take in what I'd just heard.

Corina laughed nervously. "Say something, Mom! You're making me feel guilty."

"I knew this day would eventually come," I finally responded. "You're not the kind of woman to be held down. You're twenty-six years old now, and I guess it's time for you to spread your wings and fly away from me. I'm not ready for that. But it wouldn't be right for me to stop you."

"Well," Corina huffed, "it's not like you're never going to see me again. I'm not moving halfway around the world like Wesley did."

"I know," I replied.

"Anyway," she said as she waved her hand around the yard, "you're so tied up with this house and your marriage that you don't have time for anyone or anything else."

I winced at the hint of bitterness in her voice. "Sweetheart, do you feel like I've been neglecting you?"

She shook her head. "Not really. It's just that you're so preoccupied all the time. It was so much easier to relate to you when you were single. But you've got to live your life, and I've got to live mine."

Her words almost shattered me. But instead of breaking down in tears, I pulled myself together. "Corina, darling, you deserve to follow your heart's desire. I wish you and Sarah all the best."

Two weeks later, I drove over to Corina's apartment to help her and Sarah load the last of their belongings onto the moving van they'd rented. Before they left, I clung to my daughter and cried.

"You'll be alright, Mom," she kept saying to me. "You've got a husband now. You have Andrew to lean on."

I watched the girls drive away, then got into my car and went back to my own life, a life increasingly marked by desperation.

In the winter of 1990-91, the pain in Andrew's leg became unbearable, draining him of all energy. He would come home from work and collapse on the sofa, utterly exhausted. I was forced to take on more and more of the household responsibilities, as he lacked the strength to help me.

Andrew always kept his bottle of pain pills within easy reach. I began to notice that he took the medication more often than was recommended. One day, I pointed this out to him. He instantly let me know that my advice wasn't welcome.

"You have no idea how much pain I'm in," he snarled. "So, you have no right to control how much medication I take. I know what I'm doing. Just lay off the nagging, will you?"

Several weeks later, after Andrew came home from a doctor's appointment, I found a new prescription bottle sitting on the kitchen counter. When I picked it up and read the label, my stomach knotted in fear. Andrew had been prescribed a stronger type of pain medication. This time, he'd been given a narcotic.

"Andrew!" I gasped, forgetting to guard my tongue. "You have to be careful with this stuff! It's highly addictive!"

I instantly regretted my outburst and recoiled in fear of Andrew's enraged response. But he remained surprisingly mellow.

"Don't worry," he said. "I know what I'm doing. I just took one of these pills, and it's great. It really knocked out my pain. Aren't you happy that I don't have to suffer so much anymore?"

"Of course," I replied, forcing myself to believe that those pain-curing pills could also cure the ills of our marriage.

As much as I wanted to trust my husband, I still couldn't stop myself from monitoring how he took his medication.

Every couple of days, while he wasn't looking, I would count the pills remaining in the bottle. When I'd see him reach for more medication, I'd glance at the clock to see if sufficient time had passed since his last dosage.

When I began noticing Andrew in strangely tranquil moods, I initially felt relieved. Always hoping for the best, I convinced myself that he was emerging from his winter blues. Spring had arrived, and I dared to hope for the better times of previous warm-weather seasons.

But as spring rolled on and turned into summer, I noticed that Andrew's tranquil moods alternated with periods of testiness and agitation. Try as I might, I couldn't deny the fact that I was observing the effects of Andrew's pain medication cycle. He'd be mellow after a dosage entered his system. But when the medication began wearing off, he'd become irritable again.

And so, the months passed. Andrew gradually lost all interest in projects around the house. I found myself working alone in the flowerbeds we'd planted together two years earlier. His impeccable tidiness slackened. He showed less and less interest in affection and lovemaking, and the intimacy between us dwindled to nothing.

Our second wedding anniversary came with no acknowledgement of the occasion on Andrew's part, and my attempts at a romantic dinner fell flat.

I was too devastated to sleep that night. After a few hours of lying wide awake beside my husband in his drug-induced slumber, I slipped out of bed and went to sit alone in the living room. As I contemplated the miserable state of my marriage, I could no longer deny that I'd lost the man I once knew.

By that time, I had virtually isolated myself from friends, and I felt too ashamed to reach out for their support. The only semblance of normalcy I maintained was going to work every day. There, I could be a competent person in the eyes of others, hiding the truth of what was happening in my homelife.

One Friday evening, the night Andrew usually went to practice with his band, he didn't budge from the sofa. "Aren't you going to band practice?" I asked him.

"I'm not doing that anymore," he snapped.

"Why not?" I asked.

"I'm just not." He refused to say anything else, so I left him alone. But I was dismayed. Andrew giving up on his music was not a good sign.

The following day, I did something that would've made Andrew livid if he'd known about it. When he got up from the sofa and went to pace around the yard for a while, I holed myself up in the bedroom, closing the door in case he suddenly walked back into the house. Using the bedroom phone extension, I called one of his bandmates, Chuck.

"I understand Andrew's not playing in the band anymore," I said. "He won't tell me anything about it. I'm worried, because his music meant so much to him. It would help if I knew the truth."

After an awkward silence, Chuck responded. I could tell he was choosing his words carefully. "Andy doesn't seem like himself these days. We asked him to take a break to get his act together."

I froze, imagining the worst. Had Andrew erupted in anger during band practice? Had he created scenes that his bandmates couldn't tolerate? Or was he too drugged up to play at his usual level of skill?

"He's more than welcome to come back any time when he feels better," Chuck added apologetically.

So, without the hope of his music alleviating the tension, Andrew and I were left to spend every evening together. However, we lived at a distance from each other, passing the time in different parts of the house.

Like thick, pungent smog, despair crept into the empty spaces between us. Gradually, my affection for my husband changed to bitter resentment. While he spent endless hours watching television in the living room, I sat alone in our bedroom, my mind drifting into fantasies of life without him.

I grew irritable myself, constantly on the verge of snapping at my husband. But my fear of triggering his rage kept my venom bottled up inside me.

Mercedes, you ask whether I told Elliott what was going on in my homelife. I regret to say that I was not fully open with him about that. You recall that I had sent him a glowing letter shortly after my marriage to Andrew, proclaiming that I'd found the love of my life. At the end of that letter, I had issued Elliott an invitation: "If you're ever in town, stop by to see us. I'd love to introduce you to my husband, and to show you the beautiful home we've created."

I did not send Elliott a letter the following year. I was too ashamed to admit that I'd once again been wrong, that things had started going downhill in my marriage. I forgot all about the invitation I'd offered him.

One Saturday afternoon in October 1991, I was at home alone while Andrew was putting in a day of overtime at work. I was relieved to have him gone, as I needed a break from coping with the tension between us. I busied myself with raking leaves in our yard, knowing that if I wanted the job done, I would have to do it myself.

Suddenly, I was startled by the ringing of the telephone. I dropped my rake to rush inside to answer it.

Imagine my surprise when the voice on the other end of the line said, "Dora, this is Elliott Jordan. I've come to Indiana on business, and I wondered if I could stop by and see you for a few minutes."

My spirit lit up at the prospect of a friendly visitor. "Of course!" I exclaimed.

After providing Elliott with directions to my home, I rushed around to change my clothes, scrub my dirty hands, and run a brush through my hair.

Fifteen minutes later, Elliott stood on my doorstep. When I opened the door and met his kindly gaze, I was so overcome with emotion that I almost burst into tears. I sensed that Elliott was seeing the Dora he respected and admired, not the worn down, emotionally battered woman I'd become.

"Is Andrew at home?" he inquired as I ushered him into the living room. "I was looking forward to meeting him."

I winced. "He's at work today."

Elliott looked at me quizzically, but asked no further

questions about my husband. We turned the conversation to our respective jobs, comparing notes on the rewards and stresses of his teaching career and my work in human resources.

I think I told you a few weeks ago, Mercedes, that Elliott had a son. I may have failed to mention that his son was born with Down syndrome. We talked about the challenges of raising a child with special needs. I listened sympathetically, glad to be able to offer support to my friend.

But when we'd exhausted all those topics, an awkward silence fell between us. Suddenly, Elliott's compassionate gaze made me feel exposed and vulnerable. I knew he was looking right through my cheerful façade to the pain I was harboring.

"Dora," he said, "maybe this isn't my business, but I feel the need to ask. Are you alright? You seem sad."

Elliott's caring words served as a catalyst that set off an uncontrollable reaction inside me. My reservoir of silent pain began to heave and churn, threatening to bubble up and gush out of me. I fought to hold back my tears, but they spilled out and ran down my cheeks.

"I'm so sorry," I said. "I didn't mean to break down like this."

"That's okay, Dora," Elliott reassured me. "If there's something you need to talk about, by all means do so. I'm here to listen."

So, for the very first time, I poured out the truth about my relationship with Andrew. I told Elliott about the ecstasy, the hope, the bitter disillusionment, the unbearable loneliness. All the while, I felt deeply ashamed. But my need to unburden my aching heart outweighed my desire to preserve my dignity.

Elliott listened quietly, his brow knitted in concern. After I finished speaking, he lowered his eyes and stroked his beard, as if trying to formulate a response.

"This is certainly an intolerable situation," he observed. "Are you thinking of divorcing Andrew?"

"Oh no!" I protested. "I could never bring myself to do that."

"Then you need to do something for yourself," he admonished. "Dora, you are an intelligent and capable woman. You can't squander your life locked up in an emotional prison. Get out of this house and get yourself involved in activities that interest you. Don't let your problems with Andrew keep you from living."

Elliott didn't stay long, less than an hour. As he was leaving, he said, "Dora, I'm concerned about you. Don't wait another year to write to me. Please reach out from time to time to let me know how you're doing."

So began a closer friendship with Elliott Jordan that has lasted all these years. One week after his visit, I wrote to thank him for his kindness. He wrote back with words of encouragement.

After that, we corresponded on a monthly basis. I cherished each of his letters and read them over and over again when I felt the need for consolation.

Andrew was never pleased to see Elliott's letters arrive in the mail, and he often made unkind remarks about them. I had, unfortunately, developed a pattern of giving in to Andrew's whims in order to avoid triggering his anger. However, nothing my husband said could destroy my conviction that I had a right to communicate with my friend. I was determined not to allow him to deprive me of that comfort.

I did not fail to heed Elliott's advice to break out of my isolation. Over the next few months, I ventured back into some of my former activities. It wasn't easy, as I'd lost confidence in socializing with my old circle of friends.

Gradually, I began to feel as if I was back in the land of the living. When among friends, I almost felt like the person I'd been before I met Andrew.

However, nothing could cure the pain of my homelife. I participated in all my activities with a dull ache in my heart. I couldn't access that state of bliss I'd formerly enjoyed, as my spirit felt too heavy to soar. And when I'd return home, I'd sink into the doldrums again.

In January 1992, I joined a new meditation group, where I befriended a woman named Joanna. She told me about her involvement with a Hindu ashram in Kalamazoo, Michigan, and invited me to accompany her there.

I had no particular expectations of the ashram, and didn't imagine it held anything different than what I'd already encountered in my spiritual pursuits. Truly, I went there with Joanna out of idle curiosity.

So, I was not prepared for how I felt when I walked into the meeting room. I was overcome by a powerful sense of having arrived at my spiritual home.

The meeting consisted primarily of a teaching from the Bhagavad Gita, a book with which I was not familiar. I was awed by the beauty of the teachings and their significance for my life.

At the beginning and ending of the meeting, the group chanted mantras. I was initially unable to participate, as the words were in Sanskrit, an ancient Indian language. But the melodic rhythm of the sacred lyrics mesmerized me, bathing me in a peaceful glow. For the first time in years, I experienced true serenity.

I returned to the ashram as often as I could manage the lengthy trip between Elkhart and Kalamazoo. For countless hours, I listened with rapt attention to the teachings of the Hindu swami, the spiritual leader of the group. Gradually, those strange new teachings began sinking into my consciousness, rearranging my thoughts and my understanding of life.

Slowly, I developed a new awareness of myself as a spiritual being, gaining a new perspective on my painful life experiences. The chanting of the mantras and the beauty of the sacred rituals soothed my aching heart like nothing ever had before.

Over the next few months, I dropped my other group involvements in order to devote my energy exclusively to the ashram. I believe each one of us walks our own path in our quest to find God. The way of the swami's teachings was the path that beckoned to me the strongest, the path that called my name. It was a call I couldn't resist.

I wrote to Elliott about the joys of my new discovery. I don't think he understood my attraction to the ashram, but he was pleased that I'd found a measure of inner peace.

Mercedes, you've commented before on the silk skirts I often wear. At the ashram, I associated with a number of Indians, and I always admired the colorful saris the women wore. My long skirts are made out of recycled sari silk. Corina ordered them for me on the internet, from a company that is dedicated to recycling and protecting the environment. The skirts are a lovely reminder of my time at the ashram.

Despite the improvement in my mental state, part of me remained preoccupied with my husband's peculiar moods.

I continued to keep an eye on his bottle of narcotic pain medication, to reassure myself that the supply of pills was not dwindling too rapidly. I couldn't reconcile the seemingly correct usage of the medication with the fluctuation of Andrew's moods and his ever-increasing withdrawal from our shared life. I sensed something was amiss, but couldn't pinpoint what it was.

Then one day, our tenuous coexistence fell to pieces, and the smoldering tension between us erupted into a raging inferno.

It happened on a Thursday evening in early April 1992. Andrew was watching television in the living room, while I burned off nervous energy by cleaning our bedroom.

His medication bottle was sitting on his nightstand. As I dusted the stand, I picked up the bottle, counting the pills out of habit. I found no cause for concern, as the appropriate number remained in the bottle. In fact, it looked as if Andrew was taking fewer pills than recommended.

Suddenly, I felt an overwhelming urge to check the top drawer of the stand, something I'd never done before. To this day, I have no idea where that urge came from. But something prodded me to look into that drawer, and I did.

At first glance, I found nothing amiss, just the usual items one might expect to find in a nightstand: reading glasses, tissues, cough drops. But when I rummaged around in the back of the drawer, I found the dreaded objects I was hoping not to find. My hand closed around two pill bottles.

I pulled them out and stared at them incredulously, horrified by my discovery. One bottle was nearly empty, the other half full. Both labels showed they contained Andrew's narcotic pain medication.

I compared them to the bottle sitting on the nightstand. Each of the three prescriptions had been written by a different physician and had been filled at a different pharmacy.

I began shaking so violently that the bottles clanked together in my hand. The fact that my husband had been perpetrating a massive deception slammed into my awareness. Andrew had been taking dangerous amounts of pain medication and had been hiding the evidence. He'd left one bottle out on the nightstand to control my perception, knowing, no doubt, that I was counting the pills.

I felt myself unraveling, coming apart bit by bit, the pieces of my self-control shattering and falling to the floor. With the three bottles in hand, I rushed into the living room. Thrusting them under my husband's nose, I screamed, "Andrew, what the hell is going on here?"

My confrontation took Andrew by complete surprise. I must have startled him badly, activating his PTSD, as his defensive reaction was quick and violent. He jumped up, slapping the bottles out of my hand. "Stay out of my business, you crazy bitch!" he bellowed.

Then he shoved me hard, sending me flying across the room. I lost my balance and felt myself falling. It seemed like slow motion, my body going down, down, down until I struck my head, just above my right eye, on the sharp corner of the coffee table. I felt a stab of searing pain, then the warmth of my blood oozing from the wound and running down my face.

I lay on the floor, stunned, for what seemed like hours. An oddly peaceful thought floated through my mind: "Let me lie here and die. I don't care about my life anymore."

I could hear Andrew's voice sounding distant and surreal, calling, "Dora, Dora, are you okay? Oh my God, Dora, I'm so sorry!"

It finally occurred to me that I needed to get up. Andrew extended a hand to help me, but I pushed it away. I stumbled to the bathroom, rinsed the blood off my face, and examined the ugly gash above my eye. I knew I needed stitches.

Andrew's tortured face appeared in the mirror above mine. "Let me take you to the emergency room," he begged. Nodding mutely, I followed him out of the house and to the car, holding a washcloth to my bleeding head.

I didn't say a word during the trip to the hospital. Feeling repulsed by Andrew's presence so near me, I huddled against the passenger door. Staring out the window, I watched a spring snowfall blanket everything in white. The day before, I'd enjoyed a lovely stroll in balmy April weather, hope stirring in my heart. But the cold had returned, and along with it, despair.

I could hear Andrew swallowing and clearing his throat repeatedly, as if trying to work up the courage to speak. Finally, he said, "Are you going to...?" His voice trailed off.

I knew what he was asking. He wanted to know whether I was going to reveal the cause of my injury to the hospital staff. I shook my head.

In the emergency room, I told the attending doctor that I'd tripped and fallen against the coffee table.

You say I should've told the truth, Mercedes, and you're right. But back then, I took on some of the blame for what happened. I'd been well aware of how jumpy Andrew's PTSD made him. I told myself I should've known better than to startle him the way I did. Still, he should've been held accountable for his violent action.

When we arrived back home, I gathered some clothing and personal items and set up camp in our spare bedroom.

As the shock of the incident wore off, I found myself hating Andrew, hating him with the same degree of passion with which I'd once loved him. I could hear him moving around the house. As his footsteps passed by my closed door, my stomach churned in revulsion.

I lay awake that night, my mind racing with hateful thoughts. I told myself it was time to be strong, time to stop excusing my husband's reprehensible behavior. I envisioned myself pointing an angry finger at him, ordering him out of my home and out of my life.

When I looked into the mirror the next morning, I was greeted by the sight of a blackened eye that had swollen almost completely shut. I was in no condition to go to work.

So, I spent Friday, Saturday, and Sunday in my cave of solitude, contemplating a plan of action. Each time I left the bedroom for a trip to the kitchen or the bathroom, I passed the dried pool of blood on our living room carpet. I was determined that I would not be the one to clean it up. On Sunday morning, it appeared that Andrew had scrubbed the spot, as the worst of it was gone.

Late Sunday evening, I heard a timid knock on my bedroom door. "What do you want?" I called in an icy voice.

Andrew's response sounded nervous and shaky. "May I come in?"

"I suppose so," I snapped.

The door opened to reveal my husband standing there, his face pale and haggard. I was sitting cross-legged on the bed, my back against the headboard. Andrew looked as if he was terrified to approach me. He hesitated before seating himself on the foot of the bed.

A tiny part of me felt the old urge to reassure my frightened husband that everything would be okay. But I didn't, as anger still boiled hot inside me.

"Dora," Andrew said, his voice breaking with emotion. "I want to say that I'm sorry, but I know that won't fix what I've done. When I look at you and see how I've hurt you, I feel like the scum of the earth."

His eyes pleaded for my understanding, but I lowered my gaze and made no response.

"I've been doing a lot of thinking these past few days," he continued. "I know I've gotten way out of control with the pain medication. I know I'm hooked on the pills. You don't need to tell me that. I know I'm a lousy husband, and I've been treating you like dirt. If you would tell me to hit the road, I wouldn't blame you. You'd have every right to do that."

He paused, again waiting for a response, but I had none to give. Then he hung his head and spoke in a voice so low that I could hardly hear him. "But I'm asking for one more chance, Dora. I know you've already given me lots of chances, but please give me just one more. I know I need help. So, I'm checking myself into the inpatient treatment program at Oaklawn Psychiatric Hospital in Goshen. I've already made the arrangements, and I'm going in tomorrow morning."

A wave of relief washed over me, cooling my anger by a few degrees. "Maybe," I thought, "if Andrew's addiction is treated, the worst will be over. Maybe we can find what we once had."

"Okay," I said.

Andrew's eyes flooded with tears. He moved closer and wrapped his arms around me. I did not return his embrace.

"You won't be sorry, Dora," he whispered in my ear. "I promise to make it up to you."

The next morning, I drove my husband to the psychiatric hospital. "I love you, Dora," he said as he got out of the car.

When I didn't respond, he said testily, "I know, I know, you don't love me back. Not yet, but you will someday."

I watched him limp through the doors of the hospital, suitcase in hand. Then I drove off to work, the wound on my face camouflaged with heavy makeup.

Andrew stayed in the treatment program for twenty-eight days. During those weeks, when I wasn't at work, I spent most of my time alone. I took solitary walks around our wooded acreage and sat for hours on our patio, sorting through a multitude of feelings.

After one week in treatment, Andrew was allowed to have visitors, so I dutifully made the trip to the hospital. Eager to see me, my husband talked on and on about his recovery. I mouthed supportive sentiments. But seeing him so happy enraged me, and my anger burned hotter than ever. I hated the fact that he felt so hopeful, while I remained in the throes of pain and confusion.

When I came back home after that visit, I felt as if I would burst if I didn't confide in another human being. So, I sat down to compose a letter to Elliott. As my pen moved across the paper, my troubled emotions flowed out in the written word.

After putting the letter in the mail, I felt relieved. Knowing Elliott as I did, I was sure I would receive a return letter within a week. However, I was pleasantly surprised when he called me two days later.

"I received your letter today," he told me. "I must say, I was quite alarmed when I read about what happened to you. Dora, I'm worried about your safety."

"I'm safe at the moment," I assured him. "Right now, I'm alone in the house. I'm trying to figure out what I want to do when Andrew gets out of treatment."

"You have some tough decisions ahead of you," Elliott observed. "You need all the support you can get. Have you reached out to friends for help?"

"Only you," I replied, feeling embarrassed.

"Well," he said, "I have some free time this upcoming weekend. I'll drive over to Elkhart so we can discuss your dilemma face to face."

"I don't want to take you away from family time with your wife and son," I protested.

"My wife is a kind and understanding person," Elliott replied. "She would never want me to turn my back on a friend in need."

As Elliott walked through my door on Saturday afternoon, his expression darkened uncharacteristically. I realized he was looking at the lingering discoloration around my eye.

"That's a pretty nasty bump," he observed as we seated ourselves in the living room.

"Yes," I said, feeling self-conscious.

Elliott gazed at me sadly. I knew he was wondering how I could even consider staying with Andrew after he'd engaged in such violent behavior. But he did his best to remain neutral as I mulled over the pros and cons of remaining in my marriage.

When I concluded that I needed to give Andrew one more chance, he said, "I understand." But the look on his face belied his words.

"Dora," he said as he was getting ready to leave, "I know you're doing what you think is right. But I'm afraid for you. Please stay in contact. It's important to me to know that you're safe."

That day, Elliott left me with a sense that I had someone looking out for me. That touched me deeply. I can't imagine what I've ever done to deserve his loyalty and kindness. I thank God every day for all that Elliott Jordan has done for me.

The morning that Andrew was scheduled to be discharged from the treatment program, I woke up with conflicting emotions. I'd grown accustomed to my solitude, and I wasn't at all sure that I wanted to face the unknowns involved with bringing my husband back into the home.

But just as I was getting out of bed, I received a phone call that changed the direction of my life for the next few years.

Mercedes, that call was from your grandmother Norma. She asked to speak with Andrew. When I told her he wasn't home, she gave me a message to pass on to him.

And that message was about you, sweetheart. Norma informed me that Denise had given birth to a baby girl.

"Oh!" I exclaimed. "I didn't even know Denise was pregnant!"

Norma apologized for catching me off guard and quickly explained the situation. She told me that her daughter had hidden her pregnancy under baggy clothing until she was six months along.

"When I finally found out Denise was going to have a baby," she said, "I called Andrew right away. I'm surprised he didn't tell you."

I felt a surge of resentment toward my husband for failing to communicate such critical information. But my excitement quickly overrode my anger. "How is the baby?" I asked Norma.

"She's beautiful!" she gushed. "She looks a lot like Denise, but she has black hair and dark eyes like her father. I already love her so much!"

Norma's phone call completely shifted my frame of mind. Gone were all my reservations about bringing my husband home. My only thought was that Andrew and I now had a grandchild. I rushed to the hospital to share the news with him.

Mercedes, you made your entrance into this world at the perfect time for your grandfather and me. Our marriage had almost come to an end, but your birth gave new life to our relationship. I truly believe our shared enjoyment of you kept our marriage intact for the next four years.

Those years were, for the most part, stable. During his stay in the treatment center, Andrew was prescribed medication for his depression. He was also referred to physical therapy and biofeedback therapy to treat his leg pain. So, there were no more dark moods to dread, no more pain pills to count. That was an enormous relief.

However, Andrew and I did not recover the exquisite intimacy we'd shared at the beginning of our relationship. It seemed that when one extreme left our marriage, the other extreme had to go as well. The ecstasy disappeared along with the despair.

In fact, our two lives seemed to be more parallel than intertwined. While in treatment, Andrew began a twelve-step program, and he faithfully continued his involvement after his discharge from the hospital. He became a passionate advocate for recovery and sobriety. I knew this involvement was crucial for him, and I never stood in the way of it.

But his twelve-step group was a world in which I couldn't be involved, and I often felt shut out of my husband's life. Even though I didn't want for a moment to go back to living with his addiction, it saddened me that our marriage took second place to his recovery program.

The day after you were born, Andrew and I went up to the hospital to see you. After we held you and admired you, Andrew asked to speak to Norma in private. The two of them stepped out into the hallway.

From my vantagepoint inside your mother's hospital room, I could tell what Andrew was doing. He was following the guidelines of his program by making amends to Norma for the pain he had caused her while they were married. I watched the two of them hug each other and cry. I could tell they were at peace with one another.

When Andrew reentered the room, he went to his daughter's bedside to make amends to her. Denise seemed uncomfortable with her father's apologetic overtures and repeatedly rolled her eyes. When he tried to hug her, she pushed him away, saying, "Enough already, Dad!"

About a week later, I overheard Andrew on the telephone with his estranged father. Tears ran down his face as they talked. It sounded as if the two of them were making amends to each other. I was astonished that Andrew had taken the step to reach out to his father, as I knew that had to be extremely difficult for him. That told me how serious he was about his recovery.

I kept wondering, "When is he going to make amends to me?"

Then it occurred to me that, in Andrew's mind, he'd already done so. He had apologized profusely the night before he'd gone to the hospital. He must have thought that was enough. To me, it didn't feel like enough.

Andrew joyfully returned to playing music with his band. I imagined him making fervent apologies to his bandmates, and them welcoming him back with open arms. I was glad for him. But between his practice, his concerts, his physical therapy sessions, and all the twelve-step meetings he attended, I hardly had any time with my husband.

I tried to make the best of my loneliness by doing what I'd done when living alone in my own apartment. Using the décor from my old meditation room, I turned our second bedroom into my personal sanctuary. There, I read, listened to music, meditated, wrote letters, and wrote in my journal. In that special room, my loneliness turned into blessed solitude.

One evening after he came home from a twelve-step meeting, Andrew informed me that he was going to start psychotherapy for his PTSD. *"My sponsor encouraged me to do this,"* he explained. *"He said that if I didn't deal with my baggage from the Viet Nam war, it would get in the way of my recovery."*

My husband never shared that part of his personal history with me. Once, I asked him why he never talked to me about what he'd gone through in Viet Nam.

He responded with a hint of derision in his voice. *"Dora, you were raised Amish. Your family never served in the military. How would you ever understand such things?"*

At that moment, I couldn't think of a single word to say. I turned away from him and retreated to my personal sanctuary, where I nursed my wounded feelings.

To comfort my lonely heart, I turned more and more to activities at the ashram. I felt like part of a family there, which helped to fill my emotional void.

Then, passion entered my life in a new way. One night, I had an amazing dream about my childhood, in which I was surrounded by an array of drawings I had done. My face was glowing with joy.

I woke up trembling, overwhelmed by the vividness and significance of the dream. I recalled how, in my childhood, I had filled the emptiness in my life with my own creations. I remembered how those expressions of my inner self had brought me comfort. With absolute certainty, I knew it was time to return to the world of art, to revive the talent that had lain dormant for so many years.

So, I enrolled in classes at a local art gallery. I first took a drawing class, then moved on to painting. I learned to use oils, acrylics, and watercolors. I created a studio in one corner of my sanctuary room, where I painted for countless hours in the evenings and on weekends.

Through my painting, I discovered something new about the passion of the heart. It can be channeled in a variety of directions. The same passion that I'd poured into my love affair with Andrew was now expressed through my art.

When I felt my heart brimming over with strong emotions that had nowhere to go, I would paint.

I painted all kinds of subject matter: landscapes, portraits, fantasy scenes, mystical themes. I filled the walls of my home with my creations.

As I told you before, Mercedes, this painting above my sofa is a portrait of you with your guardian angel. Now, my dear, there's another painting I want you to see. This morning, Elliott was kind enough to pull it out of the closet for me. He put it behind the sofa so I could show it to you when you came. Can you reach back there and bring it out?

Do you recognize this person? Of course, you do. It's your grandfather. I painted this portrait about two years after you were born.

I'd been missing the Andrew I'd known at the beginning of our relationship, the person no longer available to me. So, I painted my lover as I remembered him, pouring my passionate emotions into my work.

See the depth of feeling in his eyes? This is the Andrew I loved so much. This man was my soulmate.

Andrew generally paid little attention to my art projects. But as I was putting the finishing touches on his portrait, I became aware of him standing behind me, watching me as I worked.

"It looks just like me," he said, amusement in his voice. "Dora, you never cease to amaze me." He gazed at me lovingly, then averted his eyes and turned away.

"I don't deserve you," I heard him mutter under his breath as he left the room.

I stood there staring at my painting, tears rolling down my cheeks, knowing that what I'd captured in the portrait could never be recaptured in real life.

Sweetheart, when you leave this evening, please take this painting with you. I want it to be in good hands when I'm gone. I know you will treasure it.

No, there wasn't much intimacy between Andrew and me during the last years of our marriage. But there wasn't much conflict, either. I learned to embrace that as a blessing.

Over time, I reached a point where I realized that Andrew and I were traveling on very different paths. Both were worthy paths. He was deeply involved with the causes of recovery and sobriety, as he rightfully should have been. I was pursuing a different kind of self-discovery. I knew it was time for me to let go of all fantasies. It was time to recognize myself as a solitary traveler in life.

There was sorrow in that realization. On the day when that truth fully hit me, I sobbed my way through a meditation session. In the end, I came to understand that letting go of old hopes and dreams left me with a great deal of freedom.

But let me return to you, Mercedes, our beautiful little granddaughter. You truly lit up the lives of your grandfather and me the last few years of our marriage.

When you were a baby, you were lovingly cared for by your grandmother Norma. Denise clearly wasn't mature enough to take on fulltime motherhood. However, when she was angry with Norma, Denise would insist that you were her child, and that she was going to raise you the way she wanted to. To spite Norma, she'd go running with her friends with you in tow, taking you places no child should ever go.

At such times, Norma would call Andrew, frightened and crying. Andrew and I learned to be buffers in that situation. Whenever we knew Norma and Denise were at odds with each other, we would offer to take care of you. Denise would quickly accept that offer, eager to divest herself of her maternal duties.

We stocked our home with supplies for a young child. I bought clothing that we kept for you at our house. I also bought you storybooks, children's music, and a lovely little dollhouse. Your grandfather put up a swing set for you in our backyard. We ended up keeping you two or three weekends a month. We loved every minute of it.

Yes, Mercedes, your grandfather and I adored you. When there was no other common interest between us, you provided us with one.

Corina came home to visit four or five times during those

years. The first time she met you, she pronounced you a "little darling."

As my daughter always presumed to be an expert on my life, she informed me that being a grandmother was good for me. "It lights you up," she said.

Of course, I couldn't resist asking her when she planned to provide me with more grandbabies. She shook her head. "It's not going to happen, Mom. I've decided not to have children. Wesley's probably not going to have any, either. So, pour all of your love into the grandchild you have."

There was one issue, however, that cast a shadow over our lives during those years. Andrew was terribly worried about Denise's drinking. In his recovery program, he worked hard on managing his stress and maintaining serenity. But growing evidence of his daughter's addiction was the one thing that made him lose his composure.

Denise had partied a great deal during her teen years. Andrew had been hoping that she was just going through a phase. But when she moved into her early twenties, she began showing signs of a serious problem with alcohol.

Andrew couldn't bear to watch his precious child heading down such a self-destructive path. It broke his heart. He could think of only one thing: he had to get his daughter into a treatment program.

He begged her to get help, but his pleas fell on deaf ears. "Just because you had a problem, Dad," Denise would scoff, "it doesn't mean that I have one."

I think Andrew lost his perspective on the situation. He couldn't let go of trying to control Denise's life. I repeatedly reminded him that he would never be able to persuade Denise to give up alcohol, that she wouldn't quit drinking until she hit rock bottom.

"I just can't stand to watch my child sink that low," he'd tell me.

So, he continued begging and pleading, bargaining and cajoling. That was exactly the way he'd dealt with his daughter all her life.

One Friday evening in early June of 1996, Denise

dropped you off at our house with the promise to pick you up the following morning. But morning came and went with no sign of her return. The afternoon passed and evening came, with Andrew becoming more distraught by the minute. He was scared to death that something had happened to his daughter.

When he called Norma to ask where Denise was, Norma told him she hadn't seen or heard from their daughter since she'd stormed out of the house twenty-four hours earlier. "We had a big fight before she left," she informed him. "She stays out like this when she's mad at me."

Andrew asked whether we should drive you back home. Norma advised against it. "If Denise comes back to your place and her child isn't there, she'll pitch a fit. If you can, maybe you should keep Mercedes a little while longer."

So, I figured you'd be staying with us a second night. I took you to your crib, which we'd set up for you in the corner of our bedroom. I was putting you into your pajamas when your mother finally arrived. I could hear her with Andrew in the living room.

And Andrew did something he'd never done before. He blew up at Denise. I know that wasn't his intention. But he'd gotten so worked up waiting for her that he lost his temper the minute she walked through the door.

That caught Denise off guard. She'd never been confronted by her father in such a manner. She flared right back at him, screaming hysterically, and the situation instantly became overheated. From the bedroom, you and I could hear every loud, ugly word.

For the first time ever, Andrew held his daughter responsible for her behavior, although he didn't do it in the most effective manner. He yelled at her that he was tired of picking up the pieces when she screwed up. He told her he couldn't stand the way she treated Norma. He told her she was an irresponsible mother. "I'm done with all your bullshit!" he bellowed.

Denise didn't back down for a second. She screamed back at him that she wasn't doing anything he hadn't done. She shouted out a diatribe of all Andrew's shortcomings as a father, telling him he had no right to judge her.

You were frightened by the yelling, and you started to cry. I held you close, trying to reassure you that everything was going to be okay. I was so afraid of what you'd be going home to. I wanted so much to protect you from any bad thing that would ever enter your life.

When I couldn't get you to stop crying, an old Amish hymn popped into my mind. It was a song my mother used to sing when she was rocking her babies to sleep. She always sang it in Pennsylvania Dutch.

So, I sang it to you, Mercedes. Even though you were four years old, I held you in my arms like a tiny baby, pacing around our bedroom, singing and singing. You'd never before heard the Pennsylvania Dutch words, but they soothed you. They quieted you down.

Oh, Mercedes, you suddenly remember that! Oh, my dear, I can hardly believe this. You remember that special moment we shared. I'm so overcome that I'm almost speechless.

Sadly, that moment didn't last long. As the fighting in the living room continued, Denise screamed that she was going to take her child, and that Andrew was never going to see his daughter or granddaughter again. Then she stormed into the bedroom, grabbed you from my arms, and left in a huff.

That, Mercedes, was the last time I ever saw you. The last mental picture I have of you is your frightened eyes peering at me over your mother's shoulder.

After Denise drove off with you, Andrew stared at me in utter devastation. "I blew it, Dora," he mumbled. "I really blew it."

"She'll cool down and change her mind," I said. But something in me had sensed the finality of Denise's words. I knew Andrew had sensed the same.

That night, my husband and I lay far apart in our bed. Neither of us could sleep, but we were unable to talk or to comfort each other. Our precious grandchild, who had bridged the gap between us for four years, was gone from our lives.

Over the next month, Andrew called Norma several times to see if Denise was ready to allow us to see you. Norma reported that Denise wasn't budging. Furthermore, Denise had told Norma that if she allowed Andrew to see his grandchild, she would take you and disappear from her life as well. Norma, Andrew, and I all knew what a disaster that would be. So, Andrew and I kept our distance.

Andrew slid back into the same dark depression he'd experienced prior to his treatment. I was afraid that he might return to using pain pills or alcohol. Thankfully, his twelve-step group provided the support he needed to keep from relapsing.

Truthfully, I was too depressed myself to worry much about my husband's mood. We each retreated into our own cave of despair, moving past each other like shadows in our daily lives.

Prior to the falling out between Andrew and Denise, I had scheduled time off work for the first week in July. I had planned on doing projects around our property, and had also anticipated spending extra time with my grandchild. Knowing that my plans weren't going to happen as I'd envisioned, I came home the Friday evening before my vacation in a gloomy mood.

To my surprise, Andrew approached me the minute I entered the house. "Dora, we need to talk."

I sat across from him at the kitchen table, staring at his grim face. "It's time to talk about what's happening to us," he said. The tone of his voice sounded ominous, filling me with dread.

"Why now?" I asked.

His expression softened. "I know you're taking a week off. I thought it would be a good time to bring this up, so you can get adjusted to everything before you go back to work."

I knew instantly what he was leading up to. "You're leaving, aren't you?"

"Yes," he replied, averting his eyes.

I sat stunned, motionless, listening to the thundering sound of my entire world crashing down around me. In spite of all the misery I'd gone through with Andrew, I'd been loyal to him. In spite of everything he'd done, I'd made the decision not to leave my husband. It had never occurred to me that my husband would leave me.

The idea seemed incomprehensible. Inside me, a voice wailed in protest. "After all I've done for you, after all I've put up with, I don't deserve to be the one who gets abandoned!"

"Why?" I finally managed to ask.

"Dora." Andrew's voice sounded dull and flat. "I've hurt and disappointed you over and over again. I know that if we stay together, I'll keep right on doing that. The more I let you down, the more I hate myself. And the more I hate myself, the more I let you down. It's a vicious circle. I can't live like that anymore. It's not good for me."

"We can work things out," I pleaded. "We can change that pattern."

"No." Andrew said the word so emphatically that I knew there was something he hadn't yet revealed to me.

"There's something else going on, isn't there?" I said. "Tell me, Andrew, just tell me."

"Dora, no," he protested.

But I pressed on. "Andrew, I deserve to know. Just tell me!"

"Okay, okay!" he said angrily. "There's another woman. Is that what you wanted to hear? I met someone else."

I stared at him incredulously, tears streaming down my cheeks.

Andrew's face softened again. "Oh, Dora, I didn't want to hurt you like this. If it's any consolation, I want you to know that I don't love her in the same way I love you. I could never love anyone else like I love you."

"That doesn't make sense," I choked out between sobs. "Why would you leave the person you love the most for someone you love less?"

"Because I don't know how to be with you," Andrew said. "I've always wanted to be with you. You're the kind of woman any man would want to be with. I just don't know how."

He sighed deeply. "I don't expect you to understand this,

Dora. I just can't be the man you need me to be. I don't deserve you. I've never deserved you. I do nothing but fail when it comes to you. I've put you through hell with my depression and my addiction. Now, I've blown the relationship with my daughter, and my stupid behavior has cost you your grandchild."

He got up and paced around the room. "I've hurt you so much, Dora, that I can hardly stand to look at you. The sight of you reminds me of what an ass I am. With June, it's different. It's not complicated. She doesn't expect much. When I look into her eyes, I don't see pain and disappointment. She isn't sensitive like you are. You're way above me, but June is on my level."

Mercedes, I can't begin to describe my shock and disbelief when I heard those words. I couldn't fully take in what your grandfather was saying to me. "When are you going?" I whispered.

"In a few days," he replied. Then he looked at me with concern in his eyes and said, "Maybe for your sake, I should just get out of your way and go tomorrow."

I got up from the table and went outside, where I paced around the backyard in a daze. Then I sat down on a patio chair, staring into space, unable to think. Hours must have passed, as it began to grow dark.

Andrew came out and placed a gentle hand on my shoulder. "Dora, it's time to come in," he said. I followed him into the house and mechanically went through the motions of getting ready for bed.

I don't know how I managed to sleep. But I know I did, because I woke up feeling Andrew's arms around me, drawing me close to him. Caressing me ever so tenderly, he whispered, "Dora, my sweet Dora." I surrendered to his lovemaking, and for the first time in years, our spirits soared together into heavenly bliss.

Afterwards, I felt dreamy and light as air, believing that the previous evening's conversation had been nullified by our lovemaking.

But in the morning, Andrew was distant again. He sat me down for another conversation. He informed me that he would take only his clothing and personal possessions. He said I could have the house and all the furnishings, as he deserved none of it. Then he spent the next few hours packing his belongings.

Mercedes, I packed up all of your clothes and toys and added them to Andrew's pile of boxes. I dismantled your crib and put it next to the pile. I couldn't bear the thought of facing your things alone after he was gone. I knew that, in all likelihood, your grandfather would see you again someday. But I knew that I never would.

By late afternoon, Andrew was ready to go. As he was leaving, he stated rather coldly, "I'll get the paperwork started for our divorce. You don't need to worry about anything. Goodbye, Dora. I hope your life gets better after I'm gone."

"Goodbye, Andrew," I whispered.

I watched my husband walk to his car with his signature limp. Then he drove away without as much as a backward glance. And that was the last time I ever saw Andrew Covington.

So now, Mercedes, you can understand what it meant to me when you brought me your grandfather's letter. How can I ever thank you enough? You provided a blessed resolution to the love story of Andrew and Dora Covington, a beautiful ending to replace the previous harsh and broken one. The letter filled an aching hole that had been in my heart all these years.

I've always believed it could've been possible for Andrew and me to work through our problems and stay together. I've always wondered what it would've been like to grow old with him. Perhaps we would've spent all of our years together in our little bungalow on the outskirts of Elkhart.

However, my separation from Andrew set me on another path that actually turned out quite well. I've been satisfied with the years since he and I parted ways.

But the day Andrew left was one of the darkest days of my life. How can words describe the depths of despair, the searing pain of betrayal? I found it inconceivable that after

I'd remained loyal to him through all our challenging times, my husband could so easily walk out of my life and into the life of another woman.

I missed Andrew and hated him at the same time. It seemed as if he'd found an easy solution to our difficulties, a way to move on with his life without feeling the pain that I was left alone to bear.

For two days after Andrew left, I didn't eat or sleep. I wandered weeping through every room of our house, missing his presence in the kitchen, the living room, our bedroom. I wandered around our yard, gazing at the flowers and shrubs, remembering Andrew at my side as we planted them.

I felt utterly crushed by life. I'd picked myself up and moved on after other losses and disappointments, but this time, the pit of my despair felt too deep to crawl out of.

Some self-preserving part of me must have known that I shouldn't be totally alone during that time. Late Sunday afternoon, I found the presence of mind to pick up the telephone and call the friend I trusted the most.

"Elliott," I sobbed when I heard his voice on the other end of the line. "Andrew is gone. He left me."

Elliott was silent for a moment. Then he said, "Dora, I'll be there as soon as I can."

An hour later, he stood beside me in my kitchen. As he put his arm around my shoulders, I allowed his reassuring presence to calm the storm raging inside me.

After listening to my account of the events surrounding Andrew's leaving, Elliott said, "Dora, it's difficult for me to watch you endure this terrible treatment from your husband. I'm amazed to find you brokenhearted over him after all he's put you through. But I guess the ways of the heart will always remain a mystery."

Like a parent coaching a distraught child, he instructed me to eat and get some rest. "Call me tomorrow morning," he said. "Let me know how you're doing."

Elliott's brief visit acted as the catalyst I needed to reverse my downward spiral. I ate a bowl of soup, then collapsed on my bed in exhaustion. When I awoke twelve hours later, I felt refreshed and ravenously hungry. I prepared breakfast for myself and went out to sit on the patio in the morning sunshine.

As I sat there eating, an amazing idea popped into my mind, unbidden. It didn't seem like my own thought. Rather, it felt like a gift, a bestowal of light upon my dark state of confusion. I knew without a doubt that I'd been shown the right thing to do, and a plan began to form in my mind.

I set down my plate, walked inside, dialed the telephone, and said, "Elliott, I'm moving to the ashram."

That, sweet Mercedes, is the end of the story you were so eager to hear. You look as if you're deep in thought. It's a lot to take in, isn't it? I imagine you'll be mulling over the story for quite some time.

You want to know if I'll tell you about my years at the ashram when you visit next week. Yes, of course I will. My precious grandchild, I will keep on talking with you for as long as I have the strength to speak.

CHAPTER 10: DORA AND THE ASHRAM

As Mercedes stepped out of the stairwell onto Harbor Light's second floor, she heard the faint sound of music. The music became louder as she headed down the hallway, and she soon realized it was coming from Dora's apartment. The deep, sensuous tones emanated from a solitary stringed instrument.

Not wanting to disturb what was happening inside the apartment, Mercedes hesitated before tapping on her grandmother's door. She heard no sounds of stirring within, no sound at all except for the unbroken strains of the sweet music.

She knew Dora was expecting her. *I guess I'll go on in,* she thought. She opened the door and slipped inside.

The living room showed no signs of life. The lights were off, the draperies drawn, as if the previous occupant of that space had left. The music came from Dora's bedroom, a room of the apartment into which Mercedes had not yet ventured. Scolding herself for her intrusion, she tiptoed to the partially open bedroom door and peered inside.

Dora was lying in her bed, her hands folded serenely over the covers. Her eyes were closed, and her face wore an enraptured smile. Elliott was seated at her bedside, a cello between his knees.

Mercedes stood mesmerized as Elliott lovingly stroked the instrument's strings with his bow. The elderly gentleman seemed to be one with his cello, a single entity that emanated an ethereal glow.

"Oh my God!" Mercedes whispered to herself. "This is the most beautiful thing I've ever seen." Elliott's feelings for Dora were unmistakable as he poured out his love through the offering of a passionate serenade.

As Elliott brought the piece to a close, he glanced toward the door and caught Mercedes' eye. "Come on in, Miss Maldonado," he said, a smile lighting up his handsome face.

"Please keep on playing," Mercedes whispered as she tiptoed into the room.

Dora's eyes fluttered open. "Hello, my darling granddaughter," she murmured. "Come sit with me."

Mercedes seated herself on the edge of the bed, then took Dora's hand and intertwined her fingers through those of her grandmother. The two women listened with rapt attention as Elliott played a tune even sweeter than the previous one. Tears streamed down Mercedes face, but she made no move to wipe them away until the music ended.

Dora, she thought, *are you aware of how much this man loves you? He adores you. I hope you know that. After all you've been through with my grandfather and the others, you deserve this kind of love.*

Elliott placed the cello back into its case. Leaning over the bed, he kissed Dora's forehead. "I'll see you tomorrow," he said. "You ladies have a nice time."

"My dear sweet friend," Dora said as Elliott left the room. "He's been coming every day to play the most beautiful music for me, music that touches my heart and wraps my soul in love. My body is failing rapidly, but the music speaks to me, reminding me that my spirit is strong and vibrant."

With a trembling hand, she reached for a bottle of water on her bedside stand. "Sweetheart," she said after she took a sip, "can you help prop me up a bit? I can speak more easily when my head is elevated."

Using her best nursing skills, Mercedes helped her grandmother sit upright, then arranged the bed pillows to form a backrest.

Dora reached up to pat Mercedes' cheek. "Thank you, my dear, thank you. Now, I'll do my best to finish my story."

I never took another lover after your grandfather left me. My relationship with Andrew allowed me to taste the sweetness of the intimacy I had craved for so long. After he and I parted ways, I never felt the desire to seek that out again.

By the time Andrew left, I'd been involved with the ashram for more than four years and had established deep connections there. The ashram was expanding, adding new programs and building new facilities. While most of the members lived in their own homes in the surrounding community, an apartment complex had been constructed for those who wished to live on the ashram grounds.

Before Andrew and I separated, I'd never thought about moving closer to the ashram. I'd had no inclination to leave our cozy bungalow. However, I lost my desire to stay in that house after my husband left. It had been our home, not my home, and I knew it was time for me to move on.

My new plan was so unwaveringly clear in my mind that I had full confidence it would work out. The day after I told Elliott about my decision, I called the ashram to inquire about the availability of an apartment in the on-grounds complex. Sure enough, one had just been vacated. They agreed to hold it for me.

I placed my house on the market, and it sold in less than two weeks. My plan was moving forward with very little effort on my part. I truly believe, Mercedes, that when change unfolds so easily, it's a sign that what is happening is meant to be.

There was no need to change my employment right away. Although the commute between Kalamazoo and Middlebury would be lengthy, it would be manageable until I could find a job closer to the ashram.

Six weeks after Andrew moved out, the arrival of divorce papers in the mail left me in a low mood for a few days. But my sadness did not stop my forward momentum. I mailed the signed papers back to Andrew, including a note telling him that I'd sold the house and was moving to the ashram.

When Vincent and I had divorced, I hadn't hesitated to change my last name, as the name Dori Perez no longer suited me. However, after the pain of losing Andrew subsided, I found I still felt comfortable with the last name of Covington. After working through layers of bitterness and disillusionment, I discovered within myself a jewel of gratitude for the beautiful aspects of my relationship with your grandfather. I wanted to honor what had been worthwhile in the marriage by keeping his last name. So, I decided to remain Dora Covington.

My move to the ashram apartment took place the first weekend in October, three months after Andrew's departure and one week after my divorce was finalized.

Corina came up to help with the move. By that time, my daughter was thirty-two years old and was living in Florida. She was well-established in her career, having already risen through the ranks to become a supervisor in an intensive care unit. With her take-charge attitude, she engineered the details of my last-minute packing and loading, treating me as if I needed to be looked after.

I felt profoundly embarrassed by the fact that my daughter was helping me pick up the pieces after another failed marriage. Corina had never gotten to know Andrew very well, and I hadn't revealed the extent of our relationship problems to her. As we packed, she plied me with questions about the divorce, which I answered as briefly as I could.

As I've told you before, Mercedes, Corina has never married. I suspect she's observed my marital floundering and has determined not to follow in my footsteps.

Midway through that weekend, Elliott stopped by to see how I was doing and to offer his best wishes for my move to the ashram. I was glad he could see me in a positive frame of mind instead of the emotional mess I'd been the previous three times he'd visited me.

That was the first time Elliott and Corina met each other. They seemed to instantly recognize and respect each other's keen intelligence, and they got along splendidly. The two of them have remained on friendly terms since that day. The past few years, they have formed an alliance in looking after me.

As Elliott was leaving, Corina stood at the kitchen window watching him back out of the driveway. "Mom," she chided, "why do you insist on wasting your time with men who aren't good for you? Why aren't you with Elliott? The two of you seem perfect together."

"That's not possible," I told her. "Elliott is a married man. Very happily married, I should say."

Corina furrowed her brow, shaking her head slightly, a

faraway look in her eyes. "It just seems as if the two of you belong together."

When I think back on that scene, I wonder whether the strange look in my daughter's eyes reflected a moment of foresight. Because Elliott and I are now together, as well-suited for each other as any two friends could possibly be.

The first night in my ashram apartment, I felt a mixture of emotions as I gazed at the unpacked boxes surrounding me. I was sad, of course, because my life with Andrew was now undeniably over. Our divorce was final, and he was living with another woman. Our house was sold, soon to be occupied by another family. There was no going back.

But I also felt elated. My painful struggle to make that relationship work had come to an end. I was standing on the brink of a new life. I could feel newfound strength coursing through my being. My world would no longer be centered around a partner. Now, it was about me and my relationship with God.

My life at the ashram was so different from my former life that I sometimes couldn't recognize myself as the same Dora Covington who'd been married to Andrew. I have concluded that my nineteen years at the ashram were the best years of my life.

To be sure, they weren't the most exciting years, as they were relatively free from drama and emotional upheaval. Rather, it seemed as if the rollercoaster peaks and valleys of my life smoothed out, allowing my daily routine to evolve into a rhythm of quiet contentment.

For the first time ever, I felt able to savor the pleasures of a simple but joyful lifestyle. I felt the freedom to relax and breathe deeply, and to listen to the still small voice of wisdom within me.

Several times a week, I attended satsang, the form of worship practiced at the ashram. The rituals provided me with comfort and a sense of security. I spent countless hours listening to the swami, the ashram's spiritual director, teach from ancient scriptures: the Vedas, the Upanishads, the

Bhagavad Gita. His words of truth transformed my understanding of life and who I am as a spiritual being.

One of my favorite activities was joining other ashram devotees in the chanting of Sanskrit mantras. Chanting helped to clear out my troubled thoughts, replacing them with a sense of blissful oneness with God. Between chanting sessions, those sacred lyrics played like a recording in my mind.

I took better care of my health than I ever had before. I ate clean, nutritious food. I exercised regularly and practiced various types of yoga. I slept deeply and peacefully. My body felt renewed and refreshed.

I did my share of the simple chores necessary to keep the ashram running smoothly. I helped to clean meeting rooms. I participated in cooking the weekly meal we shared as a community. I planted lovely flowerbeds and helped to keep the grounds in good condition.

Within the privacy of my own apartment, I continued to indulge in my love of painting. As an expression of my devotion to God, I painted portraits of the various deities worshipped at the ashram. Many of those paintings are displayed there to this day.

Throughout my first year of living at the ashram, I continued to commute to my job in Middlebury. But my needs in my new home were simple, and I soon realized that I could live on a smaller income. There came a time when I no longer wanted to spend valuable hours traveling back and forth to Indiana.

So, I resigned from my position in the human resources department and took a retail job in a bookstore in Kalamazoo. My new employment was less stressful and consumed less of my mental energy.

Yes, Mercedes, my years at the ashram were deeply fulfilling. For so long, I had felt as if I was swimming upstream, struggling so hard against life's adversities. At the ashram, the intensity of those struggles diminished greatly. It seemed as if I was resting, floating, moving through the activities of my daily life with little effort. I felt bathed in tranquility, deeply attuned to the presence of God within me.

Some might say that I was running away from life when I moved to the ashram. That wasn't true at all. While there, I lived more fully than I ever had before. My soul needed the embrace of that environment, a place to rest and heal after so many painful life experiences.

Of course, things were far from perfect at the ashram. There were the usual problems associated with any human organization. Sometimes, conflict broke out among members. However, I managed to sidestep most of the petty quarreling, and I didn't allow negativity to deplete my energy. I enjoyed quiet friendships and a great deal of sweet solitude.

After a while, I realized I no longer yearned for an intimate relationship with a man. The desire for a soulmate, which had once burned fervently within me, had dissipated. As I looked back on my relationships with Ivan, Michael, Vincent, and Andrew, I saw that I had been looking for something from a partner that I could find nowhere else but inside myself.

I discovered that I am my own soulmate, that my truest companion is the divine spark that lives within my own heart. I no longer needed to look outside myself for fulfillment. I desired nothing more than what I already had. What a joy it was to discover that the love I'd searched for all my life had been there all along, inside me!

I had no room in my heart for bitterness. Sometimes, thoughts of Andrew would come to my mind. I'd wonder where he was and what he was doing. Since I couldn't contact him in person, I'd pray for him and send him loving energy.

I probably won't be able to say as much about ashram life as you'd like me to, Mercedes. My vocabulary doesn't hold the words to describe the deep, sweet peace I found while living there.

But let me tell you about the most exquisite gift I received during those years.

I haven't mentioned much about my son the past few

weeks. Let me remind you that when Wesley left for the Peace Corps, he didn't shut me out of his life. He wrote me monthly letters from wherever he was stationed in the world. While in Africa, he served in Malawi, Namibia, Rwanda and Uganda. He also spent some time in Central and South America: Belize, Guatemala, and Ecuador. After taking his position with the International Red Cross, he traveled all over the world to places devastated by wars and natural disasters.

His letters were always filled with interesting details about the people he was working with. Sometimes, he'd send me an article about the project he was working on. In almost every letter, he'd send me a photo.

I always kept everything Wesley sent me. I now have four or five boxes in my bedroom closet, crammed full of the letters, articles, and pictures he sent over the years. They are among my greatest treasures. Every now and then, I'll have Elliott pull out one of the boxes. We'll go through some of the photos, and I'll tell him stories about where my son was living and what he was doing at the time the pictures were taken.

In my letters to Wesley, I'd comment on what he'd written to me, expressing my pride in him and sending him my best wishes. Whenever I could, I'd enclose a small monetary donation to the cause he was working for.

But I didn't tell Wesley much about my life with Andrew. I knew he didn't trust my ability to make good choices, and that he had no interest in the details of yet another one of my marriages. When things once again started going badly for me, I didn't want him to know about it. I didn't want my son to have another reason for seeing his mother in a negative light.

After just a few years of Wesley being in the Peace Corps, I knew for certain it wasn't a phase he was going through. Humanitarian work was indeed his lifelong calling. I stopped hoping he'd come home to stay. I only wanted him to come back for a visit, even though I sensed he wasn't ready to do so.

However, when I told him about moving to the ashram, something changed in his response to me. Suddenly, he expressed interest in what was going on in my life. He seemed to approve of my decision. He started asking me deep questions about my spiritual journey, while revealing to me his own growing spiritual awareness.

In 1998, after having been gone for thirteen years, Wesley finally came back to the States to stay with me for two weeks. When I first laid eyes on my son, I was startled. My teenager had become a mature thirty-one-year-old. He'd actually grown a few inches. While still lean, he'd developed the muscular physique of a hardworking man. He had streaks of white in his sandy hair, and his face was lined from hours of working outdoors in the sun. I could hardly get over the fact that he was no longer my little boy.

After so many years of feeling like I'd missed out on my relationship with my son, I finally found the true connection between him and me. Because, to my delight and amazement, Wesley loved life at the ashram. He fit into that environment as if he'd been born into it. I discovered that under my son's quiet exterior lay great spiritual depths.

After his initial visit, Wesley adopted a pattern of coming back to see me every two or three years. He'd stay for a month in the second bedroom of my apartment. The previous two places I'd lived, I'd had a spare room waiting for him. There at the ashram, he finally occupied it.

I can't say Wesley and I ever talked a great deal. My son is silent by nature. But without hesitation, he joined me in satsang. He'd be there at my side, chanting sacred mantras to the Lord, the passion in his voice moving me deeply. He'd listen with rapt attention to the swami's teachings. I could tell that he resonated with every word the holy man uttered.

Sometimes, he'd have private meetings with the swami. While I don't know what they talked about, I do know that the swami thought highly of Wesley.

I came to realize that my son had been cultivating spiritual practices for years, and that they provided a solid foundation for his constantly changing and sometimes dangerous life. In the mornings and evenings, when I'd be meditating in my bedroom, I'd know Wesley was meditating in his own room. His serene presence in my home felt soothing to me.

It amazes me that despite my shortcomings in raising my son, life has brought us to a place where we understand each other profoundly. By all rights, Wesley could harbor resentment about the things I've done or failed to do. But I never sense bitterness in him. It seems as if he's always known that our connection is deeper than the botched mother-son relationship of his childhood.

I like to describe Wesley as an old soul. I think you know what that means, Mercedes. My son seems to have learned many lessons throughout other phases of his soul's journey. I suspect he entered my life already possessing a great store of spiritual wisdom.

Yes, the time I spent with my son at the ashram was one of the sweetest treasures of those years. Wesley still comes to see me, of course. Since I've been here at Harbor Lights, he hasn't been able to stay overnight with me. Now, his old friend David Yoder and his wife host him in their home in Elkhart. Wesley has kept in touch with David and his parents all these years.

Still, I enjoy my son's one-day visits, and the deep peace we share when we're together.

Corina visited me once or twice a year when I lived at the ashram. Whenever Wesley was there, she'd spend three or four days with us. My daughter showed no affinity for ashram life, and would always insist on taking me out into the city for dinner, a movie, or shopping.

However, she assured me that ashram life was good for me. The first time she visited me there, she said, "Mom, you look better than you have in years."

Of course, I kept in touch with Elliott after I moved to the ashram. Although I didn't see him in person for five years, we continued to communicate through letter writing. Thankfully, I had no emotional trauma to burden him with during that time.

But no matter what I've ever confided in Elliott, he's never responded with anything less than acceptance. That's just my dear friend's nature. He's had his own life challenges with taking care of a disabled son. He's suffered disappointment in his teaching career, related to racial discrimination. He's dealt with judgmental attitudes about his interracial marriage. But even though he has often spoken out against hatefulness and injustice, he's handled it all with grace. He's been blessed with the gift of serenity, a quality which I greatly admire in him.

In early 2001, four-and-a-half years after I moved to the ashram, I received a heartbreaking note from Elliott. He informed me that his wife Deborah had been diagnosed with pancreatic cancer. "Her prognosis is not good," he wrote. "Her doctor told us that she has only months to live."

Unfortunately, I had never met Deborah. Elliott had always spoken of her with the highest regard. Like him, she was a college professor. The two of them had met while teaching at the same southwest Michigan school. I knew that Elliott loved his wife dearly, and that the thought of her impending death was almost more than he could bear.

After taking in Elliott's shocking news, my mind traveled back to all the times he'd supported me during my losses and disappointments. It struck me that our friendship had been a bit one-sided, with him doing most of the giving. So, I vowed to be the best friend I could possibly be during his time of need.

I immediately wrote back to express my condolences. Knowing that Elliott would have no energy for letter writing during his wife's illness, I invited him to call me any time he felt the need to unburden himself.

I'm happy to say he took me up on that offer. About once a week, he'd phone me late at night, after his responsibilities with his son and his wife had been completed for the day. I'd listen sympathetically to updates on the status of Deborah's condition, along with accounts of grueling treatments and emergency hospitalizations.

Six months after Deborah's diagnosis, Elliott called me with the news of her passing. He sounded utterly drained.

I doubt that he expected me to be at her funeral, but I felt the need to show my support. So, leaving my comfortable seclusion at the ashram, I drove to Benton Harbor, rented a motel room, and attended Deborah's viewing and funeral.

As it turned out, Elliott received an enormous outpouring of support from his college, his church, and the community at large. I could tell how highly respected he was, and how respected Deborah had been. I felt out of place at the funeral, being Elliott's insignificant out-of-town friend whom no one else knew. But I was still glad that I went, and I think Elliott appreciated having me there.

Despite his devastating loss, Elliott quickly moved on to pick up the pieces of his life, juggling his teaching career with the care of his son Daniel. I never sensed any self-pity in Elliott regarding being left with the sole responsibility for his son's care. He simply did what needed to be done.

Some people suggested that he lighten his load by putting Daniel in a group home. However, Elliott knew that Daniel was already suffering from the loss of his mother, and that being moved out of the only home he'd ever known would compound that loss. Instead, Elliott opted to hire in-home care for his son.

A year passed, with Elliott's understandably less-frequent letters reflecting the reality of his busy schedule. Then one day, I received a call from him. He told me he was going to be in Kalamazoo that weekend, and he asked whether I would like to get together for lunch. Of course, I said yes.

Other than our brief encounter at Deborah's funeral, sitting across the table from Elliott in the restaurant was the first time I'd been face to face with him in six years. I sensed the dynamic between us had changed.

"Dora, you seem to be at peace with yourself," he observed. "I'm so pleased to see that you've found contentment in your life."

His face still bore traces of sorrow from losing his beloved wife. I could see past the pillar of strength I'd always imagined him to be, catching a glimpse of his vulnerability.

In short, we each recognized something new in the other.

That lunch meeting became the start of a new pattern between Elliott and me. Three or four times a year, he would come to Kalamazoo, and we'd spend the day together. We would talk, have dinner, or go for a walk.

Sometimes, we'd go on a day's outing, driving a short distance to places of interest. One spring, we went to Holland, Michigan, to see the tulips in bloom. We traveled to Potato Creek State Park in northern Indiana to hike the wooded trails. We went to Warren Dunes near the small town of Sawyer, Michigan. And several times, we drove to Grand Rapids to enjoy the Frederik Meijer Gardens.

No, Mercedes, I wouldn't say that we were dating. We were just enjoying a friendship that deepened over time. Elliott and I never crossed that line between companionship and romance, although the idea of taking such a step was admittedly appealing. I think we both knew that trying to sustain a love affair would strain a friendship that brought a great deal of pleasure and comfort to both of us.

Furthermore, Elliott had no inclination to join me in life at the ashram. That would have been impossible, given his teaching career and his responsibility for his son. And I had no inclination to leave.

So, we continued with what we had, which was truly priceless. We grew to know each other so well, learning each other's habits and thoughts and innermost feelings. It's a precious thing to know and be known on such a deep level.

However, we never clung to each other. At the end of our time together, we would easily part ways and return to our separate lives.

My years at the ashram rolled by all too quickly. I passed through my fifties and into my sixties. Before long, it was time to let go of my employment in the bookstore, and I entered the life of Dora Covington, retired senior citizen.

I never thought I would leave the ashram. When I'd settled into my apartment back in 1996, I had been convinced that I'd found my true home here on earth. I felt so serene at the ashram, and I wanted more than anything to have that experience last for the remainder of my life.

However, our swami repeatedly taught his devotees that the nature of life is one of constant change, and that we must learn to accept what is inevitable.

As I grew older, the swami also grew older. I wasn't concerned about the possibility of him passing on. I suppose I thought that such a highly spiritual person would never grow weak and frail. But his life followed the same course that all our human lives do.

After his death, nothing at the ashram felt the same to me. In fact, I felt rather lost.

The spiritual director who replaced the swami was young and energetic, ready to start new programs and projects. I looked around and saw that I was surrounded by people several generations younger than me, full of exuberance and new ideas.

I felt my health declining, my energy faltering. I knew it wasn't right for me to burden those young people with my dependency. It was time for me to leave.

One chilly autumn day in 2015, Elliott came to the ashram to visit me. He had just retired from his teaching career. We took a short stroll around the wooded grounds, enjoying the colors of the changing leaves. I pointed out the blooming mums and asters I'd planted in previous years.

Sadly, I quickly became short of breath from the exertion of the walk, which reminded me once again that I'd lost my youthfulness. Elliott kindly recognized my need to rest. He escorted me to a bench, where we sat down.

"Elliott," I said, "I'm going to tell you something that might surprise you. I've invested so many years of my life in this place. But I think it's time for me to leave."

He hesitated only a moment before responding. "Actually, Dora, I'm not surprised to hear you say that. I've been thinking about that matter myself."

"But I have no idea where I would go," I told him. "Corina has always wanted me to move to Florida to be near her. I've considered that. But I don't think I'm ready to adjust to that big of a change."

Elliott reached over to take my hand. "There's a new senior apartment complex being built in Saint Joseph," he said. "It's just a few miles from my home in Benton Harbor. How would you feel about living there? Now that I'm retired, we'd have more time to spend together."

And that, Mercedes, is how I came to reside here at Harbor Lights. It's been lovely living in this little apartment.

Do I miss the ashram? Of course, I do. I have moments of sadness when I long for my old life there. I've told Elliott that when I die, I want my body to be cremated, and I want my ashes to be scattered in the gardens on the ashram grounds. I hope that as my last loving act on this planet, my physical remains will provide nourishment for the soil.

As you already know, I've brought elements of my ashram life here to this apartment: my music, my pictures, my statues. I still chant my mantras daily. Sometimes, Elliott reads me passages from the sacred scriptures. These things bring me such comfort.

But my greatest comfort is the knowledge that no matter where I live, I carry God within my heart. Although I haven't always known it, God has always been present within me, and always will be.

How could I possibly complain about my life here at Harbor Lights? All of my needs have been so beautifully met. As my ability to take care of myself has declined, Corina has made sure that I am comfortable in every way.

And what my daughter doesn't do, Elliott does for me. Even though he's two years older than me, he seems to have the energy of a forty-year-old.

He is so busy with his many responsibilities. He still cares for his son at home. Daniel goes to a sheltered workshop during the day, along with other developmentally disabled adults. Elliott has served as a volunteer and an advocate for that workshop. He's also involved with his church. On top of all that, he plays his cello in the community orchestra.

Elliott gives so much to the world. But he still makes time almost every day to come and visit me. How could I ever repay my dear friend for what he's done for me? How have I ever deserved such kindness?

When I was a child, my parents were unable to provide the emotional nurturing I needed from them. Neither Ivan nor Vincent ever grew close enough to me to understand my deepest feelings. And the problems in my marriage to your grandfather didn't allow us to maintain a deep attunement with each other.

My friendship with Elliott has made up for all those deprivations. He's been like a father, a brother, a best friend, and a guardian angel, all rolled into one. It seems fitting that I have spent my last years in his company.

I know you're puzzled, Mercedes, as to why Elliott and I never married, since we appear to be so well-suited for each other. Because of our complicated life circumstances, things have never evolved in that direction. I guess we're not meant to be lovers in this lifetime.

I'll let you in on a little secret. When Andrew and I were lovers in the throes of passion, he'd ask me to promise that we'd be together for eternity, lovers in this lifetime, and the next, and the next.

But you know what? Lately, I've been thinking that if I could choose a lover for another lifetime, it would be Elliott. I can only imagine how beautiful that would be. Perhaps we'll someday go down in history as legendary lovers. We'd deserve that. The loyalty in our friendship warrants that type of reward.

You ask if I talk about this with Elliott. Of course not. I'm sure he thinks the idea of multiple lifetimes is silly. No, I keep these sweet daydreams to myself.

Mercedes, my story is now complete. There's nothing left for me to say. And I am so weary. Soon, I will be unable to muster the energy to speak. Soon, I will allow myself to lapse into silence. My dearest granddaughter, please keep coming to see me, if just to hold my hand for a few moments. Know that your presence will be of great value to me, even if I am unable to tell you that.

CHAPTER 11: DORA AND ELLIOTT

As Mercedes drove to Saint Joseph the following Saturday afternoon, thoughts that had troubled her mind all week became overwhelming. She knew full well that her grandmother was nearing the end of her life. Dread gnawed at the pit of her stomach, and sorrow weighed heavily on her heart. She had no idea how she was going to face Dora's passing when it finally came.

She desperately wanted to savor every last drop of sweetness in her relationship with her grandmother, to spend as much time as possible with the gentle soul who had so recently re-entered her life.

This might be the last time you'll see her, a fearful voice whispered in her mind.

"No-o-o!" she protested aloud. "She might have weeks ahead of her. Maybe even months. Today is not going to be the end!"

The trip to Michigan had become habitual for her, the routine second nature. Soon, the lake came into view on her left, and she passed the familiar offices and retail establishments on her right. She pulled into the Harbor Lights parking lot and eased her car into a parking space.

As usual, she fussed with her hair in the rearview mirror for a few seconds and ran a tube of gloss over her lips. Then she made the short trek to the front door.

The imposing building no longer seemed formidable to her. Weeks ago, she had stopped feeling like a stranger when she entered the facility.

As she headed toward the stairwell, she was halted by the sound of someone calling her name.

"Miss Maldonado?"

It was Audrey at the reception desk. Mercedes had passed her numerous times on her trips up the stairs to see Dora, but hadn't spoken to her in weeks. She turned to see what Audrey wanted.

"I just thought you should know they're taking your grandmother to the hospital. You probably saw the ambulance out front. The medics are up in her room right now."

Mercedes stared at Audrey, unable to absorb the shocking news. Yes, she had seen the ambulance, but an emergency vehicle parked in front of the building was not an unusual sight. She'd walked right past it, too absorbed in her thoughts to attribute any significance to it.

"I didn't want you to be caught off guard," Audrey said apologetically.

"Thanks for letting me know," Mercedes choked out. Without inquiring any further, she rushed toward the stairwell, then hurried up the stairs.

As she neared Dora's apartment, she could hear a buzz of activity. Several pieces of Dora's furniture had been moved out into the hallway, apparently to clear enough space to maneuver a gurney inside the apartment.

Mercedes picked up her pace, nearly running. As she entered the apartment, she peered through the open bedroom door and saw a gurney pushed up next to her grandmother's bed. An oxygen tube had been inserted into Dora's nostrils. Her thin chest heaved with her labored breathing.

Medics stood on either side of the bed. "One, two, three," one of them called out. They effortlessly lifted Dora's slight body onto the waiting gurney.

Then, Elliott emerged from a corner of the bedroom where he'd been hidden from Mercedes' sight. "Let me have a moment with her, please," he said, his voice breaking with emotion. The medics stepped back obligingly.

Mercedes moved closer to the bedroom door, wanting to see and hear everything that was happening. She watched Elliott take Dora's hand in one of his. With the fingers of his other hand, he gently stroked her emaciated cheek. Dora's eyes were closed, and she appeared unresponsive to her friend's touch.

"I'm here for you, Dora," he said softly. "I'll see you at the hospital in just a little while."

Mercedes stepped out of the way as the medics rolled the gurney through the bedroom door. As they wheeled

Dora down the hallway, an alarming thought rang in her mind. *Oh my God! This really might be the last time I see her!*

Giving no thought to her actions, she ran to catch up with the medics. "May I have a minute with her? Please?"

One of the medics nodded, holding up his hand to signal his companion to stop.

Mercedes lifted the edge of the blanket and took Dora's bony hand in hers. Ever so gently, she caressed the cool, dry skin. Then she bent down and placed her mouth close to Dora's ear.

"Thank you, my dear grandmother," she whispered. "Thank you for looking out for me when I was a little girl. Thank you for all the time you've spent with me these past few months. Thank you for everything you taught me. I'm so glad I got to know you again. I love you so much."

Dora's eyes remained closed, but Mercedes was almost certain that she saw her smile slightly. She held her grandmother's hand for a long moment. Then, with a deep sigh, she released it and tenderly placed the blanket over it again. She kissed Dora's forehead before stepping back.

The medics rolled the gurney down the hallway and into the elevator. As Mercedes watched the elevator door close, a sob caught in her throat. She turned and walked the short distance back to Dora's apartment.

She found Elliott pacing around the small space, surveying the contents of the rooms. When he saw Mercedes standing in the doorway, his tired eyes reflected gratitude, as if he was relieved not to be left alone with his burden of grief.

"This will all need to be packed up," he said, one hand gesturing toward the kitchen cabinets and the other toward the living room bookshelves.

"I can help you," Mercedes offered.

She thought about the fact that she and Javier were in the middle of packing their own belongings, getting ready for the move to their new apartment. Still, taking care of Dora's things seemed like a priority.

"It's kind of you to offer," Elliott said. "But I need to wait until Corina is here before I do anything. She's flying up this evening. I'm sure she'll have her own way of taking care of her mother's business."

He sank into a chair at the kitchen table, looking drained and exhausted. "I'll be going over to the hospital in a few minutes. They're taking Dora to the intensive care unit. I'll give them time to settle her in. I need a moment or two to collect myself before I see her again."

Mercedes sat down opposite him. For a few minutes, neither of them spoke. Seeing the strain on Elliott's face made her heart ache. She knew the depths of his sorrow was even greater than her own.

She glanced around the kitchen and living room. Dora's furnishings appeared forlorn and shabby without her gentle, warming presence. The apartment seemed deathly quiet without the usual background of the sweet, droning music. The only sound was the relentless ticking of the kitchen clock, reminding Mercedes that time was marching toward an inevitability that neither she nor Elliott were prepared for.

"So, you and Dora have been friends for a long time?" Mercedes knew the answer to her question, but felt compelled to distract the elderly gentleman from his heavy thoughts.

Elliott's face brightened. "Oh, yes. We've known each other for almost fifty years."

Has Dora told you how we met? Back in the early 1970s, when I was teaching at Goshen College, she was a student in my sociology class.

I don't believe I even noticed her the first few weeks of that semester. In the midst of the noisy, high-spirited students around her, she hardly stood out.

However, once I did notice her, she captured my attention. She was small and thin, with long curly hair falling around her shoulders and hiding her face. Her clothing was shabby and unfashionable. She reminded me of a portrait of a peasant girl I'd once seen, painted by one of the great masters of old.

Despite her unremarkable appearance, there was an

unusual light about that young woman. But her light seemed tentative, wavering, as if she wasn't well-connected with her power source.

I don't believe I ever saw her speak to any of the other students in the class. She always sat in the back of the room, as if she was afraid of being seen.

She usually kept her eyes downcast. But one day while I was lecturing, my gaze sweeping the room, she suddenly looked up. For a moment, we locked eyes, and I saw that hers were filled with tears. Her face reddened when she realized that I'd noticed her, and she quickly lowered her head.

That brief moment of eye contact unnerved me. I was forced to pause and collect myself before resuming my lecture. I knew I'd been looking at a pure soul, albeit a troubled one.

The weeks of the semester passed. Every class session, Dora sat in the same spot in the back of the room, her eyes downcast. Whenever she'd momentarily raise them, they'd always appear to be tear-filled. She seemed so fragile, so unsure of herself. Sometimes, I feared she'd be trampled by the other students as they rushed out of the classroom at the end of the hour. She'd always move aside and allow them to pass, then would trail out after them.

It got to the point where I knew I would be remiss if I didn't ask about her wellbeing. If something about her campus experience was troubling her, then it was my duty as a faculty member to inquire about it.

One day, I stopped her as she was about to slip out the classroom door. "Is everything alright, Miss Graber?" I asked her in a quiet voice.

She startled, almost as if I'd shouted at her. But she stopped and turned to face me. For the first time, I saw that she was not a nineteen-year-old like the other students in the class. She was several years older than that. I could see the lines of worry and strain etched on her delicate features.

That day and in the weeks to come, I came to know Dora's story. I learned that she was a mother of two, and tragically, a widow.

When she revealed to me that she'd come from the Amish community, I understood why she appeared so shy and tentative. She was having tremendous difficulty adjusting to mainstream American culture.

Being a member of a minority group myself, I understood some of what she felt. You're nodding your head, Mercedes. As a Hispanic woman, you've had your own challenges.

Dora's plight moved me emotionally. But as a social anthropologist, I was intrigued on a scholarly level as well. I wanted to know more about her transition from the sheltered Amish community to life in mainstream society.

After she finished my class, I spent several weeks interviewing her for an academic paper I was writing. The article ended up being published in a professional journal. I'm proud to say that it was well received among scholars in my field. I don't think Dora has ever fully realized that her story was the subject of interest in the eyes of others.

After spending so many hours in the interviewing process, I ended up gaining a great deal of respect for my subject. Dora was such an intrepid soul, bravely facing daily life despite being encumbered by tremendous challenges. But even though I saw her strength, I still felt concerned about her wellbeing. So, as we parted ways, I suggested that we stay in touch.

I'm sure Dora has told you how a friendship developed between the two of us. At first, it was characterized by letters exchanged once a year, usually around the holidays. Early on, she told me about the older neighbor couple who had taken on a grandparenting role with her children, after her own parents had turned their backs on her. I was so pleased that she'd found that source of support.

She told me about entering the world of employment. Despite the lack of any previous experience, she stepped up to become the sole provider for her children as they were growing up.

When she took up dancing, I was glad that she'd ventured out to do something for her own enjoyment. For a short while, she dated a fellow named Mike. He seemed to care a great deal about her. However, I could tell she was unsure about moving forward with that relationship.

Then, out of the blue, she married her dance instructor. For the next few years, I heard very little from her. I sensed she was consumed by the flamboyant lifestyle in which she'd immersed herself. I didn't quite know what to make of it, but I feared she was somehow in over her head.

It didn't take long for that world to come crashing down around her. She was devastated. I knew she needed someone to believe in her. So, I did the best I could to be there for her, to assure her that she had the ability to rebuild her life and move on again.

And she did. After her second marriage ended, Dora focused more attention on her work, making great strides in her professional career. In her correspondence with me, she began sounding more mature, more self-assured. She was doing well as a single woman. At that point, I was confident that she'd be alright, no matter what came her way.

Then she met your grandfather, Mercedes.

Let me pause here to give Andrew Covington the respect he deserves. He sacrificed a great deal while serving his country during the Viet Nam war. That experience left him with scars, both physical and psychological. I know he had to work hard at overcoming his PTSD and his problems with addiction.

Despite his challenges, he was a good man with a great deal of potential. It's most unfortunate that Andrew and Dora couldn't work things out. I know that Dora's deepest desire was to spend the rest of her life with him.

I've always felt somewhat responsible for the pain Dora endured in that marriage. She'd had two previous marriages that fell far short of the mark. When she met your grandfather, I could tell she was caught up in magical thinking about having found her soulmate. She seemed a bit ungrounded, unrealistic in her expectations. I thought about cautioning her to slow down, to take some time to look at the situation carefully.

Regrettably, I didn't. I held back, telling myself that Dora was in charge of her own life. I wish I would have said something.

It was difficult to watch things deteriorate in that marriage. Against all reason, Dora kept hanging on, her unrelenting heartache draining the life out of her. I knew she needed my friendship more than ever.

Sometimes, I wanted to shake her to make her stop clinging to hope, to insist that she open her eyes and see the reality of her circumstances. But I knew that would do no good. As much as I wanted to rescue her, she had to find her own way through that dark passage.

After she and Andrew finally parted ways, she announced that she was moving to the ashram. I was incredulous at first, afraid that she might be making another misguided decision.

However, the last twenty-five years of Dora's life have been altogether different from her previous years. They have been remarkable. Dora is now securely plugged into her power source. Her light is brilliant, steady, unwavering. I am in awe of her.

Her brilliance, of course, is on a spiritual level. On a human level, Dora's insecurity about being an Amish girl in an English world has never fully left her. After all these years, I still sense her trepidation, her vulnerability. Even though she's of the Caucasian race, she is far from mainstream.

During Dora's years at the ashram, she and I grew to be the dearest of friends. I stopped worrying about her. I simply admired her and began to treasure her company.

Mercedes, I know you're curious about whether Dora and I were ever lovers. No, we never were, not in the physical sense. In that regard, my wife Deborah was the one and only love of my life.

My love for Dora is different. It has nothing to do with the body. It's a deep understanding between our two souls. I've never experienced that with anyone else. Truthfully, it's beyond my comprehension, and I hardly have the words to explain it.

It feels as if Dora has always been with me and always will be. Our souls have become so deeply connected that even though she's about to leave her body, I know we will not be apart.

Miss Maldonado, I think it's time for me to run over to the hospital now. I need to be at Dora's side. Thank you for keeping me company for a few minutes.

Let me also express my deepest gratitude for what you've done for your grandmother. When you were taken from her as a child, her grief knew no bounds. Getting to know you again has given her endless happiness. And, in some way that she hasn't fully explained to me, I think your reappearance in her life has put to rest some lingering unfinished business she had with your grandfather.

Now, if you'll be so kind as to give me your phone number, I'll keep you updated on her condition.

CHAPTER 12: MERCEDES AND JAVIER

Saturday night was a restless night for Mercedes. Every time she closed her eyes, she pictured her grandmother's frail body lying motionless on the medics' gurney. She repeatedly went over what she'd whispered into Dora's ear, wondering whether she'd said the right things and whether Dora had heard her. She told herself she should have arrived at Dora's apartment an hour earlier, before the medics came, so that she could have spent more time with her grandmother. She thought of a hundred things she wished she'd said or done, imagining herself to be negligent.

In the dark, lonely hours before dawn, her overwrought emotional state became unbearable. "I let Dora down," she berated herself. "I wasn't there for her like I should've been."

Just when her painful rumination threatened to consume her, she felt a wave of soft, sweet energy pass over her. The memory of Dora's smile flashed in her mind, along with the whispered words, "It's okay, my darling girl."

Stunned by the extraordinary experience, Mercedes lay perfectly still, not wanting to break the blissful spell. She felt light as air, as if she'd been washed clean of something. Within moments, she drifted off into a deep, peaceful sleep.

Several hours later, she awoke to the sound of voices in her son's bedroom. Javier was instructing Javi in how to pack his belongings for the family's upcoming move.

Exhausted as she was, Mercedes forced herself to get out of bed. She knew she needed to keep working hard to stay on track with their timetable of vacating their old apartment and taking possession of their new place.

She was in the kitchen labeling a box of pots and skillets she'd just packed when her phone rang.

Dropping her felt-tipped pen, she pulled her phone from her pocket. "Oh no!" she cried out when she saw the name *Elliott Jordan* on the screen.

Javi looked up from his seat on the kitchen floor where he was sorting piles of toys into boxes. He stared at his mother in alarm.

"What's wrong, mi amor?" Javier called from the living room where he was packing up his books.

Without a word to either of them, Mercedes ran with the phone to her bedroom and shut the door. "Hello," she said, her voice trembling with anxiety.

"Miss Maldonado, this is Elliott Jordan," the voice on the other end of the line intoned. "I'm sure you've guessed why I'm calling. Your grandmother passed away early this morning."

Elliott's words punched Mercedes in the chest, knocking the wind out of her. "Oh, Elliott," she said when she finally found the breath to speak. "I wasn't ready for this yet. I knew it was going to be soon, but not this soon. I was hoping to visit her in the hospital in a couple of days. I wanted just a little more time with her."

"I understand," Elliott said kindly. "I think we all wish we could've had more time with Dora."

Tears began coursing down Mercedes' cheeks. Phone in hand, she moved into the bathroom to find a tissue. "How was she?" she choked out. "How were her last hours?"

"Everything was peaceful," Elliott assured her. "Corina flew in yesterday evening. She'd contacted Wesley a few days earlier, telling him their mother had only a short time to live. He immediately made arrangements to come home, and he arrived at the hospital around midnight. I believe Dora was waiting for him. She died an hour after he got there."

"Oh...." Mercedes suddenly felt so weak that she sank down onto the edge of the bathtub. "I'm so glad that Dora had her children with her at the end."

"Yes," Elliott replied. "It was a beautiful experience."

"And were you there all that time?"

"Yes, I was." Elliott's voice quavered. "After I left you yesterday afternoon, I stayed at Dora's bedside until she took her last breath. All that time, she was in a peaceful sleep, completely unresponsive to those around her. I'm certain she knew her children and I were there, loving her to the very end. But her worn-out body could no longer communicate that awareness."

"You must be exhausted," Mercedes said.

"I am," he sighed. "It was a sleepless night for Corina, Wesley, and me. I'm still too emotionally overtaxed to relax. But I'll get some rest later today."

Mercedes tried to imagine the magnitude of the elderly gentleman's loss. "Elliott," she ventured, "I'm not good at saying the right thing at times like this. I just want to thank you for taking such good care of my grandmother. After all she'd been through in her life, she was lucky to have you at the end."

"And I was so blessed to have her," Elliott said. "I count myself as most fortunate to have known Dora."

"It has to be really hard on you to lose her," Mercedes said. "The two of you had such a strong bond."

Elliott did not respond. Mercedes heard a stifled sob as he struggled to contain his emotions. She wanted to ask, "What will you do, now that you don't have Dora to look after?"

But she held her question, knowing that he was on the verge of breaking down. She sensed he would prefer to avoid that embarrassment.

After a long pause, Elliott spoke again, his voice resuming its usual dignified tone. "Dora requested that her funeral ceremonies be conducted at the ashram. Corina and I left most of the arrangements to Wesley. He's acquainted with the people there, and he knows how they handle such events. There will be a cremation service this evening, a very small affair with just Corina, Wesley, and me in attendance. Next Saturday afternoon, there will be a memorial service for anyone who wishes to pay their respects to Dora. It will be held in the ashram temple. I hope to see you there. Let me know if you need directions."

"I'll be there," Mercedes assured him. "My husband and son and I will all be there."

Six days later, Mercedes walked through the door of the ashram temple, anxiety coursing through her body. With one hand, she clutched Javier's arm, and with the other, she reached for her son.

The previous night had been the family's first night in their new apartment. Too stirred up from the stress of the move to fall asleep, she and Javier had lain awake for hours while she recounted the stories Dora had told her. When she'd broken down into gut-wrenching sobs, Javier had gathered her into his arms, holding her tenderly.

That morning, she had scrambled to find suitable clothing among the unpacked boxes and suitcases strewn across their living room floor. Thinking it best to wear a dark color to a memorial service, she'd tried on a black mini-dress. But she'd decided it was too short and too low-cut for such an occasion. She ended up wearing the maxi skirt she'd once worn when visiting her grandmother. The bright colors reminded her of Dora's skirts.

As they entered the temple foyer, Mercedes desperately hoped her tears of grief had all been shed. She swept her gaze around the room, trying to orient herself to her strange surroundings.

The foyer opened into a spacious sanctuary. She watched people, both Indian and Caucasian, remove their shoes and place them on shelves in the foyer before filing silently into the sanctuary. She was relieved to see that her colorful skirt fit in with the bright patterns of the Indian women's saris.

Some of the people seated themselves cross-legged on the sanctuary floor, while others sat on chairs lining the periphery of the room. Mercedes marveled at the number of people present, grateful that so many had turned out to pay their respects to her grandmother. *Dora deserves this honor,* she thought.

The far end of the sanctuary was elevated by two steps, and a row of ornate life-sized statues stood at the back of the riser. Mercedes guessed them to be the ashram deities Dora had described to her. An altar stood in front of the statues, filled with lush bouquets of flowers and strange objects similar to those she'd seen in Dora's apartment. She assumed them to be artifacts of ashram worship.

Several dark-skinned men in flowing white robes sat regally in chairs flanking the altar. A cluster of musicians sat on the floor at the edge of the riser. The sound of droning instruments and the muted chanting of strange words filled the room with an otherworldly ambiance.

Mercedes realized she'd stepped into the realm that had provided Dora with a haven of peace for nineteen years of her life. Although she felt awkward and out of place, her heart overflowed with gratitude for the solace this mysterious world had offered her grandmother.

"This is really strange, isn't it?" she whispered to Javier.

"Yes," Javier whispered back. "But I think it's interesting."

"What should we do?" she asked. "Should we take off our shoes and go on in?"

"I guess so," Javier replied.

Then, Mercedes spotted Elliott Jordan standing with a small group in one corner of the foyer, the only African American man in the crowd of white-skinned and brown-skinned people. Relieved to see a familiar face, she steered Javier and Javi in his direction.

Elliott's tall, robust frame towered over those around him, except for the woman with whom he was conversing. The beautiful statuesque lady appeared to be in her mid-fifties. Her dark shoulder-length hair was expertly styled, and perfectly applied makeup accentuated her lovely features. She wore a simple black dress accessorized by a string of pearls. Her stunning dark eyes flashed with energy, and she exuded the air of one who's in charge.

Mercedes gasped in recognition of the woman who'd so frequently appeared in her grandmother's stories. "That has to be Corina!" she whispered to herself.

The woman looked every inch of the brilliant, capable person Dora had described her daughter to be. Corina had almost become a mythical superheroine in Mercedes' mind. But here she was, a real person. Mercedes suddenly felt small and ordinary, intimidated by the stately woman.

A slender man of slightly shorter stature stood behind and to the side of the tall woman. His long hair, nearly pure white, was tied into a tail that hung down his back. Large, luminous blue eyes dominated his weathered, deeply-tanned face.

The man's attire intrigued Mercedes. He wore a suit made of crisp white cotton, consisting of a long collarless tunic over a pair of loosely fitting trousers. Strands of wooden beads encircled his neck and one of his wrists. Mercedes glanced down and saw that his feet were bare.

Elliott's face lit up as Mercedes approached. Smiling, he extended his hand. "Thank you so much for coming, Miss Maldonado," he said.

Mercedes shook his hand, then gestured toward Javier. "Elliott, this is my husband, Javier. Javier, this is Dr. Elliott Jordan. He was my grandmother's...."

Elliott supplied the word. "Companion."

The two men shook hands and exchanged pleasantries. Then Mercedes guided her son forward. "And this is Javi."

Elliott bent down and extended his hand. Javi offered his own hand, responding to Elliott's greeting with a polite, "Pleased to meet you, sir."

All the while, the darkhaired woman was looking at Mercedes questioningly. "Corina," Elliott said, "This is Mercedes Maldonado. She's the granddaughter of your mother's former husband, Andrew Covington."

A smile of recognition lit up Corina's face. "Mercedes! Little Sadie! I remember seeing you when you were a baby. My mother adored you. Several months ago, she told me you'd looked her up, and that the two of you were enjoying some lovely visits. She was so thrilled to have you back in her life."

She paused, then added, "She said something about helping you with a school assignment?"

"Yes, that's true," Mercedes replied. The fact that an assignment had been part of her involvement with Dora now seemed irrelevant.

"My mother lived a complicated life," Corina continued. "I think her talks with you helped her put some things into perspective. I only regret that I wasn't able to spend more time listening to her."

She held Mercedes' gaze for several moments. The sadness in her eyes made her seem more ordinary. "Thank you," she murmured.

Mercedes felt her own eyes flood with tears, but she willed herself to hold them back.

Corina turned to the man in the white tunic. "Mercedes, this is my brother Wesley. Wesley, this is the granddaughter of our mother's husband Andrew. Remember Mom talking about her when she was a baby?"

Wesley! Mercedes thought. *Dora's silent, mysterious son!*

Wesley acknowledged Mercedes with a nod, and a slight smile broke the placid lines of his face.

Suddenly, Corina turned her head toward the doorway, and the rest of the group followed her gaze. An elderly man and woman had just entered the foyer. They seemed hesitant, disoriented, unsure of themselves. The bearded man wore a black high-collared suit and held a black hat in his gnarled hands. The woman, whose large blue eyes seemed strangely familiar to Mercedes, wore a long dark dress and a black bonnet.

Corina moved toward the newcomers immediately. "Aunt Katie! Uncle Eli! Thank you so much for coming!"

She led the couple toward the group and made introductions. "This is my aunt Katie Schrock and my uncle Eli Miller, my mother's sister and brother."

As Mercedes shook the hands of the elderly couple, she felt so overwhelmed that she thought she was going to swoon. This man and woman were part of the family Dora had so painfully left behind many years earlier. She could hardly believe they were real, that they were more than just characters in her grandmother's story. And she was deeply touched by the fact that they'd traveled so far to remember their sister, the sister from whom they'd long been estranged. Once again, her eyes welled with tears.

To distract herself from her overwhelming emotions, she glanced around the foyer again. Her eyes fell on a large painting hanging in a niche on the wall opposite her. It was partly obstructed by the people standing in front of it, so she moved a few steps to one side to get a better view.

The painting portrayed a radiant young man with blue-tinged skin wearing a turban and a garland of flowers around his neck. Gentle adoring animals surrounded him, and he held a dove in his hands. Mercedes gasped when she saw the artist's signature in the lower righthand corner: *D. Covington.*

Forgetting herself, she exclaimed, "Did Dora paint that?"

Corina turned, following Mercedes' pointing finger. "Oh, yes! She certainly did. That's...." She furrowed her brow, then nudged her brother. "Who is that deity?"

Wesley glanced at the painting. "That's Lord Krishna."

The conversation was abruptly halted by a sudden change in the music. From the edge of the sanctuary riser, a high, pure female voice sang out a sweet melancholy melody. Mercedes didn't understand the meaning of the strange words, but she knew they conveyed the yearning of the human heart. A soft male voice echoed the plaintive phrases.

The entire group—Elliott, Corina, Wesley, Katie, Eli, Mercedes, Javier, and little Javi—stood riveted by the haunting beauty of the music, united in a reverent hush.

The singers repeated the verses several times before the music faded into a silence that seemed to last for an eternity.

Wesley's voice finally broke the stillness. "That was Mom's favorite Sanskrit mantra. She used to sing it in her apartment when I stayed with her at the ashram. She said it was a love song to the heart of God."

A tear spilled from one of his blue eyes and trickled down his weathered cheek.

The sight of Wesley's tear broke all of Mercedes' resolve. The tears she'd been holding back poured from her eyes, and her body heaved with sobs. She felt Javier's strong arms around her.

"I'm so sorry," he whispered in her ear as he held her close. "I know how much your grandmother meant to you."

Javi slid his arm around his mother's waist, "Don't be sad, Mommy. You still have Daddy and me. We're right here."

"I know, sweetie," she sniffled. "I know."

Easing herself from Javier's arms, she fumbled in her purse to find a tissue. When she looked up again, she found herself gazing into Corina's teary eyes. Without a word,

Corina stepped forward and drew her into a long hug.

"Mercedes," she said after releasing her embrace, "two weeks before Mom died, she talked with me about what she wanted done with her things. She insisted that you have the painting that hung above her sofa. She said you'd know why. I have it wrapped up in the back seat of my car. Stick around after the service, and I'll give it to you."

Then she reached into her purse. Mercedes inhaled sharply when Corina pulled out a rumpled coffee-stained envelope with the name *Dora* etched on the front.

"She wanted you to have this, too." Corina pressed the envelope into Mercedes' hand. "She said you brought it to her, and that it's important that you have it back."

Mercedes stared down at the envelope through tear-filled eyes. Once again, the letter seemed alive, its sizzling energy almost burning her hand. She looked up at Javier, whose face was filled with questions.

"I'll tell you about this later," she whispered to him.

Two hours later, Mercedes, Javier, and Javi set out on the long trip from the ashram back to their home. Grateful for her husband's offer to drive, Mercedes sat in the front passenger seat in a motionless trance, reflecting on the beauty of the service they'd just attended.

The haunting music, the chanting, and the prayers played over and over in her mind, along with the numerous heartfelt testimonials to Dora's life. She could still picture the opulent flowers and the colorful statues, and the musky fragrance of the incense lingered on her clothing. She felt mind-blown and disoriented, as if she'd just visited another planet. She wasn't sure she was ready to return to her own world.

Sensing his wife wasn't in a mental space to talk, Javier wisely refrained from attempting conversation. Javi fell asleep in the back seat.

As he pulled the car into the lot of their new apartment complex, Javier's chuckle roused Mercedes from her silent reflection. "I almost drove us back to our old place," he told her. "I almost forgot that we're living here now."

When they walked into their spacious, newly refurbished apartment, Mercedes was greeted by the sight of the countless boxes they would need to unpack in the upcoming days. An image came to her mind: Dora sitting among her unpacked boxes on her first night in her ashram apartment, on the threshold of a beautiful new life. *Am I also on the brink of something new in my new home?* she wondered.

Javier set down the massive painting he'd carried in from the car, leaning it against one wall. The blanket it was wrapped in fell away, revealing the blissful scene of the little girl with her guardian angel. "Where should we hang this?" he asked.

Mercedes replied without hesitation. "Above the sofa. That's where Dora always kept it. That's where it will always belong."

Newly invigorated from his nap in the car, Javi began rifling through the boxes to find the toys he'd packed, while his exhausted parents collapsed on the sofa. "We've got a lot to do to get this place in order," Javier commented.

Mercedes nodded wearily. "I don't even know where to begin."

"Well, let's not try to do too much tonight," Javier said. "You've had a draining day."

The two of them watched their son dive excitedly into the boxes containing his toys, as if he'd just discovered buried treasure. Loading his arms with Lego packages and electronic games, he carried the booty off to his bedroom.

"What are you up to, Javi?" Mercedes called.

"I'm putting my stuff away," he called back. "I want everything in my room before I go to bed tonight."

"Well, at least one of us has some energy," Mercedes laughed. "I should probably go check on him."

As she made a move to get up, Javier said, "He's okay. Let him figure this out on his own."

Sighing deeply, she sat down again, snuggling up in the crook of Javier's arm. The two of them sat in peaceful stillness. Mercedes watched the rise and fall of Javier's abdomen as he breathed, realizing her own breath was in sync with his.

After a few minutes, Javier broke the silence. "Tell me about that envelope Corina gave you."

"It's the letter," Mercedes said, shaking off her drowsiness. "The letter from my grandfather to Dora."

She reached for her purse lying on the couch beside her. Pulling out the envelope, she said, "I've been wanting to know what's in this letter for a long time. It hit Dora really hard when she read it. It shook her up, but in a good way. It seemed to make her feel better. She said it brought her peace."

She clasped the letter to her chest. "I've been wanting to look at it all afternoon. But I'm kind of scared. Should we read it together?"

Javier nodded. Taking a deep breath, Mercedes took the single sheet of paper out of the envelope, unfolded it, and began to read her grandfather's words aloud.

My Dearest Dora,

I don't know how you will feel about receiving this letter, but I know I need to write it. My days are coming to an end, and there's much to be said before I go.

I've screwed up a lot of things in my life. But by far the biggest mistake I ever made was leaving you. I knew the moment I walked out on you that I was doing the wrong thing. But my stubborn pride kept me from turning around and coming back. It kept me from throwing myself at your feet and saying, "Dora, I love you more than life itself."

I kept thinking about coming back to you and asking for one more chance to make our marriage work. But after a while, it was too late. I knew you'd moved on with your life, so I moved on with mine.

Dora, you are a wonderful, beautiful woman. I never deserved you. I never felt worthy of you. I think that's why I treated you so poorly at times. I hated myself for not being good enough for you.

Sometimes, my love for you overwhelmed me. The feelings frightened me, and I didn't know what to do with them. So, I pushed you away and treated you harshly. Words can't even begin to express how sorry I feel for all the times I treated you unkindly.

Most of all, I deeply regret that I didn't have the courage to stick it out with you during our difficult times, to do what it took to get our relationship where it needed to be. I truly believe you and I were meant to be together. But I ruined the opportunity we had.

Over the years, I've wondered whether you found another man to love you. If you did, I hope that he's taking good care of you. I hope you are happy with him. I'm sure he's a better man than I am.

Please understand this, Dora. I have loved you more than I have loved anyone else in my entire life. I have never stopped loving you. Even after my death, I will continue to love you.

Yours forever,

Andrew Covington

Mercedes dropped the letter into Javier's lap, then bent forward with her head in her hands. "Oh Grandpa!" she wailed softly. "Oh my God, Grandpa!"

She'd thought she had no more tears to shed that day. But now, grief welled up inside her again, this time for the tragedy of her grandfather's life.

For a few minutes, she sat curled forward, sobbing, while Javier caressed her back.

When Javi returned to the living room for another load of his things, he stopped short when he saw the state his mother was in. "Why is Mom crying like that?" he asked his father. "Did something bad happen to her?"

"Son," Javier explained, "sometimes people cry like this when their hearts are touched."

Mercedes sat upright, and Javi came over to give her a hug. "I'm okay, sweetie," she assured him.

She stood up and began pacing around the living room, then stopped to stare out the large window facing the woods behind the apartment complex. "This is such a nice view," she commented. "We're lucky we got this unit."

Resuming her pacing, she reflected aloud. "Now, I understand why Grandpa was so quiet and withdrawn. He'd given up on life. He stopped doing anything that mattered to him. He lost the will to stand up for himself. He let my mom and June boss him around and run all over him."

She walked over to the sofa and sat down next to Javier, who was perusing the contents of the letter again. "I think Grandpa stopped living the day he left Dora."

Javier turned to her, a determined expression on his face. "We need to learn from this, Mercedes. We can't ever let this kind of thing happen to us. I moved out once. But I'm telling you now, I'm never going to leave you again."

"You're serious about this, aren't you?" Mercedes said.

Javier nodded. "I never want to end up like your grandfather, giving up and walking out. And then, living the rest of my life with regrets. When a man finds the kind of love Andrew had for Dora, the kind of love I have for you, he should have the courage to hold onto it, even during the most difficult times."

He beckoned to Javi, then pulled his son into one arm and Mercedes into the other. "If I can be the husband and father my family needs, then I will have lived the best life I could possibly live."

"You're the best dad ever," Javi said as he wriggled away and ran off to look through the boxes again. "I have the best mom and dad in the world."

Mercedes sat in silence, her head bowed, deep in thought. Her time with Dora was over. The memorial service was over. The mystery of the letter had been resolved. That surreal chapter of her life had come to an end. She felt profoundly exhausted, but peaceful and fulfilled.

"Maybe your grandfather and Dora are together in heaven," Javier ventured.

Mercedes shook her head. "I'm not sure of that. I think she's there waiting for Elliott. The two of them belong together." But after a few moments, she added. "Maybe it's both ways. We don't know how things work in the afterlife."

She sat up straight, raking her long hair out of her face. "I need to get out of this skirt and put on something more comfortable." Laughing, she waved her hand at the boxes. "If I can remember where I packed my sweats."

Javi poked his head out of his bedroom door. "I'm hungry. What are we going to have for dinner?"

"I don't know, sweetie," Mercedes said. "We'll have to figure that out. We don't have much of anything on hand. I was planning on getting groceries tomorrow."

"We can go out to eat," Javier suggested.

"No," Mercedes replied. "I'm too tired. Let's just order a pizza."

An hour later, Javier and Mercedes sat lingering at the kitchen table with the remnants of their dinner, while their son ran off to play in his new bedroom.

"Last year at this time, we were adjusting to living with the Coronavirus pandemic," Javier observed. "That was the craziest thing we'd ever been through. But you've just come through another strange summer."

"I know," Mercedes said. "Never in my wildest dreams had I imagined getting to know a grandmother I hadn't seen since I was a toddler. These last couple of months have been unreal."

She picked up an uneaten pizza crust, absentmindedly breaking it into pieces. "I'm totally worn out. But somehow, I feel stronger. I think I have more confidence in myself."

"How is that?" Javier asked.

"Do you remember the way I used to be?" she said. "Not wanting to listen to anybody?"

Javier grinned, saying nothing.

"Well, for some reason, I listened to a voice inside myself. It was the voice that told me to find Dora and give her my grandfather's letter. That turned out to be one of the best decisions I've made in my entire life. So, I've learned not only to listen to other people, but to myself. Not to my bratty self. To the wise voice deep down inside of me. That makes me feel like I can handle more than I ever thought I could."

She tossed the broken crust back into the pizza box, then closed the lid. "Getting to know Dora was unbelievable. Yes, I had only a couple of months with her. Losing her has been really hard. But the whole thing was worth it. I wouldn't have missed that experience for anything in the world."

"What made it so meaningful for you?" Javier asked.

Mercedes paused to think. "Dora lived a hard life. She wasn't perfect. She made a lot of mistakes. But I think she learned from those mistakes. In the end, she found peace."

Tears began trickling down her cheeks again. She reached for a napkin to wipe them away. "Dora was the most kindhearted person I have ever known. She was the first person who really understood me, who really saw me for who I am. She never judged me. She saw goodness in me, goodness I didn't even know was there."

Javier lifted his hand to stroke her cheek. "Mi amor, I hope to see more of your goodness and your beauty every day for the rest of our lives."

Mercedes smiled through her tears. "Dora helped me understand how important you are to me, Javier. She helped me find my love for you."

She stood up to gather the plates and carry them to the kitchen counter. "You know what I think? Dora is going to keep on helping me. Even though she's gone, she's left some of her light in this world. I know her spirit will always be with me."

"So, what happens now?" Javier asked as they lay in bed that night. "What's coming up next for you?"

Mercedes thought for a moment. "For now, it's getting settled into this apartment and getting Javi situated in school. It's going to be an adjustment for him, after doing virtual learning for so long."

She sighed deeply. "And of course, I'll keep helping June take care of my mom. That responsibility is going to be on my plate for years to come."

Javier reached over to take her hand. "Remember, I'm here to help you with that. You and I are in this together."

She snuggled close to him, laying her head on his chest. "On top of all that, I have to get through my last two semesters of nursing school. It's going to be a hard year, but I know I can do it."

"We'll have to celebrate after you graduate," Javier mused. "We'll have to do something really special. What do you think you might want?"

A thought popped into Mercedes mind, accompanied by a surge of energy. She sat bolt upright in bed. "I know exactly what I want. Next summer, I want to us to go on a trip to Mexico. First, we'll find my father and visit with him for a week or so. Then, we'll go to Mexico City to stay with your family for a while."

Javier jumped up, switching on the bedside lamp. "Really, Mercedes?" he asked incredulously. "Do you really mean this?"

"Yes," Mercedes replied. "I'm one hundred percent sure of it. You can go ahead and start planning our trip if you want to."

She laughed at the excitement on his face. "Knowing you, you'll be online tomorrow looking at flights."

"Oh, I will be!" Javier chortled. "Mercedes, this is the best news I've heard in a long time."

Reaching for her hand, he eased her out of bed. "Come, mi amor, come dance with me."

He led her into the living room, which was illuminated only by the faint light from the streetlamp in the building's parking lot. He put a record album of his favorite Mexican opera music onto his stereo system, turning the volume down so as not to wake their sleeping son.

Then, as the soft strains of the beautiful music filled the room, he took her into his arms. Mercedes closed her eyes, swaying to the music, her body floating so lightly that her feet felt as if they barely touched the floor.

How does this man have such an effect on me? she wondered dreamily.

AUTHOR'S NOTE

The idea for this story first came to me in 2005. I was so excited by the inspiration that I promptly wrote the first draft. Sadly, I was unsatisfied with the outcome. The story didn't feel quite right. I set it aside, doubting that I would ever publish it.

That initial draft languished in a drawer for years. I picked it up again in 2010 and made a series of changes. Still, it didn't seem ready to present to readers.

I returned to the story several times over the intervening years, making improvements but never achieving what I was striving for. Between attempts at fixing this story, I wrote and published a number of other books.

In late 2019, after all my other projects were completed, I again returned to this story, wondering whether I should give up and consign the manuscript to the fate of the shredder. I decided to make one last effort at refurbishing it.

This time, the story came alive in a new way. As the tragic year of 2020 rolled in, I suddenly realized why the book hadn't worked out in previous years. It was meant to be set in the current era, the era of the Covid-19 pandemic and sharp political divides. I knew I was now ready to complete and publish the project.

So, I began reworking the story, giving it a brand-new title, changing the nature of the characters, making changes to the plot, enjoying every minute of the project. At last, this story has been told the way I wanted to tell it.

OTHER BOOKS BY LOIS JEAN THOMAS
www.loisjeanthomas.com

Me and You—We Are Who? (The Sambodh Society, Inc., 2006)

All the Happiness There Is (The Sambodh Society, Inc., 2006)

Johnny and Kris (The Sambodh Society, Inc., 2013)

Daughters of Seferina (Lois Jean Thomas, 2013)

Days of Daze: My Journey Through the World of Traumatic Brain Injury (Lois Jean Thomas, 2014)

Rachel's Song (Lois Jean Thomas, 2014)

A.K.A. Suzette (Seventh Child Publishing, 2014)

Blessed Transgression (Seventh Child Publishing, 2015)

A Weekend with Frances (Seventh Child Publishing, 2016)

Hope's New Season (Seventh Child Publishing, 2017)

A Different Frame of Mind: Living a Full Life with Traumatic Brain Injury (Seventh Child Publishing, 2018)

Hold Me One Last Time (Seventh Child Publishing, 2019)